Broken Reflection

Broken Reflection

A Mirrorverse Novel

Book 1

Ravyn Brown

Made for Success Publishing
www.MadeForSuccess.com

Copyright © 2025. All rights reserved.

Distributed by Blackstone Publishing

First Printing

Library of Congress Cataloging-in-Publication data
Brown, Ravyn
Broken Reflection
p. cm.

LCCN: 2025933962
ISBN: 978-1-64146-921-0 *(PBBK)*
ISBN: 978-1-64146-922-7 *(eBook)*
ISBN: 978-1-64146-923-4 *(AUDIO)*

Printed in the United States of America

For further information, contact Made for Success Publishing at
+1 (425) 526-6480 or email service@madeforsuccess.net

To Cammie,

Thank you for being my biggest inspiration during my hardest time.

Department 1, Day 1

As someone who has spent almost a decade adventuring the impossible, I have witnessed many unbelievable things. But nothing compared to what happened all those years ago on the beach. Long before I met Sander, but perhaps the reason why.

It was my mistake, the start of the end. A foolish, imprudent mistake that sent a tsunami of chaos into motion. For even love is a thing that cannot be trusted.

It seems silly now, all the problems swimming in my brain before. They seem so small, so inconsequential. And, in fact, they were. But I wish they were all I had to worry about now. It is as if my life has been thrown into a sack and shaken about. And I am stuck with the pieces, desperately trying to put them back together.

Yet there's no hope.

There never was, I realize now. We were foolish to think otherwise.

Maybe there is hope for others, but it is a dwindling flame, growing smaller and smaller by the day.

The wind is hot as it brushes across the desert. Death's welcoming embrace is approaching. I always expected I would die alone, but this is not the end I anticipated. So much for trusting a higher power.

But trust is dead. Trust is for children.

I am sorry for rambling, but you must understand that this is not a happy story.

It is the story of a man by the name of Sander Fox, who once thought of himself as insignificant and, perhaps, still does. But he is the reason the world you stand in is still safe. He is the reason any world is still free.

So, remember him. Honor him.

For he is the reason your world is still your own.

-Elyane

CHAPTER ONE

Someone was in my room.

I noticed them the moment I woke up. Standing at the end of my bed, with a face shrouded in shadows, their presence seemed to take up the entire space. The way the shadows bent around them, so startlingly real, proved to me this wasn't one the normal figures that haunted my dreams.

My window was still sealed shut. My bedroom door was locked. Fear tightened its grasp on my lungs and sent a wave of ice down my limbs, freezing me in place.

The person shifted, and my heart lurched in my chest. Did they know I was awake? Could they see my face?

Moonlight spilled through the crack between my curtains, outlining the thickset figure before me. They moved again, and something glinted at their side. The silvery flash of a knife.

In an instant, my mind was bombarded with dozens of terror-driven thoughts. But before I could react, they spoke.

"Are you Sander?" It was a woman's voice.

The ice crept over my lips. It would have taken over my heart, to, if it hadn't been beating so hard.

The woman moved. Clothes rustled as she moved toward the head of my bed.

Oh, God. I was going to die. An image of my sister bent over my grave flashed through my head, tears streaming down her face. And Mama, one hand on Sadira's shoulder and one over her mouth, doing her best to hold back the tears but failing miserably.

I didn't have any friends, so at least they wouldn't have to send out many invitations for my funeral.

"Don't be scared." The woman's voice was rough, as if something was stuck in her throat. "Listen, some very bad people are coming here. They're looking for something. Your father—"

There was a thump.

The woman's head whipped toward my door as muffled voices sounded from the hallway. Too many to be my family.

"Clear in the kitchen," someone said.

"Keep searching," demanded a gruff voice, a humanoid version of a wolf's growl. "She's in this Department somewhere. No one gets dinner until Jones is dead or cuffed."

I scrambled upright, but the woman moved faster. Her footsteps were almost nonexistent as she lunged toward me and clapped a calloused hand over my mouth.

"Don't move." Her whispered words cut like a knife.

Even if I had wanted to, I wasn't sure I could. My body was paralyzed with fear.

She took a step away from me, glancing toward my door. Through the slight crack along the floor, shadows moved in the hallway. Toward Sadira's room.

A blinding crack split through my soul, crushing the ice that had taken over my body. I jumped out of bed, reaching for a soccer trophy on my dresser. I held it like a bat, trying to ignore how violently my arms were shaking. The woman lunged toward me, and I swung frantically. Stepping to the side with ease, she grabbed my wrist and the back of my neck and threw me onto the ground. I let out a pained cry as she twisted my hand, and the trophy fell from my fingers.

The woman shifted behind me as she braced me in a headlock.

She hissed into my ear, "I was supposed to bring you back, but they've found me quicker than I anticipated. I'll keep them off until morning. Then, you must run."

She began squeezing, cutting off my circulation. I gasped and clawed fruitlessly.

"Your father's code. His symbols. Use them as he taught."

I didn't know what she was talking about, but I couldn't respond because I was already unconscious.

"Sander?"

Someone was shaking me.

"Sander, why are you on the floor?"

My eyes flitted open, revealing my sister's worried expression. She gently slapped my face. I mumbled and lazily pushed her hand away.

"Why are you on the floor?" she asked again.

I blinked. Once. Then twice.

The events of the previous night washed over me. My hand shot to my neck, fingers brushing over the space where the woman's arm had been.

Panic swept through me, and I frantically ran to the bathroom. In the mirror, among the golden bronze of my skin, I could see faint red marks, ones that could easily have been acquired in sleep.

I went still. What had happened? Had it just been a crazy, vivid dream?

I thought of the way she'd thrown me to the floor and the resulting pain. I could still feel her hands against my wrist and neck, warm and calloused. The voices had been too real, but they'd left us untouched. Mostly.

My heartbeat thrummed loudly against my ribcage, sending blood rushing through my head so fast that a wave of nausea swam through me. I gripped the counter and forced my breath through my teeth.

"What the hell is wrong with you?"

I spun, snapping out of my trance, and faced my twin. She stood in the doorway, hands on her hips, and glared at me with accusation in her bottle-green eyes.

I opened my mouth to respond, but the words stuck in my throat. I wasn't even sure what was going on. Instead, I went back to my room and inspected the trophy, which was back on my dresser.

"There was someone in here," I finally said. My voice was raw and threatened to crack. "Last night. There was a woman in my room."

Sadira grabbed my wrist, pulling me to face her. She pressed the back of her hand to my forehead. "Are you feeling okay?"

I pushed her hands away. "I'm not lying. There was a woman in here and—" My words tumbled out faster and panicked. "She was running from someone. She said something about Dad and his symbols?" My heart dropped to my stomach. "Where's Mama? Is she okay?"

I didn't wait for an answer before making my way down the hallway and slamming open the door to Mama's room. Her bed was empty, the old blue comforter pulled straight with perfection. The top drawer of her dresser was slightly open, but other than that, it looked normal.

Sadira stepped up beside me. "She already left for work. What is going on with you?"

"I'm not lying," I insisted, turning to face her. Though I wasn't even sure myself, the more I said it, the truer it felt. "There were people in our apartment last night."

She scrunched her face, doubt creeping over her warm features. Her rounded chin and doe eyes were similar enough to mine that any passerby would assume we were siblings, but it was the sharpness of my cheekbones and my lean build that made them doubt we were twins. I had taken after my father, whereas she had inherited the compact and round edges of our mother.

A sigh passed through her plump lips. "I think you just had some weird dream." She spun on her heel, deep brown curls bouncing as she strode away.

Defeated, I sulked back to my room, doubt creeping into my thoughts. Maybe it had just been a dream. It wasn't uncommon for me to confuse my imagination with reality, nor were delusions uncommon in our family.

After the fire that had burned down our previous home, Dad's delusions manifested in the form of nonsense written across the walls in our basement and sketches and theories written in journals. Mama had been unfazed by it, but it had kept Sadira and me up for many nights. Questions left unanswered had eventually faded into dust, slipping through the layers of dirt that now hugged Dad's casket.

I sighed. Perhaps it was a biological thing.

Sadira called from her bedroom. "Sander, we're leaving in ten. Get ready if you still want to come."

I rubbed my thumb across the palm of my hand as if it could soothe the growing worry.

Taking a deep breath, I pulled open the drawer of my dresser and grabbed a T-shirt. My memory of last night was already beginning to blur.

Perhaps it was best I forget about it.

Two hours. For two hours, we scoured the antique stores of South San Diego, searching for a gift for Mama, and we hadn't picked out a single thing. We were friendly with some of the shop owners, having gotten her gifts from these places before. But even with our combined knowledge of my mother's interests, they had nothing to offer. Eventually, Sadira had grown tired of my complaining and sent me home while she'd gone to another shop.

But it was a weekend, and I found myself drifting further from the familiar streets I'd grown up on.

The grass bent away from my feet as I walked in between the lines of gravestones. A light breeze blew across the cemetery, salt from the ocean tinging the wind and dancing on my tongue. Behind me, I could hear the roar of cars as they whizzed past.

If it weren't for my lack of money and my crippling dependency on my family, I'd have left the city long ago. But unfortunately, I didn't have a job, and I still had a year of high school left. Plus, I'd never been without Sadira or Mama for more than a week.

I'd spent hours at a time thinking about where I'd go. I'd always imagined a little cabin in the mountains, somewhere windy and quiet. There, I had a farm with horses and a German Shepherd named Tucker.

But I couldn't see anyone with me. I couldn't decide if I liked that or not.

The cemetery was relatively empty, save for a hooded figure bent over a faded headstone. I kept my head down as I passed him, tucking my hands into my pockets and making myself as small as possible to avoid social confrontation. Not that he looked like he was going to initiate a conversation; it was just a habit.

Dad's gravestone sat at the end of the row, underneath the shade of a Ficus tree. Etched into the stone in a cursive font, his name mocked me. William Patrick Fox.

Though the rest of the memory was fading, the woman's words from last night had stuck with me. What symbols? It didn't make any sense. But then again, nothing my dad ever did made sense. He had been a strange man, haunted by the monsters in his head.

Monsters, I was beginning to fear, he might have passed down to me.

Glowering at the letters, I imagined what he would say had he known I was here.

"Silly boy, mourning a soul long passed. You have more important things to be doing with your life. Go find Sadira."

I mumbled a response to the fictitious conversation, bending down to pick up the bouquet of wilted flowers I'd left there last week and replacing them with the roses I'd bought on the way here. Some might say it was heedless to keep buying flowers for someone who couldn't even appreciate them, considering what little money my family had.

I closed my eyes, letting out a long sigh. It was odd, the way I'd grown closer to him after he'd died. Living, he'd been distant, taking trips for work seemingly every month. Even when he was home, he was always tired, stressed, and worried. We had shared no interests. He'd always urge me to see things from another point of view, muttering things about infinite stories. I had been a child, and he'd spoken to me like I was a scholar.

But he'd tried his best. He'd make us breakfast as much as he could. Mama had mentioned multiple times how much he'd loved doing it. It made him feel like he was important in our lives, even if it was in such a small way.

"Excuse me?"

I jumped, startled, and turned to face the newcomer.

It was a young man, probably a few years older than me. He wore a pleasant expression on his chiseled features, but it seemed forced. "Sorry, I didn't mean to scare you."

"You're fine," I responded, rising to my feet. Anxiety-ridden thoughts raced through my mind. Why was he talking to me? I didn't know him, did I?

He gestured to Dad's grave. "You knew him?"

"He was my dad." My words came out harsher than I intended them to be. I bit my lip. "How did you know him?"

"My parents worked with him. I met him a couple of times through them." He held out his hand. "I'm Troy Coldwell."

I shook it hesitantly. "Sander."

"I wish I could've met you sooner. Your father talked about you and your sister a lot. I would've come to the funeral, but unfortunately, I had my own family problems to deal with."

"The funeral was private. It was only me, my sister, and my mom."

"Not even extended family?"

I shrugged. "Mama's not on the best of terms with hers, and we never met Dad's."

Troy gave a slight smile, the sun glinting off his slate eyes. "He was a very secretive person indeed. If—if you don't mind me asking, how exactly did he die? I heard rumors but—" he trailed off, having seen the stilled expression that had fallen over my face.

As soon as he had asked the question, the memory shot into my head. I remembered the fear and the screams as Mama shoved me out the back door. The flames and the smoke. Blood stained my hands as I scrambled toward my father's body.

Back in the cemetery, I pressed my hand to my mouth. "I need to go," I choked out, pushing past him and speed-walking out of the cemetery.

CHAPTER TWO

Mama had to work late again. She texted Sadira and me, saying one of her coworkers had gotten sick and she needed to cover their shift.

I sat at the counter, staring at the bouquet of roses, tulips, and lilies I'd picked up for her on my way home last night. I shouldn't have been as disappointed as I was. This was normal. But it was Mother's Day.

Although we hadn't done much, I had been looking forward to this evening. It felt as though we were never together as a family anymore.

Mama was always working; Sadira was usually at a party or her best friend's house. Most nights, I was alone in the apartment. Don't get me wrong, I enjoyed my time by myself, but it got a little tedious.

I ran my fingers over the tan, square tiles of the countertop over the bumps and dents that made up not only our story but the stories of all the people who'd lived here before.

The man's questions had stirred something in me, a growing unease that I couldn't shake or dim. I'd said nothing of the encounter, and was so lost in my memories that I didn't think too much about why the stranger had approached me.

Distant as he had been, our dad had been the centerpiece of our family. He'd taught compromise and insisted on peace above all else. His teachings had failed when we needed them most. When he had left.

Now, the responsibility had fallen upon me to pick up the pieces. It was the last thing he'd asked of me.

But our family was falling apart, and there wasn't anything I could do about it. I watched as Mama dove headfirst into her work, scarcely coming up for breath. When her job as a news reporter had crumbled beneath her, she had no safety net to fall into.

And Sadira was desperate to get out of the house whenever she could. There would be times when she'd be gone for days without a word. She and Mama used to get into arguments about curfew, some of which even resulted in our neighbors asking me if I was safe. It was hard to pinpoint when exhaustion had taken over Mama and she'd stopped trying.

But in the end, Sadira always came back. Mama too. As long as they did that, we could figure the rest out together.

There was a knock at the door.

There was a moment of silence before Sadira called me from her room. "Sander, can you get that? My hands are full."

I peered through the peephole and saw the rounded face of a tired-looking man. My heart seized with fear at the sight of his blue uniform.

The hinges squeaked as I opened the door to greet the cop.

"Is this the home of Safiya Fox?" His voice carried a heaviness that went deeper than the dark circles beneath his eyes. But a soft smile played on his lips as he surveyed me and the cramped apartment beyond.

"Um, yeah. That's my mom. She's not home right now." My hand was still clutching the doorknob.

"Is there another adult here?"

I shook my head. "Just my sister and me."

As if in response, Sadira stepped out of her room, head tilted with curiosity. When she saw the cop, her shoulders straightened, and her eyes narrowed. She walked up next to me, one hand coming to rest on my elbow in a gentle but protective gesture.

"Can I help you, sir?"

I winced at the bitterness in her tone.

The cop didn't even blink. "May I ask for some form of

identification to show that you are, in fact, Mrs. Fox's children?"

Sadira opened her mouth, but I shushed her and sped to our rooms to grab our student ID's. My sister's cold mask hadn't budged by the time the cop handed them back to us, his head tilting in confirmation.

"We received a call a few hours ago from Fairview Cemetery, alerting us that one of the graves had been dug up sometime last night."

My stomach dropped.

"It appears someone attempted to rob the grave of William Fox."

"Attempted?" Sadira choked out, her face twisted in disgust.

"It seems they didn't find anything they wanted because nothing was taken. However, the casket was completely wrecked. They must've taken a hammer or a bat to open a hole."

Disbelief struck me like a tidal wave, hard enough I had to sit down. Sadira followed me into the kitchen and offered the cop a glass of water. He declined and scribbled a phone number on a notepad tucked into his belt.

A wave of sympathy passed over his face, and he rubbed his chin. "We already have a detective on the case. She'll be stopping by later. Please call this number if you think of anything that might be of use."

"Yes, sir," Sadira said quietly and locked the door behind him when he departed.

I listened to his footsteps receding down the stairs. When he was gone, I spoke up. "It was the people who were in our house the other night."

My twin let out an exasperated sigh. "Sander, I thought we were past that."

"Who else would it be?" I bristled, ready to start an argument. "They were in our apartment. The woman mentioned Dad!"

"You said they were looking for a person, not a grave. Connect the dots for me, and I'll believe you."

I went silent. There wasn't any evidence, only every nerve in my body telling me it was true. "But—"

Her eyes narrowed. "Will you please take your crazy delusions elsewhere? I can't deal with them right now."

My face fell. Sadira didn't notice because she'd already turned away and dialed Mom's number. I stood silently for a moment, stunned, and then numbly made my way back to my room.

She was upset, too, I told myself. She was tired. She'd had a long weekend partying and hanging out with her fancy friends. She didn't really understand how much those words hurt me. She didn't understand just how much I wanted to prove her wrong.

I wasn't crazy.

Angrily, I dumped out the school supplies from my bleach-painted backpack and began shoving things inside. A sweater, my rusty Leatherman, my sketchbook, and a pencil pouch.

Curiosity and anger had taken over me. Both were reason enough to get out of the apartment. The walls had already begun to close around me.

I peeked out of my room. Sadira was down the hall in her room, whispering in a hushed tone as she informed Mama of what the cop had said.

Slinging my backpack over my shoulder, I crept toward the front door and slipped on my shoes. Heart like a drum against my ribs, I pulled open the door, casting one last glance toward Sadira's room. She was facing away, still on the phone. I let out a breath in an attempt to calm my nerves and turned to face the hallway.

It's not like I'm not coming back, I reminded myself. I'd see them again in a few hours.

My original plan had been to go to the park tucked in the back pocket of our county. It was a place I liked to sit when things got crowded. But my legs had other ideas. Perhaps I let them drag me in the opposite direction, if only because I wanted to see things for myself.

Fairview Cemetery was busier than usual, especially considering the fact that it was almost nine o'clock. Most of the people seemed to be part of the same group. They huddled together, their conversations drifting on the humid wind. Even in the dim light of the faded sunset, I recognized one of the figures almost immediately.

I slipped my hood on and ducked behind a tree as the man I'd met the other day turned away from the group and began stalking toward the exit.

Why was he here?

I watched him greet an older woman, old enough to be his mom. He lowered his head in a gesture akin to a bow and began speaking to her. They were too far away for me to hear the whole conversation, but I could see the woman's face tightening with disappointment as the man continued.

Another figure slid up beside the woman. They were smaller than both of them and short enough to be a child. I couldn't tell, however, because their face was shrouded in the shadow of a hood.

I felt their gaze slide over me, and I shuddered, turning away abruptly.

My father's grave had indeed been demolished. The six-foot pit was surrounded by yellow caution tape as well as a discarded shovel and pile of dirt. Something twisted the knife in my chest when I saw the flowers I had laid on his gravestone thrown to the side.

I placed my hand on the Ficus tree, swallowing a lump in my throat as I peered into the coffin.

My father's soulless skull stared back at me, mouth agape as if in awe. Whoever had dug up his casket really had no respect for the dead. His rotting corpse had been shoved about carelessly; the culprit had obviously been searching for something.

Nausea crept up my throat. That was my dad. The pile of bones and decaying flesh lying before me had once been my dad. Alive and breathing. That body had been his.

My chest began to tighten. I stepped back on wobbly knees.

"Who are you?" demanded a deep voice from behind me.

I started, turning around frantically. Any chance I had at responding vanished when I locked eyes with the person who had spoken.

Deep blue eyes stared back at me, illuminated by the lanterns that dotted the cemetery. He was a terrifying sort of beautiful, I noticed in awe, with a cold and predatorial complexion and a warmth in his eyes that seemed misplaced. The sort of beauty that made you want to get closer, even though every nerve in your body was telling you to run.

"This area is closed to the public," he continued, though in his leather jacket and jeans, he looked just as much a part of the public as I did. "I'm going to need you to leave."

"Yes, sir. Sorry, sir." I ducked my head against the breeze, which brushed my hood off. I began to make my way past him, but he grabbed my arm and pulled me back to face him.

I went still as he looked me over. Then, a grin crept over his charming face.

"You're Sander Fox, aren't you?"

I couldn't do anything but nod.

He let out a small chuckle that made my heart stop beating. "My, my, you certainly just made my job ten times easier."

I was about to ask for clarification, but before I could, he lifted his fist and rammed it into my chin.

The room I woke up in smelled like antiseptic and mold. It was an odd combination, reminding me of the art classrooms in the basement of my school.

My eyes opened to a blinding white light, and I immediately shut them again, hissing. I raised my hand to my aching head. Groaning, I sat up.

Panic. Pure, undiluted panic zapped through me as I took in the white, polished walls, the cot, and the heavy door with a small, barred window.

I jumped to my feet and ran to the window, peering out. The hallway was stark white, with bright lights illuminating the walls and floors. More cells lined the walls, extending past my vision.

Blood rushed in my ears, and my breath came in short bursts.

"Hello?" Fear threatened to crack my voice.

I took a few steps back, patting down my body to ground myself to reality. But as I did so, I noticed my jeans and sweatshirt had been replaced with a slate blue prison uniform, the number 75634 printed on the chest.

"Oh, God." I tugged on my curls anxiously.

Perhaps the cops had discovered I was at the grave the day before it had been robbed and thought I was a suspect. Maybe the person who had done it pinned it on me. Maybe they'd gotten DNA samples of mine while they'd been at my house so they could frame me.

I banged my head against the wall in frustration and instantly regretted it. Pain splintered through my skull.

Down the hallway, I heard a door slam.

I peered through the small window.

Two men wearing blue and silver guard uniforms and helmets with black visors walked down the hall. Their whole outfit looked as if they had come straight from a sci-fi movie set. The guns buckled to their hips were white and sleek, with strips of bright blue lining the handle.

They stopped at the cell a few doors to the left of mine and pulled out a sagging figure. The boy, seemingly around my age, was limp and whimpering. As they came closer, I had the feeling that I knew him. He seemed startlingly familiar.

And then I realized why.

The young man was me. Or at least, a version of me.

If it weren't for the bruises and cuts on his face, it would've felt like looking into a mirror.

He had the same short, coffee-colored curls, the same golden bronze skin tone, and a lean build. When he glanced up at me, I glimpsed terror in his bottle-green eyes, the same ones I shared with my sister.

He was dragged past me, and I was left staring, mouth agape and heart a hollow cave.

When another door opened and closed again, I pulled my gaze away and stumbled back a few steps. As I did so, I noticed a pair of dark eyes staring at me from behind the door across the hall.

"I've heard it's a weird feeling." The girl's mouth curved into a playful smile. "Seeing your Reflection."

I stared at her, forgetting how to speak.

She tilted her head at me. "I've never seen mine, but I've met people who have. My dad had a bad encounter with his, but I wasn't there, so I've only heard stories."

"What is going on?" I managed to choke out.

"Ah, you're one of the newbies, aren't you?" The girl blew a strand of dark hair from her face and let out a chuckle. "My name is Ivy. Ivy Harrison."

She was quiet for a heartbeat before I realized her silence was an invitation for me to introduce myself, too. "Sander Fox."

"Well, Sander, welcome to Blackford Correctional Facility, First Department."

"Correctional Facility? As in, prison?" Shock rippled through me. "But I haven't done anything wrong."

She laughed again. "You don't have to do anything wrong to get locked up in here. The SSD likes to hide all their problems in their prison. She made quotation marks with her fingers around the word prison.

"SSD?"

"Scientific and Security Division," she responded, then let out a sigh. "Let me explain this as simply as possible so your premature brain can handle it." She paused for a moment, thinking. "The multiverse is real, and you, my friend, are in the prison of the SSD—a branch of the Inter-Dimensional Government."

My eyes widened. This couldn't be happening. "Um… no. I don't think so."

Ivy raised an eyebrow.

"Son of a—" I turned around. "This is a dream. Sadira was right. I'm going crazy. Good night!" I waved to her. "I'm going to sleep, and I am going to wake up in my bed at home. I'll see you never."

She chuckled, her deep, melodious voice ringing in my ears. "Good night, Sander Fox."

CHAPTER THREE

I'd never liked waking up. But doing it today was especially annoying, considering I was snapped out of my slumber by a blaring alarm and flashing lights. What made it even worse? I was still in the white-walled cell.

This had to be some stupidly vivid dream.

Despair and panic became my most prominent emotions, resulting in a cold sweat that clung like cobwebs to my skin. I raised my hands to cover my eyes. It seemed like ages passed before the lights stopped flashing and the alarm went silent, though it had only been a few seconds.

There was a hissing noise. The door creaked and slid to the side, revealing the unnaturally bright hallway with blueish-tinted lighting.

I rolled off my cot, landing on the floor with a groan. Someone nudged my shoulder with their foot. I turned to look at them, squinting against the LEDs.

The girl from across the hallway grinned at me. Long, dark hair cascaded in messy waves over her broad shoulders, swishing as she leaned down to help me up.

I brushed away her hand, rising on my own.

"So much for this being a dream." The freckle in the corner of her eye folded in on itself as her grin turned triumphant.

I frowned, my belief wavering.

She grabbed my elbow and led me out of the cell and down the hallway toward a big steel doorway.

"Where are we going?" I questioned.

"Breakfast."

Ivy pushed open the double doors, and a loud clamor filled my ears. We stepped into a large rotunda as a laughing couple shoved past us, causing me to stumble into the railing. The ramp we were currently standing on hugged the walls of the circular chamber as it curved downward. A quick glance told me I was on the fourth floor, and five more stretched above me. On the ground floor of the rotunda, there sat several dozen cafeteria tables, packing the room to the brim. Much to my disappointment, Ivy led me that way.

Doors leading to more hallways appeared every twenty or so feet. More prisoners ran into me, not stopping to apologize. I wasn't complaining, though. In fact, it reminded me of high school despite the prisoners' varying ages. The youngest I saw shocked me at about ten, and I saw no one older than fifty.

What had they done to end up here? Stories ran wild in my head as I stared interrogatively at each person I passed. Each daydream escalated, becoming crazier and bloodier, and suddenly, all I wanted to do was lock myself in my cell again. At least in there, I was by myself.

Ivy waved to a white-haired girl standing outside one of the doors. When we approached, I felt her cold gaze slide over me, and I suppressed a shudder.

Ivy, seemingly oblivious to the girl's hostility, introduced us. "Eden, this is Skyler. He's new here."

"Sander," I corrected.

"That's what I said."

Eden narrowed her gray-blue eyes at me. They were a stunning feature, an uncommon match to her dark skin. But what really made her stand out was the white lines that followed the shape of her cheekbones and ended on the skin that connected her pointed ears. At first, I thought it was painted, but with a second look, it seemed to be permanently etched into her skin. A tattoo, maybe?

She grunted and pushed herself off the wall and then led the way down the rest of the ramp.

As we made our way to the end of the slow-moving food line, I stared wide-eyed at the rest of the prisoners. Many of them seemed normal, but every now and then, my eyes would wander over a person who was completely out of the ordinary. One of them, a girl, I assumed, had faded red skin and unnatural bumps along her forearms and neck. Another prisoner was missing an arm, but where the shirt was cut away for the remaining shoulder, I spotted veins bulging and dusty cracks in their skin.

This had to be a dream.

I pinched myself. A sharp pain shot through my lower arm, but nothing changed. I frowned.

Everything felt real. Extremely real. When I was dreaming, it was usually as though my vision was limited and everything was kind of fuzzy.

A sinking feeling began to form in my gut.

God. What would happen if Ivy was right? What if this was all real? The multiverse? An inter-dimensional government?

Or maybe I had been drugged. Was it possible to hallucinate something this vivid while on drugs?

I shook myself out, only to find I'd been so lost in my thoughts that I hadn't noticed a hush had fallen over the prison. I followed everyone's gaze to a set of heavy metal doors that were propped open.

A man stood there, flanked by at least a dozen guards. He wore a black suit with a pristine white shirt underneath, the minimalist look completed with his slicked-back blonde hair. My heart dropped into my stomach when I recognized him. Both times I had seen him, he had been at the cemetery, so it was extremely disorienting to see Troy here. His eyes raked across the mass of prison uniforms until they landed on what they were searching for. Me.

My heart lurched.

Troy pointed. "There."

All sets of eyes swiveled to me. At that moment, I wished I could be a turtle, sinking back into my shell and not having to look at anyone.

Two of the guards peeled away from the group and approached me.

Panic seized my chest. Should I run? Should I scream? Instead, I went completely still. I barely reacted when they grabbed my elbows and pulled me toward the doors.

I cast a glance over my shoulder just in time to spot Ivy's solemn expression, and then they shut the doors behind me. I turned to see another set of doors, seemingly thicker and stronger.

Something beeped. Then, a line of green light swept over our group. An automated voice echoed through the room. "Prisoner detected. Please state the number, name, home Department, and purpose for leaving."

Troy replied. "75634. Sander J. Fox. Home department: 523. Meeting with the Director."

"Verifying." There was a slow beeping for a few seconds before the voice spoke up again. "Verification complete. Please move forward."

The doors slid open. I was shoved forward into an enormous hallway that extended too far for me to see the end. Other than a few other guards or people in white doctor's coats, it was empty.

There were no windows, I noticed as we made our way down the hallway. Perhaps we were underground.

The youngest of the guards surrounding us, seeming fifteen or sixteen, kept eyeing me. He stood out from the others. While they all had close-cut haircuts, his blonde hair fell to his shoulders in messy waves. He caught my gaze and grinned, the piercing in his septum twisting with the movement.

One of the other guards grunted and said something to him, but I didn't hear. My focus had gone to a man in a long white coat walking out of a room we were passing. Someone called for him back in the room, and he paused to reply. He nodded to the guards as we passed, not giving me any notice.

I didn't care.

My attention was on his hands. He wore gloves stained with blood.

When he propped the door open for his colleague to walk out, I caught a glimpse of the room behind them.

A body hung from the ceiling. A man. His skin was cracked and peeled like chipped paint, and he was an unnatural white. His veins bulged, and blood dripped from his eyes and ears. His arms seemed too long, his legs too skinny. The whole corpse was irregular and disproportionate.

I froze, unable to peel my eyes away from the mess of a body.

Someone pushed me forward, saying something.

"What is that?" I pointed to the room. "What the hell is that? *Where am I?*"

The man with bloodied hands slammed the door closed, and guards rushed for me. I struggled, terror rising in my throat.

"*Where am I?!*" I screamed again. I attempted to jerk away, but the hands around my arms were like steel.

"Calm down," growled one of the guards.

Around us, people had begun to crowd. The tightening of the space and the dozens of judging gazes pointed in my direction made nausea swirl in my gut. A hot flash ran down my neck, and if it weren't for the adrenaline pumping through my veins, I knew I would have passed out seconds ago.

I struggled to keep my breathing steady as I saw someone rush up to me. The youngest guard, the one with the blonde waves, grabbed my face and looked me dead in the eye.

I couldn't move.

"It's going to be okay," he assured, then stepped back and whipped his hand. "Take him to the Director."

"It's not your place to tell us what to do, Coldwell," Troy snapped.

Coldwell snickered but said nothing as I was dragged down the hallway.

My heart raced. Surely, it wouldn't be too long before it burst right out of my chest.

Stuck in a cycle of frightened thoughts, I let the guards shove me into a room, strap me to something that looked like a dentist's chair, and then leave. I squeezed my eyes shut.

"Sander Fox, is it?"

A woman stood a few feet away, peering through glasses at a holographic file projected from a thick black wristband. Though the last time I'd seen her it'd been too dark to catalog all of her features, I did so now, heart dropping when I recognized her as the woman Troy had been talking to in the cemetery.

"Born in San Diego, California. Department 523. Your father died when you and your sister were twelve. Your mother raised you alone afterward." She looked at me. "Tell me if I get anything wrong." Her angular face seemed as if it had been purposefully sharpened, and the slant of her eyes had me looking anywhere but her gray irises.

"Who are you?" I croaked, "How do you know all that? Are you the FBI?"

She chuckled humorlessly. "I'm the Director of the SSD, the Security and Scientific Division of the Inter-Dimensional Government."

"Are you high?"

The Director raised a perfectly trimmed eyebrow. "No."

"Then tell me the truth." My voice came out weaker than I had intended it to, traces of fear and panic prominent in my words. "Why am I here?"

She dismissed my question with a flick of her hand. "I'd like to hear your retelling of the night your father died. Now that your mind is… clearer."

My eyebrows knit together.

A video appeared on the screen before us. Security camera footage.

All thoughts in my head vanished as I laid eyes on the young boy who lay curled on a hospital bed, blood-covered hands pressed to his eyes. Warm ceiling lights sent the shadows in the ICU scattering, but it didn't stop the boy from shaking.

Though my memory of this was hazy, I could still smell the rubbing alcohol a nurse was now dabbing on the boy's forehead.

Twelve-year-old Sander Fox didn't flinch at the touch. His deep green eyes lay on the detective who sat beside his hospital bed.

"Where is Sadira?" His voice was hoarse from screaming.

The detective gestured to the wall. "In the room next door. She and your mom are being tended to, but I came here to have a conversation about what you saw today, Sander."

"I didn't see anything." Young Sander rose from his fetal position as the nurse pulled away. "It was smoky. I heard screaming. I went outside as soon as I could."

The detective leaned forward in her chair, ponytail shifting with the movement. She grabbed young Sander's hands and ran her fingers over the rashes on his wrist. "And how did you get out of the ropes?"

I could feel it now, the way my whole body had shut down at the question. Tears had risen, but my eyes refused to allow them through.

A coldness swept through me now, and I turned my gaze away from the screen. "Why did you bring me here?"

The video stopped. The woman before me, stone-faced and calculating, leaned forward in the same way the detective had. But her touch wasn't warm or comforting. Her skin sent sparks up my arm as she released one of the cuffs, inspecting the wrist beneath.

The rashes were long gone, but the feel of them still haunted the depths of my mind.

"Did you speak to your father before he died?"

I swallowed the lump in my throat. "Tell me the truth. Where am I, and why am I here?"

"What I said was the truth. You are in the SSD. But I suppose if you need proof…" She sighed and waved her hand, expertly avoiding my last question. There was a click, and the clamps around my ankles and wrists swung open. I lunged forward, but as soon as I stood up, my legs gave out and I crumpled to the floor.

A door opened and two guards came in, Coldwell being one of them.

They grabbed me by my shoulders and hauled me up. The feeling drained back into my legs, and I tentatively took a step forward. The Director walked out, and the guards shoved me after her.

I was led to a room with a heavy door. The Director grabbed the handle, and there was a click. It slid open soundlessly to reveal four men dressed in black suits standing before a one-way window, Troy among them. They saw the Director, and each gave a small bow.

"Director," Troy said. "We've taken care of Haley Jones."

"Then tell Mr. Wolf and Ms. Styx to give their report to you and send them back to Blackford."

He nodded and then departed.

The Director addressed the others in the room, gesturing to me, "This is Sander Fox. He is having a hard time wrapping his head around the multiverse. Show him."

Coldwell split off from me and took position by the door. The other guard pulled me past a thick black curtain, and when I looked up, I went still.

A mirror took up the far wall, bordered with strange writing in white paint. But that wasn't the weirdest part.

When I looked in the mirror, where I should've seen myself, there was nothing. Not even the reflection of the guard.

I reached out to touch the glass, but the guard pulled me backward so forcefully I tripped and stumbled back a few feet.

"Don't," he growled.

"Why?" I asked.

He didn't reply.

The Director stepped through the curtain. "I suggest stepping away from the Mirror, Mr. Fox."

I spun toward her. "Explain."

"You are standing in front of a portal to another dimension. Stepping through it would mean waking up in a different world, a different time. It would mean knowing no one and nothing about where you are."

"Tell me again why I shouldn't just run through it?"

"Because my guard can pull his gun faster than you can take a step."

Indeed, there was a gun strapped to the man's waist, and by the way his hand rested comfortably on top of it, I doubted he would hesitate to use it.

I shifted. "What about that mangled meat sack I saw? What the hell was that?"

"That was… " she hesitated, "that was an experiment gone wrong."

"An experiment gone—" I cut myself off and began backing up, "Who did you have strung up and skinned? Who did you have tortured beyond recognition and why?"

"Mr. Fox—"

"Don't!" I shouted. Fear clutched my chest. "Let me go. I didn't do anything."

The Director's expression didn't change as she flicked her hand, and once again, I was dragged away.

Back in my cell, my arms and legs throbbed, and my muscles groaned as I forced myself to sit up. The door was locked, and the lights had been dimmed. Either that or my eyes had adjusted to them.

I rubbed my forehead, my heart still racing. This was real.

I hadn't done anything. Why couldn't I just go home? I had a family to go back to. A sister. A mom. We'd suffered enough. We didn't need to add this to the list.

I let loose a shaky breath and then laid back on the cot. Tears began to brim in my eyes. I pressed my palms to my eye sockets. Please. I just wanted to go home.

CHAPTER FOUR

I remained in my cell the next morning, ignoring Ivy's attempts to get me to leave and instead counting the voices in the hallway. It was a numbing activity, one I used to enjoy. But my mind repeatedly snapped back to the bombshell that had been dropped on my life.

I was pretty sure Ivy was pitying me. She visited me regularly, offering me the snacks she managed to bring from the cafeteria, all of which I declined. I didn't think I could stomach shoveling food down my throat after seeing that mangled body.

When I finally forced myself to step into the rotunda, nausea swam giddily in my gut, threatening to empty what little contents were in my stomach. My fingers clutched at the railing shakily as I descended the ramp, eyes landing upon a familiar couple playing cards with two newcomers: a young girl with brown braids and—I swallowed—the beautiful boy from the cemetery, the one who had punched me.

I shoved past the anxiety in my gut and ducked underneath the piercing gazes of the other prisoners. Ivy sent a dazzling grin my way as I approached, and as she started to introduce me to the new faces, I couldn't think of anything other than my overwhelming desire to run back to my cell and throw myself under the blanket.

The boy, seemingly slightly older than me, slid a pair of deep sapphire eyes in my direction. I couldn't tell if he was glaring or if that was just his normal expression.

"Hello again, Foxy." His voice was deep, lingering in my ears even after he closed his mouth. A hint of a smirk danced on his thin lips.

I struggled to find words.

It was almost difficult to look at him, yet all I wanted to do was study every inch of his face and then draw it. My eyes clambered clumsily over the slight crook in his nose, the black hoops and studs decorating his ears, and the sun-painted blush that ran atop his pale skin.

It was there that my attention lingered. The vibrancy of the pink suggested it hadn't been too long since he'd been in the sun, but I had seen no windows in the building nor any outdoor access points. He'd been outside when I'd encountered him in the cemetery, but what was he doing here now? It was a shock to see him dressed in a prisoner's uniform when he'd acted so freely before. I could only wonder what he'd done to end up in prison so quickly or if he had truly been free when we'd crossed paths before.

"Don't call him that, Amias," Ivy grumbled and dealt out a new hand. "It sounds weird."

Amias rolled his eyes, then gestured to an empty seat. "You going to play?"

My eyes flicked over his companion, whom my gut told me was the other figure I'd seen that night. She raised her head to look at me, and a chill rushed down my spine. Her skin was almost deathly pale, and her youthful features rested in a stony mask of apathy. Though her mouth wasn't moving, I could almost hear her cold words ringing through the tombs in my mind.

Welcome to the end.

A flash of anxious heat shot up my neck, and she tilted her head almost knowingly.

"Excuse me," I muttered and spun on my heel. Their gazes seared my back as I disappeared into the bathroom.

Stumbling for the sink, my fingers shook as I shoved them under the running faucet.

God. God. God. God. What the hell is going on?

When I lifted my head to face the mirror, I expected to see only the empty bathroom behind me as I had earlier in the

Director's office. When I stared into my own eyes instead, confusion intertwined with anger and, shot straight up my spine, blinding the backs of my eyes and heating the tips of my ears.

I reached out to touch the mirror. Cold, solid glass met my fingertips.

"You're pretty new to this whole multiverse thing, aren't you?"

Half-expecting the voice to be in my head, I turned reluctantly. Amias let the bathroom door swing shut and propped himself against the cement wall. The sleeves of his prison uniform had been rolled to his elbows, revealing a winding snake tattooed around his right wrist, a forked tongue flicking across the back of his hand. On his left arm, a singular lily stretched from his inner elbow to his wrist. More designs curled along his skin, disappearing beneath his shirt.

"You were at the cemetery." I swallowed, mouth dry.

He nodded once, toying with the black hoop in his ear.

I could hear my heart thudding beneath my bones, anxious under this strange boy's stare, but I pushed on anyway. "You knocked me out."

He nodded once more, unnaturally calm.

His silence invited anger into my words. "Why?"

"My boss told me to." He offered a nonchalant shrug. "The Director. She controls what I do, so don't hold a grudge against me."

It explained the sunburn and why he'd been at the cemetery.

"I—I don't—why?" I stuttered, throat closing. "Why are you in here then? Why am *I* here? Why did you take me? Where is my family?"

He raised his hands submissively. "Easy on the interrogation, Foxy. Your questions will be answered in due time. I followed you in here to see if I could help with that." He stalked over to the sinks and hopped atop the counter, patting the space beside him.

I remained standing, arms crossing as I watched his reflection shift. That wasn't what I meant, and he knew it. But if he was offering to help, I might as well see what I could get. "Why can I see a reflection in this mirror but not the one in the other room?"

"Because that's not a Mirror." He gestured to the glass behind him.

"Yes, it is."

He chuckled. "There are two different kinds of mirrors. The first ones are portals, which can be activated by a series of symbols written on the rim. The other ones are just regular mirrors. Like that one."

"How do you know which one is which?"

He shrugged. "You typically can't. Unless you and your Reflection are displaced from your original worlds. The imbalance in the multiverse shows itself in the portals."

"About Reflections," I began, fighting the nervous shaking in my legs, "how many does each person have? How many duplicates do I have?"

"One or two."

I raised an eyebrow. "How many dimensions are there?"

"Billions."

"That—" I frowned. "How does that work?"

"They're not all in the same timeline," Amias said. He held out his hands as if he were going to use them for visuals but ultimately decided against it and went back to picking at his nails. "For example, how old are you?"

"Seventeen."

"What year were you born?"

"2004."

"See? I'm eighteen, yet I was born in 2046 in my world."

"What year is it in this dimension?" I wanted to ask him where his world was, but that topic seemed littered with time bombs. My shoes squeaked on the tile as I shifted and cast a glance at my hands. My fingers jittered, weak from the hunger gnawing in my stomach.

"I'm not sure." He reached up to scratch his chin, the snake on his forearm creasing with the movement. "It was the first dimension recorded in the SSD's system."

I let out a breathy sigh.

Amias seemed so peaceful for someone who had been stalking my father's grave and kidnapping innocent teenagers just a few days ago. His relaxed demeanor was nearly overwhelming, one I would have succumbed to had we been in a normal setting. But despite his comfortability, his words lacked empathy. There was a cold darkness lurking behind them. Like the depths of a lake underneath frozen sheets of ice.

I raised my gaze to find him studying me. Amias cocked his head. My eyes trailed back to the ground. "What did you mean by the Director controls what you do?"

He shrugged. "Renna and I are the SSD's personal dogs. We're sent out to do the Director's bidding when and however she wants. My latest mission just so happened to be related to you."

Realization crashed into me like a boulder. "It was you." My words stuck in my throat, coming out as little more than an exhaled breath. "You were one of the people in my apartment that night."

He tilted his head, a black strand of hair falling in front of his eyes. "You were awake?"

I nodded vigorously. "I woke up in the middle of the night. There was a woman, and I heard voices. My sister didn't believe me, but now that—" I caught myself. If I could get him to Sadira, he could help me prove to her that I hadn't been dreaming.

"Well, there's no need to worry about the woman anymore. She's been taken care of."

I fell silent, not sure I wanted him to elaborate on that. And he was wrong; it wasn't completely taken care of. Some small part of me worried about her. Her words lingered in the back of my mind. I was itching to get them out, to tell Amias everything. To tell *anyone*. But were the people here the ones I should be telling? Especially after what he'd just revealed to me.

Amias deemed the interrogation over and waltzed out of the bathroom. Had it not been for fear and anxiety, I would have demanded he stay and tell me everything. But that wasn't my style. And something about the way he moved suggested he wasn't going to be as compliant should I push him.

Back at the table, Ivy was pulling in the cards. Eden was helping her, and the new girl, Renna, was staring at me.

The hairs on the back of my neck rose.

As I sat beside Eden, Amias leaned down to whisper in Renna's ear. Her empty expression shifted toward mild curiosity as her eyes slid over me.

I turned away but could still feel her gaze on me as I reached for the cards Ivy had passed my way.

There was something unsettling about her. Not just the fact that she hadn't spoken a single word—I was fine with that. I liked quiet people. But being around her flipped a switch in my brain, triggering unsettling waves of hyper-awareness.

CHAPTER FIVE

There wasn't much to do in a prison. I came to that realization quite quickly after the initial shock wore off.

We were woken up at eight o'clock every morning by flashing lights and blaring alarms. Which, if you asked me, was a bit overkill. Lights-out was at ten, followed immediately by the guards' nightly rounds to secure the cells. We were locked in our cells for the rest of the night.

Most nights, I got maybe two hours of sleep, and even then, it was inconsistent. My mind was clouded with thoughts of worry. Worry for myself. For Sadira and Mama. For the mangled body in the room. Images of my family with the same pale, cracked skin drew me from sleep and kept me staring at the dark ceiling throughout the night.

During the day, we'd talk, throw a ball, or play cards. I didn't speak with any of the other prisoners. Ivy knew most of them and pointed out the ones to steer clear of and the ones to talk to. It was easy to slip under their attention now that I'd already been "claimed" by Ivy and her group.

Whether or not these prisoners were in the same situation as me, I couldn't view them as anything other than a threat. Worries ran rampant in my mind and, on multiple occasions, made themselves known to others by sending my meals back out through my mouth. Ivy assured me that as long as I stuck close to her, the others wouldn't harm me. I had no choice but to heed her warning, even if it didn't make me feel any better.

The day after meeting them, Renna and Amias disappeared after lunch. I'd watched them slip out the double doors, guards flanking them like a pack of cubs. They hadn't been called; they'd just gotten up and left without a word.

Eden and Ivy didn't say anything about it, so I didn't bring it up. Amias's words from the bathroom held back my questions. The SSD's personal dogs.

I ached to know more about what he'd meant, but my curiosity was held at bay by the crippling fear of being killed for asking too many questions. With the image of the body lingering in my mind, I nervously kept my mouth shut, but it didn't stop me from wondering what their role was in this government. I tried picturing them giving orders but found it hard to do when I had only ever seen the two of them in prison uniforms, aside from the first night in the cemetery.

The way Amias had phrased it, it sounded like his orders came from the Director herself. And though he hadn't mentioned any prejudice against his position, something in my gut told me he wasn't the type of guy to easily take commands.

Two days passed before they returned.

If Renna and Amias hadn't looked so different from one another, I might've passed them as siblings. Renna, with her soft eyes and unnerving demeanor, was nearly the opposite of Amias, with his deep voice and strong, wolfish features. However, despite their differences, they expressed easy comfort and familiarity around one another.

Seeing them so close brought my thoughts circling back to Sadira. After Dad died, we hadn't been as close. There hadn't been a real reason; she'd just drifted away from me. Or at least, I thought she had. It might've been me who'd pulled away from her. I didn't feel like I fit in with her type of people. With her friends. Despite her best attempts at making me get to know them.

That was what was different about life in prison with these people. Despite the anxiety I felt in their presence, I was grateful I was so easily welcomed into their group. From the looks of it, the rest of the prisoners weren't as friendly as my hallmate and her friends.

I couldn't go so far as to trust them. During the nights, I'd tug on my cell door to make sure it was locked. Ironically, it eased my mind to know that I couldn't get out if only it meant no one could get in.

"Your turn, Fox," Amias said.

Ivy nudged my shoulder.

I blinked myself away from my thoughts and glanced over the cards in my hands.

My new "friends" and I sat in a circle between Ivy's cell and mine, a deck of cards sprawled in front of us in a shape that was new to me. It was a game I'd just learned today. Apparently, I was the only one in the prison who knew nothing about it because they'd all looked shocked when I said I didn't know how to play. I couldn't even remember what they'd called it. Heads, Arms, and Tails—or something stupid like that.

Ivy raised an eyebrow at me and chuckled as she played the obvious move. The one I should've made. "Did you even look at the cards?"

I bristled. "In my defense, I wasn't really paying attention when you were explaining this."

"It seems so," Eden said. I frowned as she set down all her cards. "I believe I win."

Amias cursed, throwing down his cards. "I was so close."

Ivy laughed again. Renna pulled the cards in and began shuffling.

The door at the end of the corridor swung open, the chatter of the rotunda spilling into our hallway. My heart lurched as a guard nudged the heavy door closed behind him. A tug of his helmet had blonde hair spilling out. Coldwell sat down beside us. "Is this an open table?"

Amias smiled. "I thought your mom put you on dog duty for slacking off."

"She did. I'm not really sure why she thinks that's a punishment, though. I like dogs."

"Even cleaning up their shit?"

"Good point. But I still like them. It's not that bad." The guard seemed to finally notice me. "Sander, right?" He stuck out his hand, "I'm Aven."

I shook his hand, wary.

Amias chuckled. "Relax, Fox. They're our friend."

They. Whoops.

"What dogs?" I asked, curious.

"The SSD keeps dogs to help manage some security checkpoints. You know, like you guys have at, what do you call them? Um…" They frowned. "The flying machine launchers with snacks?"

"Airports, Aven." Amias rolled his eyes.

Aven snapped their fingers. "Right. Airports."

My eyebrows knit together. How did they not know about airports?

They must've seen my confusion because they let out a small chuckle. "That's right. I forgot how new you are. You seem calmer than you were before. I take it that means you're feeling more comfortable here?"

I wasn't sure what they meant by comfortable, but I nodded anyway. Across from me, Renna dealt out the cards again.

Ivy seemed surprised. "You've met before?"

"Mhmm." I nodded again. "I met him—them—when I met with the Director. Sorry."

They shrugged. "No worries. At least you come from a planet where that stuff even exists."

I raised my eyebrows at their casual use of that phrasing. "I have so many questions about everything," I mumbled, not really expecting anyone to hear, much less answer.

"I'll tell you what," Amias challenged, annoyance lacing his voice. "Each time someone plays, we'll answer one of your questions."

"Learn some patience, please, Mr. Wolf." Eden set a few of her cards down, then gestured for Renna to play.

"Wolf? That's your last name?"

He glared at me. "You're one to talk, *Fox*."

My tone must have come out differently than I'd hoped because that wasn't what I'd meant when I'd sounded so surprised. The Director had mentioned him before. Mr. Wolf and—my gaze turned toward Renna—Ms. Styx. They were kind of funky names.

"Question number one," Amias said as Renna played. "Go."

"What's the SSD?" I asked. "How does it work, and why does it exist?"

"Stands for the Security and Scientific Division," Amias replied. "It's run by the Director and her husband, Warren, Head of Experiments. Their main job is to keep the crossing of dimensions in check. They also train and supply soldiers for the other branches."

"And they're only one part of the government?"

Aven continued for Amias, "Yeah. The whole government is run by a man called the Reflector and his council, which is made up of the two leaders of each of the three branches."

It was my turn. I struggled to figure out what to play and ended up throwing down a random set of cards. "Who created this government? What are they trying to keep the multiverse safe from?"

"Chaos," Aven answered almost immediately. "Years before the Inter-Dimensional Government was founded, quantum researchers discovered that each time someone crossed into a dimension they weren't born into, the universal vibrations would change. The more it would shift, the more... dangerous consequences would occur. From what I've heard, it's why most worlds are wastelands. My mother oversees maintaining the order of the crossings, while my dad is more focused on finding new ways to protect the borders." Aven's face tightened in anger and something more, and I couldn't help but notice that their words sounded preached.

Ivy scoffed. "That's what their job description says on paper."

Renna hissed disapprovingly at her.

Ivy lowered her voice and continued, "Some people say Aven's mom, the Director, is plotting something huge. Blackford was supposed to be a place to store prisoners temporarily while the CLS—the criminal and law system branch—made their decisions on what to do with them, but some people here haven't left in decades. Those who do leave…" Her gaze drifted to Renna and Amias.

The latter continued Ivy's words, his voice uncharacteristically empty. "She's creating soldiers. People similar to Renna and me, capable of things most normal people aren't."

A chill rushed through me as I struggled to take in this new information. I let loose a tight breath and found my words stuck in my throat despite it.

"She has this whole plan." Aven tilted their head back thoughtfully. "She's spent pretty much her whole life working on this, and still, she doesn't expect it to be done by the time she's dead. She has my whole life planned out."

The hallway lights flashed once, signaling we had five minutes until we would be locked in our cells for the night.

Silence fell over our small group. Without a word, those who weren't in my hallway rose and left.

I said goodnight to Ivy and slipped into my cell, flopping onto the cot with an *oomph*, limbs heavy with the weight of the knowledge that had just been dropped onto me.

Create soldiers.

Was that what I had seen in the hallway? Was the experiment gone wrong supposed to be a soldier? If so, what did the successful experiment look like? Amias and Renna? Or something worse?

I couldn't wrap my head around the possibilities. Amias hadn't said much about it, and I wished I'd asked. If only so I wouldn't have to fear all the options that were displaying themselves in my mind.

How many of the other prisoners here were hiding something? How many of them were working for the Director, just like Amias and Renna?

I wrapped my arms around myself, praying to a god I didn't believe in for a chance to get out of this nightmare.

Department 1, Day 2

In my opinion, helplessness is one of the worst feelings. At this point in his journey, I imagine Sander must have been feeling that way. He was realities away from his family, stuck in an unfamiliar prison with an odd group of people.

It is true; I pitied him. But being around him was somewhat annoying. His ignorance felt like a burden. As I got to know him, however, I realized how hard he had been trying to fit in.

Sander is the type of person who dumbs himself down to match another's personality, but when he is the uneducated one, he feels pressured into acting like he knows more than he does. If he can't, he tends to sink back into his comfort zone and pull away from people.

He is a gifted boy. Truly. It is hard to find people as kindhearted and compassionate as he is. He understands how to listen to other people's side of the story, even if he believes it to be wrong or immoral.

But even the kindest people have a dark side. And Sander had yet to dip his toes into the shadows.

-Elyane

CHAPTER SIX

I dreamed of that night.

My hands were bound. My feet were bound. The voices were jumbled. The smell of blood and beer choked the air from my lungs. My temple throbbed, and I found myself worrying about the punch I'd taken and the bruise it would leave.

But then Dad came into view. He was tied to his own chair, pleading at the men who hit him. His lip was cracked and bleeding. A bruise had already bloomed on his jaw, and I was sure that the white specks on the carpet were his teeth. His tears mixed with blood as they rolled down his face.

"Please!" he cried. "Please! Just let my son go!"

The man hit him again, and I saw the tattoo on his wrist. A shattered mirror.

The words of the attackers grated my ears like static. They were demanding something from my dad, who shook his head violently. My pleas ripped from my throat, tight and hoarse, but the men paid no attention as if I wasn't there.

Dad shook his head again, his next words quiet enough that I strained to hear them. "I don't know where she put it."

"Then you are of no use to us," the man declared, pulling an impossibly long blade from the sheath on his forearm.

I screamed through my gag. Dad turned to face me.

His words were distorted as if he were speaking through a buffering screen. "Don't worry, Sander." His mouth curved into an attempt at a comforting smile. Too fake. His body was shaking, pupils dilated with terror. "Help your mom and sister. Trust me.

Everything is going to be fine."

And then I was falling. Falling through an endless, empty void. I was still bound. Helpless to do anything as I plummeted into nothing.

Images lit up the abyss.

Dad screaming as they cut into him, screaming as his insides spilled out onto the rug.

Tears streamed down my face, and I writhed against my bindings. But I kept falling. Falling. Falling. Falling.

Dad was screaming.

The tattooed men were laughing.

The carpet started burning.

I was crying.

I lurched upright, reaching for nothing. My hand grazed the smooth wall beside my cot. I gasped for breath, veins throbbing in time with the thundering of my heart. I breathed in and then out. And again. In. Out. In. Out.

I rubbed my forehead, then pinched the bridge of my nose and collapsed backward.

I hated remembering the way the ropes felt around my wrists. Hated remembering the smell and the sight of the blood. I hated all of it.

I took a few shallow breaths before climbing off of my cot. I sat cross-legged on the floor of my cell and stared at the wall. My mind wandered and I let it because I couldn't do anything else.

At some point, I must've fallen asleep because I woke up to the sound of my door swinging open. When I opened my eyes, two figures silhouetted in dim light stood in the doorway. I blinked and hesitantly stood up.

A man stood by the Director. He wore a long white lab coat that hung loose over his spindly body. Brown hair tinged with specks of gray suggested he'd just woken up or that he hadn't slept at all. He seemed old, but not physically. He'd aged in a way that made me question what type of life he had lived. Despite the exhaustion that hung over him, he wore an eager expression.

"This is him?" The man's voice rose with glee.

The Director nodded. "Sander Fox, this is Warren Coldwell. He would like to have a chat with you."

Warren. The Director's husband. Head of Experiments. Aven's father.

The Director flicked her hand, and a set of guards came in from behind them. I didn't bother resisting as they gripped my elbows and guided me out of the cell.

The state of the hallway told me it was early: dim, empty, and quiet, save for the echo of our footsteps. After various steps for security, we stepped into an elevator. My heart squeezed in response to the cramped space.

I could see my reflection on the metal walls. Although my vision was somewhat warped, I looked tired. Broken. Just like my Reflection, or whatever I was supposed to call him. The person I'd seen dragged through the hallway on my first day here lingered in the back of my mind.

The machine hummed almost silently as we descended. It was a long ride, long enough that when the elevator beeped and stopped, I was jolted out of the tired trance I'd fallen into.

The Director stayed in the elevator. I gave her one last glance over my shoulder as I was guided down the new hallway. Her face was as stoic as ever.

Troy met us in the room I assumed to be our destination. He didn't move. Not a bit of recognition flashed across his expression as his gaze trailed over me.

The skinny man in the white lab coat—Warren—moved toward a metal desk drilled into one of the white walls. He ran his hands over the metal, and to my surprise, a holographic screen flickered to life, as well as a keyboard. As he logged in, he waved off the guards and spoke to Troy.

"Troy, this is Sander. But from the report I was given, you two have already met."

"We have, sir."

Warren shuddered. "Don't call me sir. Save the formal stuff for your mother. She's the one who cares."

"Sorry, s-" Troy bit back another sir. "Sorry."

I tilted my head. So, Aven was Troy's sibling. Seeing him again made me realize just how much he looked like Aven. So much so that if he had been a few years younger, I could've easily mistaken them for each other.

Chuckling, Warren turned away from the screen and faced me again. "Sander Fox, I have waited so long to meet you."

I lifted my gaze to his, words dry in my throat.

He straddled a nearby swivel chair and drew in a deep breath, suggesting he was going to start telling a story. He didn't disappoint. "My title in the SSD is the Head of Experiments, meaning it's my job to oversee and conduct all sorts of research projects and such. But this wasn't always my job. Before me, the position belonged to a brilliant woman named Samrah Mahmud."

Beside him, Troy stiffened.

"The word genius doesn't even cover half of how amazing this woman was." Warren's face was full of awe. "She was an amazing scientist, and she created our government's biggest weapon yet. Substance A."

He spun on the chair and pulled up an image on the screen. A picture of a young boy appeared. He was maybe ten or eleven, lifting a car above his head with an excited grin on his face. Although I was surprised to see what he was capable of, my gaze was pulled to his arms and neck, which were covered in bandages.

"Substance A, the A standing for 'aggrandize,' gives an individual enhanced strength and reflexes and shortens their typical healing time. And that's just the beginning of it."

His voice grated my ears. I hated the way he talked like it was something to be proud of. Experimenting on kids until their entire body was covered in bandages. My stomach tightened.

He continued, "This boy right here was our first successful use of the serum, whom you've already had the pleasure of meeting."

I snapped my head away from the picture and faced him. "What?"

Another picture appeared beside the image of the young boy lifting the car. It was a face I recognized, with sapphire eyes, charcoal hair, and wolfish features. Amias.

My stomach tightened even more. I lifted a hand to my mouth, sickened. All the anxiety I had felt around Amias dissolved into sympathy and pity.

"What's the matter?" Warren tilted his head, genuinely interested in my discomfort.

I held back my retort, not sure if I would be able to talk at all. Did he truly have no morals? No regret or disgust for experimenting on a kid? Amias was around ten in the first picture, and he was eighteen now, which meant he'd been working for the SSD for eight years, maybe more.

When I didn't answer, he sighed and moved on. "Unfortunately, we were attacked after our second success. Samrah was killed. Her research, stolen."

I noticed Troy's fists clench.

"As the second-in-command, I rose to the top and was tasked with recreating her work. But it was hopeless; I am nowhere near her level. And I had nothing to go off. All her work was gone." For the first time since the conversation started, the glimmer in his eyes vanished. It turned to an accusing glare pinned on me. "Or so we thought."

A sinking feeling began to arise in my gut. I had a feeling I knew where this was going.

"The woman who stole Samrah's research came up on our radar a few weeks ago. We had trouble tracking her down, but we finally caught up to her in Department 523. Your home Department."

"What are you saying?" My voice was shaky. I swallowed.

"It seems you had a run-in with this woman." He leaned forward, elbows on his knees. "My question for you, Mr. Fox, is what exactly happened that night?"

Sweating, I clenched and unclenched my fists. Fear overtook me. So, I lied.

"I—I don't really know. I remember waking up, and there was a woman in my room. I heard voices, but that's about it. I thought it was a dream, so I ignored it. I must've fallen asleep because the next thing I knew, I was waking up, and it was morning."

Troy spoke. "It's not a good idea to lie to us."

"I'm not lying," I pleaded. "I swear I'm not. I don't know anything."

"The woman." Warren pulled up another image on the screen. A frizzy-haired brunette with the name *Jones, Haley*, underneath. "Did she look like this?"

I shrugged, shaking. "I'm not sure. It—it was dark."

They both seemed skeptical. But why wouldn't they be? I wasn't the best liar. My hands shook despite my attempts to hide it.

Troy opened his mouth, but a siren cut him off.

Lights flashed red. An alarm blared.

Warren jumped up, and fear flashed in his eyes. Troy faced him and demanded, "Get to your room! Lock your door and turn off the lights!"

Warren didn't waste any time before racing out the door.

Troy disappeared, and I heard him say, "Get the prisoner back to his cell. Once you do, report to me straight away."

Two guards appeared and cuffed me. My limbs were still shaky, but they hauled me out the door and began leading me through the halls.

Guards ran past, carrying guns as they went. Men and women in black suits brushed past, shouting orders. People in lab coats fled, books and papers in their hands.

We took the elevator again, which seemed like a thoroughly stupid decision. The silence on the ride was only interrupted by the faint sound of chaos in the halls we passed. When the doors pinged open, the level we entered was a mess.

Guards in their blue and gray uniforms battled strangers in dirty, torn, and stained clothes. Despite their lack of uniform, they moved with surprising speed and skill as they shot and slaughtered the guards.

Gunshots rang out. Blood sprayed across the once-clean walls. Bodies littered the hallways, and the guards who were dragging me ran. I gaped in horror as an SSD soldier nearby crumpled to the ground, a knife protruding from his back. My limbs began to go numb, and I was grateful for the guards dragging me along. Without them, I would've shut down like a pill bug, curling into myself until the madness ended.

Then, the guard on my left toppled to the ground. The second guard lunged for him, releasing his grip on me. But another shot rang out, and he fell, too. I stifled a scream as the man crumpled to the floor, a hole through his helmet's visor and between his eyes.

Someone grabbed my shoulder and spun me around. I came face to face with a woman with dirt-stained skin and goggles propped on her messy hair.

"Please," I held up my cuffed hands. "I'm just a prisoner. Don't kill me."

She hesitated for a moment, turning to look at a photograph in her hands. Finally, she raised her hand and rammed the blunt of her gun against my temple. The world went black, but not before I saw the tattoo of a shattered mirror on her wrist.

CHAPTER SEVEN

"Sander?" Someone nudged my shoulder. "Sander, are you awake?"

I groaned in response.

"Oh, thank god." Ivy's voice sounded in my ear.

My eyelids flitted open. Save for Aven, the worried faces of my group stared back. Renna hung back outside my cell, boredom expressed through her slouched posture.

Behind Ivy, Amias grinned. "Welcome back, Fox. It's been lonely without you."

I sat up and groaned again as splitting pain shot through my temple. My whole body ached, and the springs jutting out of the mattress of my cot didn't help much. "What happened?"

"The SSD was attacked," Eden replied, her gray-blue eyes flashing with an emotion I couldn't comprehend.

"No shit, Sherlock," I mumbled.

She tilted her head. "Who is Sherlock?"

I arched an eyebrow, but Ivy cut in before I could say anything.

"It was the Rising. They managed to sneak through the walls and slaughter hundreds." Her words spilled quickly from her lips as if they tasted like poison.

"But not me?"

She shook her head, the dark waves of her hair bouncing in the LEDs. "Only members of the SSD. None of the prisoners."

"The Rising. I'm assuming this is some sort of resistance against the SSD?" I swung my legs over the side of the cot and rubbed my head.

"Yes. They've been trying to get into this place for years. We all thought they were going to free the prisoners, but…"

"But they didn't," Amias finished for her. "Much to our disappointment. Oh well, we have backup plans."

Hope sparked in me. I was cut off before I could ask him to elaborate.

"Then why attack at all?" Ivy retorted. "Were they just trying to weaken their enemies?"

"I heard they were looking for something," Eden said. Everyone turned to her, and she dipped her chin. "Just some of the rumors spreading around the prison."

"Does anyone know what they were looking for?" Ivy questioned; her gaze was pointed at Amias. Something like accusation sharpened her rounded, warm features.

"Why are you looking at me?" he snapped. "I had nothing to do with this."

"You know what my question is?" I spoke up. They turned to look at me. "Why didn't they let you and Renna out? You guys are supposed to be their weapons, right?"

Silence fell.

Finally, Amias huffed, "I don't know why they didn't let us out, okay? They haven't told us. Normally, we would be the first ones to respond to a situation like that. But maybe they didn't have enough time."

"Why didn't the guards let you out?" I shot back, anger bristling. "Surely, they know who you are?"

"Of course they do," Amias scoffed.

His bravado made heat rise in my neck. I clenched my sweating fists. How had I felt sorry for this arrogant boy?

"Does anyone know anything?" I snapped, rising to my feet. "About this revolution or why they attacked?" My chest squeezed, locking my heart in a state of fear.

No one answered.

"What about Aven? Do they know anything?"

"We have yet to hear from them," Eden replied. Her voice caught me off guard, the calmness in her words.

The peace it brought me was short-lived. "So, for all we know, they could be dead?" I threw my hands up and turned toward the wall. "Dear god, we're all going to die." Clutching my uniform, I pressed my forehead against the cool white tile.

The butterflies in my stomach happily showed off their dagger-tipped wings, searing the inside of my gut as they fluttered about. In response, I squeezed my eyes shut and swallowed the lump forming in my throat. The tattoo of a broken mirror burned brightly against my eyelids.

The Rising had something to do with my father's death. The thought burned like acid.

It had been a trivial detail from that night but had somehow stuck with me in the five years since. I'd spent the majority of my sleepless nights since then attempting to sketch an exact replica. For what? In hopes of giving it to the police as some sort of clue? I'd never gotten the lines right. The direction. The number of cracks in the mirror or the swirling darkness beyond the glass.

But it had been the same. Seeing it again brought those dormant emotions to the surface.

Rage boiled in my gut, fueling me to scream, but my body seemed intent on collapsing onto the cot and staying there. I did neither, limbs going numb as the walls in my mind thickened.

The familiar darkness loomed, beckoning with comforting malice.

Warm skin brushed against my wrist. A crack of lightning.

My eyes flickered open to find Eden's dark hand resting atop mine, only a few shades lighter. Her nails were short and the skin around them was peeling. A few had been covered with Band-Aids. The back of her hand was home to a white crescent, much like the lines across her cheekbones.

A quick turn of my head showed the rest of the group had

departed.

"Do you have family?" Her words sent the darkness skittering.

I swallowed. I blinked a few times and watched hesitantly as she ran her fingers over the lines in my palm. "A mom. And a twin sister."

"Tell me about her."

"Um, well, she's a big people person. She's got lots of friends. I don't know. She's a nice person but kind of fake. She presents a mask to those she's not comfortable with or with those she feels the need to impress."

Eden flipped my hand over, rubbing the spot between my thumb and index finger. Her touch was rough, digging deep into my skin. "Mhmm. Ivy's kind of like that."

"Yeah…" I trailed off, studying her face. The odd, blue-gray eyes and the white lines across her cheekbones. "What are you doing?"

"Calming you down." She looked up at me.

It took a moment for me to process her words. Another moment to realize the fluttering of the daggered butterflies had stopped.

"Oh. Thanks."

She smiled again, then pressed her hand over her heart. "I would suggest getting some air, but there is not really a place for you to do that around here."

I blew out a laugh.

"I'll be in the cafeteria if you need anything."

The day went on as if nothing had happened. It was odd, the way the prisoners and guards were able to act so normally. Well, somewhat normal.

A tension had settled over Blackford. The guards were doubled. Even with the black visors covering their faces, I could sense an uneasy feeling around them.

Aven didn't show up. Amias and Renna were called away. After roaming around for a little bit, I slipped back into my cell to take a nap.

Relaxation was a mere wish, however. Though the panic had worn off, my mind still swirled with the thoughts of the woman in the hallway and the tattoo she'd borne.

Had Dad been connected to the Rising? What did he do to get them to kill him? What had he known?

And why had they let me go free? Both then and now. Perhaps, now, it *was* because I was a prisoner. I couldn't help but wonder if I had some sort of value to them. Had they let me go all those years ago because they'd wanted me alive or merely because I was a child at the time?

The bloodbath I'd seen mere hours ago made me doubt the Rising had that sort of mercy in their hearts.

It's pointless to keep thinking these things, I told myself. *It's not your problem*. But maybe it was. I was connected to the SSD and the Rising now. Somehow.

I pressed the heels of my hands into my eyes. Too much thinking. The thinking was bad.

I stepped outside my cell, peering down the hallway. Eden and Ivy had gone for lunch, and I'd meant to join them but had been too swept up in my worries.

When I walked through the heavy door leading to the ramp circling the rotunda, the noise was overwhelming. Prisoners laughed and chatted; others yelled. I brushed past a few prisoners and made my way up the ramp.

The crowd thinned the further I ascended, and soon, I was alone on the ramp. For a moment, I gripped the railing and stared down at the view below. I could just make out Ivy and Eden sitting at our table, bonding over a bowl of soup.

The faint sound of piano keys drifted from a few levels up. Curious, I followed the sound down a vacant hallway. Dust coated the walls, but the ground had about a dozen sets of footprints, all the same size as if someone had come this way often.

At the end of the hallway, there was a rusted door. Broken chains, which I assumed had once been wrapped around the handle, lay discarded on the floor. I pulled open the door, and the music flooded through.

I let out a marveled breath, my worries momentarily forgotten. The music came from a piano in the center of the room that looked like it had suffered years of neglect. Dust-covered, old prison furniture had been shoved along the walls. Cots, chairs, cafeteria tables. A storage room. I wondered how the piano had made it in here.

But the music… it was wondrous. More so than any other music I'd heard before. But when I recognized the hulking silhouette that sat at the piano, I couldn't help but let out a startled laugh.

The music stopped. "Surprised to see me, Fox?"

"I didn't peg you as a piano guy," I told Amias.

He chuckled and patted the bench next to him. "Come on. I'll teach you."

I hesitated only for a moment before obliging. I ran my fingers along the keys, cool underneath my skin. It was an old piano, but it sounded as if it had just been made. "This is beautiful," I whispered.

"I know." There was a hint of a curve on his lips. "I found it on one of my first nights here." He played a short melody that rang out beautifully in the near-silence.

I blinked, surprised at the fact that he hadn't always been here. I decided to pry. "Where did you learn to play?"

"Back home, I used to sneak into the music shop at night and play the piano there. The shopkeeper caught me one time and took pity on me. She taught me everything I know." He smiled at the memory, an old sadness in his eyes.

He shook himself and played the same melody again.

"Try it," he said, doing it slower so I could watch. I tried. The sound came out slow and harsh.

"Don't press too hard," he instructed.

I attempted to do it again, but my fingers stumbled, and a horrible, sharp note rang out. I winced, and Amias laughed.

After a few more failed attempts, I gave up with a dispirited sigh. "This is impossible," I complained.

"It's really not," countered Amias. "You just have clumsy fingers."

"I do not."

"That was a lousy comeback." He poked me. "You just need to keep practicing. Then, maybe one day, you'll become half as good as me."

"Maybe?"

"In like a decade or so."

I laughed, and with a heart-wrenching jolt, I realized it was the first genuine laugh that had come out of my mouth in a long time. My heart sank a little at the realization that it was this man—the one who had captured me and put me in here—that had made me laugh like that.

After about an hour, I left Amias after he made me promise not to tell anyone about the piano room. Ivy found me on my way back to my cell and reported that Aven had been freed from their job for the day and had changed into a prisoner's uniform to sneak into our hallway unnoticed. They'd said their mom didn't want them talking to us. That we were "miserable, filthy prisoners that weren't worthy of speaking to them."

Aven didn't seem to care, though. They were lying on my cot when I stepped into my cell.

"Ever think of brightening the place up a bit, Sander?" they asked, tossing a red ball up and catching it again.

"I don't have much to brighten it up with." I hung back near the door, wary of the SSD member before me. I liked Aven. Truly. But their mom was the Director. She was sure to have influenced them in some unhealthy way.

"True." They caught the ball and sat up.

"What do you know about the Rising?"

Aven shrugged. "Not much. Just that they've been trying to get into the SSD for decades."

"What were they after?"

They raised an eyebrow. "My mom said they were here to kill her."

"Why?"

They scoffed. "You have to ask? She's the leader of a multidimensional terrorist group hellbent on achieving uppermost power. Of course, there are people who want her dead."

"Do you want her dead?" I leaned against the wall.

They went silent, contemplating. After a long moment, they finally said, "I don't think so. She's not a good person, but she's still my mom."

I hesitated before asking, "Are there any other people the Rising want dead? Or were there?"

"I'm not sure. Why are you asking?"

"I—" I swallowed, unsure of how to respond. "I was just wondering."

They looked at me skeptically but didn't say anything. We kept talking, but they didn't seem to know anything new about the rumors or why the Rising had attacked. Nor did they know anything about my dad, though I didn't ask them directly. I didn't dare risk sharing that information.

Not if it could connect me to this whole mess.

CHAPTER EIGHT

The following morning, I was sitting at our table in the rotunda, bouncing a ball between Amias and me, when the double doors swung open and the room fell silent.

A high-heeled, blonde-haired figure stepped through the entryway. The black and white of her immaculately tailored dress suit seemed stark and cold against the blues of the guards trailing her. A mere nod to the nearest one had him stomping toward me.

My limbs turned to lead.

The guard unceremoniously grabbed me by the arm and dragged me to the door. I sent a panicked look at Amias, whose expression had gone blank. He rose, avoiding my gaze, and stalked away.

I was led up an elevator and to an office and shoved into a black leather chair. When I made to race toward the door, the cold barrel of a gun nudged my temple. The Director took a seat behind the desk and leaned back, scanning me.

She was silent for a few minutes, the only sound a faint ticking from a clock on the wall behind her. To my right, the wall had been taken over by black cupboards stretching from floor to ceiling. On my left, an outward slanted window overlooked a sprawling cafeteria with people in black suits and lab coats moving about like ants among the snow. There were no pictures on the desk or the walls, the only colors being from the pens neatly lined up beside a stack of papers on the desk.

My heart stuttered to a stop as the Director pinned her gray-eyed stare on me. The silence between us was thick with tension. Although she seemed relaxed, my body was rigid.

Finally, she spoke. "Your father... he died a few years ago, correct?"

I nodded, worried about where this conversation was headed. The guard seemed to acknowledge that I knew I wasn't going anywhere and lowered his gun.

"My knowledge is that the police were never able to find any leads as to who was responsible for his murder."

"Is that a question?" The words felt slow, stuck to the sides of my throat.

"I want you to tell me your story. What did you see? The people—was there anything unusual about them?"

Why was she asking about this? She couldn't possibly know about the tattoo similarity, could she? I hadn't spoken about it to anyone other than a brief description to the police. The drawings I'd done had long since been thrown out.

The guard beside me shifted, nudging the barrel of his gun in my direction once more.

A reminder to talk.

I shook my head cautiously. "They looked like normal people. Knocked on the door. My dad was the one to open it and—" I fell silent. Unwanted memories emerged from the corner of my mind I'd shoved them into. "Mama and Sadira were able to get out unnoticed. They called the cops, but it—"

"It was too late," the Director finished for me.

"They burned our house down and vanished." I let out a shaky breath. "No one knows anything. The police stopped looking years ago."

She drummed her nails against the desk, a look of contemplation crossing over her face. Running her fingers over the desk space in front of her, a keyboard flicked to life. A holographic screen was cast into the air between us. She pulled up an image of a man with chestnut skin, deep brown eyes, and a lip piercing. In the picture, he was smiling, his arm thrown around a person whose face had been cut from the frame.

"Was this man at the scene of your dad's murder?"

"Um, no. Why? Who is he?"

She gave no answer. "You witnessed William's death firsthand. In the police report, they mentioned you heard part of a conversation between the attackers and the victim."

A lump formed in my throat.

"Can you recall what they spoke about?"

My mouth was dry as I dredged up the memories, spilling them out as fast as possible as if the words were rotten.

It had been years ago, but some of the conversation still lingered in my mind. I told the Director as much as I could, some part of me hoping that my cooperation would be rewarded with freedom. A foolish thought, but it was there, nonetheless.

The group had been looking for something. They'd mentioned names, none of which I could remember. I did recall them speaking about a family that would be coming after them. Coming for us. That part was vivid in my memories. The look on Dad's face after they mentioned that had been one I would never be able to forget.

I couldn't bring myself to mention the tattoos.

By the time I was done, my body ached.

My insides swam with nausea as I was guided back to my cell, and I wasn't able to keep up the conversation Ivy attempted to start with me.

"What happened?" she asked. "What did you guys talk about?"

I swallowed, unable to answer, and collapsed onto my cot. Shoving my face into the pale sheets, I felt the mattress shift as she took a seat next to me.

"I want to go home," I croaked out as I buried my face in my hands.

She patted my shoulder awkwardly. "Don't worry," she said under her breath, her voice laced with a sobriety I hadn't heard from her before. "We aren't going to be here for much longer."

CHAPTER NINE

I stumbled down the rotunda's ramp early the next morning, a yawn creeping into my mouth. Despite it being barely ten minutes after the cells had unlocked for the day, the cafeteria was filled to the brim, each table seating more than its capacity. Other than ours, of course. It seemed as if everyone knew to steer clear of Renna and Amias. But they weren't the only ones who'd made a name for themselves. I'd seen people speed-walking just to get out of Eden's way.

It wasn't hard for me to imagine why, but the memory of her soft voice calming me down was so different than what I'd expected from her.

Again, I was struck by the oddness of the people in this prison. I bumped into a purple-skinned woman with something that looked like seaweed replacing her hair.

I muttered my apologies, grabbed my breakfast, and sat down.

It wasn't until I took my first bite of grainy bread that I noticed the others staring at me. I chewed, gaze sliding from face to face. Renna's expression was empty, as usual, but Eden, Ivy, and Amias all shared a look of worry.

I swallowed. "Is there a bug on me?"

Amias cleared his throat. "I overheard a conversation last night. Between a few of the guards."

"Okay, and?" I prompted, lifting the bread to my mouth.

"Apparently, you're to be executed. They're taking you tonight."

I choked on the bread.

Eden patted my back sympathetically as I launched into a coughing fit. Blinking back tears, I looked up at him. "What?"

"That's what I heard." He shrugged, then a grin lit up his face. "But fear not, I have already put together an escape plan. Well, I've had an idea for a while, but now, we have a more compelling reason to try it."

I put my head in my hands. The breath in my lungs turned to ice.

I was going to be executed. The world drained away as this reality sunk in. I truly was going to die. The possibility of this had been in my head since arriving here, but now it was happening. It—

"Hey, Fox. Snap out of it." Amias reached over the table to poke my shoulder. "Did you not hear what I said? I put together an escape plan."

I couldn't get words out of my mouth, but I tilted my gaze toward his face.

His grin grew wider. "God, I should've done this years ago. We're leaving this shithole, Foxy. And we're not going to die in the process."

"Hooray," I muttered bleakly.

I'd never thought I'd be able to say I broke out of prison. Yet, here I was, standing in the piano room and waiting for Amias to blow a hole in the ceiling.

Even though he'd explained the plan to me multiple times, I still didn't understand what we were doing. I'd spent the majority of my day trying desperately to act normal and calm my anxiety-ridden mind. If the plan went sideways, I had no doubt the SSD would love to make an example out of my execution.

Eden, Renna, and Ivy had spent their time trying to keep me distracted. Whereas Amias had scampered off when Aven faked a summoning from the Director. In reality, Amias was making his way to a room above the prison. The room above the one we stood in.

Soon, he'd blow a hole in the floor, making an opening into the crawl space above us, and then open the sealed trap door to let us in.

After that, I'd gotten a little overwhelmed and couldn't comprehend the rest of the plan. Something about maintenance stairs. Terror had blocked my ability to understand prison break explanations.

But the overthinking had somewhat stopped a while ago. I'd started counting backward from ten thousand in my head. Right now, I was at five thousand. For the second time. Not counting all the times someone had talked to me and caused me to mess up.

This was supposed to be the most secure prison in the whole multiverse. How the hell were we supposed to get away unnoticed? That was what I'd asked, but Amias told me to leave that to Aven. Apparently, they were going to disable the lasers and alarms.

I checked the dusty clock on the storage room wall: 9:28.

Amias said he'd be ready at 9:30, which meant we would only have thirty minutes before we were supposed to be locked in our cells and the guards did their rounds.

I tapped my foot impatiently. 4,981. 4,980. It was fine. We weren't going to die. 4,979. 4,978. 4,977.

There was the sound of a muffled explosion. My gaze shot up.

"It's okay, Sander," assured Ivy. "It's just Amias up above."

I nodded, biting my lip nervously.

There was a stomping sound. The ceiling shook. Plaster rained down on us. I blinked and coughed, taking a few steps back. Then, a loud crack split the air, and a trap door swung down from the ceiling.

Amias peeked his head out, a grin plastered on his dirtied face.

"What happened to you?" Ivy questioned, noticing the soot that covered his features. "Did you get in a fight with a chimney sweep's broom?"

"Yes," he replied. "Get the piano bench thingy. We don't have much time."

Renna did as he instructed, and one by one, we filed into the crawl space. Once I'd latched the trapdoor closed, I remained on all fours and followed the others, who had already begun to maneuver over the electrical and plumbing work.

The claustrophobia that settled over me didn't help with my anxiety. Head pounding with tension, thousands of what-ifs filled my mind. Sweat beaded on my brow. I gritted my teeth against it all.

It wasn't long before Amias stopped in front of a vent. He whistled to get our attention. "Fox first. After all, he's the one we're breaking out of here."

The others scooted out of the way to let me approach.

"Are you really that nice to let me go first?" I peered into the darkness of the vent.

"No," Amias chuckled and pushed on my feet. "You'll just get the spiders out of the way."

I didn't speak, afraid my voice would crack. The vent was bigger than the ones in typical houses, but I still had to lay down in order to fit. The metal pressed against my shoulders as I wormed my way forward.

"Probably should've gone in feet first," muttered Amias from behind me.

"What? Why?"

My question was answered when I felt the surface I was lying on slip away from underneath me. I let out a yelp and scrambled backward, accidentally kicking him in the face. "Sorry."

A blue glow lit up the space behind me, and Amias's deep voice rippled through the space. "Vent should be dropping away now. Fox, do you see it?"

"I can't see anything," I snapped. "But I felt it."

"Okay, gimme a second." I felt him rustling around, and then something hard hit the back of my head.

"Ouch." I reached for the object, which turned out to be the source of the blue light. It was a wristband, about as thick as a phone. A hologram projected from it, picturing a 3D map of what looked to be the vents.

"The red dot is you," Amias instructed. "You see the vent a little bit above you, to your right?"

"Yeah."

"You're going to reach into that, pull yourself out of here, and chimney crawl down."

"Oh, dear god," I mumbled and slipped the band onto my wrist. With the light of the map illuminating the tunnels, I managed to hook my arm into the vent to my right. My muscles screamed in protest as I wiggled my hips forward.

"Oh, this is not fun." I talked into my arms, which were clinging desperately to the ledge of the hole. It indeed was an awkward position. My body was half hanging out of the vent I'd been in previously.

"Get a move on!" Ivy shouted.

"You think I'm not trying?" I yelled back and pulled my legs out.

Fortunately, my shoes were grippy enough that they stuck to the side of the vent. After a little more maneuvering, I had my back against one wall and my feet pressed against the opposite one.

"Wonderful job, Fox," Amias congratulated, although I could've sworn he was teasing me. "Now get going."

I began inching myself down, my breathing getting more ragged by the second.

10,000. 9,999. 9,998.

I clenched my jaw.

9,997. 9,996.

In. Out.

Don't panic. Don't panic. I told myself repeatedly in between the numbers.

Survive this, and you can see Mama and Sadira again. You can go home.

The thought of home brought tears to my eyes. I bit my lip, forcing them back. Home. The smell of coffee, cinnamon, and Mama's pecan pie-scented candles. The feeling of my worn-out sheets pressing against my face. God, what I would give to hear Sadira yell at me again.

Amias snapped me out of my thoughts when he told me to check the map.

I did so and noticed the dropping vent came to a halt. I lowered my feet, relief rushing through me when they met solid ground. After checking the map one more time, I spotted a small hole by my knees. Unfortunately, this vent was covered by a grate.

"Um, Amias," I looked up at him.

"Yeah, yeah. I see." He grumbled and landed next to me.

The space was barely big enough for the two of us. His body brushed against mine as he nudged the grate with his foot. I pulled away as much as I could, ears flushing.

He turned to face me. "Can I see the map?"

His breath blew against my face. I nodded, panic and fear momentarily replaced by something unfamiliar.

He peered at the map. The small vent appeared to open into a duct big enough for us to stand up in. I wasn't sure what he was checking for, but he must've found what he needed because he told me to back up.

I did as much as I could, ducking behind him as he crouched, raised his fist, and swung a punch at the metal.

My breath left my lungs.

From the picture of ten-year-old Amias holding a car, I knew Substance A gave him superstrength, but seeing it in action was more surprising than I thought it would be.

He'd busted a hole through the metal. The steel sheets. With one punch.

In the dim lighting, I could see liquid dripping from his knuckles as he punched the hole wide enough for us to fit through. Blood. He peeled away the vent with breath-taking ease and ducked through, nimbly dodging the sharp edges despite his hulking shape.

"Careful," he warned as I followed him through.

A gust of air blew through my hair as I stepped through the vent and into the duct. It was about two arm lengths wide, and I could reach the top if I stood on my tiptoes. More vents split off behind us, leading to different parts of the facility.

I peered down the large duct. There was a light further down, but it was faint.

"Why are the vents so big?" My voice bounced off the walls, reverberating down the ducts.

"Blackford," responded Ivy, "as well as the rest of the SSD's main base, is all underground. It's a big facility, bigger than any building you've been in. It's practically a city, so they need as much air as they can get."

"Why did they build it underground?"

"Easier to keep safe." It was Renna who responded this time. She slipped through the hole Amias had made, turning to offer a hand to Eden. "They only have one door in this whole place."

A chill swept over me. "Then how are we getting out?"

From the light of the holographic map, I could see a small smile creep over her delicate face. It surprised me, being the most emotion I'd ever seen her show.

"Let me rephrase that," she said. "They only have one *safe* door to this place."

I wrapped my arms around myself, suddenly cold.

"This way," Amias instructed, and he headed off in the direction of the light.

It was a long walk, longer than I'd expected it to be. The more steps I took, the louder the space became. A loud humming caused the floor to tremble beneath our feet. Yet Amias didn't stop. The others didn't waver.

So, I clenched my shaking hands, rolled back my shoulders, and strode forward.

I was going to see my family again. I didn't care what I had to do.

The tunnel opened up into a circular ventilation shaft, ascending hundreds of feet upward. About two-thirds of the way up was the home of the humming sound. A large fan spun slowly, pulling the air up and out of the hole above it. I could see the star-lit sky peeking through in flashes of light as the fan spun.

Hopeful giddiness arose in me. We were almost there. So close.

"This way, Foxy." Amias pulled me back and pointed to a door in the side of the duct labeled MAINTENANCE. He broke the lock and pulled it open, revealing a metal stairwell lit by small lights every few feet or so.

Eden was the first one through. I stuck close to her, liking the sense of protection she gave off.

After a few flights of stairs, my legs were trembling. Whether from fear or physical exhaustion, I couldn't tell. But it was only made worse when an alarm started blaring.

"Shit, shit, shit," Amias cursed, grabbing my arm and brushing the wristband with his thumb. A clock popped up.

My heart sank. 10:03.

The guards had noticed we were missing.

Eden burst into a sprint. I stumbled after her.

Voices echoed from below us, and bright lights switched on. I sent a panicked look down the stairwell. Below, I could see a group of guards filing into the bottom of the stairwell, peering up.

"I see them!" I heard someone call.

"Don't look, Sander, just run!" Ivy yelled at me.

I put all the energy I had into my legs. A voice sounded in the back of my head. *Now Sadira can't say doing cross country was useless.*

I would've laughed if I hadn't been so utterly terrified.

I was so focused on keeping my legs moving that I didn't notice when Eden stopped. I ran into her, accidentally slamming her into a door.

"Oh my god, oh my god. I'm so, so sorry." My breathing was erratic, panic seeping into my words.

She didn't answer. Instead, she yanked the door open.

A gust of wind blew past us.

I tried to peer over her shoulder, but she just pushed me back and let Amias go first. He peered out the door and then turned his head to look up.

"Dammit," he cursed. "Aven said they'd be here by now." He came back inside and checked the guards.

"Ivy, Eden," he instructed. "You're in charge of keeping Fox safe until Aven gets here. Renna and I will take care of the guards."

I gaped. "Renna? Are you sure? She's kind of—"

Her glare cut me off, pure anger in her sky-blue eyes. I bit back my words, deciding it'd be best if I kept quiet.

Eden pulled me out the door and into the ventilation shaft I'd seen earlier. The fan was below us now, the exit maybe forty feet above us.

We stood on an outstretched metal platform surrounded by a rusted railing. I gripped the railing as Ivy and Eden backed up into me.

"Keep an eye above us," Eden shouted, loud enough to be audible over the drumming of the fan. "Aven should be here soon."

I glanced up.

Grunts and screams sounded from the stairwell, but Eden and Ivy were blocking my view despite me being taller than both of them.

I heard the faint sound of someone screaming my name.

My head shot up. At the top of the ventilation shaft, I could see Aven peeking over the side. They were lowering something down. A rope ladder.

I tapped Eden. "Aven's here."

She glanced up and then yelled at Amias.

A few more seconds passed before the ladder was within our reach. Eden ushered Ivy onto it and then turned to me. But my attention wasn't on her.

I'd stepped back into the stairwell. Renna was running toward us, blood staining her hands and a manic grin on her face. Bodies littered the steps. Visors had been shattered. Uniforms had been drenched in red.

I held back a gag.

Renna pushed past me and scrambled for the rope ladder.

"Sander." Eden was shaking me. "Sander, we need to go."

I'd frozen.

The blood. The smell of it brought back the memories. I clutched a hand to my mouth, my dinner threatening to make a reappearance. Tears blurred my vision, so much so that I didn't notice the guard in front of me until it was too late.

I felt the pain before I heard the shot.

It split through my side, and my legs crumpled from the shock. I barely had time to register what had happened before Amias grabbed me and dragged me toward the rope ladder.

I let out a cry as white-hot pain flashed through my body. I bent over myself, gripping the rope as Amias screamed at Aven, telling them to pull it up.

My vision was starting to fade. The coppery tang of blood filled my mouth.

Then, the rope started to move. Or maybe the wall was moving. Either way, all I could feel was Amias's arm around my waist and the pain shooting through my side.

More shots were fired. I heard them ring out, but I didn't think any hit me.

"Don't pass out on me," growled Amias. "God, you really are a pain."

"Sorry" was the only word I could get out of my mouth.

I was vaguely aware of being dragged up onto solid ground. I tasted sand, and a cold breeze swept over me. I made to sit up but cried out and crumpled as my side spasmed.

"Oh, so you wake up after the hard part is over?"

I blinked. Amias was leaning over me, anger written on his wolfish features.

I opened my mouth to speak, but no words came out.

"Do not try to talk," Eden said. "We need to move."

I whimpered at the thought of moving, and then leaned on her as she helped me to my feet. Aven finished pulling up the rope ladder, flipping off the guards below with a cheeky smile.

"Aven!" Ivy yelled at them. "Get your ass over here. You're the only one who knows how to fly a helicopter."

Helicopter… I peered into the darkness. Sure enough, I saw the machine's outline a few feet before us.

They began racing toward it.

Something moved in the corner of my eye. Another figure was running toward us. They raised something.

I cried out to Aven and Ivy, but my words were too late.

The figure launched the bomb. It landed on the helicopter and exploded with a flash of heat.

I was blown to my back, my ears ringing. The flames of the wreckage illuminated Eden's figure as she raced toward a crumpled Aven and Ivy. Her screams were faint, but all the same, they ripped through me.

I glanced toward the figure who was stalking toward us. The one who had fired off the bomb.

It was a familiar face. One that sent chills down my spine as I got a good look at it.

Troy spotted me, a grin falling over his features.

My body succumbed to the heaviness tugging me downward, and then I promptly passed out.

CHAPTER TEN

4,223. 4,222. 4,221.

In. Out.

Counting. Breathing. No matter what I tried, nothing could distract me from the pain that was ever so slowly spreading through my body. Somehow, my wound wasn't bleeding any more. Instead, a chill had settled on my skin, encompassing it. But the pain ravaged my hip and across my ribs.

A contrived, stale breeze blew through my hair and ruffled my blood-stained prison uniform. I'd woken up on frigid, smooth cement. It was too dark to make out much of where I was, but Aven, Ivy, and Eden were tied up and knelt on the ground beside me. Beyond them, I could barely see the figures of a dozen guards surrounding us and the cement walls past them.

We sat in silence, staring into nothing as our minds reeled. A taste of freedom, that's what we'd felt, only for it to be stripped away.

As I looked around, I realized with a heart-stopping jolt that I sat surrounded by a group of people I barely knew anything about.

But the weird part… I think I trusted them.

Because as crazy as they were, they'd tried to save me when they'd found out I was supposed to be executed. And yes, they were probably killers and murderers, and yes, that made me uneasy, but they'd saved me. As stupid as it sounded, they were killers for the right reasons.

For a moment, this realization ebbed the terror that threatened to consume me.

I wasn't sure how long it had been when the lights finally buzzed and switched on. I let out a groan against the sudden brightness. Blinking against the tears that threatened to form, I squinted at the room around us. We were in what looked to be a garage with a couple dozen heavily armed, advanced-looking vehicles. Before us, embedded into a concrete wall, a set of commercial steel doors swung open to allow entry for the Director, Troy, Warren, and a group of others I had yet to recognize. They trailed the Coldwells with their heads bowed and shoulders hunched, taking up as little space as possible.

"Apologies for making you wait so long," the Director said. "We had a few things to sort out before we could get to what we were planning to do with you."

In the light, I could now see the white powder that had been dumped over my wound. "What did you do to me?" I rasped.

"What did we do *for* you?" Troy corrected. His eye was bruised, and dried blood dotted his cheekbone and forehead, yet he still wore a smug expression. "You come from a reality of little scientific progress, so it's no surprise you wouldn't recognize HemoSeal when you see it."

The Director sent a glare at her son and he shrunk. She then turned to Aven, her glare shifting to despondency. "I'm disappointed in you."

They clenched their jaw, biting back an angry retort.

She went on, "You deserted your post, aided in the escape of the prisoners, and betrayed the SSD—"

"All right, shut up," Aven snapped. "Are you just going to stand there and read my crimes? Because, honestly, none of us give a damn. And yes, I betrayed the SSD. So what? The place was shitty anyway. If you ask me, I didn't do it soon enough."

Her eyes flared, and she opened her mouth to speak but was cut off when a roar echoed nearby.

Everyone went silent.

Another muffled growl rippled through the air. The Director's face went pale.

"Ma'am?" Troy asked.

"Someone let them out," she said in disbelief, her eyes going wide.

The door burst open. Amias ran through with a wild grin on his face. Renna ran beside him, her expression mirroring his.

"What did you do?" Aven hissed as the duo raced toward the guards surrounding us.

"I let the monsters out." Amias grinned, snatching a pistol from the nearest guard's hands, who seemed hesitant to shoot someone who had been on their side a few hours ago. At Amias's movement, however, the rest of the guards snapped their guns toward him. But Renna moved faster.

I had a sinking feeling he wasn't speaking metaphorically.

"We need to move—*now*," Renna said. One blow to the visor of a guard had the screen cracking, revealing the terrified expression of the brunette beneath. Another one sent her crumpling to the ground, out cold.

How old was Renna? Thirteen?

She focused her efforts on the remaining guards, half of whom had chosen to protect their leader and raced for the Director.

Amias made his way toward us, unveiling a knife in his sleeve.

As the chaos swarmed around us, I locked gazes with the Director. Something like a smile painted her red lips, but I didn't have time to read into it. Amias sliced through the ropes on my wrists just as the roaring thing crashed through the doors. I caught a glimpse of white mottled and cracked skin, a large hulking figure complete with claws and fangs, and then Amias pushed me away and shouted to the others.

He shoved us into the back of a nearby truck and then scrambled into the front seat. After everyone had climbed in, Renna slammed the doors shut and yelled to Amias. My heart raced. The engine roared into action, and the tires skidded. I clutched the edge of my seat so hard I heard a knuckle pop.

Before I could even form a thought, the world went flying. Glass shattered. The truck tumbled through the garage and slammed into something. A roar echoed through the room. Pain ripped through my arm, and my head slammed against something hard.

"Fox?!"

I heard Amias shout my name, but it was faint.

"Renna?!" he shouted again, coughing. His massive frame came into view, and he knelt before me, shaking my shoulders. "Hey, hey. Get up, Foxy."

I blinked and crawled to my hands and knees, then up to my feet. Adrenaline had taken over; the pain in my side was a mere throb. Amias pushed me toward the truck's door, handing me a gun before he went to help the others.

I staggered out of the truck, which had been thrown upside down against the wall. My head was bursting with pain, and when I brought my fingers to my forehead, they came back covered in blood.

Across the room, I heard a snarl and a crunch. I squinted toward the sound. My vision was blurred, but I could just make out the creature from before as it lifted something—a man—into his mouth and tore away a piece. A bloodcurdling scream ripped across the space, then abruptly went silent. The Director and her followers were nowhere to be seen.

My heart stopped. "Amias..." I said, turning back to him. "Amias, what the hell is that?"

He winced. "That's a story for when our lives aren't in immediate danger."

"Amazing plan, Amias," Renna noted, helping Aven crawl to their feet.

Ivy was leaning against Eden, biting her lip in pain. My eyes trailed to her foot, which was dangling at an unnatural angle.

"It was the only plan we had," Amias countered.

The creature threw the bloodied body—little more than a sack of meat—to the side and spun toward us. Blood dripped from its jaws, its long, pointed teeth stained red. I thought of the body I'd seen in the hallway all those weeks ago. The thing in front of me looked like that, but as if it had more time to evolve. It was around fifteen feet tall, with pale skin and bloodshot eyes. It crept toward us on its hind legs, but the abnormal length of its forearms caused its claws to drag along the floor.

"Shit," Amias cursed. "Shit, shit, shit."

"I feel that word perfectly describes our current situation," I said.

"Go, go, go!" He began herding us toward a tunnel sloping upward toward the surface.

Eden lifted Ivy onto her back, and we ran. But we weren't fast enough.

The creature leaped in front of us, blocking our path to escape the garage. Its mouth dripped with blood, and it let out a snarl as it took an advancing step. We spun around and began running the other way. It ran after us. Its footsteps sent tremors through the ground.

There was a scream.

I spun around to see that the creature had snatched Ivy from Eden. Ivy reached for her gun, but the creature shook her, and it fell out of her hands and onto the ground. I aimed the one Amias had given me and shot, but the bullet just bounced off the creature and clattered to the floor.

Eden's expression had frozen with deathly rage. She slid underneath the creature, slicing its forearm with a piece of broken metal she'd picked up from the wreckage of the truck. Blue blood sprayed across the floor, but the creature just turned to Eden, barely flinching. It let out a roar and tossed Ivy aside. She skidded across the garage and slammed against a pole. She didn't move.

Eden leaped away from the creature, but it caught her easily. It lifted her to its mouth, teeth snapping hungrily.

"Put her down, you big freak!" Renna screamed.

The creature froze.

I looked at her. We all looked at her. Renna tilted her head.

The creature seemed to forget Eden as its bulging eyes flicked toward Renna. An indecipherable expression crossed its face, and it tossed Eden to the side. The creature began stalking toward Renna. It seemed curious, but its hesitant steps suggested wary thoughts, if a beast like that could even think.

"What the hell is that thing?" Ivy snapped through pained grunts as Eden eased her onto her feet. Both moved shakily toward us.

Amias's face was ashen. The muscles in his throat moved as he swallowed. But he remained silent as he hustled the six of us into a rover while the creature was docile.

"Stop moving," Amias snapped at me.

"Tell Aven to stop driving like a lunatic," I retorted, digging my feet into the floor to brace myself against the jolting of the rover.

"Tell the desert not to be so bumpy." Aven was at the wheel of the rover, their fingers drumming against the leather to the beat of imaginary music.

The stars freckled the night sky, stretching over the desert in a blanket of darkness. The wind nipped through the cracked window at Ivy's side, ruffling her hair as she rested against the glass. According to Renna, desert was the only thing on this planet. It was a world destroyed by humanity's own stupidity. A world the SSD had decided to make their own.

Pain jolted through my side as Amias adjusted my bandages, taping the gauze to my skin. I clenched my jaw.

I watched warily as he moved to put the first aid kit back into the cupboard beneath the bench.

There were only two seats in the rover. Aven and Ivy occupied the driver's and the passenger's seats. The cabin of the rover, where the rest of us sat, consisted of two benches, a cupboard, and a bunch of covered electrical work. I sat on a bench with Eden while Amias moved to sit with Renna across from us.

I still couldn't wrap my head around what had happened. What we'd seen. And especially what Renna had done. I hadn't confronted her or Amias about the look I'd seen them exchange. They knew what that thing was. It had nearly killed Ivy and Eden, and yet, they still hadn't mentioned what they knew.

"Sander," Ivy said, peering over her shoulder to look at me, "is your forehead feeling okay?"

I nodded, unconsciously reaching to touch the bandage she'd put on it. Thankfully, Ivy was fine after being slammed into the pole, if only a bit dazed. Aven had diagnosed her with a mild concussion but nothing too serious. As for her foot, her ankle had been dislocated, but Eden had popped it back into its socket without hesitation. It was obvious to me that they had experienced things like this before, though I still felt hesitant to ask about their pasts. It was a delicate subject that I feared I didn't have the pondering expression sanction to touch.

The silence was deafening, disrupted only by the growl of the rover's engine as we plowed through the desert unforgivingly. I grazed my fingers across the bandage beneath my bloody prison uniform, wishing for something to change into. But our previous search of the vehicle had turned up empty, save for a few jackets and medical kits.

Agitation boiled beneath my skin. No one had said a word about where we were going. Nor had Amias or Renna explained what the creature in the garage was. I'd risked my life trusting these people. Trusting *Amias* as he'd let loose a monster that nearly tore us apart.

"Say something already, Sander," Renna grumbled.

I blinked, unaware my feelings had been on display. "Excuse me?"

"Your jaw will break if you clench it any harder." She pulled her foot onto the bench, leaning against Amias tiredly.

How was I supposed to respond to that? I searched for the words but fell short and turned away, tension knotting in my chest. I feared if I started talking, I wouldn't stop until a panic attack had rendered my ability to speak.

Thankfully, I didn't have to say anything at all because Eden did it for me. "Amias," she started, crossing her legs and inspecting a cut along the back of her wrist. "I can't say I understand why you aren't overwhelmed with a desire to tell us what you unleashed."

He shifted uncomfortably, brushing one of Renna's braids off his face. "I can't say I'm sure where to begin." Something bitter laced his voice.

"Hm," Ivy feigned a pondering expression. "How about starting with *what the hell* that thing was?"

"Why don't you tell them?" Amias nudged Renna.

She elbowed him. Hard. "You're the one that set it free."

He glared at her before submitting. "That was Warren's attempt at recreating the SSD's greatest success. Renna and I." He puffed his chest a bit at the last bit, and I resisted the urge to roll my eyes. "Before Warren, the Head of Experiments was a woman named Samrah Mahmud. She was assassinated shortly after completing Renna and me five years ago." His bravado faltered at the mention of this woman.

"I've heard that name before," Ivy said. "I think my parents knew her."

I blinked at the mention of her parents.

Aven cut in. "Probably. She was close with my mom as well."

"I already know all of this," I grumbled. "Warren told me."

Amias blinked. "Oh. Did he tell you about his failures?"

I shook my head slowly.

"For years now, he's been trying to replicate her work. But as you've seen… he hasn't been that successful."

"That's not really true," Renna countered. "The monsters he created could be even more powerful than us, once he finds a way to control them."

"So, the thing that attacked us," I rubbed my temple. "Just to recap. That was Warren's failed attempt at recreating the serum that was used to create you and Renna?"

Amias nodded. "Substance A."

"Right. Right. Right," I muttered and let out a shaky breath. I cupped my hands over my ears and curled my shoulders forward. I had almost been killed by the result of a genetic experiment gone wrong. And Warren was doing that work *willingly*?

A thought struck me hard, as if a church bell had sounded in my mind. Samrah had known the woman who had broken into my apartment. Warren had told me that much.

"Five years ago, you said?" I found myself asking.

Amias gave a shallow nod.

Five years ago, my dad was killed. Was it a coincidence he'd been killed the same year as the woman who'd created the SSD's greatest weapons? Surely, lots of people got murdered, but when a suspect of one of the murders happened to show up in the room of the other victim's kid? There had to be something there.

The rover had gone quiet again. Processing.

Amias had to know more. If I could find out more about the day she'd been killed, then maybe I could find some other correlation.

But part of me didn't want to know. In fact, most of me didn't want to. This wasn't my mess. As soon as I got off this godforsaken planet and back into my apartment with my family, it'd all be in the past.

The thought drove me to rest, but I wasn't sure what led me to keep quiet about my suspicions. Maybe it was the way Renna was staring at me, her gaze calculated, as if my thoughts were projected before her in bubble letters.

I bundled into myself, the thought of home luring me away from the rover and eventually into sleep.

Department 1, Day 4

My final resting place is getting colder. I have no way to decipher the months, but I can sense winter taking over. That does not mean much. No one else is here.

After breaking out of Blackford, news of us spread fast throughout the Inter-Dimensional Government, the ID. We had done the unthinkable. Broken free from a prison that was supposedly unbreakable.

Something in me had not sat right about our escape. This prestigious, impenetrable facility, and we had gotten out without a single death. It felt too easy. However, I decided to brush it off, grateful that we had made it out without any fatalities.

We celebrated. Praised ourselves. Thought us to be invincible.

Oh, the naivety.

If only we could have seen. If only we could have spotted the secrets behind those predatorial eyes. Perhaps our ending would have been a little more peaceful.

–Elyane

CHAPTER ELEVEN

I slipped in and out of sleep throughout the following day and night. When I finally arose from unconsciousness for longer than five minutes, Amias sat at the wheel. The morning sun slipped through his hair, illuminating the outline of his face.

I was lying on the bench, a backpack underneath my head and a thin wool blanket stretching across my body. I felt a stab of guilt when I spotted Eden asleep on the ground. I must've pushed her off at some point, but I couldn't really remember when.

She seemed content, though. Her arm was around Ivy's waist, and her face was buried in her back, the blanket barely big enough to cover both of them. I laid mine down on top of them and stretched.

I reached to move the backpack, but it fell from my hands and the contents clattered to the floor. I mumbled a curse and made to pick them up but stopped when I noticed a familiar leather-bound sketchbook.

"Amias?" I called. "Why is my sketchbook in here? This is your backpack, right?"

"Oh yeah," he chuckled. "I nabbed that before they put it in the incinerator. Thought it was cool. Took me a while before I realized it was yours."

"Did you look through it?" I bristled.

"Yup. You're really good."

I frowned, unnerved at the thought of Amias looking through my drawings. Not that they were embarrassing or anything, but they were a little… creepy. I had a dark mind, and it was easy to put those types of thoughts onto paper instead of talking about them.

I shook myself off and changed the subject. "How long do you think we have until the SSD finds us?"

He shrugged. "The wind blew away our tracks last night, but with their helicopters, it could be anywhere from a few hours to a day."

He spotted the concern on my face in the rearview mirror and grinned. "Don't worry, Foxy. We came up with a plan while you were napping."

"Which is?" I raised an eyebrow, rubbing the tender muscles surrounding the spot where I'd been shot.

"We're going to the nearby Rising camp. We'll break in and use their Mirror to get off this hellhole."

I forcibly turned from anxiety and instead faced my curiosity. "Isn't there nothing but desert here? How do you know about the camp?"

He laughed almost mockingly. "You underestimate the SSD. We have eyes everywhere. We're going to know if a little rebellion sets up a camp to keep an eye on us."

I frowned at his light use of the term "we" but leaned back and flipped open the sketchbook. I'd been drawing pretty much my entire life, but it really became a hobby after Dad's death. My therapist had recommended it, saying it'd be good to put the things I had seen on paper, considering I wasn't good at putting them into words. I'd been terrible at first, but over the years, I'd progressed. I still wasn't the best, but I tried.

I flipped to the nearest empty page, about a quarter of the way into the book, and began sketching.

I wasn't sure how much time had passed, but the sun had slipped higher into the sky by the time I heard a voice beside me. "That's really good."

I jumped, panic rushing through me for a split second before I recognized Renna. I'd been so invested in the drawing that I hadn't noticed her make her way over to me. I put my pencil down and looked over the drawing. It depicted the man I had seen hanging from the ceiling, complete with cracked skin. "It's a little gruesome," I noted.

"I've seen worse."

I turned to face her. She didn't seem to be joking at all. Her expression was curious but hesitant. I'd rarely talked with Renna. She made me nervous. It was hard to get a read on her.

She sat down on the bench and crossed her legs. "You're an interesting person."

Unconsciously, I shrunk into myself. "Um, thanks?"

"But I don't know you," she continued. "You have yet to prove to me that you don't mean us harm." Her voice dropped, eyes darting to where Amias hummed quietly to himself. Other than the three of us, no one else was awake. "I'll be watching you. The minute you do anything remotely suspicious—" She leaned forward, her breath on my cheek as she traced my neck with her fingertip. "I'll slit your throat."

Amias pulled the rover to a stop. "We're here. Wake up the others."

Renna let out a light giggle and pulled away from me.

The others rose from their slumber groggily, and we poured out the doors and into the blinding heat. Aven pointed to a misshaped building at the bottom of the dune we currently stood on. For a moment, I struggled to distinguish it, but then I realized it was an airplane, or rather, what was left of it. Only one of the wings remained, the other replaced by makeshift tents. In the distance, small figures milled around the plane, probably armed.

"The Mirror is probably in the cockpit of the plane." Ivy squinted at the plane. "Considering it's the most heavily guarded. Plus, it's kind of the only part that hasn't fallen apart."

Aven cut in, "I can change the symbols to get us out of here, but it will take time."

Symbols. Something clicked in my brain—your father's symbols.

The woman had said that before knocking me out in my room.

"We'll give you time," Ivy promised. She pointed to the maze of tarps that replaced the missing wing. "Looks like the entrance is there."

"We create a distraction," Renna cut in. "One or two of us. And then the rest sneak through the back. Aven will get the Mirror ready and send a signal, and then the ones creating the distraction will run in, and then we leave."

"Just like that?" I asked.

"Just like that." Amias grinned.

"This is a stupid plan," I grumbled.

"I call being the distraction," Ivy said.

"I shall go with her." Eden pulled a gun from Amias's backpack. "Grab what you want from the rover. We will not be coming back."

"Actually," Ivy said, a smile growing on her face, "I think I know what the distraction will be."

⁂

Despite the heat of the morning sun, Renna and Amias were barely panting as the four of us ran down the sandy dune toward the back of the plane.

Ivy and Eden rode in the rover toward the entrance. Already, I could see the Rising readying their weapons and gathering to meet them.

When the hill leveled out, we slowed to a walk, watching from a distance as Eden confronted the Rising. Ivy was still in the rover, and I frowned.

Eden and a woman I assumed to be the leader of the Rising exchanged harsh words and angry gestures. Then, a Rising member stepped up to their leader and whispered something in her ear.

The leader's head snapped up. She shoved past Eden and toward the rover. Ivy raced out of the rover, grabbed Eden, and dashed toward the entrance to the plane.

The leader stepped up to the rover, and just as she set her hand on the door, it exploded.

"Guess that's the distraction," Amias muttered, and we burst into a sprint.

I couldn't see what was happening near the explosion, but I heard shouts and saw more figures pour out of the wreckage.

Renna and I followed Amias through a tarp covering a hole in the plane. We stepped into a small, cramped room with a full-length Mirror taking up one side. Aven had beaten us inside and was already fixing the symbols with white paint. Renna pulled a satchel from over the back of the pilot's chair and began stuffing it with junk I could see no use for.

A second later, Ivy and Eden burst in, the former's face flushed red, an excited gleam in her eyes. Eden, however, was splattered with red, and I found myself hoping it wasn't blood, but my mind knew otherwise.

"We need to go," Eden panted. Her face was panicked but, in her eyes, glittered a bloodlust I knew hadn't recently been discovered. "Right now."

"I'm not done," Aven said.

"We don't have time," Eden shot back.

"Unless you want to end up dead in the middle of space, I suggest you buy me time," they growled, the first I'd ever heard them say anything in a harsh tone.

"We'll get you time," Amias cut in. "Just get that done." He ducked under the tarp flap, and when Renna started to follow him, he shook his head. "You're staying here."

"I can help," she insisted. "I'm stronger than Ivy and Eden."

I raised my eyebrows.

"I don't care," he snarled. "You're staying here, or so help me, I will tear you apart."

Renna rolled her eyes but slumped into the pilot's chair. Eden gave her a sympathetic glance before she and Ivy followed Amias out the door.

"He always sidelines me," Renna grumbled, catching my glance. "I'm nearly as skilled as him."

"Amias?" I asked in disbelief.

When she nodded, I didn't know whether to believe her or not.

Shots fired into the air, and I jumped, but Renna and Aven didn't so much as flinch. I began to wonder if shooting people and escaping terrorist groups was a regular thing for them.

Sounds of fighting echoed from behind the tarp curtain. I wanted to see who was winning, but when I moved forward, Aven stopped me.

"Don't," they said. "Your presence will only distract them."

I pulled my hand back from the tarp.

"Yes!" Aven clapped their hands after a few more moments. "I got it." They rushed past me and poked their head out of the tarp. "Get a move on, guys. Our ride's ready."

Ivy came first. She tore through the tarp, turning once and ringing a shot into the air. I heard a grunt and a thud. Eden followed, hands bloodied and eyes sparkling. Amias was last. He ran for us, but then a shot rang out.

He stumbled and brought his hands to his stomach, and when they came up, my heart stopped. He was bleeding. That much I knew. But his blood wasn't red as it should have been. It was blue.

He looked at Renna, then at Aven, and then at me. And he fell.

And behind him stood Dad, a grin on his messed-up face as he lowered the gun. He turned his gaze to me, and his grin turned from joyful to sinister. "You did this, Sander. It was your fault they even tried to escape the SSD in the first place. You got him killed."

My heart stuttered to a stop. It was Dad. He was standing in front of me.

"Sander!" Ivy screamed, punching me in the leg. She was bent down beside Amias's body. "Sander, give me your sweatshirt."

I pulled off the loose SSD jacket I'd found in the rover and handed it to her, eyes darting back to the space where Dad had been. He was gone.

Rising soldiers rushed through the tarp, guns raised and aimed at our heads. "Don't move," one of them growled.

No one did. We'd be dead before we made one step toward the Mirror, and even if we tried, we wouldn't be able to bring Amias.

A slender, brown-haired woman stepped through the crowd. The others parted around her, giving her a wide berth as she came forward.

"What should we do with them?" a Rising soldier asked.

The woman pointed to Amias. "Stitch him up. Lock up the others."

The same soldier seemed startled by her order. "They've just killed Tasya. It's obvious they are not friends."

The woman spun toward the man. "Did I stutter?" she spat, enraged. "I am Tasya's Shadow. Now that she is gone, I am the acting Chieftain until Maverick gets back. Lock them up before I give in to the craving to rip your throat out."

The man lunged for us immediately. I didn't bother fighting as firm hands gripped my wrists and shoved me forward.

Amias was taken to a separate part of the plane while we were led into the emptied cargo hold, stripped of our belongings, and bound. They shoved us to the ground and placed four Rising soldiers to guard us.

The rope they'd bound me with felt sickening. My stomach tumbled, and my chest tightened. I tried to ignore the panic in my gut as the woman pulled up a chair in front of us.

"Let's start easy," she said, flipping a braid over her shoulder. "What are your names?"

Ivy spat in her face.

The woman brought her hand to her cheek, a smile dancing on her lips. She leaned toward Ivy. "I like you. Perhaps I'll keep you."

Eden tensed beside me.

"What did you do with Amias?" Renna asked, surprisingly calm.

"Don't worry. Your friend will be patched up in no time. We are trained to survive under conditions worse than these."

"All right." Renna leaned back and rested against the wall of the plane. "When do we get fed? I'm starving."

The woman raised an eyebrow. "You're awfully calm for a prisoner."

Renna smiled. "I am trained to survive under conditions worse than this."

The woman let out a sharp laugh.

"Listen, lady," Aven cut in, "you really need to let us go. We all need to move. The SSD has been tracking us ever since we escaped. Unless you feel like you're up for dying—"

"You did what?" she interrupted. "You escaped? Blackford?"

"That's what I said. So—"

"No one's done that before."

"We're special," Aven said, exasperated. "Will you please let me talk?"

They kept talking, but I couldn't hear them because my mind was slipping away, back to what I'd seen in the cockpit. Dad. He'd been here. He'd spoken.

But that couldn't be. I'd watched the light fade from his eyes all those years ago. I'd seen the blood stain the carpet. There was no way he'd survived that.

My chest began to tighten; my breath began to quicken. The ropes around my wrists and feet burned.

I had to get out. I needed air.

I closed my eyes, feeling tears brimming. Oh, dear god.

In. Out. My breathing was getting increasingly faster. I felt trapped, more trapped than I'd been since the day of Dad's murder. A longing itch to get outside overtook me, and I began struggling at my bindings.

"Sander?" Eden noticed me. "Sander, are you all right?"

I could feel the panic showing in my eyes as I turned to look at her. She spoke again, but my heartbeat was in my ears, preventing any other sound from getting in.

"Eden," I breathed, but the world went black, and I plummeted from consciousness.

CHAPTER TWELVE

The clouds were stained pink when I opened my eyes the next morning. The color of tulips, to be exact. I noticed the beauty faintly through a narrow hole in the broken and cracked ceiling, from which I was able to assume we had an hour or so before the sun rose.

A chilled breeze swept through the plane wreckage, fluttering the tarps. Someone stirred. I heard soft breathing around me and saw bodies lying in sleeping bags or under old blankets all around us. Sometime last night, someone had thrown one over me.

I shifted, my muscles aching. When I tried to move my hands, I realized with a start that they were still bound.

After feeling a small burst of panic, I drew in a deep breath. It had just been a panic attack. I hadn't really seen Dad, had I? The stress of the past few weeks had finally caught up to me. I chuckled to myself. *God, Sander, you're going crazy.*

With my limited range of motion, I stretched out my legs and did my best to kick off the blanket.

At my movement, I felt Eden shift beside me. Her eyes were closed, but her breathing was shaky. Beads of sweat coated her forehead.

"Eden?" I whispered. "Eden, are you awake?"

She didn't answer.

I nudged her with my feet. She jolted up, gasping and lunging for blades that weren't there. When she seemed to remember her surroundings, she let out a shaky breath and leaned back.

"Good morning?" I offered.

She started and faced me. "Sander! Are you feeling all right?"

"I—" I hesitated. "I'm okay. It was just a panic attack, I think."

She regarded me with a monotonous expression. After a moment of awkward silence, she said, "Just a panic attack? You fainted."

"Um, yeah." I let out a light laugh lined with mock humor. My chest grew tight. "It's happened before. I'm fine. Are *you* okay? You seemed like you weren't having the best dream."

She hesitated for a long second before something shifted in her expression, and she spoke. "I often have nightmares of my time before Blackford. I attracted the SSD as a result of my immaturity and put my family in danger." She swallowed and shifted her gaze away from me. "I am wholly unaware of their well-being."

Words felt utterly useless, but I whispered to her anyway, "I'm so sorry." We were in similar predicaments then.

She shook her head slightly, meeting my gaze once again. "It is all right. Why are you so used to panic attacks?"

"I had to watch my dad get killed when I was twelve," I said, startled at how fast the words had come out of my mouth. A weird feeling rushed through me. I hadn't said them out loud before. Not even to Sadira. But now that I had, something between relief and sorrow crushed me.

"My feet and hands were tied. I… I was hopeless to do anything. I couldn't. I just watched." My voice broke. "I just watched. And then when they put the ropes on…" I didn't turn to face Eden, but I could feel her gaze on me. For some reason, I took comfort in her silence. But it felt strange. When I looked at her, there wasn't pity or sympathy in her eyes. They were empty. No emotion. And I kind of felt relieved.

"Hmm," she tilted her head back.

"That's it?" I asked. "You're not going to tell me I didn't have a choice? That there was nothing I could do?"

"I am not going to tell you what you have already been told," Eden said. "My time in prison has been beneficial toward my personal growth, absurd as it may seem." Her eyes drifted toward

Ivy. "I am fortunate enough to have gotten help. But I cannot say I have the ability to expedite that kindness toward others. Forever and always, Sander Fox, *you* are in charge of allowing yourself to heal."

Allowing myself. I blinked, letting the conversation drift away with the breeze.

Eden closed her eyes once more, and within minutes, her breathing deepened and relaxed.

———

I didn't fall asleep again. I wasn't sure it was a feasible option. But by the time the others began to stir, I had just begun to drift off. As the sun began to shine through the crack in the ceiling, my eyelids fluttered closed. Someone elbowed my arm.

"Wake up, Sander." Aven's voice was far too bubbly for a morning brought about by gritty winds and ropes around our wrists.

"I'm awake," I mumbled, sinking further down.

They elbowed me again. "Are you okay? Are you going to tell me what happened yesterday?"

"No." The word came out far too harshly, but I didn't have the energy to care.

"As long as you're not dead, that's fine."

I opened my eyes, meeting their wide grin with a scowl of my own.

The Rising members had dispersed, though many still resided within the walls of the plane wreckage. It seemed as if the number of rifles had tripled, with one strapped across each person's back. I noted the absence of children and wondered if this camp was temporary. Or perhaps newly built. Its buildings and inhabitants suggested a knock-off war camp.

The woman who'd interrogated us yesterday slipped through a tarp and approached us. She wore a leather jacket atop a heavily armed vest. I spotted more than three knives hidden among the fabric.

"Good morning," Aven said cheerfully. "Maybe now that you've had time to cool off, we could talk about breakfast?"

She sighed, reached into her bag, and tossed us a small bag of field rations. They shrugged their shoulders, gesturing to our bound hands.

She grumbled a curse and reached over with a blade. One by one, she sliced through our bindings. Aven released a happy sigh and shook out their wrists, then ripped apart the rations, dividing them among the five of us.

"Eat," the Rising leader demanded. "It's not going to do you any good to starve yourself."

Eden reached for the food, but I didn't. The swirling nausea in my gut threatened to reject anything I attempted to eat.

The woman turned to me. "Is there a reason you passed out last night?"

I glared at her. "No. I just felt like fainting."

A proud grin crept over Aven's face.

She sighed. "Listen, I like you guys. I really do, but you killed my friend. Tell me your names, and perhaps I'll let you go."

The Rising members around her stiffened. Someone on the far side of the plane muttered harshly to their friend about her incompetence.

"Why don't you go first?" Ivy asked, handing the rest of her rations to Eden, who frowned but grudgingly ate them.

"Tanith," the woman said. "Tanith Lexington."

"All right, Tanith," Ivy said, leaning against the wall. "Which Department are you from?"

"435," she replied.

"Do you have a family?"

"Two sisters."

"Parents?"

"Dead." Tanith pulled up a rusty stool. "I've answered your

questions. Now answer mine. What is your name?"

"Ivy."

"No last name?"

Ivy shook her head, the smile on her lips innocuous. "We're not close enough for me to give you my last name."

"Hmm. Family?"

"All dead."

I blinked, not able to tell if she was lying or not.

"What were you doing at Blackford?" Tanith asked.

"Being a prisoner," Ivy smiled.

She sighed. "Why were you a prisoner?"

"The SSD didn't like me."

"How did you get out?"

"How did you get *in*?" Ivy shot back. "Your people were just at the SSD. If you were able to do that, then surely it wouldn't have been too difficult to help the prisoners."

"Those in Blackford were not our concern." Tanith gritted her teeth.

"Then what—or who—was?"

"A very important individual. She's invaluable to the Rising."

Ivy smiled, baring all of her teeth. "Thank you for that information. We appreciate it dearly. Now, we would also appreciate it if you let us go."

Tanith stood up, her chair scraping across the ground. "You're impossible."

"So I've been told."

She glared at us for a moment. "I'll be back. I really hope by then you have changed your minds about being so difficult."

"What about Amias?" Renna called lightly.

Tanith paused. "Your friend is alive."

Aven let out a relieved sigh, which I echoed internally. Renna didn't seem to be worried in the least. She rolled her shoulders and lifted her wrists.

"Since we're all done eating, I suggest tying us back up. Don't want us running away while you're fighting off the SSD."

Tanith turned to her and scoffed. "The SSD? Little girl, they're miles away. Besides, they don't bother themselves with abandoning their test tubes and guns to tramp through the desert."

Renna raised an eyebrow but silently declined to elaborate.

Blood rushed past my ears as I heard the roar of a wave of engines. Through one of the cracked windows, I spotted a dozen rovers breaching the dune. All was silent for a long moment as reality sunk in. I couldn't imagine what the Rising was feeling, but it was incomparable to the terror that wracked through my bones with such force I felt dizzy.

People began yelling and running. Tanith wasted no time before racing outside and screaming orders.

A wave of gunfire splattered into the sand. Shooters on top of the incoming rovers fired machine guns without care, sending the scrapyard of a camp into disarray and chaos.

The commotion startled the guards surrounding us. Half of them split from the group, either heading for the battle or for the Mirror. The remaining two hesitated, casting wary glances toward us before ultimately deciding to stay. But their moment's hesitation had given Ivy and Eden time to move. Feet still bound, they moved in startling unison as they leaped from a crouch into a closed-legged cartwheel, bringing their feet down on the heads of the guards.

They all tumbled to the ground, wrestling for the guns. As they did so, Aven frantically began untying the bindings holding their feet. Renna, I noticed dizzily, was long gone. Her ropes lay torn on the ground beside us.

I knew I should be moving, but fear had paralyzed me. It had taken hold of my body and pinned me in the spot as if my limbs had been turned to stone. The beating of my heart was impossibly loud as I watched the chaos unfold.

Eden managed to snatch the gun from her opponent's hands. In one movement, she rammed the hilt of it into the Rising member's temple and swung the barrel toward Ivy's opponent.

"Drop the gun," he snarled. He had the barrel of his gun pressed against Ivy's chest. "And she lives."

"Think again," said Aven, who pressed a blade against the man's throat. "You have to the count of three."

I saw the man grit his teeth in indecision.

"One."

He didn't move.

"Two."

His grip on the gun loosened. "Okay—" he started to say, but Aven had already sunk the blade into the man's skin.

Blood sprayed. I felt my breath leave my chest, but the warm liquid that landed on my face snapped me out of my stupor. I scrambled for the ropes around my ankles to find that Eden was already slicing through them.

I swallowed and rose, my legs like gelatin. "How are we supposed to get Amias?"

"Renna's already on it," Aven responded. "But we should go back her up. You go wait in the cockpit; we'll be there in a second."

Ivy gave me a pitying glance as they departed the plane. I peered through the exit. The Rising soldiers didn't seem to notice them, and if they did, they didn't bother to lock them back up. They were all running toward the entrance, guns and blades in hand. Through the maze of tarps and bodies, I saw a flash of gray and blue uniforms. SSD soldiers.

I slipped through the tarp to enter the cockpit, plugging my ears to drown out the muffled gunshots and screams. The Mirror was intact. It didn't seem to me that any of the symbols had changed, but then again, that wasn't my area of expertise.

I ran my hand over the dirtied desk, fingers drifting over a discarded crowbar.

There was a sound behind me, the tarp moving. I spun, grabbing hold of the crowbar as if it were a bat.

The Rising member who entered had an irritatingly familiar face. The pale blue of his eyes would've been stunning on almost anyone else, but paired with his disgustingly dirtied buzzcut and see-through eyebrows, they were horrifying.

"My god," he breathed, revealing a line of crooked teeth. "It really is you."

"What?" I snapped.

"Sander Fox. You sure have grown since I last saw you."

I gripped the crowbar tighter. "How do you know my name?"

"Really? You don't remember me? I would've thought I'd left more of an impression," he chuckled.

My gaze trailed to the tattoo peeking out from underneath his sleeve.

"Sorry, let me give you a hint." Ferity fueled his movements as he raised a finger gun. "On the ground, and we'll let your family live!"

The world came to a halt as the realization hit me. I was back in my old living room once more. Blood was on my tongue, and my cheek pounded from the blow I'd taken. The one I'd taken from the man before me.

He'd been there that night. It was his fist that had knocked my tooth out and his orders that had brought about my dad's death.

The anger that rushed through me was so blinding I couldn't think. It washed away all my other thoughts and drowned them in waters of rage. I lunged.

The man didn't have time to move before I smacked the crowbar across his face. Over and over again. I couldn't stop. I sent blow after blow across his face. Blood bloomed and ran down his features, and I felt a sick thrill pulse through my veins. I wanted to see him pay. I wanted to see him bleed.

He deserved it. He deserved that and so much worse.

I rammed the bar against him again and heard a crack. Blood sprayed across my face. Stained my hands. I didn't care. I couldn't have cared less.

Again and again, I hit the man.

"Fox!" A deep voice snapped me out of my trance. A firm hand grabbed my wrist.

I panted, looking up to lock eyes with Amias. He was clutching his side, leaning against Aven. He gave me a sad look, then ripped the bloodied crowbar out of my hands.

I looked back at the man and only saw a mangled face staring back at me. He gave a small wheeze, and I saw his chest fall. It didn't rise again.

I fell to my knees, horror crashing down on me.

I held out my hands. Blood had stained my skin. I crumpled, falling back. Sobs rippled out of me as I rocked back and forth, head in my hands.

Had I really just done that? Had I really just become like the monster that had butchered my dad? I'd beaten a man—to death.

Amias helped me up, and when he looked at me, I didn't see disgust or horror in his eyes. The recognition and pity in his eyes made me wonder if he'd felt like this before.

He didn't say anything; he just pulled me in. I leaned into him, tears streaming down my face.

I'd just killed a man. And I'd enjoyed it. If not a monster, then what did that make me?

From what I could tell, there weren't any people in the new reality we entered. We entered through an old apartment building. By the way vines had climbed over the crumbling walls and how cobwebs and dust hung in the corners, I'd say it was safe to assume the building hadn't been touched in years. Decades, even. Grass and weeds had sprouted through the cracks in the floor. Some windows had been shattered, and when I peeked out, more of the same met my gaze.

The building we stood in belonged to part of an old city. The houses and stores lining the streets had been overtaken by nature, skyscrapers cloaked in a blanket of green. But as far as I could tell, the city was empty. It looked like it had been for a long time.

Now, Eden and I were the only ones awake after deciding to spend the afternoon in the apartment building. Amias had taken over the moss-covered couch, his snores rippling through the silence. The other three were curled around the fireplace, in which Eden had managed to light a piece of an old dresser and was slowly feeding the flames.

I sat huddled in the corner, staring at the afternoon sun that streamed through the broken windows. Arms around my legs, I hummed to myself and rocked back and forth.

I did my best to focus on the sounds in the present—Amias's snores and the crackle of the flames—but I could only hear the sound of metal against bone. I saw myself hitting the man over and over again.

The smell of blood still hung heavily over me. The red on my hands felt like a new tattoo, itchy and permanent.

I swallowed the bile rising in my throat. Tears brimmed in my eyes.

I'd never believed myself to be a good person, but deep down, I knew I was wrong. But now… how was I supposed to come back from this? How did Amias still think so highly of himself? Surely, he'd done worse things than I had.

He probably doesn't, said a voice in my head. *He probably loathes himself more than anything in the world.*

I pressed my palms into my eyes.

Eden didn't say anything as the sobs ripped out of me.

CHAPTER THIRTEEN

A heavy fog hung over the green-encased city the next morning. The frigid air held damp clouds. Wind ruffled the dark waves of Ivy's hair as she walked next to me, arms crossed and face tucked into her new leather jacket, which she'd taken when we raided an old mall.

I'd woken up to Amias kicking me, saying he wanted to check out the city before the SSD found and slaughtered us. He had recovered slightly from the gunshot, enough that he didn't show any discomfort at walking. We'd spent our first hour redressing the bandages for our wounds and pillaging resources. Despite my gunshot wound being less disastrous than Amias's, I'd groaned and complained all morning about the lack of painkillers. Eventually, everyone got tired of my complaining, so Renna tossed some small white pills to me and told me to take them or shut up.

As we walked, I became increasingly sure humans didn't exist on this planet anymore. I saw a few rats and birds, but other than that, there didn't seem to be much life left.

"Do you know what happened here?" I asked no one in particular, grateful the stinging in my side had numbed.

Aven ran their hand along the wall of a shop. "I'm pretty sure we're in Department 236. They were wiped out by disease in 2022."

"Departments. That means dimension, right?"

They nodded. "Departments are what the ID Government calls the dimensions they've counted. Sub Departments are ones that haven't been counted."

"How many have they counted?" Eden questioned.

"Almost seven thousand."

The conversation dropped away, and silence hung over us again.

I glanced over at Aven. They ran their hand through their blonde hair, leaning into the wind. Their new outfit consisted of a brown flannel over a tan T-shirt with a smiling cartoon flower. A gun bounced against their leg as they walked, residing in the unnecessarily large pocket of their army green cargo jeans.

I wore a similar outfit, my blue jeans similar in style but a looser fit. It had been gratifying to leave behind the prison uniform, littered with more blood than just my own. The wind snapped my sweater strings against the thin fabric, and I wished I'd grabbed something warmer.

I kicked a rock and watched as it skidded across the cracked pavement. As we stepped up to it, Amias kicked it again. Then Ivy. Then Eden. Then Renna. When Aven kicked it, it rolled into one of the sewer grates.

"Come on," Ivy groaned in disappointment.

"I'm not a soccer player," Aven snapped back. "I don't have telekinesis either."

"It's not that hard, though."

The corner of my mouth curved. I glanced at Amias and found him looking at me with a curious expression. When he saw me catch him, his expression flashed with something between shock and disbelief for a moment before he glared at me and walked a few paces ahead.

Confused, I followed him as we ducked inside what I assumed to be an old hotel.

"What are we doing here?" Renna asked Amias, catching up to him. I blinked. She was so quiet that there were moments I forgot she was even there.

"I thought we'd look for a Mirror," he replied. "Since I smashed the one back at the apartment."

"Why?" Eden ran her finger over the front desk, picking up a layer of dust. "It is nice here. Quiet."

"That's exactly why," he answered and opened the door to the staircase. "There's no one here. I feel vulnerable. The SSD could show up any minute and we'd be toast."

Eden's brow furrowed. "Why would we become bread?"

"That's not—" He sighed. "Never mind. All I'm saying is I don't think it's a good idea to be someplace without other people. The SSD won't attack us in the middle of a crowd. It would only raise questions."

We followed him to the first room we could find and into the bathroom.

"Aven, how long will it take you to write the symbols?"

They frowned. "I don't have anything to write them with. And besides, where are we even going to go?"

"I don't care," Amias said. "As long as it's a place that has people."

Take me home! I wanted to scream. *Take me home so I can forget about all of this.*

Would that really put an end to it? Probably not, but reason never seemed to agree with desire.

"Amias," Ivy cut in. "Can I talk to you?"

They disappeared into the hallway. Aven hoisted themself onto the counter and put their black Converse into the dusty sink. They leaned against the mirror and let out a sigh. "You know, I always thought life on the run would be more fun. But I'm really bored."

"Do you want me to tell the SSD where you are?" Renna asked, her expression annoyed. "Perhaps that'll spice up your life a little."

Aven rolled their eyes, but their mouth curved into a smile.

She fell silent again, her expression slightly amused.

I sat down on the ground and began picking at the carpet. Amias and Ivy's conversation floated through the walls, consisting of angry shouts, but I couldn't distinguish their words.

I ran my fingers through the matted knitting and pulled out a few knots. I didn't know what I was doing here. I didn't know what the hell my life had become. I was on a planet where humanity had been wiped out, and yet I felt as if I couldn't get far enough from the stench of society.

"Guys," Aven said, scrambling down from the counter. "We have a problem."

When I turned my head, I caught sight of the rippling Mirror, and then a gun poked through.

I leaped to my feet and called out to Amias and Ivy. The door to the bathroom opened, but it wasn't either of them that came through.

The man with bug-like blue eyes grinned, the same grin he'd worn right before I'd bashed his head in with a crowbar.

A chill swept down my spine.

"Hello, Sander," he tilted his head, pulling a crowbar from behind him. "Miss me?"

"How—" I choked out.

His grin widened, and he slung the crowbar over his shoulder like a bat. I drew in a breath, bracing myself as the blow came. It landed against my ribs, a crack splitting the air.

I let out a cry, falling backward. I scrambled underneath the sink, desperately gasping for breath.

"Don't hide now," the man crooned. "We're just getting started."

I heard shouts. Gunshots and grunts sounded as SSD soldiers poured through the Mirror.

I didn't see the fighting. The man had crawled underneath the sink and grabbed my arm. He shoved me onto my back and knelt over me, then started beating me again.

Pain burst through me. And it didn't stop. Didn't even ease. Over and over again, it came crashing into me, like I was on a beach and a wave had slammed me into the sand, and every time I tried to get up, another one would roll in and slam me down all over again.

I attempted to push him away, but my efforts were useless.

I bit my lip so hard the coppery tang of blood spilled into my mouth.

In the corner of my eyes, bodies fell to the ground. Blood sprayed across the tiles. Amias snapped at Renna.

It wasn't until the gunshots faded that a face looked underneath the counter. It was Amias. His blood-splattered face was set in a scowl.

"What the hell were you doing?" he snapped and grabbed my foot, dragging me out.

I tried to speak, but the words were caught in my throat.

The man with the crowbar was gone. He'd vanished into thin air. But a few broken bodies of SSD soldiers littered the tile. Glass from the Mirror lay scattered and glinting like rubies when mixed with the splatters of blood.

Amias pulled me up. "What were you doing, huh?" I couldn't tell if he was shouting; his voice was loud enough on its own. "I understand you're useless in a fight, but cowering under the sink? Was it really beyond you to *try*?"

I clawed at the tattoos on his arms, trying to break free of his grip on my sweatshirt. "It was the man—" I choked out. "The one from the plane."

"The one you killed?" He tilted his head.

I winced. "He wasn't dead. He was right here. He was—"

Amias released me, face twisted in disgust. "The man's gone. You bashed his brains in."

"He was right here!" I protested. "I swear, he was—"

"How stupid do you think I am?" he spat. "I was in here. I didn't see the man."

"But—"

"Don't try to justify your actions by making up some dumb shit like that. Face the facts, Sander, you're a coward." He looked down his nose at me, despite being barely two inches taller. "I can't believe I ever thought differently of you." He spun on his heel, stepping over the fallen SSD soldiers as he stormed out. Renna shot me a glare before following him.

It was silent for a long moment. Eden, Aven, and Ivy were

staring at me like they were waiting for something. An explanation? I couldn't give them one.

I just sank to the ground. The bloodied glass bit through my clothes and into my skin. They tried to get me to talk for a few minutes, but after they realized I wouldn't, they gave up and left. I was alone, staring at the bodies before me, wishing once again that none of this had ever happened.

I didn't move until Eden came in an hour later, holding out a can of beans.

"Where did you get this?" I asked hoarsely as I took it from her. The pain was gone. The bruises and blood had vanished. I was completely untouched, as if I really had been.

"Ivy found it on one of the soldiers," she replied. They'd hauled the corpses out of the bathroom at some point, and I'd once again been too useless to help. "And there's no need to save any. We found another Mirror. We're leaving."

"Off this dimension?"

She nodded. "Aven's working on the symbols right now. They should be done soon."

"Okay," I whispered and stared at the can of beans, too scared to ask where we were going.

She crouched and set a warm hand on my wrist.

I looked up at her. "How mad is he?"

"He will be all right. He will forgive you once you tell him what happened."

"I did," I insisted. "At least, I think I did."

The corners of her mouth tilted downward, and her eyebrows knit together. A look of worry flashed through her blue-gray eyes. My gaze drifted to my hands, heat flushing my cheeks and neck.

"I'm fine, Eden," I insisted. "I think the stress of these past few weeks has finally caught up with me."

Her worry didn't fade.

I rolled my shoulders, fiddling with a loose strand on my pants as a newfound wave of discomfort washed over me.

"I will respect your privacy," Eden's voice dropped a notch. Her expression was pitying, so different from the looks she'd given me when we'd first met. We'd gotten closer. Closer than I'd thought we'd ever be. "But I am here for you. I have been told in the past that I come across as threatening, so I would like to change that with my new friend if I could."

"New friend?" My voice caught in my throat, a smile threatening to appear on my lips.

She returned my joy. "Yes."

My delight dropped away like a stone plummeting from a cliff. "But why?"

As soon as the words escaped from my mouth, regret replaced all my thoughts. *Goddammit, Sander. Why is it so hard for you not to doubt every good thing in your life?*

To my surprise, Eden let out a low laugh.

I raised an eyebrow.

She rose to her feet, offering a hand, which I took tentatively.

"You're a rather demure person, Sander. If only we had met a few years ago, perhaps I would not have turned out to be as heartless as I am today."

She led me out of the bathroom. I pondered her words as I trailed her into the hotel lobby, where the others were gathered around a golden-trimmed mirror.

Aven was finishing up the last of the symbols with a can of spray paint. Where they'd gotten it, I didn't know and I didn't necessarily care. Amias was leaning against the wall, his glare pinned on me.

Renna sat on the ground next to him, cross-legged and cleaning her gun. When she saw me, she gave me an empty smile. A spider-like chill walked down my spine.

Ivy was aggressively stuffing a backpack she'd gotten from the closet. Her gaze paused on me for only a second before her mouth formed a thin line and she looked past me.

I gritted my teeth, shame falling over me. Eden squeezed my fingers in an attempt to comfort me, but the tension never faded.

I was the last one through the Mirror. As I stared at the glass, empty of my reflection, I wondered if it would be so bad if I stayed behind. But the overwhelming desire to see Mama and Sadira someday took control of my thoughts and I stepped into it, a cool silvery liquid falling over me. It chilled me to know that a group of murderous criminals were my only hope for getting home.

CHAPTER FOURTEEN

My face was bruised. I couldn't see it, but by the pain that was splintering through my eye, I had to assume so.

Ivy sent yet another punch flying for my jaw, and I stumbled backward. She didn't waste a second before kicking me in the gut and then hooking her foot underneath mine. I sprawled across the cement.

I groaned, rolling onto my side and clutching the wound that was painfully slow to heal. Renna had run out of the pills fast, so I had to make do with my own tolerance.

"Get up," she said. "We're going again."

Grudgingly, I climbed to my feet and held up my arms. The bullet wound groaned in pain. She shifted one of my feet.

"Keep your stance wider, and stay on the balls of your feet," she instructed.

I did as she said. I threw a lazy punch, exhaustion already creeping through me despite not having been at this for even an hour. She side-stepped easily and sent one back at me. I raised my hand to block it, but I wasn't fast enough. She struck me across the face. I grunted and brought my hand up as blood trickled from my nose.

Ivy knocked me to the ground and pressed her knee to my throat. "You hesitated."

"You broke my nose."

"You think the SSD's going to apologize for making you bleed?" she growled and helped me to my feet. "Again."

I groaned once more, knowing I had brought this upon myself

with my request for training. Amias's words had cut deep, and sitting around doing nothing wasn't an appealing option.

"Ivy, give the poor man a break," Eden said, pushing away from the pole she'd been leaning against. "He's still recovering."

Ivy grumbled a curse under her breath but gave in and ran a hand over her mouth. Then, she muttered something and walked off.

I approached Eden, who popped my nose into place with a painful crack. Then, she handed me an ice pack wrapped in a towel. I pressed it to my aching nose.

When we arrived three days ago, Amias had demanded we move to a place closer to the city. After quite a bit of arguing, the rest of us finally gave in and found an empty storehouse. We'd spent the last few nights sleeping on hard floors with nothing but jackets for warmth. As uncomfortable as it was, I'd learned they didn't appreciate my complaining.

The world we were in seemed relatively similar to my home world. Almost identical, in fact, so much so that I had thought it was the same one until I had been told differently. Much to my disappointment.

"Here." From their perch on top of a stack of crates, Aven handed me a bottle of water.

"Where did you get this?" I asked as I unscrewed the cap. "I thought we didn't have money."

"I don't need money to get what I want."

I took a sip, glancing around at the empty room. "Where did Amias and Renna go?"

"Supply run."

"You mean to steal more things."

Aven laughed. "Yeah, that's what I meant. But they should be back soon."

As if on cue, the doors slammed open and they came running through. They raced up to us, faces flushed. It was then that I heard the distant sound of sirens.

"It wasn't my fault," Amias insisted and began packing supplies into Renna and Ivy's backpacks.

"It was all your fault," Renna said.

"What did you do?" Eden growled.

"It was not!" Amias snapped at Renna. "I didn't know he would have a gun."

"Seriously?" She let out an exasperated laugh. "Did you really expect him not to?"

"What did you do?" Eden snarled again.

Amias flashed a grin. "I ran into an old friend."

"Your obscurity will be the death of me," Eden muttered angrily as she tossed me Ivy's now-stocked backpack. I pulled it on just as Ivy came back through the doors.

"What's going on? I heard sirens."

"Amias didn't move fast enough, that's what," Renna answered.

"Argue later," Aven said, hopping down from the stack of crates and shoving a gun into Amias's hands. "Run now."

We went out the back door, but we were met by a swarm of cops, guns trained on us.

⁂

"We have a witness telling us that your friend shot and killed Derick Stevenson," said the cop before me, hands folded neatly on the table in front of him. "Is this true?"

"How would I know?" I replied and leaned back in the hard metal chair. I was handcuffed to the table in the center of the small room. A one-sided window reflected the back of the man, and I stared at myself through it. I knew more cops stood on the other side, watching us.

I tried to ignore the ever-looming heaviness of the metal around my wrists. Whenever I remembered they were there, I felt my chest tighten with fear.

"You were hiding out in the old storehouse with your friend, were you not?" he asked. In my mind, the cop looked like every other middle-aged white man out there, complete with neatly combed brown hair and brown eyes dark enough that they seemed black. He wasn't attractive, but he wasn't ugly either. Just… normal. Normal enough that nobody would look twice.

"I don't even know who Derick Stevenson was," I said. "One minute, I was standing in the storehouse; the next, they came running in. And then you guys came seconds after."

His expression didn't reveal anything. "And why were you in the storehouse in the first place?"

"Um… party," I tried.

"Just the six of you? And no alcohol or anything?"

I nodded. "That's right."

He sighed. "Since you're so keen on explaining things, why don't you explain this? We ran your fingerprints, and apparently, you, Sander Fox, are a twenty-seven-year-old living in an apartment in Chicago and engaged to a woman named Kara Taylor. And yet here you are, looking sixteen and hanging out with murderers."

Kara. I knew that name. That was Sadira's friend. I let out a chuckle, and the cop raised an eyebrow.

"Something funny?"

"I'm getting married to my sister's friend," I replied, still laughing. "Man, I honestly didn't think I'd get that far in life."

"Oh? And why is that?"

"I—never mind," I groaned. "Listen, can't you just let us go? We'll leave and no one will ever see us again."

"Your friend is a suspect in a murder. If you really think we're just going to let you go, then you truly are out of your mind."

"Amias didn't—" I banged my head on the table. I couldn't lie. Amias had killed that man. But hopefully, he'd deserved it. I tugged against the handcuffs. "Let me talk to them, then I'll tell you everything you want."

"I can't do that," he said.

"Sure, you can. Just free me from the table and lead me to my friends."

"Your friends," he leaned forward. "Let's talk about them."

"Let's not," I grumbled, but he didn't seem to hear. Or care.

"Amias Wolf. Suspected of murder and wanted for multiple charges of theft and one account of arson. Last seen four years ago in New Jersey. Ivy Harrison. According to her fingerprints, she's barely four years old. And the rest of your friends, we ran their prints three times, and apparently, they don't exist."

No shit. I wanted to shout. I ran my finger in a circle, then scraped dirt from underneath my nail. Amias had to have a plan. They'd locked him up somewhere, but my guess was they didn't know what he was. He could get out. He could get the rest of us out.

But then I remembered the angry glare he'd been sending my way for the past few days, and I wondered if he'd even bother to come get me. I doubted it. And honestly, I didn't even feel sad about it, as long as the rest of them got out. They would. They would get out, and I'd be tossed in prison. But it didn't matter because, sooner or later, the SSD would catch wind of me and come pick me up. The horrible truth settled over me, and I let out a sigh.

"I killed him," I blurted. "I killed Derick Stevenson. Now take me to jail."

"Not three minutes ago, you were saying you didn't know who he was."

"I was lying," I snapped. I flicked my gaze back to the man sitting before me. "That's what criminals do, right?"

His eyes narrowed. "I know you didn't kill him."

"Then why are you even bothering with interrogating me?"

"I am trying to understand!" he snapped, slamming his hands on the table. "How the hell are you here? We have eyes on a twenty-seven-year-old you right now. Yet your fingerprints say you are Sander Fox. But you can't be! You're sixteen!"

"Seventeen," I corrected.

"That doesn't matter," he rose to his feet, rubbing his chin tiredly. After a long moment, he stepped out of the room. The sound of the door slamming shut was the last thing I heard before the room fell into silence.

I watched the clock on the wall, but my mind couldn't stay focused.

Tick. Tick. Tick.

The hands moved. I stared as they did, the numbers and stripes blurring until they became a sea of white and black. The long, thin lines of the hands were the only things that weren't bleary. They were sharp, moving as each minute went by.

Tick. Tick. Tick.

I began doubting Amias. Maybe he wasn't as strong as I'd thought and couldn't break them out. Or maybe he was dead. Maybe they'd shot him.

Tick.

The SSD would be here soon enough. Eden, Amias, and the rest of us would be taken back to Blackford.

I stretched my legs, remembering the man with the bloody crowbar. A flash of guilt ran through me, so hot and sudden that I cringed. I flexed my fingers and then closed them again.

The door opened, and the detective from earlier walked in. I stayed silent and directed my gaze back to the table.

The chair screeched as the man took a seat on it. "Mr. Fox—or whoever you are—I know you didn't kill Derick Stevenson. Tell me why Amias did it, and I will let you go."

"I don't see a reason," I sighed. "They're going to kill me anyways."

"Who? Amias?"

"No," I scoffed.

"Then who?"

I remained silent. He wouldn't believe me even if I told him the truth.

"Who, Sander?"

"None of your damn business," I shot back.

He let out a groan.

I rolled my shoulders, wincing at the pain in my wound. But then, I looked behind the cop. Symbols began taking place on the rim of the mirror. The glass rippled. My reflection disappeared.

Fear clutched my chest.

I yanked against my cuffs as a gloved hand reached through the silvery liquid.

CHAPTER FIFTEEN

It was late. Around two-thirty. At least, that's what the clock in the Director's office read when I squinted at it, my vision still half-blurred from the blow to my eye.

Based on Troy's angry commands as he and a pack of SSD soldiers shoved past the Director's office, I knew the others had escaped.

I watched the clock tick as I'd done back at the police station while the Director sat across the desk from me, scanning silently through a digital file. Her hair was pulled back in a tight bun at the base of her skull, and her expression was empty, as usual.

They hadn't cuffed me, but they didn't need to. Two guards stood behind me and four more on the outside of the door, all clutching their guns too comfortably. Trigger-happy freaks. Surely the only reason they hadn't shot me already was because they wanted me as bitter and scared as I could be.

Finally, the Director leaned back, flipping a pencil in her hand. "You, Mr. Fox, have been unbearably annoying. Do you have any idea how many resources I wasted to find you?"

"Thanks?" I tried, surprised at the ease with which the word had been spoken. Anger had finally overcome my crippling fear. It ran through my blood white-hot and boiling. To pinpoint the source of my rage would be as useless as sweeping a forest.

She set her elbows on the desk and clasped her hands. "You managed to escape. I can't afford to put you back in Blackford."

"So, you're going to kill me?" I nearly laughed.

"No," she said. "I think I'm going to give you to my husband. A little anniversary present."

My eyes widened. The anger dipped for a brief moment before skyrocketing. My body followed the movement, shooting out of my chair and bracing myself to scream. But what could I say? I had no power here.

As the guards moved to grab me, I feared I would burn at their touch. Terror and fury sparked beneath my skin, but I could do nothing as they dragged me toward the door.

"Have fun, Sander." The Director gave a small wave as the door slammed shut.

CHAPTER SIXTEEN

I sat curled in the corner of a white room, unsure how much time had passed since the Director had thrown me to Warren. It had felt like a few days, but I couldn't make assumptions. For all I knew, it could've been months.

The tiles were cold beneath my bare feet and sloped slightly to a small grate in the center of the room. The concrete walls were empty, and it smelled of antiseptic and blood. Blue-tinted lights embedded in the ceiling sent rays bouncing off the metal chair above the grate.

I hadn't stepped out of this room since they'd tossed me in, and the only people who'd come in were Warren and Troy. I'd been stripped of my sweatshirt and jeans to make room for the baggy T-shirt and shorts they'd been replaced with. The pale fabric was damp with sweat despite the blasting wave of cold, stale air the AC sent my way.

At seemingly random times, Warren and Troy would enter the room wearing gas masks and draw my blood, along with various other health tests. Something shifted in me one of those times, but I couldn't pinpoint when. At some point, it began to hurt to move my body, my head swam, and sounds were muffled as if I were underwater. Every time I tried to speak, the words clung to the sides of my throat like unrelenting cobwebs. Even the room seemed to be tinged with a fuzziness I knew was coming from my eyes.

Every few hours, a slit in the door slid open, and someone shoved a tray of food through it. I'd crawl to it as best I could, pained whimpers slipping from my lips. Even eating hurt. My arms would shake as I attempted to lift the food to my mouth, and most of the time, I'd only manage to eat a little less than half of what they'd given me. It was out of pure instinct that I shoved the food down my throat. Motivation had left my soul entirely. I spent the hours miserably awaiting the arrival of Troy and Warren, if only because they offered me some semblance of company.

My thoughts mushed together into a clump of grays and desaturated oranges. I couldn't form any words in my mind. Letters swam giddily away from me, dancing through the haze with horrifying delight.

I forgot my name. I only knew what I looked like because of some blurred memory sitting quietly in the back of my mind. A dizzy reflection of myself, the once bright green eyes faded to the color of stones.

A few hours after a meal of beans and stale bread, the door swung open once more, and I bit back a pitiful whimper at the sight of the duo dragging along a woman, gagged and bound. It wasn't the gash that ran down her temple that shocked me. Though the last time I'd seen her, the only light had been from the moon, there was no mistaking the heavy-muscled figure before me as the woman who'd broken into my apartment many nights ago.

Her eyes widened at the sight of me, a confirmation of my realization.

"I believe you two have already met," Warren grunted through his gas mask. His mood certainly had gotten worse throughout my time here. Today seemed especially sour. The circles beneath his eyes had darkened, and the T-shirt beneath his lab coat was outrageously wrinkled. A sense of gloom and enervation wafted from him. "But I'll introduce you again." He gestured to the woman, "Sander, this is Haley Jones. Haley, this is Sander Fox."

Her eyes brimmed with tears at the sight of me.

Troy untied the gag and let it drop to the floor, then departed the room without so much as a glance in my direction. My blood boiled with anger at his disinterest.

Warren addressed Haley, his voice echoing the exhaustion on his face. "You have five minutes. Please do keep in mind the terms of our agreement." He trailed after his son, the door slamming shut forcefully behind them.

Haley Jones lunged for me. The tears that filled her eyes now spilled onto her cheeks as she cupped my face in her hands. "What did they do to you?" she whispered.

I lacked the words to respond truthfully.

My eyes anxiously darted across her face, scanning for any sign of familiarity beyond the figure who had been in my apartment all those weeks ago. I needed something to explain her sudden kindness and care. Was she a relative of Dad's? The thought vanished as soon as it came. Though I had trouble remembering the exact contours and edges of my father's face, I knew it was nothing like the curves before me.

Pain echoed through my motions as I pulled away from her and tucked myself further into the corner of the room. Mustering the motivation to speak, I asked her the first question that came to mind. "Did you see my family?" The words scratched against my tongue and ripped apart the roof of my mouth, but I spoke again. "Are they okay?"

Her face twisted into an ugly picture of worry. "I have no idea."

Something cracked once more inside of me. I'd had little hope this woman would know the whereabouts of my family, but her response made me inch closer to falling into the looming pit of despair.

"Sander, you can't worry about them." She gripped my face once more. I'd lost the energy to pull away. "You're the only one that matters."

I wanted to scream. Her words made no sense to me, just as they had our first encounter, but I couldn't bear to hear such blatant disrespect toward my family. My sister and my mom were *everything*.

My silence must've spoken volumes. Haley pulled back, noting the confusion and rage in my expression.

"Your dad told you of me, didn't he?" She spoke faintly, almost too quiet for me to hear.

I did not respond to that. I had neither the energy nor the will to do so. "If you are not here to help," I mumbled weakly instead, "then leave."

"Help you?" Her eyes widened. "You're supposed to help *me*. Sander, you're supposed to get us out of here."

It was only my incredible frailty and pain that stopped me from slapping her across the face. Was she so stupid that she couldn't see the state I was in? I could barely lift a finger, let alone break out of the SSD.

She fell away from me, despair crumbling her expression. "He didn't tell you." Again, her words were so quiet I strained to hear them. She snarled at me. "William chose not to tell you."

The hatred in her words was enough to send birds flying.

I watched helplessly as she rose to her feet, let out a bloodcurdling scream, and kicked me in the gut.

I doubled over, coughing and scrambling away from the sobbing woman.

She cursed at the ceiling, swearing at the soul of my father. Her tantrum had reopened the gash on her face and sent blood spilling across her skin. The crimson liquid mixed with tears and dripped onto the white tile. Haley threw herself to her knees. Her screams ripped through the room and split apart my eardrums, filling my head with nothing but her heart-wrenching anger and grief. They lingered in my mind even after Troy and Warren pulled her out of the room, like needles repeatedly prickling my scalp. The screams left gouges in my ears long after Haley Jones was gone.

CHAPTER SEVENTEEN

The days passed in an endless blur of pain, vomiting, and fear. The droning of the AC had lessened, giving room for my thoughts to ravage the confines of my mind. Troy and Warren stopped coming to visit, and I couldn't help but wonder if I'd disappointed them in some way. The only person who came by was a janitor sent to clean up the food my stomach rejected.

Cracks had appeared throughout my skin, clustering heavily around my joints. I could only theorize what they were doing to me.

They were trying to turn me into one of those monsters, perhaps.

The door opened again, but this time, the Director and Warren and a swarm of men in black suits entered. Their lack of gas masks stirred a thought, reminding me of the AC and its lack of air. He gestured to me and started talking as if I wasn't there.

"As you can see, there are notable differences between Mr. Fox and our previous subject." He walked over to me and pulled at my arm to display it. "His veins aren't as significant. He seems to be moving more. And he isn't showing as much pain."

"The previous boy was also taken off his treatments. But for him, it seemed to get worse." The Director demanded, "Explain."

"That's the fascinating thing." Warren's eyes lit up. "I can't figure it out. Normally, my attempt at Substance A causes a heavy release of dopamine in the subject. It's like opioids, if you will. It causes so much pleasure to the subject that they disregard the damage it's doing to their body."

I nearly gaped. Though I didn't know the full context of the situation, it seemed as if they were saying I was doing well. My condition wasn't as bad as it was supposed to be.

Warren continued. His big words flew past me. I didn't understand most of them, except for the basics. He mentioned a change in DNA, which intrigued me.

Another man came through the door. Troy. My blood went cold. The only difference between him and his father was Troy's cruelty. Sure, Warren was cruel, but he didn't enjoy seeing others in pain. Troy, however, relished in others' misery. It was easy to see why Aven had been so eager to get off this planet.

The Director and the others continued talking, but I felt my mind slip away from the present and into my thoughts. When I finally snapped back, I felt a cold hand wrap around my bicep. Panic rushed through me, but I was in too much pain to do anything about it. The guard hauled me toward the chair in the center of the room and clasped the cuffs around my wrists.

I tried to look up at the people surrounding me. My heart pounded. Blood rushed in my ears. I wanted to pull away. I wanted to scream or curse. But I couldn't even move my finger. Every breath I took felt like I was inhaling toxic air.

I felt the familiar sting of the needle in my neck, and then a whole new wave of pain washed over me. I let out a choked cry.

"See?" Warren said. "You all saw what happened to the other one."

His words faded in and out. My ears rang. Pain splintered through my head, and my vision began to darken. It felt like my skull was splitting open.

I squeezed my eyes shut and screamed.

No sound came from my mouth.

My eyelids peeled back, and I was met with nothing but darkness. An endless void stared back at me.

The pain was gone. A blanket of peace wrapped itself around me, seeping through my skin and melting into my bones.

I took a step forward, noting that I was not chained down

anymore. My body felt as if it were made from feathers. I moved through the void weightlessly, wondering if I had died. Lights began to flicker throughout the void. Distant stars illuminated themselves before me. Galaxies stretched beyond my vision.

A feeling began to arise in me. One that I'd never felt before. It felt like the final piece of a puzzle. It completed me.

This feeling… It felt like freedom.

From here, from this state, I could do anything. I could go anywhere. No limits.

I smiled.

I never wanted to go back.

Back. Back to the SSD. Back to the pain and suffering. To the white walls and metal chair. To the grate in the floor and the handcuffs.

My smile fell.

At that moment, a voice rang out. It was difficult to tell whether it was in my head or in the air around me. But the voice, like the echo of a piano in an empty hallway, spoke softly with clear words.

"Sander, you've found me at last."

Then, something was dragging me. Fast. Faster than I could see because, the next thing I knew, I was waking up on the floor of a white room.

CHAPTER EIGHTEEN

I had changed rooms. They'd strapped me to a table in a sterile, updated room. It was still completely white, but cabinets lined the walls, along with a desk and an impossibly thin computer. In my limited vision, I could see two men standing at the foot of my makeshift bed, speaking indistinctly to one another. When they noticed I was awake, one of them came forward. Warren.

I let out a small whimper.

He reached behind me, and something clicked. Then, a machine lowered over my head. Cold metal bit against my forehead and cheeks, clamped around my neck, and covered my peripheral vision. Through a gap in the metal, I could see Warren fussing around the room. He opened drawers, and machines whirred to life somewhere out of my view. The other man in the room stood quietly by the door, his hands clasped behind his back in a pose of respectful protection.

Warren grumbled under his breath, then addressed me. "If you'll excuse me a moment, I have to fetch my wife." His footsteps faded, and the other man followed.

I took a few sharp breaths and struggled against my bindings despite knowing the fruitlessness of my attempts. My body screamed against the action, and I had no qualms with succumbing to its cries and going limp.

I couldn't feel any bit of hope. It had been days since I'd believed my so-called friends were coming to save me. Their continued absence should have brought fear, worry, or even anger, but I hadn't felt anything except self-pity. I was scared for my future—or lack thereof. It was a feeling I had trouble recognizing, considering it had been so long since I'd truly brought such attention to myself.

My friends weren't coming to save me. Whether they were unable to do so or simply didn't want to, I didn't care. They'd done enough for me already, and I'd proven not to have anything to offer in return.

A few minutes slid past before I heard the door open. My fear had settled already, but a new wave crashed over me. I swallowed a lump in my throat, readying myself for Warren's prodding questions.

But they didn't come.

Instead, the machine over my head lifted, and a masked face greeted me. The figure before me wore a black bodysuit, blades strapped across their toned limbs. The gas mask and hood only allowed the slightest glimpse of deep brown eyes and arched eyebrows.

"Who are you?" I asked, my voice raspy.

They didn't respond. Instead, they released my binds and reached out their hand to help me up. My muscles screamed as I rose, knees buckling under the sudden weight of my body. I crumpled against the figure.

They strapped a mask to my face. I watched them warily but didn't resist as they pulled me into a hallway filled with gas so thick it made my eyes water.

I breathed through the mask, my inhalations becoming raspy. The edges of my vision blurred.

Bodies began to appear in the fog, slumped against the walls or sprawled across the floor. I winced, praying they were just asleep, although I knew better.

"Who are you?" I asked again, reaching for the wall to brace myself.

They pressed a finger to their mask, indicating that I should stay quiet. I shut my mouth.

We took a flight of stairs at the back of the facility. Unfortunately, the path didn't exit the building because we entered another hallway.

The gas was gone, and after the person took off their mask, I did the same.

They shook out their head, hood slipping off and revealing chestnut waves. The woman smiled at me, brown eyes crinkling. Her face was truly striking. The warmth of her features contradicted the coldness in her stature and gaze, but it was mesmerizing. Her tanned complexion suggested roots in Central America, but with the addition of new worlds. I couldn't dare to make assumptions.

She pulled out a blade and peeked through the doorway at the end of the hallway. She pulled back, seemed to contemplate the odds, and then pushed through. I followed her, limping and in pain. My head was fuzzy, but I managed to take it in as she snuck up on the guards standing by an elevator, slitting one's throat and driving her blade through the heart of the other. She then sliced off one's finger and pressed it to the keypad. The keypad beeped, and the elevator doors slid open.

She jerked her chin toward the elevator. I followed her in, movements fueled by desperation alone. The doors closed just as guards rounded the corner and started shooting at us.

I sagged against the railing, breathing hard. "Can I talk now?"

She laughed, a joyous sound once again countering the sharpness behind her eyes. "Feel free. Those hallways are horribly echo-prone."

I rubbed my fingers across my face, desperately trying to ground myself.

She noted my movement with wary eyes but said nothing about my condition. Instead, she tilted her head and held out her hand. "I'm Nevena. Nevena Harrison. You probably know my sister, Ivy."

I stared at her extended hand, knowing the polite thing would be to shake it. However, if I moved to shake it, I would certainly collapse into an embarrassing heap before her. I instead focused on the new piece of information she'd just provided me. "Did she send you?"

Nevena chuckled and faced the elevator door. "Please. She voted against rescuing you."

The fragile sliver of hope I hadn't known was there dissipated. I looked at the ground. "What do you mean, voted against me?"

"You'll see," she replied as the elevator pinged open. Guards spun and raised their guns, but Nevena was quicker. She jammed her dagger into the ribs of the first guard, grabbed his gun, and shot a hole through the head of the second. However, the gunshot only made the guards further down the hall turn to us.

Nevena shoved me back into the elevator as bullets ricocheted off the wall. She poked her gun around the wall and fired a few times. The bullets stopped.

"Move," she said.

I stumbled forward, barely able to stay on my feet. She grumbled a curse and slung my arm over her shoulder. The ground sloped away from my feet, and I became dimly aware of sunshine. How had we gotten out? Where were the guards?

My knees crumpled as my shoes met sand. A UTV sat a few feet away, and Nevena helped me onto it. She shoved a helmet onto my head and then on her own before taking her seat beside me and gripping the steering wheel. The engine roared to life, and soon, we were speeding across the golden sand.

I barely processed the wind whipping my clothes because my head bobbed, and soon, I was unconscious.

CHAPTER NINETEEN

The hoot of an owl lured me from sleep. The wind whistled through rustling leaves, and the muffled clamor of voices rose above the crackle of a fire.

I shifted, and for the first time in a long time, severe pain didn't follow the movement. Though a tight soreness grasped my muscles, I could move without much trouble. I nearly let out a whimper of relief. Then, I took a deep breath. The clean, fresh air smelled of smoke and tickled my nose. It was the best thing I'd smelled in over a month, or so I estimated. I opened my eyes.

I lay on a pile of old pillows and blankets underneath the thick canopy of a yellowish leather tent. A chair and table sat to my right, and a lantern flickered atop it. Outside the tent, the glimmer of a fire silhouetted less than a dozen people.

It took a long minute for me to adjust to the reality of the situation. My escape with Nevena was hazy and blurred, like a fever dream.

I threw off the blankets and changed into the jeans and sweatshirt that had been laid out for me. At least, I assumed they were for me.

Outside, there were about a dozen or so tents, some with lanterns glowing inside and some without. The sun had set a while ago, and the darkness of the looming forest was fought back with the firepits surrounding the camp. At the one in front of me, a familiar figure waved to me.

"About time," said Aven. The golden glimmer of the fire couldn't hide the tired shadows across their face. Their exhaustion didn't seem directed toward me, however. My worries vanished as their genuine smile grasped my attention. I took a seat on the log beside them and cast a long glance at the small crowd of men and women chatting quietly with each other. They paid no more attention to me than they would an ant. A tightness eased in my chest.

I brought my attention back to Aven, who seemed preoccupied with the bowl of soup before them. Hoping to get some answers, I asked them the question that had been nagging me since I'd been thrown into the white-tiled room. "How long have I been gone?" I kept my voice low, fearful of disturbing the peace.

"A little over two weeks," they replied. "But Nevena brought you back a few days ago. You've been in and out of sleep since then."

"Oh." I frowned, still pondering the length of my absence. "I don't remember that."

"Of course you don't." They laughed, though it was a hollow sound. "You were barely conscious enough to form a sentence."

I looked around. People were starting to stare at me and talking in hushed whispers. Far across the camp, Nevena was talking to a man, but I didn't see anyone else I knew. "Where are the others? Are they here?" I wasn't sure what answer I was hoping for.

"Not at the moment," Aven shook their head. "They went with a hunting party a few hours ago. I stayed behind in case you woke up." They seemed to notice my confused glances at the space around us. "We're at one of the Rising outskirt camps."

I snapped my gaze toward them. "We're *where*?"

"Calm down. They're not going to kill us."

"They nearly have. Multiple times."

"And we killed nearly twenty of their own," they shot back. "I'd say we're even. Besides, they need Amias and Renna to destroy the SSD. And Amias and Renna only agreed to help them if we all stayed alive."

"And me?" I asked, despite having a sinking feeling that I wasn't going to like the answer.

They gave me a pitying look. "We weren't sure it was worth the risk to come and get you. We took a vote. Eden, Ivy, and I voted yes. Renna, and Amias…" They paused for a moment, contemplating their next words. "I'm not sure what happened to you back in the bathroom with the SSD, but if Eden is right and it's more than what it seems, I'm not going to push you for answers. But the others, they might forgive you if you tell them."

I shook my head vigorously. "I'd rather have them hate me than think I'm crazy."

"You're not crazy. You're just…" They searched for the right words. "A little messed up."

I glared at them.

They raised their hands. "In my defense, we're all a little messed up. I mean, have you seen Eden when she kills? She's like a death machine. And Ivy—"

"I get it, Aven. We're all crazy. Still, I-I'm not even sure what happened. So how can I explain it to them when I am still so confused?"

Aven sighed and ran a hand through their hair. "All right. But you better figure it out eventually."

"Thank you," I said and got to my feet. "I'm going to take a look around."

They nodded and went back to their soup.

I started to walk off, but they jumped from their seat and jogged over to meet me. "And Sander, the Rising—they don't know about my mom. Like, who she is. So, if you could—"

"I'll keep it to myself," I promised.

Relief flooded their face.

I walked away.

The camp was lined by an oval of tents. Rising members kept their distance, watching me as I ambled around the camp. Eventually, I wandered off into the surrounding forest. When I did so, an unusual feeling washed over me, as if all my thoughts had gone silent.

Moss blanketed the trees in thick layers, stretching up toward the night sky. The ferns were abundant, as well as white flowers that seemed to shine in the moonlight. But that wasn't the part that shocked me. It was the butterflies.

Dozens of blue and purple butterflies glowed with a fluorescent light that illuminated the forest. They hugged the trees and flapped between branches, and when I set my hand on one of the sequoias, they flapped away in a frenzy.

A wondrous smile danced on my lips as I watched the beauty unfold around me. The grandeur tipped me closer to believing I wasn't here at all and just asleep back in the cell.

I kept walking, and as I did, the sound of rushing water grew louder. I pushed past a wall of ferns and emerged onto a large boulder overlooking a small pool. On my right, a waterfall plunged into the water below. At the end of the boulder, Ivy sat utterly still with glowing butterflies dancing around her. When I took a step forward, however, they shot away.

Ivy spun around her gun already drawn. She relaxed when she recognized me. "You're awake," she said. She certainly didn't seem pleased, but she didn't sound angry either.

"I am," I said and walked up to her. "Much to your disappointment," I couldn't help but add.

She glared at me as I sat down beside her. "I'm not mad you're alive. I still care about you, no matter how angry seeing your face might make me."

It could've been a joke, but her tone made me second-guess. "I'm sorry about what happened. If I—"

"Are you even going to tell me what happened?" she asked. "I think we deserve an explanation."

"You already know," I answered. "I'm a coward. I hid under the sink while the SSD attacked."

She shook her head. "It's more than that. Tell me the whole

truth, Sander."

"That is the whole truth," I insisted.

"You don't want to tell me, that's fine. But for god's sake, Sander, at least tell Amias. Friendships aren't free, you know. Especially his. Sometimes, you must do the hard thing to keep your friends."

"And what if doing the hard thing would just end up driving them away?"

Ivy studied me for a long moment before saying, "Then at least you'll know."

CHAPTER TWENTY

Early the next morning, when the sky was pink and the sun was just a strip of gold behind the mountains, I sat in a wooden chair and picked at a pencil while half-listening to the conversation flow before me. The light of the dawn spilled through the opening of a tent similar to the one I'd first woken up in.

Nevena stood beside a tall man with black braids falling over his broad shoulders. They leaned over a makeshift table composed of logs and a rectangular piece of wood covered in a tarp. A map was sprawled out before them, and they were pointing at the worn, yellowing paper and muttering to each other. On the other side of the table, a young girl slumped over the wood, her ginger curls rising and falling with the movements of her chest.

Nevena had found me wandering about earlier, unable to sleep, and invited me in. I hadn't done anything since I'd sat down, but I doubted I'd be much help anyway. I had no idea what they were talking about, and I'd stopped listening minutes ago.

Nevena nudged the girl at the table awake. "Go fetch our guests. And tell Asher and Kenneth to get their stuff ready. We leave in a few hours."

The girl blinked before nodding and racing off.

"Where are you going?" I asked Nevena.

"Primos," she replied, rubbing her deep brown eyes, now caramel in the sunlight. "You're coming too."

"What's Primos?"

"Rising headquarters and capital. You're going to meet our leader."

"So you can kill us?" I questioned.

The man beside her chuckled. "Why would we do that? You and your friends are our best shot at taking down the SSD once and for all."

"Wha-" I trailed off, pondering his statement.

"Sander," said Nevena. "This is Aslen. He is the Chieftain of the Second Station."

I frowned. "So, he's the boss? I thought the lady we met at the airplane was the boss."

"Tanith was their Chieftain's Second. Most of their numbers were wiped out after your little group riled the SSD," she explained. "We have stations set up in multiple Departments. The Chieftain of the station you came upon is Maverick. Aslen leads the Station on Department 56. Overall, we have seven different stations on seven different dimensions."

"Which one do you lead?" I stood up and walked over to them, running my hand over the map. It showed a country I didn't recognize, complete with mountain ranges, lakes, and cities.

Nevena laughed. "I don't lead anything. I'm a Shadow."

"A what?"

"A Shadow. It's like a personal spy slash assassin assigned to a person of power. I'm the Major's Shadow."

"The Major," I repeated. "I'm assuming they're the big boss?"

She nodded.

I decided then that I liked her. The directness with which she answered my questions was something I felt I had lacked since being taken from my home. The coldness still lingered behind her every movement, but I found that comforting. She felt… real. Like if I reached out and grabbed her hand, my fingers wouldn't pass through her skin.

It was then Amias and the others walked in. My heart seized in my chest, and the warmth Nevena had eased me into vanished. After my conversation with Ivy, I'd managed to avoid the rest of them until this moment.

Amias's cold gaze brushed over me impassively as if I were nothing more than a piece of furniture in the background. Renna followed suit, and Ivy gave a tight-lipped smile. Eden and Aven both acknowledged me with a dip of their heads, and the latter moved to greet me, but Renna grabbed their shirt and whispered something harshly. Aven's face fell, and they turned away from me.

I sunk back into my chair as Nevena addressed the group.

"We leave for Primos in two hours. I don't know whether you have belongings, but if you do, pack up."

Amias tsked, "My, my, I think I remember agreeing to work *with* you, not *for* you."

Nevena's dark eyes slid toward him, unspoken threats lingering in her gaze. "Watch your tongue, Blood Bringer. I'll kill your friends where they stand."

Ivy snorted. "Have you really sunk so low you'd kill your own sister?"

"You're hardly family of mine," Nevena said. Her expression didn't change, though Ivy flinched.

Aslen cleared his throat. "You have agreed to work with us. Nevena was merely telling you the plan." Before anyone could talk back, he spoke again. "Once we get you to our capital, you will meet with the Major to discuss your plans with the Rising."

"Any idea what that will include?" Renna piped up.

"Please don't put me on dog duty," Aven said.

A quiet laugh escaped my mouth, and they sent me a smile.

Nevena ignored them. "You're going to be mapping out the SSD. Give us detailed layouts of the building, point out their weaknesses, strengths, and anything else you deem important."

"And after?" Eden prodded.

She shrugged. "That's not for me to decide."

We rode high-tech dirt bikes to Primos. Two men joined us as we left. Nevena told me that the first, Kenneth, was the Chieftain of the Seventh Station, and the other, Asher, was his Shadow. Aslen was to meet us in the city within the week, but no one else seemed eager to join our group.

The glowing butterflies had vanished, much to my disappointment. But their beauty had been replaced with breathtaking views as we rode through canyons, tunnels, and on cliffsides.

We stopped every two hours or so for a snack and to shake out our legs. On our fourth stop, Nevena pointed from her seat on the mountainside toward the sprawling grass hills beyond. I followed her gaze and spotted skyscrapers stretching into the horizon.

By the time we rode through the scrap metal gates, the sun had started to slip behind the mountains.

The city—despite being built on an otherwise deserted planet—was surprisingly beautiful. Skyscrapers sprung toward the clouds, and the streets were filled with hovering cars. Ornate streetlights glowed purple and seemed to grow in number the further we went. The neon lighting bounced off the sleek sides of the towering obsidian buildings, each one styled exactly like the other.

Everyone but Eden and I was uninterested in the sight. The former's face was startled. When she saw my gaze, she said, "I did not think I could be surprised by these things anymore."

I nodded in agreement.

"Hey!" Nevena called over to us. "Press the blue button on your bike."

I found the button and pressed it. "What does it do?" I asked her. But before she could answer, the engine coughed. Machines whirred. The bike tilted upward, and the wheels turned horizontal and began rotating like a propeller.

Beside me, Eden gasped. "It is exactly like riding a dragon. Except smaller."

I couldn't tell if she was joking or not.

Nevena stood up on her bike and whipped in front of us, laughing. We followed her to a building shaped like a capital A, although one side was completely vertical, so it was more like a slanted *A*. She led us to the top and set her bike down on a landing pad. I followed her, although with more difficulty.

Asher and Kenneth had disappeared, probably to go to a different part of the city. But they were the only ones missing.

Aven was the last one to land. But they forgot to hit the brakes and almost went flying over the edge. Thankfully, Nevena grabbed them by their hood and pulled them back.

They gave her a sheepish grin, then looked over the drop. Their grin fell.

"Come on," Nevena said. "I'll lead you to your rooms. You'll meet the Major first thing tomorrow."

"First thing, as in before or after breakfast?" Aven asked, wanting to make sure their priorities were heard.

"As in, you'll meet him during breakfast."

"Coolio." They saluted.

The guest rooms were near the center of the cross part of the A. We were each given our own room. Mine was impossibly dark with black walls and flooring. A white rug spilled out from underneath the bed. The headboard was drilled into the wall, but the rest of it hovered above the floor. I sat down tentatively, feeling as if it were going to crash to the floor. When it didn't, I lay down and stared at the bronze tree chandelier.

As much as I tried, I didn't fall asleep for a long time. I couldn't stop thinking about that white room. The metal chair.

I curled onto my side. Something akin to hopelessness settled on my chest. It felt crushing, as if someone was sitting on me.

I thought of Sadira sitting beside me on my bed after our dad had passed. She didn't say anything. She didn't try to comfort me. But her presence was enough. Now that she wasn't here, I couldn't help but feel like someone had ripped my world in half.

I missed her. I missed Mama.

I pinched the bridge of my nose, trying to keep the tears from falling. It didn't help. They came anyway.

Department 1, Day 5

Since my forced departure from my home world, I have learned about the differences and similarities of many universes. One phrase I have heard across many worlds is, "You can't choose your family." I truly think that belief is utter nonsense.

While you can't change those you are related to, you can choose who you consider family. There are few who I have considered mine. Sander is one of them. He is the type of person I believe everyone should know, and I feel sorry for those who do not know him the way I do.

While he may not know it, I regard him as my brother. And like the rest of my family, both blood-related or not, I will protect him for as long as I can. Until my lungs give out and I am separated from the physical dimension, I will keep him safe.

-Elyane

CHAPTER TWENTY-ONE

Regardless of being on the short side, Nevena walked remarkably fast. Even I, a long-legged person, struggled to keep up with her.

She'd barged into my room not thirty minutes ago, announcing it was time for our meeting with the Major and handing me a change of clothes. The clothes I was currently feeling bad about sweating in. I adjusted the forest green blazer for the fortieth time as I followed Nevena onto the stairs.

The staircase, which zigzagged across the slope of the A, was lined with glass and steel railings, overlooking the steep drop down. At each turn of the staircase, a landing jutted out and connected to a long walkway that stretched across the space. More walkways and bridges spiderwebbed around us, but Nevena kept to the stairs.

As we walked, she spoke to me. "Now, before you meet the Major, be warned that he can be a little intense at times. Also, the last time I talked to him, he wasn't very fond of the idea of having people from the SSD become allies."

"And you convinced him otherwise?" I brushed a few curls out of my eyes, turning my anxiety toward the lengthy locks instead of the growing panic in my gut.

The necessity of my presence at the meeting seemed highly irrelevant. It was my desire for the Major's resources that drove me from my bed. Amias and the others had shown no intention of getting me back to my home world, so I was left with little choice but to see what deals the Rising could offer.

"Eh, more like asked for a chance." She gave me a hard look, which did nothing to quell the rising storm in my mind.

"Compliment him. A lot. He enjoys flattery."

"What am I supposed to compliment?" I inquired.

"I don't know. His shoes. His hair. His clothes." She shrugged as we reached the top of the stairs. She set her hand on the door handle. "But whatever you do, don't insult Mr. Giggles."

"What? Who—"

Nevena opened the door, and I was left standing in shock as she strolled up to the head of the table, kissed a man—whom I assumed to be the Major—on the cheek, and took a seat next to him.

The room was grand, with tall windows framed by a rainbow of tulle curtains. Morning sunlight cast the colors of the fabrics across the white-stained wood flooring. The rainbow theme spread along all the furnishing in the vast room, mainly supported by the long table stretching through the middle. The chairs were each a different color, from red to deep sea blue framed with silver. I took a seat on a black wooden chair pillowed with maroon cushions, trying not to gawk at the eyesore before me. Though the jigsaw maximalist vibe might be favorable to some people, I was certainly not one of them. It was difficult to find a safe spot for my eyes, but eventually, I was drawn to the person at the head of the table.

In a golden and lime throne-like chair, a man with chestnut skin and close-cropped pink hair lounged with a goblet in his hand. A snake carving rested along the back of his throne, eyes closed. His yellow shirt was topped with a peach blazer, and beaded sunset-colored trees hung from his ears. His bottom lip was pierced with a single silver ring, which rolled to the side as he frowned. "You must be Sander Fox."

"I—I am, sir," I stuttered, lowering my head.

"No need for that," he let out a sigh. "I read the reports sent my way. You were the one who beat Leland to death with a crowbar, correct?"

I flinched, and he seemed to take it as a yes.

Leland. Something about putting a name to the face made me sick all over again.

There was silence for a long time. When I finally managed to lift my gaze back to his, he was still staring at me, deep brown eyes narrowed with amusement. He drummed his fingers on his goblet and looked at Nevena. "You did tell the others we'd be dining together, did you not?"

"I did, sir," she replied and leaned back in her chair. "They should be arriving shortly."

As if on cue, the doors swung open, and Amias, Renna, and Aven walked through. They silently took seats, the latter next to me and Amias and Renna across from us.

Amias wouldn't meet my gaze, but I couldn't take mine away from him. His hair was still a mess, but it fit the clothes he'd been given, a blue and black rose-patterned button-up and onyx pants. He'd adorned himself with two guns and a few more knives strapped along his thighs, which earned a disapproving glare from the Major.

For the first time, I studied the tattoos that trailed up his arms. A three-eyed cat on his bicep peeked out from beneath his rolled-up sleeves, and a phoenix curled around his elbow. My gaze flicked back to the tattoo I'd seen before, a snake slithering down his forearm, tongue flicking across the back of his hand. From my position, I couldn't see his left arm, so I made a mental note to study it later. If only so I could draw it accurately, I told myself.

A few minutes later, Eden and Ivy came through the doors, taking seats on the other side of Aven.

"Well," the Major said. "Now that you're all here, I suppose we shall get straight to it. As I'm sure my dear Nevena has already told you, I am not thrilled with the idea of working with you six. After all, you killed more than thirty of my people."

Amias cleared his throat. He knitted his fingers together on the table before him. "I'm sorry, sir. I do hope it doesn't affect our chances of becoming your allies."

The blatant artificiality in his voice made me cringe.

"Hmm." The Major frowned but then clapped his hands together. "I can't talk like this on an empty stomach. Let us dine."

Dishes were brought in swiftly. Plates piled high with waffles, sausages, eggs, and fruit were laid out in front of us. Aven was the first one to reach for the waffles.

I forced myself through a few bites of eggs and half a piece of toast but stared emptily at the rest of the lavish feast. The food felt stale and cold in my mouth, as though I were eating freeze-dried paper.

The clinking of dishes was the only sound that echoed through the large room for a long time. When the Major spoke again, he did so much happier than before.

"Allow me to introduce my pet," he said. "Mr. Giggles."

It was then I realized the snake carving on his chair wasn't a carving at all. The snake's eyes opened, and the Major stroked its chin.

It was a large snake. Larger than any I'd ever seen in person. Its scales were yellow and gold, matching the chair it was lying on. I felt a chill run down my spine as I met its pale eyes, staring at me with an empty gaze. There was nothing about him that made me feel like giggling.

"He is an albino African Rock Python," the Major continued. "A rare species. I found him a few days south of Primos. Isn't he beautiful?"

We all nodded hesitantly, except for Renna, who seemed to do so with enthusiasm.

"What does he eat?" she asked eagerly.

"Oh, anything really. Mostly rodents. Rabbits. Raccoons. He's not picky."

"He's gorgeous," Renna breathed.

The Major beamed.

"Can we get back on topic, please?" Amias asked, picking at his food from a distance.

The Major's smile turned to a scowl, but he didn't object. "Listen, Nevena insisted you all would be good assets to the Rising. I disagree, but because I admire her so, I have given you a chance to prove yourself. So, tell me, what can you do for me?"

"Renna and I can give you information that will get you into the SSD. We grew up there. We know their weak points. With what we know and a little bit of firepower, you could take them down once and for all." He shoved a piece of waffle into his mouth, then chewed and swallowed before continuing, "However, I cannot say with certainty that you would leave alive. But you'd have much better success with us. We only ask for a few things in return."

The Major's brown eyes narrowed. "Which are?"

"Your protection and a place to stay."

"I can promise that," the Major said. "But you and Renna will join us in the battle."

Amias's eyes flared. "Like hell."

Nevena cut in. "Amias, you and Renna are the most powerful people here. You have a better chance than anybody at getting out alive."

"We can still get shot," he snapped.

"Then we'll provide you with armor."

"They could capture us."

"We'll make sure they don't," she said.

"How?" Amias growled. "You say you will give us your protection, then demand to throw us into battle. Real hypocritical of you." The fury in his eyes burned brightly, and I had to wonder why he was taking this deal at all. Maybe his bravado and arrogance could only take him so far. As if he felt my gaze on him, he turned toward me slowly. I lifted my chin and held his gaze despite every nerve in my body ordering me to do the opposite.

"I'll do it," Renna cut in. All eyes went to her.

"Over my dead body," Amias snarled, shooting to his feet.

Renna mimicked the motion, and the room went dead silent

as the two stared each other down. Even my breath caught in my throat, afraid to move an inch through the deadly tension.

"I'm not some little girl for you to boss around, Amias. I never was, no matter how much you like to believe otherwise."

"You are fourteen." His eyes narrowed, and to my surprise, Renna didn't balk.

"And you're eighteen. It doesn't matter." Her voice was uncharacteristically emotional, wavering with frustration bordering on fury. "We've trained side by side for years. My age does not determine my abilities."

He turned to the Major, who was watching the spectacle with caution. Amias glowered at him. "If there are no other options, I will fight beside you. Renna stays far away from any battle."

"Dammit, Amias!" Renna slammed her hands down on the table, making everyone jump. "Stop treating me like I'm a replacement for your sister!"

He went still. I could see his mind churning as he stood motionless, trembling with rage. His nostrils flared. In a rush, he stormed out of the room, the door slamming behind him with an echo that shook the walls.

Renna sat down, her features smoothing over. She took a bite of her waffle.

Even the Major was stunned into silence.

I looked at Renna. I didn't think she'd ever spoken that much in one conversation. Let alone shown that much emotion.

"Is breakfast over?" Aven asked and was greeted with yet another wave of silence. "I guess so," they answered themselves, grabbing a stack of waffles before chasing after Amias.

"Thanks for breakfast," I said. No one protested as I rose and left.

Rain fell over the city, turning the concrete streets into ranging shades of gray. A harsh breeze swept through my hair and ruffled my clothes, accompanied by the looming presence of a not-so-distant storm. I tilted my head to the sky, a feeling of peace settling over the torrent of my worries.

Nevena walked beside me, her chestnut hair tied back into a tight braid. A few loose strands waved in front of her face despite her fruitless efforts to keep them tucked behind her ears. She was pointing out different places to me, where to get the best coffee and whatnot. I wasn't really hearing what she was saying, but I nodded and smiled as appropriate.

My mind kept circling back to Amias and Renna's argument.

Stop treating me like I'm a replacement for your sister.

"Sander." Nevena punched my arm.

I turned to her.

"Have you been listening to a word I've said?" she asked.

"Not really," I admitted. "Sorry."

"It's fine," she sighed.

I glanced down the street. "How long have you lived here?"

"Almost eight years," she replied. "I became the Major's Shadow about five years ago."

"You climbed the ranks fast," I noted.

She gave a half-smile. "That's what my parents taught me to do."

I bit back the urge to ask more, my curiosity blocked by a wave of anxiety. I didn't feel like it was my place to ask stuff like that. Small talk or not, her family seemed like one I would regret asking about later.

"How did you hear that we escaped from Blackford?" I asked instead. "How did you know to come looking for Amias and Renna?"

"The Blood Bringers are all our enemies talk about," Nevena replied. "So, when they escaped, you can bet it caused a big commotion. One big enough for the Rising to catch wind of it. Plus, after your little massacre at the Fifth Station's outskirts, Maverick came complaining to us to put you down."

I flinched, a habit I'd picked up anytime someone mentioned our time at the airplane wreckage and the ensuing SSD massacre.

"Maverick…" I prompted.

"Leader of the Fifth Station, or Shora, the name of its city. His Second, Tanith, was the one you met."

And got killed.

"This is confusing," I muttered under my breath.

She laughed. "You'll get used to it. I have a feeling you're going to get to know the Rising pretty well."

The thought didn't sit well with me.

CHAPTER TWENTY-TWO

It was well past midnight when I woke drenched in a cold sweat. Heartbeat in my throat, my vision blurred with tears, and as I lifted my hand to wipe my cheeks, I noticed it was shaking.

I wasn't entirely sure what I'd dreamed about. I grasped at a vague memory of someone falling from a cliff or building, but the longer I was conscious, the more the image started to fade.

I swallowed the lump in my throat, then rubbed my eyes and glanced at the clock. I'd slept for an hour and a half or so, yet it hadn't felt like more than a few minutes.

Despite every fiber in my body telling me to go back to sleep, I pulled back the covers and fumbled to turn on the lamp beside my bed. After a few futile attempts to find a switch, I adjusted my position and ran my hand over the lampshade.

It switched on, and I jumped in surprise.

I tapped the lampshade again. Darkness overtook the room.

"Wow," I muttered to myself as I turned it on one last time. The backpack I'd borrowed from the Rising camp lay discarded beside my bed, unzipped, with my sketchbook and pencils spilling out. I scooped them up, my mind wandering as the lead met paper.

I'd never seen Renna show as much emotion as she had at breakfast. Part of me had wondered if she was incapable of doing so. Evidently not.

What exactly had she meant by what she'd said?

The look on Amias's face after she'd spoken those words dug a hole into my gut.

I shook my head. It wasn't my problem. I had my own shit to

worry about. I'd been told by Sadira that I had a habit of distracting myself with other people's problems so I didn't have to deal with my own. It was true, I realized now. I'd been so worried about the Blood Bringers siding with the Rising that I had barely even thought about my previous experience in the SSD labs.

As soon as the thought crossed my mind, a wave of heat washed over the back of my neck, followed quickly by a shudder of fear.

Troy's cold, cruel gaze flashed through my mind. Warren's intrigued expression.

Tears welled in my eyes. I blinked them away furiously.

Shut up. Shut up. Shut up. I snapped at myself. *You're so weak, Sander.*

What had they done to me?

Now that the pain had lessened and my mind had cleared, I deduced that the AC must have been the source of whatever was going on. It would explain the gas masks and why they'd come in without them near the end when the AC was shut off. So, I'd been breathing in toxic air for two weeks, but I was still alive. My mind spun with the endless possibilities of what the air could've contained.

I shifted my gaze to my hands as if they would dry and crack once more. But the bronze skin remained normal, healed, though my worries only grew.

It was then I heard a soft knock at my door. To my surprise, Amias stood before me when I opened it.

He looked surprised to see me. "Why are you awake? It's one o'clock."

"Why are *you* awake? And why are you at my door?" I shot back, pretending to be busy with my hands so I wouldn't have to meet his gaze.

He stood silently for a long time. His eyes darted over my face. I didn't speak. Worried thoughts about the coming conversation buzzed around my mind.

"Never mind. This was a stupid idea," he said and turned away.

He made it about ten feet before I called out to him.

"Wait!" I jogged over to him. "Um, can I ask you a few questions?" I didn't know what had driven my body to do that. He certainly wasn't the ideal person for answering my endless barrage of nervous inquiries.

A muscle in his jaw twitched. "Sure," he said through gritted teeth.

I winced. "Um, never mind, actually."

"Just spit it out, Fox," he grumbled, spinning on his heel to face me.

Something in me snapped. Oddly, I was grateful for his sudden anger. It gave me an excuse to get mad, too.

"What is your problem?" I burst out. "I get that you don't like me. I messed up back then, okay? But is it that hard for you to just forgive and forget? Or hell, just forget."

His eyebrows rose, then knit together. "You put the people I care about in danger." His voice was low, sending a shiver down my spine. "I don't let go of things like that so easily."

I bristled. "Oh, I get it. You're a protective asshole with trust issues. But unlike you, Wolf," I mocked, "I'm not used to this type of life."

He blinked.

My ears heated. "I had a normal life. I was fine until you and the SSD came and ruined everything."

"Really?" he snapped. "You're looping me in with those narcissistic fascists? I was just following orders."

"Why shouldn't I? You are part of them, aren't you? Tell me, Amias, how many people have you killed in their name, claiming you were just following orders?"

Beside us, a night light glowed deep indigo atop a metal framed console table. It illuminated Amias's face, causing dark circles to appear around his eyes. He opened his mouth to respond, but words were already spilling from my mouth. Thoughts I hadn't even known were in my mind.

"You know who else said they were just following orders? Nazis. Someday, you're going to have to take responsibility for your mistakes. I understand that may be hard for your egotistical brain to handle, but you'll get it once you mature a little."

I knew I would regret those words later. But at the moment, I didn't really give a damn. My fists were clenched, knuckles paling.

"You think you're such a victim," Amias snarled, lip curling. "That you have nothing to do with this. If we didn't need you, I would've left you to die in the air shaft."

"Need me? What on earth could you need me for?"

He gritted his teeth. Ignoring my question, he spat, "You're a burden, Fox. Do you want my forgiveness? Learn how to defend yourself first. Hell, learn how to throw a punch. Otherwise, you're nothing but an extra thing to worry about."

"Well, then why am I here?" I snapped. "You had plenty of chances to leave me behind."

"You want me to be honest?" He lifted an eyebrow.

I gestured for him to go on. "Please."

"I thought you and I could get along."

I gaped at him. "You brought me along on your murder road trip because you wanted someone to talk to? How insane are you?"

He didn't answer. I could see his chest moving up and down heavily, even in the dim lighting. When I didn't speak again, he turned on his heel and stormed toward the elevator.

"Oh yeah," I muttered, then raised my voice. "Walk away. Ignore everything that makes you uncomfortable. Real mature."

He spun abruptly, face twisted into a mixture of anger and grief. "I just wanted a friend!" he shouted.

"And I just wanted to go home," I cried back, voice cracking.

I didn't see his reaction because I turned away so fast I almost ran into the wall. Slamming the door behind me, I stormed into my room and pressed my forehead against the wall.

I groaned, smushing my palms into my eyes in an effort to hold back the tears.

Why couldn't I just go home?

The next morning, Nevena got me for breakfast again. The Major wasn't there. His Shadow told us that he had had a rough night and wasn't feeling good. I interpreted that as him getting drunk last night and being too hungover.

Amias ignored me all throughout the meal. I tried to corner him afterward, but he easily avoided my attempts to question him. Anger still ran through my blood, heating the skin along my arms and chest as I watched him slip away from me for the third time. I'd been the one to walk out, but our conversation wasn't over. I didn't think it would ever be, but the fiery knot in my chest would only grow tighter if I didn't get his thoughts about what I'd said.

It seemed, however, that I would have to suffer from its heat for a little longer because not only was I expertly bad at trying to talk to Amias, but it seemed as if the others wanted nothing to do with me. My presence at yesterday's breakfast was just as I'd thought, a way for the Major to put a face to the name.

I wasn't necessary for any future plans.

Nevena and Renna went out for the day, the former saying something about mapping out the SSD. Aven had insisted on going with them. Eden and Ivy were training, and Amias was avoiding me, so I had nothing to do.

I wandered through the slanted A-shaped building, but most sections were blocked off to me. Eventually, I left the building and found myself in the dirty streets of the city's outskirts, kicking a rubber ball against a wall. Hands in my pockets and hood over my head, I kicked it again.

I wasn't sure why I'd drifted here. The inner city was certainly a lot nicer.

Shouting kids played nearby, their footsteps racing past me. I watched them go, despondency lingering through my actions and clinging to my limbs. The kids, though dressed in oversized shirts and near-soleless shoes, laughed joyfully as they turned a corner and disappeared.

Yesterday's storm lingered. Thick clouds blotted out the sun, threatening a downpour later in the evening. I took the chance to walk the damp streets, the air relatively warm despite last night's weather.

The housing in the outer city ranged from wooden shacks to shipping containers. I spotted more than one family huddled on the side of the road, passing what little food they had amongst the kids. I became even more grateful for Mama's perseverance after our father's death, knowing how easily that could've been us. Though our third-story apartment in the suburbs of San Diego wasn't five-star, it had given us a roof and a place to sleep.

I tried to keep my gaze to myself, though I offered my sweatshirt to a boy who begged for help. It did little to ease the tightness in my chest, seeing as how the sweater wasn't mine to begin with.

My wandering took me to an old highway stretching off into the grassy horizon. The clouds faded away further from the city, allowing the sunlight to stretch across the pale hills.

I wondered how deserted this planet was. Had humans been here before the Rising came along? Were there other creatures living amongst the trees and oceans?

My heart tugged in my chest, pulling me away from the city.

It occurred to me that no one would notice if I left. They'd shown time and time again that I was not needed. I had no purpose. I was a burden. Another thing to worry about amid a battle. Another useless mouth to feed.

The tug in my heart grew stronger.

Away. It seemed to scream. *Away from these people and the fear.*

Run.

But how would I get back to Mama and Sadira? Even that urge had been diminished, however. My murderous actions clung to my body like a shadow I could never get rid of, no matter how much light there was.

I sighed. Amias's words ran through my mind once more, and the anger that followed was blinding. It hurt, like a scream I couldn't let loose. It shattered my bones and crushed my organs.

No, I told my heart. I would not give up. I still had some fight left in me, if only from wanting to shove Amias's words back down his throat.

I ignored the insistent tugging and turned back toward the city.

I limped off the elevator, wincing as pain lanced through my muscles. I was pretty sure that within the next few days, bruises would cover nearly every inch of my skin. I was also sure pain wasn't supposed to be shooting from my shin every time I stepped.

I'd asked Nevena to train me. Back at the SSD, I'd nearly forgotten about my bullet wound, considering all the other pain I'd been in, both mentally and physically. But now, I had time to realize that it was nothing more than a big scab that caused minimal pain with movement. It'd leave a cool scar, though.

Nevena, despite me asking her to, hadn't gone easy. At least, she hadn't gone by my definition of easy. She'd taught me a few things—how to throw a powerful punch, how to block a kick, and so on. I felt like I'd done pretty well, all things considered.

As tired as I was, I was also angry. Over and over again, I'd been thrown to the mat. By the time I'd declared it over, Nevena hadn't even been breathing hard.

There was someone standing by my door. Multiple someone's. Ivy, Aven, and Eden. Ivy knocked on my door and called out,

"Sander, it's us. Open up."

"Hey," I said, and they spun toward me. "What is it?"

"We need your help," Ivy said.

I blinked in surprise, shoving away the bright flare of hope that flickered in my gut. "With what?"

"Breaking into the Major's office," Aven said. Ivy elbowed them in the ribs. "Ow. What was that for? I'm right."

"Anyone could be listening," she shot back. "Be careful what you say."

Aven grumbled a curse as I led the group into my room. The door closed, and I began untying my shoes.

"Why do you need to break into the Major's office?" I asked.

"Reasons," Ivy's eyes darted to my neck. "Is that a bruise or a hickey?"

"It's a bruise. Courtesy of your sister."

"Speaking of Ivy's sister," Aven cut in. "We need something from you."

I picked at a hangnail, glaring at the floor. There was no other reason they would ask for my help. "Uh oh."

"Nevena has the access codes to the security room," Ivy explained. "Normally, I could get in without much effort, but getting the codes would be easiest and wouldn't trigger any alarms. Once we get into the security room, Renna will mess with the cameras, and we can break into the Major's office undetected."

"Mhm," I crossed my arms. "And why do we need to break into his office?"

Ivy tilted her head in genuine confusion. Then, she sighed, rubbing her forehead with her palm. "To put it simply, I don't trust him. I don't trust anyone in this city. I feel that if we were to find anything suspicious, it'd probably be in there. Seeming as that's where he spends most of his time."

"So, you're telling me you don't have any actual proof that these guys can't be trusted, and you want to break into their leader's office so we can find evidence that may or may not exist?"

She nodded.

"And what do we do if there is none?"

"Then I suppose we can trust them."

I resisted the urge to roll my eyes. "Even if I wanted to help, I don't know if I could. I have zero skills in this arena, and I don't even know Nevena that well."

Ivy shrugged. "She likes you. She thinks you're helpless. You have all the right reasons for her not to suspect you."

I frowned. "I'm not doing it."

CHAPTER TWENTY-THREE

I had breakfast in my room the next morning. Sitting cross-legged on my bed, dressed in flannel pajamas and a sweater, I picked solemnly at my food while staring at the clouds and tips of skyscrapers out the window. My stomach was in knots. I couldn't eat the food on my lap, nor had I slept very well. Not that I ever did.

Ultimately, Ivy won the argument. The word "argument," however, was a bit of an overstatement. We'd exchanged a couple of opposing thoughts, and in order for me to avoid a fight, I'd backed down.

I had no idea how I was supposed to get the codes from Nevena. It's not like I could just go up and ask for them. Why did Ivy need to get into the Major's office anyway? Weren't we supposed to be allies? And didn't allies not sneak into each other's offices?

Though my lack of details was unnerving, I desperately wanted to get the codes for them. If only in an attempt to regain their trust. There weren't many lines I wouldn't cross for friendship, even breaking and entering, it seemed.

Finally, I pushed myself out of bed. My muscles groaned in protest, still sore from yesterday's training. I stretched them out for a bit, pulled on jeans and a green hoodie, and stepped out.

The previous days we'd been here, the building had been relatively empty of people. I'd passed office workers with stacks of files in their arms, along with groups of intimidating men and women donning black uniforms and armed to the teeth with knives and pistols. Today, such groups seemed to have multiplied by a dozen, stampeding down the staircase like a herd of frightened elephants. The Rising soldiers—I assumed they were, anyway—were cold and strict-faced, and no one was wearing a uniform, so finding someone willing to tell me where Nevena resided was a challenging task.

It turned out she had a whole level to herself below the Major's penthouse on the vertical part of the A.

The elevator opened up to a hallway painted black with white wood flooring and violet lights illuminating the way. The hallway spilled into a kitchen and open living room. The far window overlooked the city, taking up the entire wall and slanting outward.

"Nevena?" I called out, walking into the kitchen. I ran my hand over one of the sleek, black marble countertops and instantly felt out of place. "Nevena?"

A door opened, and I spun around. Nevena came out of her room. "Sander? What are you doing here?"

"Um, I—"

My gaze followed her into the kitchen, where she pulled a tub of ice cream from the freezer. She leaned against the counter and raised a prompting eyebrow.

My eyes trailed over the fridge, and I said the first thing that came to mind. "Do you have cheese sticks?"

She snorted, bringing her fingertips to her nose. "You're joking. You really came all this way for cheese sticks?"

God, Sander, I cursed at myself. *You're a terrible liar.* "Yes," I said, my voice squeaking. "I'm missing home. Those have helped in the past."

"Wow," she chuckled, opening the fridge. She tossed me a pack of a dozen cheese sticks. "Take them all. I never eat them."

"Thanks." My heart raced. I wiped my sweaty palms on my pants, then gingerly held the cheese sticks in front of me. How the hell was I supposed to do this?

Curses swam in my head, all aimed at Ivy and her stupid idea. I just had to start a conversation. Maybe I could have her give me a tour of the building and nudge her toward the security room?

Even if that didn't work, perhaps I could go "ask" Ivy to do it for me. She could figure something out.

"Do you think you could give me a tour of this building?" I asked. "I tried giving one to myself, but I got lost so fast."

Nevena's lips curved into a playful smile. "Why not? I've got nothing better to do."

According to the Major's Shadow, the wonky A-shaped building was used as an apartment complex for higher-ranking personnel and guests as well as a base of operations of some sort.

It was structured that way so the Major could be close to the things he needed to watch over. Most of them, at least. There were also outposts along the city's border, where soldiers and guards lived, for those of them who didn't have a home. Nevena told me that most of the soldiers in their army were refugees from attacks or just needed somewhere to live.

As grateful as I was to them for housing them, it hurt me to know that people needed a place to stay. But I supposed, in the multiverse, stuff like this was inevitable.

I adjusted my grip on the bag of cheese sticks as I followed her into the elevator.

"Is there something in particular you want to see?" she asked.

My heart began to pound. "Some stuff, I guess. I was up late last night, just overthinking everything, you know. Then, the thought of the SSD attacking us came to my mind. I just wanted to know how exactly you guys keep them away."

Something like compassion filled her face, and she gave me a small smile. "I understand. Let me show you something."

In the middle of the building, peeking out from the slanted side of the A, sat a curved balcony, divided from the inside by a double set of glass doors.

My clothes ruffled in the wind, which slipped through the cotton and caused goosebumps to form on my skin. I placed my hands atop the metal railing, taking in the city stretching out below us. Then, I followed Nevena's gaze as she pointed to a circle of cell towers encompassing Primos.

"That's how we keep the SSD from finding us," she explained. "The cell towers have been modified to manage unwelcome interdimensional visits. Now, it doesn't keep them from attacking outside Primos, but we have security measures for that, too."

"Such as?" I prompted.

"Curious today, are we?"

My cheeks heated, and I ducked my head as she led me back inside. Once inside the elevator, Nevena opened a keypad. My heart lurched.

I pinched myself, relief flooding through me when she didn't move to block the code from my view. She punched in the numbers 6-7-9-1-0. I repeated them in my head as the elevator lurched into motion.

It opened into a blue-painted hallway, bustling with workers and, to my surprise, dogs.

"Why are there dogs down here?" I asked, reaching to pet one as he brushed against me.

Nevena shrugged. "The Major's a big animal fan. He travels a lot and always brings home strays."

I kept repeating the numbers in my head as she began explaining how the security system worked, all the while passing rooms lined with screens. Most of it went over my head, but then again, I wasn't really trying to pay attention.

I'd done what Ivy had asked me to do. I just had to make it through this.

"Did you get it?" Ivy scanned my hands the moment I stepped into my room.

I repeated the code to her and flopped onto the bed beside where Eden sat. She patted my head.

"It is hard work being a spy," she said comfortingly.

I pulled away from her, frowning. "Don't patronize me."

Renna, from her spot in the chair by the window, chuckled. I jumped, having not realized she was there. "Better get used to it. This probably won't be the last time you have to do something like this."

I groaned, stuffing my face into the pillows.

The door opened, and Aven jumped onto the bed beside me. "Did you get it?" Then, they noticed the cheese sticks. "Why do you have those? Can I have one?"

"No," I said. "I earned them." They reached for one, but I pulled away. "I said no."

"But there's so many," they whined. "And I'm hungry."

"You just ate, you pig," Renna said.

"I have a high metabolism," they snapped back at her. "Startling high, my dad says."

"I earned these cheese sticks," I said, rising from my spot on the bed. "Through hard work and dedication."

They raised their eyebrows skeptically.

"Fine. Nevena gave them to me."

"Therefore, you didn't earn them." They moved toward me. "And, therefore, I can eat one."

"No," I shied away as they reached for one. They gripped my elbow, pulling me against them as they tried to pry the cheese sticks from my hands. I fell to my knees, bending over myself.

"You guys are so stupid," Renna muttered.

"Shut up," Aven said and flipped me over with surprising strength. I curled inward over the food. "Give it to me!"

"Just give it to them, Sander," Ivy urged.

"No," I protested, a smile sneaking its way onto my face.

"It's not that big a deal. Just one."

"No," I said again.

Aven slid their hand underneath my arms and tried to pull the cheese sticks away. I kicked at them, but they sat on my legs. "Give up!" they shouted, holding back a laugh. "I dominate you physically. There's nothing you can do about it."

"Liar!"

"What the hell is going on?"

We both froze and looked toward the doorway, where Amias stood, face twisted in anger and disgust as he surveyed the tangled mess of bodies that created Aven and me. They scrambled off me, something akin to panic in their movements.

Amias raised an eyebrow.

"Cheese stick," Aven said and pointed.

I held out the pack.

"Never mind," Amias said, throwing up his hands and turning away. "I don't really care."

I rose and took one last glance at them before racing after Amias. I wasn't even sure why I followed him. To tell him there wasn't anything going on between Aven and me? Why did I even care? Amias had said he didn't.

I grabbed Amias's arm. He lifted his fist as if he were going to punch me, and I quickly took a few steps back. He relaxed his arm.

"What do you want?" he growled and pressed the button for the elevator.

"I just—I—There's—"

He glared at me. "Why are you telling me? I don't care."

"I—I don't know. It kind of seemed like you do," I stuttered.

"Well, I don't," he snapped.

The elevator doors opened, and Amias stepped inside. I didn't go in. "Why do you hate me so much?" I asked. "I mean, I know because of what happened in the bathroom. But it feels like more."

He pressed a button, and the doors slid closed.

I stayed in my room for the rest of the day, drawing and sleeping. After Dad's death, I'd been hammered with nightmares. Eventually, getting only three or four hours of sleep became a regular thing for me. But now that I had nothing to do all day, I managed to get in a few more hours. Spread out as they were.

It had started raining a while ago, and I found myself wondering what season it was here. It had been mid-spring back home when I was taken. I had no idea what it had been at the SSD, but given the endless desert and seemingly unyielding sun, I doubted it mattered much.

For Primos, I guessed early spring. Back at camp, the flowers had just been buds. There weren't many plants in the city, but the ones I could see seemed new.

Ivy knocked on my door at nine. She ushered me to the elevator, where Eden and Aven were waiting. The latter reported that Renna was already making her way to the security room to cut the cameras.

"What's the plan?" Aven asked as the doors opened and we all stepped inside.

Once again, I was wondering how necessary my presence was. But I had little to lose.

"Knock out the guards. Get inside."

"Right. Amazing plan. And what is it exactly that we're looking for?"

"I don't know. Anything suspicious." Ivy shrugged. "The Major seems… off."

"Of course, he seems weird, Ivy," Aven chuckled. "He's drunk half the time and high the other."

"I realize that!" she snapped, then groaned and put her forehead on Eden's shoulder. "I just want to make sure we know who we're allying with before we actually ally with him."

"Right," Eden nodded. "We want to know all his deep, dark secrets."

Ivy pulled her head back as we all chuckled. "If you don't want to help, then feel free to get off this elevator."

Eden smiled; the warmth within her eyes only seemed to appear when Ivy was around. "No need to fret, darling. We will help this dumb plan of yours succeed."

Ivy turned away, rolling her eyes, and the doors opened. We filed out.

"Excuse me." Ivy approached the single guard outside the door to the Major's office. "Is the Major in there? We're looking for him."

"He's not," the guard said. "But if you're looking for his party, I'm pretty sure it is in his penthouse."

"Thank you, sir." She stepped up to him, a sly smile curving the corner of her mouth. "Actually, there's one other thing I need from you."

He tensed, eyebrow raised. "Yeah?"

Ivy's grin grew wider. "Get out of my way." In a flash, she snatched the gun strapped to his hip and rammed the handle into his temple. He crumpled. She turned to us and spread her arms wide. "See? I told you it would work."

"Now we just have to make sure no one else comes," Aven said.

"That's what you're here for," Ivy said and flicked the gun toward the guard. "Put his uniform on."

"I'm not going to strip a man and put his clothes on," they said. "That's rude."

Ivy shrugged. "If you want to get caught and executed, be my guest. But if you don't want to die, I suggest you put it on."

"What makes you think I don't want to die?" Aven grumbled as they reached for the guard.

Ivy picked the lock to the Major's office and held the door open as we filed inside. She headed for the desk and began rooting through the drawers. Eden and I took the shelves.

The books were coated in dust as if they hadn't been pulled out in years. I scanned them anyway, reading the titles. Most were in languages I couldn't understand, but the ones I did weren't suspicious at all.

Eden hummed quietly as she worked, climbing the ladder that leaned against the bookcase. Ivy wore a frustrated expression, eyebrows knit together and mouth drawn into a thin line. They acted as if they'd done this before. And honestly, I wouldn't be surprised if they had. In fact, I half expected it. The comfortability with which they did illegal things suggested a history that had probably landed them in Blackford in the first place.

Ivy chuckled. "Look at this one." She held a book out to us, but before I could read the title, a voice sounded from outside the door.

"Sir, I told you, you can't go in there," Aven called louder than necessary.

"But it's *my* office!" The Major exclaimed. "Why can't I go into *my* office?"

Ivy began cursing. We scrambled for a place to hide.

"Uh, gas leak," Aven tried.

"Gas leak? There's never been a gas leak before!" The Major's words were muffled. I heard a grunt, and someone bumped against the door. "Let me go! I'll have you fired!"

"Sir, please. It's not safe."

I made my way toward Ivy but tripped and fell against a shelf. Books fell to the ground, and I winced at the noise. Ivy bent down and began helping me pile the books back onto the shelf.

"What was that?" the Major snapped. "Who's in my office?"

"Uh, the people fixing the gas leak. They don't want anyone else in there."

"I knew your idiocy was going to get us caught," Ivy hissed at me.

"Then why bring me along?" I shoved a book back onto the shelf and began reaching for more but stopped when I saw a book on the shelf that didn't have a title; in its place was a smiley face. I pulled on it, but it was stuck. I pulled harder and heard a *clunk*.

The floor hummed, accompanied by the muted sound of grinding metal. The bottom half of the bookshelf slipped into the floor, revealing a dark hole.

I looked at Ivy. "Maybe not."

She rolled her eyes and shoved me into the hole. Eden followed closely. I ran my hands along the wall, looking for something to close it.

The doorknob rattled.

"Hurry!" Ivy snapped.

My fingers landed on a lever, and I pulled hard. The bookshelf slid closed just as the door swung open.

"What are you talking about?" the Major asked just as we were immersed in darkness. "There's no gas leak. There are no people here." There was a moment of silence. "Hello? Guard? Where'd you go?"

I let out a breath. Aven must've split when the Major got past him. Cowardly, but smart.

I heard the Major start laughing. "Man," he mumbled. There was a crash, and he laughed even more.

He kept talking to himself. Ivy flicked on a light, and I took in our hideout.

It was a small room full of plush red, pink, and purple pillows. Red wood shelves took up the back wall, littered with small trinkets, including glass ballerinas, stuffed flamingos, and more. Blankets covered the mattress that took up most of the room, facing a TV installed above the exit. Oddly, a disco ball hung from the ceiling, glittering in the lights.

Ivy chuckled, but her smile fell as the same clunk from before sounded. The machines whirred, and we all dove underneath the pillows.

I heard the muffled sound of the Major sighing in contentment.

I snorted and tried to bury the sound in the pillows.

A few moments later, the cushions shifted, sinking as the Major laid down. His snoring echoed in the small room. No one moved. No one dared to.

His breathing was steady, but I was afraid moving would wake him. So, despite my cramping muscles, I stayed still. In the meantime, we shared hushed whispers. Every now and then, the Major moved, causing us to go tense, ready to bolt if he caught us.

It wasn't long before The Major let out a long sigh and pushed himself onto his hands and feet. Through my congested view through the pile of pillows, I watched him make his way to his desk, pour a glass of whiskey, and take a seat. He left the door to the room cracked.

It was dark outside. Meaning we'd been in here long enough for the sun to set. I wondered what Aven was doing, if they'd met up with Renna or not.

"What's he doing?" Ivy asked Eden in a hushed tone. She lay on the opposite side of the room, unable to see the Major.

"Drinking," Eden whispered back, lying next to me.

"That's it?"

She nodded.

"He's opening a book now," I reported.

Ivy scoffed. "Surprising. He doesn't seem like a person who can read."

"Maybe it's a picture book," I suggested.

She snorted and shifted beneath the pillows.

"He's moving now," Eden reported. "He's coming this way."

The conversation dropped away. I pulled a blanket farther over my head and peeked out from underneath it. In my limited vision, I could see the Major peering at one of the bookshelves. He pulled off a deep blue book and flipped it open. He took out a gray sphere and made his way back to his desk.

"He has a gray ball," I whispered to Ivy. I kept talking to her as he set it on his desk and pressed something. A holographic image shot out, displaying the image of a young girl sitting cross-legged with a book in her lap. The picture began moving. A boy walked away from the camera as if he'd set it up, and then he stood behind her. He began braiding the girl's hair while she read her book aloud.

After a minute or two, she paused. "Are you almost done, Ambrose?"

Ambrose laughed. "I'm not even close to finishing the first one. Keep reading."

The girl did the opposite. She closed the book and set it aside. "I don't want to read that book anymore. It's boring. Besides, I'm not going to lead the SSD, despite what my mom says."

"You're not?" the boy asked. "And why is that?"

"Because I want to be free. I want to build a city for the poor and give them shelter and food," she looked up at the boy with a happy smile on her face. "Wouldn't that be great, Ambrose?"

Ambrose nodded, but when she brought her head back down, I saw worry on his face. "You know," he started, "building a city like that is going to cost money. Money your mom won't give you."

The girl frowned. "Then I'll make my own."

"Verena…" He looked down with a sad expression. She looked up at him, confused. His sadness broke, and he forced a smile onto his face. "You'll build a great city. What will you call it?"

She thought for a second, then decided on "Primos. I'll call it Primos. And it will be as close to heaven as we can get."

The Major flicked the video off. He put his head in his hands. His shoulders started to shake.

"What's happening?" Ivy hissed. "What's he doing?"

"He's—he's crying," I whispered back in disbelief.

The Major looked up, eyes red, and blinked back tears. He pinched the bridge of his nose, then finished off the last of his whiskey. Slamming the glass on his desk, he pinned his glare on the gray sphere. Then, he snatched the ball and tossed it at the wall. I heard it shatter somewhere out of my view.

The Major stood there for a moment, eyes blazing and chest heaving. Then, the anger melted away and his body sagged. He slumped to the ground, his head in his hands. His hands began to shake, and his sobs rippled out in waves. He pressed a hand to his mouth and squeezed his eyes closed.

I didn't know what to think. I watched in horror as he grabbed the bottle of whiskey and slammed it down on the ground. The glass broke, and the liquid spilled over the wood flooring. Fumbling, he grasped a shard of broken glass and clenched it tight. Blood seeped through his fingers.

"It's your fault," he whimpered. "It's your fault. You could've saved her. But you didn't. Dammit, Ambrose!" he shouted and slammed the piece of glass into his thigh. "Why didn't you save her?" he screamed, spittle flying from his mouth.

I clapped a hand over my mouth, eyes wide.

The Major sobbed into his hands for a while before swallowing back his tears and rising to his feet. He limped out of view, blood in his wake. The door to his office opened, then closed.

Eden, Ivy, and I didn't speak for a long while. After making sure no one was waiting for us, we made our way out of the office and, after promising to meet each other in the morning, slipped into our separate rooms.

I crumpled onto my bed, exhaustion creeping into my bones. Despite this, I couldn't sleep.

Who was the girl? *Verena*, I recalled. Who had she been to the Major?

I thought of her words. *"I'm not even going to rule the SSD."* Did the Director know who she was? Had the Major and the Director known each other?

If so, what had happened to make them so different from one another?

CHAPTER TWENTY-FOUR

As promised, I met the others in Ivy's room the next morning. I was barely able to drag myself out of bed without stumbling, much less down the hall. They were talking when I walked in. I took a seat on the ground, my mind swimming with questions.

I rubbed my face and yawned.

"Did anyone get any sleep?" Renna asked. Her usual braids were replaced with messy pigtails, and she was draped in a T-shirt twice as large as mine. Her collarbones seemed painstakingly prominent, jutting through her skin with quiet malice.

Nobody replied, leaving the answer hanging in the air. As much as I had tried, I had only gotten a good hour.

It was then that Aven came bursting in. "Oh my god, guys!" they exclaimed and collapsed onto me, wrapping me in a hug. "I thought you were dead! I told Amias, and he freaked out." They pulled away from me and went to hug Ivy.

Behind them, Amias hung back. "I didn't freak out," he said, eyes on the floor.

"You totally did," Aven countered and reached for Renna. She shook her head, and they stepped back, frowning.

Renna smiled and gestured to her hair. The meaning behind her movement eluded me, but Aven seemed to understand. They rolled their eyes, a soft smile spreading across their lips.

"I knew you were fine," Amias grumbled.

Ivy chuckled. "You can admit you were worried, Amias."

"I wasn't worried," he snapped. "I was…"

"You were worried," Aven finished for him.

"Can we just drop it? What even happened last night, anyway? Why didn't you invite me?"

As Eden, Ivy, and Renna filled them in on the previous events, I found my gaze pinned on Amias. He took a seat at Ivy's desk, shifting uncomfortably as he caught me staring at him.

I forced myself to peel my gaze away.

"Have you talked to the Major since?" Aven asked.

Eden shook her head. "No, but we were about to head to breakfast if you want to join."

They began heading out, but I stayed sitting. I wasn't sure why. I had no serious objections to the idea of breakfast. In fact, my stomach was practically yelling at me. But I remained in place as they strode away.

"Are you coming, Sander?" Amias asked.

I shook my head. "I'll catch up with you guys later."

He hesitated, looking as if he wanted to say something, but he decided against it and stepped out.

Maybe he was why I didn't go with them.

That afternoon, Nevena knocked on our doors, tossing outfits onto our beds and announcing that we were invited to a party tonight.

I pulled on my outfit, then stared at myself in the mirror for a while, trying to identify the person who stood before me. He looked good, wearing a forest green blazer with white stripes over a tan turtleneck and black pants. But there was a tired sag in his stance, like something heavy was riding on his back.

I rubbed my face and rolled my shoulders back. I tried to put a confident look on my face, but it looked unnatural. Forced.

There was a knock at my door, and then Nevena called to me. "Stop primping and get out here!"

I yanked open the door. "I'm not primping."

She whistled. "Look at you, Sander. You look nice."

"Hm. You look good, too," I said, barely casting a glance at her outfit.

"Oh, I look more than good." She gestured to her black knee-length dress. "Now, come on. Let's get our gorgeous selves to the party."

"Did you tell the others?" I peered behind her as if they'd be there.

A frown tugged at the corners of her mouth, but she forced a smile. "Yeah, yeah. I just told them. They'll meet us there."

The party's building was within walking distance, but even then, Nevena insisted we take a cab.

"The rain will ruin my hair," she complained as we climbed in.

My chest was already beginning to tighten, and my heart was racing. I desperately wanted to run back to my room. When I expressed those thoughts to Nevena, she chuckled.

"You only need to make an appearance. You're one of the stars, after all."

"How so?"

"The Major needs to announce our alliance with your group to the other Rising stations. And given the attention-seeker he is, he decided to turn a simple announcement into a whole party. So, there will be many higher-ups at this place, which means you and your friends need to be on your best behavior."

I swallowed and decided to ask the question that had been tugging at the back of my mind since I'd woken up in the camp. "Why *me*? What do I bring to the table that's so important I need to be at every single event?"

She seemed almost surprised by the question, but then she laughed, her golden earrings clinking. "Mr. Fox, your friends were rather insistent you were a part of their group. I fear they'd have objections if you weren't included."

The cab came to a halt. As we stepped out, Nevena slipped her arm into mine. The warmth would've felt nice, but my mind was anywhere but in my body.

There were so many people. Oh god, there were so many people. I drew in a breath as she pulled me through the crowd. The room was huge, complete with domed ceilings, marble columns, and frescoes on the walls, reminding me of a Greek cathedral.

The chatter and laughter of the finely dressed guests nearly drowned out the elegant music. I felt a little underdressed despite having had Nevena pick out my outfit. But above that, I felt anxious. Besides school, I'd never been in a room with so many people. Especially people who seemed to know who I was.

They sent curious glances my way and whispered to their friends as I passed by.

Nevena led me to the Major, who was laughing with some people I remembered from the camp. Kenneth, Asher, and a man and woman I didn't recognize. He spotted us and waved us over.

"About time," The Major said. "I was beginning to wonder where you were."

I glanced down at his thigh, but of course, it was covered by his pants, concealing his injury. His eyes were lined with golden paint, and sapphires dripped from his ears. There was no trace of the broken man I'd seen in his office last night.

Nevena grabbed the glass of wine he had in his hand and took a sip, then handed it back to him. "Sander spent a little too much time in front of the mirror."

They chuckled, and I felt my cheeks flush. "I—I didn't," I said, but my words were weak.

The Major looked me over. "It sure was worth it. You look nice."

"That's what I said," Nevena laughed.

"You remember Kenneth and Asher, yes?" The Major gestured to the men who stood next to him.

I nodded.

"This is Rosa." He set his hand on the shoulder of the woman

I didn't recognize, who seemed to be in her late forties. Her mouth was set in a disappointed frown, but I didn't think it was directed at anyone. It might've just been her resting face. "She is the Chieftain of the Third Station."

"I'd say it is nice to meet you," she said. "But you killed Leland."

The Major cleared his throat. "This is Carlos, her son and Shadow."

The boy greeted me with a cold smile. "It's a pleasure."

It didn't sound like it. I tried to smile back, but it felt like a wince.

"Sander!"

I turned at the sound of my name. Ivy was shoving her way through the crowd and getting rewarded with disgusted glares. She wore a tight black dress that hugged her slender body, cut off just above the knees. The thin-strapped sleeves showed off the muscles rippling across her arms. She held her shoes in her hands.

"There you are," she said. "I've been looking for you forever." She noticed the Major and gave what seemed like a mocking bow. "If you'll excuse us, I need to steal Sander from you."

Nevena frowned. "He's talking with us."

"His *friends* are looking for him," Ivy glowered.

"I'm right here," I muttered, but they didn't notice. My heart swelled at Ivy's words.

"It's his first party," Ivy continued, "Sander should be with people who appreciate his company and don't just want to sleep with him."

Nevena looked startled.

Without leaving much room for argument, Ivy grabbed my hand and pulled me away.

"Does she really want to sleep with me?" I asked her as we made our way to the far wall.

She snorted. "Nevena wants to sleep with everyone. Especially the hot ones."

"I'm not—"

"Yes, you are."

"Oh," I said awkwardly. Feeling flustered, I decided to change the subject. "What happened between you and Nevena? Why do you hate each other so much?"

Ivy glanced at me. "That's a story for another time, but the short version is she's a traitorous, lying freak and the reason I ended up in Blackford in the first place."

"Oh," I said again. "I'm sorry for befriending her then."

She gave me a half smile. "I don't blame you. We Harrisons are very charming when we want to be."

"And very scary," I added.

She laughed.

We approached the corner of the room where the others were waiting.

"Found him," Ivy announced. "Nevena dragged him over to the Major."

Amias and Renna stood, each on opposite sides of the bench Eden and Aven sat on.

Eden nodded at me from her seat. A long silver dress fell over her body, shimmering in the light each time she moved. She had her hair up for once, pulled back into a loose bun circled by a braid. Her white tattoos and pointed ears were on display. "We used to have balls like this at my home," she said.

"At your home?" Aven raised their eyebrows. "Man, how rich is your family?"

She chuckled. "Perhaps I could show you one day. I believe you would like it. It is very beautiful."

"Beautiful home for a beautiful lady," Ivy said, extending her hand to Eden. She took it, and they stepped out onto the dance floor.

Renna took Eden's seat, and I saw Amias take a small step away. So, they hadn't resolved their problems then. No surprise there. Amias's solution for every problem was to ignore it.

I sighed and leaned against the wall a few feet away from him. Aven started chatting with Renna, who seemed to do so grudgingly.

I stared at Eden and Ivy. They laughed as they spun around the floor.

Was this how parties usually went? Sitting around waiting for someone to talk to you? I could think of more than a dozen things I'd rather be doing.

"You look really good," Amias said, his voice gruff.

I looked over at him. "Thanks. You look… " I trailed off as I took him in fully for the first time. He wore a suit the color of the deep sea, with a light blue undershirt and a tie the color of his eyes. He'd combed his hair back, except for a small strand that dangled in front of his face.

"You look amazing," I finished, then immediately regretted it. My cheeks flushed. "Sorry," I muttered.

The corner of his mouth curved.

I smiled at the floor, happy to get a good reaction out of him for once. Maybe our friendship wasn't shattered after all.

My eyes caught on a duo of young girls giggling and looking our way. They saw me staring at them, shrieked, and turned away. That might've been a bit of an overreaction. Aven winked at me and made their way over to them.

Renna rolled her eyes. "I need to go to the bathroom," she murmured and walked off.

Amias muttered something under his breath.

"So, you're Sander?"

I turned to the new voice. There were two of them, a man and a woman. Their gazes were pinned on me with such deadly anger that I didn't have to guess who they were.

"Who are you?" Amias stepped in between me and the newcomers. "What do you want?"

"Amias," I said slowly, putting my hand on his arm.

"We're here for him," said the man, pointing to me. "I want him."

"Get in line," Amias snapped.

If I hadn't been so terrified, I would've looked at him in surprise. Did he want to kill me as well? I didn't have time to wonder about it because the woman spoke.

"Sander Fox killed our brother." Her voice cut like shards of ice. "Beat him to death with a crowbar like an animal."

"Your brother gutted his father," Amias snarled. "I'd say you're even."

I blinked in surprise. I hadn't said anything about who Leland had been. I didn't have time to consider it because the man's face went red with anger.

"Even?" the man roared. "*Even?*"

"Amias," I said, "let's just go."

"You're not going anywhere." The woman took a step forward and pulled out a gun. The people around us gasped. The dancing slowed to a stop. "Not until we're done with you."

Amias lunged for her, but the man pulled a gun on him as well. He pressed it against Amias's temple. "Move, and I'll blow your brains onto the wall."

A muscle in Amias's jaw twitched.

The woman stalked toward me. Gun still trained on my head, she gripped my shoulder and began guiding me toward the door. The crowd parted.

The man started walking backward, still aiming his gun at Amias.

"Kayson," the Major's voice rang through the air, and he stepped from the crowd. "Put the gun down."

Kayson didn't. "Put me in jail if you wish," he snapped, "but I won't go knowing I haven't gotten justice for my brother."

"Put the gun down," the Major repeated. "That's an order."

Kayson swung the gun toward the Major. The room fell deadly quiet. "I will shoot you, too. I will shoot you all!"

The Major raised his hands, a seemingly exhausted expression on his face. "Amias here is the key to getting rid of the SSD. Kill Sander, and he won't help us. Are you really so selfish that you'd risk the fall of the Rising over the life of one man?"

"We're not going to kill Sander," Kayson snarled. "We're going to make him bleed just like my brother did. First, we'll break his fingers. Then his wrists. His feet. Then, we'll take a crowbar, just like he did with Leland, and beat him until he's bloody and begging for death. That's when—" his words were cut off when something came through his chest.

He looked down with a startled expression at the bloodied hand protruding from his skin. Then, he went limp. The hand darted out, and Kayson's body crumpled to the ground. Standing over him was Amias, his face filled with a fury I'd never seen before. Something red rested in Amais's bloody palm. Kayson's heart.

He looked up at me, sapphire eyes filled with a crazy rage.

"No!" the woman screamed.

I shut my eyes, expecting a bullet to tear through my skull. But it didn't.

I heard the clatter of the gun on marble and turned around. The woman was looking at her hand—or rather, where her hand used to be. Eden stood beside her, blade red. It was astonishing, really, how she'd been able to hide such a long, wicked sword underneath her dress. She didn't waste time and promptly ran it through the woman's heart.

CHAPTER TWENTY-FIVE

I didn't bother changing my clothes when I stumbled into my room late that night, half-dazed, and collapsed onto my bed with the intent to sleep. Alongside the weariness that threatened to pull me into unconsciousness, there was a nagging fear that someone would get hurt if I did so. I tried to push past the feeling, but it weighed me down like heavy chains wrapped around my chest.

I sat at the end of my bed, staring out the window at the night sky. The violet city lights outshone the stars, but the moon's halo glowed deep within a layer of clouds. Every now and then, my eyelids began to flutter closed, but I continued to wake myself by splashing water on my face.

Slowly but surely, the paranoia crept along my skin like a mass of spiders chipping away at their prey. It took over my body, my nerves, and wiped away any logic I had left. I had no reason for such a high level of anxiety, but every bone in my body was telling me to *move*.

I slipped my shoes back on and made my way into the hallway. Aven's room was the closest. I knocked once, panic rising in the few seconds they didn't answer. I knocked again. When they didn't reply, I pushed the door to find it unlocked.

Pain burst through my jaw as someone slammed me against the wall. A gun clicked.

I cursed my body as it went still but met Aven's gaze with a look of my own that made them pause.

"Sander? What are you doing?" They took a step back and released their grip on me.

I turned to face them, rubbing my jaw. A quick survey of their jostled pajamas and messy hair told me they were safe. The relief I felt couldn't douse the raging fire that consumed my mind. "I was just making sure you were okay."

They turned on the lights. Worry was etched across their features as they scanned me. "Are you feeling all right?"

"I'm fine." I brushed off their question and exited the room, heading toward Ivy's. I didn't bother knocking this time and barged into the shadows seeping across the room. My gaze landed on a lump silhouetted by the window.

"Sander?" Ivy's voice echoed from the dark.

I fumbled for the switch. Light illuminated the room, revealing Ivy sitting by the window, a bag of chips in her hand.

"Are you okay?" she asked. "Why are you awake?"

I checked her over once more before turning on my heel and pushing past Aven. I sped-walked toward Renna's room.

Being the only semi-sensible one of us, she was asleep. But that changed fast when I flicked on the lights. She sprung from her bed and slammed me against the wall, arm to my throat.

"Why are all of your first instincts so violent?" I shouted, feebly shoving against her superhuman grip.

"Why are you sneaking into my room at three in the morning?" she snapped, stepping back.

Heat rushed through my cheeks, and the panic subsided so abruptly that I crumpled against the wall. "I wasn't sneaking in. I was making sure you were okay."

Ivy bent down before me. "Why wouldn't we be?"

"Because—" I stuttered. "I just—I couldn't sleep and—"

"I don't give a shit what's going on," Renna grumbled. She brushed a strand of hair behind her ear, braids undone for the night. Her sky-blue eyes narrowed and pinned on me. "He woke me up. Get out of my room."

Ivy offered to help me up, but I brushed her hand away and rose on my own. Fists clenched in embarrassment, I kept my head down as I made my way back to my room, doing my best to ignore the worried stares of Ivy and Aven.

The door behind me closed harder than intended, and I became grateful for the absence of other residents in this hall. I threw myself onto the bed and shoved my face into the pillows.

Amias and Eden had been locked up for the night while the Major decided their punishment. With the combined obstacles of the time, location, and the trust we'd just lost from the Rising, it wasn't possible for me to check on them, too. The paranoia seemed to have dulled, like a pool smoothing over after its occupants had left. But it was still there, waiting quietly for its next chance to attack.

They couldn't kill Amias. They needed him. And they couldn't kill Eden. Amias and Renna wouldn't work for them otherwise. But they could keep them in jail, at least until they needed them.

I ran my hands over my face.

My door cracked open, and Aven came in. Expression solemn, they gave me a tight smile.

I propped myself onto my elbows, too tired to try to return it.

"What happened just now?" They sat down on the end of my bed.

I kept silent, averting my gaze.

"Okay, fine." They let out a sigh. "That's understandable. You've seen a lot today."

"Don't pity me," I snapped.

They tilted their head. "I wasn't. I was simply stating that you had a rough day."

"And you didn't either?" I grumbled. "I'm sick of this. You guys treat me like I haven't seen shit. I can deal with it. I'm not a child."

They laughed incredulously. "That's not what I'm saying, Sander. I just know you aren't as… experienced in this arena as the rest of us. I'm trying to be empathetic toward that."

I scoffed. "Have—" I swallowed the words. I didn't need to tell them. No good would come of it.

But I needed to get it out.

I clenched my fists. "Have you ever tried to put your dad back together while he lay dying in pieces?"

Aven fell silent for a moment. Their posture shifted, shoulders sinking with something mixed with relief and sorrow. When they did speak, their tone was gentle. "All the more reason why today was hard for you. It was hard for all of us, Sander. I admire your bravery, actually. If I were in your position, I would not have been able to make it as far as you have."

I swallowed, heart sinking. "You seem strong, though."

They shrugged. "Appearances can be deceiving. Truth is, after what Amias did today, I nearly threw up. I'll never be able to get used to all of this death."

I tried to smile. "I don't think any normal person would, if that makes you feel better about yourself."

"Are you?" they asked. "A normal person?"

I couldn't answer. I didn't have one. Instead, I said, "Amias seemed pretty comfortable with what he did today."

Aven ran a hand over the back of their neck, face distraught. "Let's be glad that's all he did."

"What do you mean?"

"When they first injected Renna and Amias with the serum, they went crazy. They killed thirty men before they managed to restrain them. There are times when the crazy comes out. When the serum takes control of them. Renna is better at controlling it than Amias is. But let's just say it could've been a lot worse."

My heart lurched, and I thought of my time under Warren's supervision. Was that going to happen to me, too?

"I don't know what we're going to do, Sander," they muttered.

"There's no antidote?" I asked hopelessly. "There's nothing that can fix them?"

They shook their head. "Fixing them was never the SSD's focus."

The door opened again, the hallway lights illuminating the

room for a brief moment before sending the room cascading back into darkness as Renna and Ivy approached. The former crossed her arms. Ivy nudged her forward.

"Renna has something to say," Ivy prompted.

Renna sent her a glare, then turned to stare at me for a second too long before saying, "I'm supposed to apologize for how I acted earlier."

I was taken aback. She was doing what?

Ivy elbowed her.

Renna's lip twitched. "I'm sorry. I was rude."

"You-you're fine," I stuttered. "It makes sense that you're a little tense with everything that's going on."

"That, and I just don't like you," she replied. "But actually, when you talk to Amias, please make sure you're careful with him. I think he's going to feel bad about what has happened."

I was confused. Amias had killed plenty before and hadn't shown even a bit of guilt. What made this so different?

She must've read my expression because she clarified, "He never wanted you to see him like that. Any of you." She grabbed a throw pillow and began playing with the long strands of fur. "Amias thinks of himself as a monster. You can't change his mind. I know because I've tried. I spent years trying. He tries his hardest not to show anyone that monster, but sometimes… he can't."

I stared at her.

Amias thinks of himself as a monster.

I looked at my fingers, my head filling with the image of them curling around a bloodied crowbar.

Maybe Amias and I weren't so different after all.

The next morning, a knock sounded at my door. I forced myself to rise from the position I'd been resting in for the few hours since the others had come into my room. When I opened the door, a man with a shattered mirror tattoo displayed on his wrist announced that the Major would see all of us in his office in twenty minutes.

I thanked him and ran to grab breakfast before heading back into my room to wake up the others.

Ivy had fallen asleep with Renna in her arms, and Aven was sprawled on their stomach at the end of the bed. I nudged them all awake.

They got up and groggily ate the waffles I'd brought up. I took a seat at my desk, legs hanging over the armrest of my chair. "The Major's meeting us in ten minutes. He's going to tell us what he's decided to do about Amias and Eden."

Ivy mumbled something through a mouthful of food. She held up her hand, swallowed the food, and spoke, "Do we know if Amias and Eden are going to be there for the judgment?"

I shook my head. "The messenger just said to go up to the office."

Aven took a sip of coffee. "After we get them back, are we planning on staying in Primos?"

No one answered. No one knew the answer.

"I think Amias should decide," Renna said, and we all nodded in agreement.

After everyone finished eating, we took the elevator to the office. The guard didn't bother stopping us as we pushed through the doors.

The Major frowned at us from his seat on the lip of his desk. He held a near-empty wine glass filled with coffee and a tired look in his eyes.

Two guards stood to his left, and at their feet, forced to kneel and chained like dogs, were Amias and Eden. The former looked up at me, an emotion in his eyes I couldn't decipher.

"Sander Fox," said the Major. He set his glass down and pushed himself off his desk. "They're always saving you, aren't they? Don't you think for once that you should be able to fight for yourself?"

I clenched my fists and forced myself to stare at my shoes. "I—"

"You know," he interrupted. "I knew your dad. He was a great man. Ambitious. But it was his ambition that got him killed. Thought he could sell information to the SSD without us hearing about it. So, I ordered him killed."

My head shot up. I had begun to suspect someone had ordered him killed, but I hadn't suspected the Major. Just how deep did my dad's influence run in these worlds?

He laughed dryly. "Yes, yes. That was me. And I'm sorry, I truly am. He was one of my greatest friends."

"Just get to the point," I snapped, my mind going white with rage. All the questions that burned in my throat couldn't seem to make their way onto my tongue. Getting Amias and Eden out of here was more urgent.

He didn't seem to hear me. "Your daddy was a smart man when it came to battle strategy. When it came to friends, he drifted toward the unruly type," he flashed me a smile. "Much like you. I tried to stop him, but he didn't want to hear what I had to say. He became friends with shady characters, and their betrayals are the reason he is dead."

"Apparently, *you* are the reason he's dead," I spat. It wasn't like the Major was such a saint, either.

He tsked. "But I wouldn't have had to kill him if his friends hadn't convinced him to make deals with the big bosses." He finished off the last of his wine. "Your friends are going to get you killed, Sander. Trust me on that one."

"You killed one of your greatest friends and expect me to trust you?" I scoffed. Why was he talking to me? Why not Renna or Ivy? Or Aven? I'd been the first person he'd addressed as soon as we'd stepped into the room without so much as glancing at the others.

They now stood behind me silently, taking in every single thing that was being said. Their presence felt like a warm fire at my back, empowering and warm.

Before he could reply, I straightened. "I'll take my chances with the shady characters. Now, what are you going to do with Amias and Eden?"

"Murder is a crime," the Major said bluntly, seemingly disappointed in my change of subject. "And you'd be surprised how little crime happens in Primos. It can't go unpunished. Your 'friends' will be released but will have guards stationed outside their bedroom doors and be with an escort everywhere they go."

I released a breath. It wasn't terrible. Not as bad as I'd feared.

"But know this," the Major added. "Amias Wolf and Eden Kavan will have to earn back their full freedom. They will contribute to helping the city in every way I order."

I nodded. "Give us our friends back."

He sighed and gestured for the guards to unlock the chains. Once they clattered to the ground, Amias rose to his feet, rubbing his wrists and glaring at the Major. Eden went to stand beside Ivy, and Amias approached me.

"Are you okay?" he whispered and scanned me.

"Am *I* okay?" I whispered back, my heart jumping. "Are *you* okay? You were the one who spent the night in jail."

"I'm fine," he growled.

The Major waved us out, saying he'd already spoken with the criminals about the details of their release. We departed with four guards trailing closely behind.

Amias led us, face set in a scowl that could send children running. The blood was still on his hand. Aside from that, I didn't see any other signs of injury.

I suddenly felt angry. Angry at the Major for tossing them in jail. Angry at Amias for killing a man—even if the man had been an idiot. Even if the man had been trying to kill me. I clenched my jaw. They were always protecting me, and I hated it. I hated how useless I felt. I was a burden to them, nothing else.

No one spoke until the door to Amias's room closed, leaving the guards standing outside. I took a seat on the leather chair facing the window and stared at the purple street lights fading beneath the golden glow of the sunrise.

"Are we leaving?" Ivy asked in a hushed voice. "We can get rid of the guards. Easily."

"No," Amias said, and we turned to look at him. He leaned against the window, tattooed arms crossed in front of his chest. His gaze was focused on the streets below. "We're not leaving."

"We have no reason to stay," Aven argued.

"I agree with Aven," Renna added. "There's nothing left for us here. They know the symbols. We can find a new world and never look back."

Eden rubbed the back of her neck. "I know of a place."

Amias's gaze snapped toward her. "Can I talk to you? Alone?"

Eden followed him into the bathroom. The door closed, and we were left in silence.

After a long moment, Amias's voice rose.

"Did you forget what he told us? No way in hell am I risking it!"

"We have options. Remaining here does not have to be one of them," Eden countered.

Their voices died down again. I found myself counting the threads in the shag rug. I had just counted past two hundred when the door to the bathroom opened and Eden and Amias walked out.

We all looked to the former. She gave a subtle incline of her head. "We will carry on in Primos."

My heart sank. I didn't want to stay in Primos. I wanted to go home.

"The smart move would be to get the hell off this planet," Aven snapped. "Did Amias knock you senseless? The Major's crazy. He had Sander's dad killed."

Amias looked at me. I glanced at my hands.

Eden continued, "He has provided us with shelter. Food. The SSD is unable to find us, and if they do, the Rising has an army. If anything were to happen, we could be long gone by the time they got to this building."

"What makes you so sure the Rising won't take the rest of us prisoner?" Ivy argued. "Amias and Renna are useful to them. They could end the war."

"We came to an agreement on that," Amias cut in. "I won't help him unless he keeps you all safe. We have an advantage here. He needs us. We don't need him."

I fussed with my curls. He was right, of course. We could live on our own without the help of the Major and the Rising. In fact, maybe I would even have a chance to go home. To see Sadira and Mama. My throat began to close at that thought.

I rubbed my face, trying to pull myself back from that feeling. The others continued arguing, but I drifted off, stuck in my mind.

I wondered how they'd react if they saw me. It had been, what, two months since I'd disappeared? Three? Did they think I was dead? Were they even sad that I was gone?

For some reason, that thought didn't leave me as sad as I thought it should.

"Earth to Sander," Aven said, waving their hand in front of my face.

I blinked and met their gaze.

"We came to a decision," they said and waited for my response. I didn't answer. They sighed and continued, "We're staying. But the minute things get heated, we're out of here. Sound good?"

I nodded. "Sounds good."

After a few more hours in Amias's room, Ivy and Eden left, and a few minutes later, so did Renna. Then, it was just Aven, Amias, and me. While they talked, I sat cross-legged on the floor at the end of the bed, listening to their conversation. Somehow, we'd gotten onto the topic of families, and Aven was explaining how their parents' relationship worked.

"Basically," they said, "they chose to marry each other, not for love, but because, with their combined brain power, they could make freedom become a fantasy."

"That's sick," Amias laughed. "They literally decided to spend the rest of their days together creating a world where everyone would bow to them?"

"And not just one world," Aven continued, "everything. All the dimensions. They want to make mind control a real thing. They want soldiers who won't hesitate even a second to follow orders. Hell, they want them to be able to kill a child without flinching or even feeling guilt. I've heard they almost succeeded, too. They got close to obtaining the way to do it."

"Why?" I asked. "Is universal domination really that important that they have to devote their entire lives to it?"

"Not just *their* lives. They know they won't be able to finish by the time they die. That's why they had Troy and me in the first place."

"So, you weren't an accident?" Amias asked.

Aven punched him. "No, believe it or not, I wasn't an accident."

Chuckling, Amias took a seat on his bed.

Aven leaned against the window and looked at their feet. "I don't know why my parents want to do it. I never got the courage to ask, and they certainly never told me. But I think it has something to do with my mother's parents. What happened to them."

I looked up at them questioningly.

"I don't know much. Just that they died before Troy was born. Murdered."

"You think it's revenge?" The humor in Amias's voice was gone. "On the person that did it?"

"Maybe." Aven shrugged. "I don't know." They shook themself out and clapped their hands. "I'm bored. Let's go do something."

"Like what?" I stood up and reached for my sweater. I'd changed out of my party clothes and had pulled on jeans and a T-shirt, as had Aven and Amias.

"We'll fight," Amias said, nudging my shoulder. "You need the practice, Fox."

It wasn't until the sky had faded from blue to navy that Aven and I stumbled out of the training room. Amias, on the other hand, strode out as if we hadn't just spent the last few hours throwing punches and getting slammed into the mat. Well, Amias had done most of the slamming and punching.

"It's not fair," I complained as I pressed the button for the elevator. "You being a super soldier while Aven and I are just normal human beings. I bet you can't even feel pain, can you?"

He tipped his head back, laughing. "I can feel pain. I've just gotten so used to it that it's more of an annoyance now."

His words were joking, but I saw the sad truth behind them.

I frowned.

The doors pinged open and we filed in, Amias's guards coming in after us.

The whole time we'd been training, they'd stood by the door, watching Amias like hawks stalking their prey. I had no doubt that they were ordered to report Amias's every move to the Major.

We stepped out onto our level and said good night to Aven as they headed into their room. I made way for mine; however, Amias grabbed my shoulder before I could open the door.

"I'm sorry I couldn't get you home. I know it must hurt, being away from so many people who love you." His voice was laced with jealousy.

I shrugged. "Don't worry about it. It's not that many people, anyway. Just my mom and my sister."

He nodded slightly, and then his sorrowful expression shifted into something akin to forced happiness. He gave a small salute. "Night, Foxy."

"Good night, Wolf."

His words had stirred something inside of me. The pity I'd been sent through small glances and muttered apologies had finally gotten to me. What *was* keeping me from my family after all? Nothing I couldn't get past with a little bit of work.

Department 1, Day 6

Our time in Primos was brief. I am not one for big cities, but being there, with everyone at least somewhat safe, felt nice. Food was plentiful, we slept under a roof, and most importantly, we were all together. The memories from that time are ones I have cherished for a lifetime. It was the best time I had ever had.

But I realize now that my thoughts on this were not reciprocated by my friends. Sander, for one, had only recently been pulled away from his life and thrust so violently into a new one. And there were others who lived life constantly on edge. I had taught myself over the years to find peace in the chaos, to always take a moment and find something to be grateful for.

It was not an easy skill, but it was helpful for keeping my grip on sanity. As were friends. If any one of us had gone on this journey alone, I truly believe that we would not have made it out as right in the head as we did.

If it were me alone, I would not have fought. I cannot fight for myself. I do not hold myself to such a standard where I deserve to be fought for. But there are a few specific people for whom I would burn the universe. And if it meant giving her *them a happy ending, then I would do anything.*

-Elyane

CHAPTER TWENTY-SIX

Nothing made sense. From the moment I'd been thrown into Blackford, it was as if nothing had a solution or answer. Every question I asked myself just ended with more questions. But last night, I'd lain in bed, pondering the previous week's events and conversations, when something had clicked.

Last night's discussion with Amias had brought up yearnings I'd tried my best to hide.

Home. That was all I really wanted. I'd become so entangled within the conflict of the SSD and the Rising that I'd neglected this feeling because it felt insignificant. An impossible dream.

But Nevena had talked about the use of the cell towers. The SSD couldn't track our movements through the Mirrors here.

So, I went to see Aven the next morning before the sun had even risen. It was just a sliver of pink in the sky; clouds crumpled like tinfoil spreading across the sea of colors.

They were lying on their stomach, their face smushed against their pillow. The blankets were hanging off the bed, and their shoes were still on.

I flicked on the lights and started rummaging through the TV stand.

"What are you doing?" Aven's voice startled me. They let out a groan, and I heard the sound of blankets shifting. "Man, it's not even six o'clock."

"I'm looking for a marker," I replied. "Do you have a marker?"

"How should I know? I don't live here," they grumbled.

I rolled my eyes but didn't say anything back because I spotted a thick blue marker hidden beneath a stack of stationery.

Aven stumbled after me, rubbing their eyes. "What are you doing now?"

I pressed the pen into their hands. "I did some thinking. Nevena says the cell towers block the SSD from the Rising when they use the Mirrors."

"Yeah, we—they knew something was keeping them from doing that but weren't able to ever figure out what it was."

"Which means it works, and she wasn't lying." I went to the hallway and checked for guards. Other than the ones standing at Amias and Eden's doors, there were none. I went to Aven's bathroom and waited for them to follow. "We're in Primos. The heart of the Rising." I didn't wait for Aven to acknowledge before continuing, "Meaning we could go through any Mirror without the SSD knowing."

Their eyebrows knit together. "We can't know for sure. Maybe it has something to do with the people of the Rising themselves. Their biosignatures?"

"I don't know what that word means." I tapped the marker. "But that's not all."

They eyed me. "Did you even sleep at all?"

"I don't sleep," I answered. I swallowed hard. "Do you know the symbols for my home Department?"

Understanding fell across their face, followed closely by pity. "Sander, I know you want to get home."

"No, no, no." My throat closed up. "You don't know. Please, Aven. I need to see my family."

They chewed their lip. "If the Major finds out you're gone… If Amias finds out—"

"Neither of them will care. Besides, all you have to do is write the symbols. I go through and bam. Nothing happened. You were sleeping."

They let out a deep sigh, combing their hair back. "Having you gone could cause a lot of problems for us.”

“Then I won't stay gone.” I just needed them to write the symbols. Once that was done, I would be free. “I'll just check in on Sadira and Mama, then come back.”

They contemplated, drumming their fingers on the black countertop. After what seemed like too long, they sighed. “This is not a smart idea, but… fine. But I'm coming with.”

“No, you have to stay and make sure no one comes in here,” I said. They couldn't come. They'd make sure I came back to Primos.

“I'm writing the symbols,” they said, “and I'm coming with you.”

“Well, how do you suppose we keep the guards or Amias and the others out of this room?” Think of something. Anything to get them to stay.

They shrugged. “I don't know. Put up the Do Not Disturb sign?”

“I don't think that'll keep any of our friends out. If we even have one.”

“We'll be fine,” Aven assured. “It's five o'clock in the morning. No one will be awake for at least an hour. We can be in and out in under thirty minutes. I think I remember how to get back into your hometown.”

Fine. I'd lose them somewhere in that dimension. “Just write the damn symbols,” I demanded.

“Pushy much?” They chuckled and climbed up onto the sink.

It took them a few minutes to get the symbols up. I climbed through the Mirror first, coming out in the first-floor boys' bathroom at my school. I hopped down from the counter just as Aven came through.

They grunted and shook themself out. “Where are we?”

“My high school,” I replied, voice shaky as the familiar graffitied stalls and smoky air filled my senses. It was far from pretty, but I felt like sagging to the floor with relief. I never thought I'd be so excited to be in this bathroom.

They glanced around. “Where would Sadira be?”

"At five o'clock in the morning? Still asleep, if she was sane."

"Well, it might not be five o'clock here."

"What do you mean?"

They frowned for a second. "It's kind of difficult to explain, but… think of the multiverse as a train," they explained. "Each train car is a dimension. They're moving at the same speed but in different places. Or, in our case, different times."

I led them through the bathroom doors, the words sinking in. We exited into the hallway, which was packed to the brim with students. My chest tightened, and I suddenly remembered why I hated school so much.

Aven, on the other hand, seemed exhilarated. There was a fascinated smile on their face as we pushed through the crowd.

"You know, I've never been to a school before," they said. "I learned everything I know from my dad or books."

I didn't answer; I was too busy keeping my head down. I could feel people's eyes on me. Either they didn't know who I was, or they knew who I was and knew I was supposedly missing.

"Sander?"

I snapped my head up at the heart-joltingly familiar voice.

"Sander!" A girl pushed through the crowd toward me. Libbie Bates, Sadira's eccentric best friend, grabbed my hand and dragged me into an emptier hallway. Then, she wrapped me in a hug. "You're back! What have you been up to?"

"I—that's a long story," I stammered, confusion rippling through my thoughts.

She pushed her round glasses up her nose and squinted at me through the lenses. "You look sick."

"I'm exhausted."

"Why did you leave so suddenly? Is your family okay?"

"I—"

She brushed a short brown wave out of her eyes. It was then that she noticed Aven. She took them in, then gasped. "Oh, Sander, did you finally make friends?"

Aven stuck their hand out. "Hi. I'm Aven Coldwell."

"Libbie Bates," she replied and shook their hand. "I want to hear everything. I want to know how you two met."

"Um, later."

"Mmm hmm," she replied skeptically, then hooked her arm in Aven's. "Come on. I can skip science. You're going to tell me everything."

Aven and I trailed Libbie to the back of the school, then hopped the fence and slipped into the suburbs. Once we'd crossed the street, Libbie began bombarding us with questions.

"How was the East Coast? Warm? I wanted to check the weather, but your mom didn't specify where you were going. Do you have pictures? Oh yeah, is your grandpa okay?"

I looked at her. "What do you mean?"

She frowned. "The East Coast? You were there for two months."

I shook my head, blood rushing through my ears. "No, I wasn't."

"Then why did your mom say you were?"

I fell silent, mouth going dry. Her words were barely audible, blocked by the thundering rhythm of my heart.

I watched Aven deflect her questions with some of their own. They sent an imploring glance my way.

I knew I should be answering Libbie's questions.

All I had to do was ask a simple question. Just a few words. Then I'd know if my sister was safe. But the sentence stuck to the sides of my throat like glue, even when I opened my mouth to get them out.

Libbie and Aven fell silent, the former sending an understanding look my way. She led us to a park where Aven and I took a seat on the swings. Libbie sat before us, picking at the woodchips warily.

"I get it if you don't want to talk to me," Libbie started. She adjusted her glasses. "But we need to go to the police. You've been gone for two months, Sander. We can go home first, get you guys some food and rest, and then head over to the station."

"We're not staying," Aven said, with a pointed look at me. "We have friends waiting for us."

It was difficult to swallow. Right. Friends. Was that even what they were?

She looked away. "What have you all been doing? If you weren't visiting your grandpa?"

"All?" I echoed.

She frowned. "Yeah, which gets me to my next question. If you're here, why isn't Sadira?"

The whole world went silent. All of my previous plans to stay in this world melted away.

I stared at Libbie, hardly able to perceive the words that fell from my mouth. "What did you say?"

"Sadira? She's not with you?"

I rose. Aven followed suit.

"We're going back to Primos," I growled in a raging voice that I didn't recognize. "Right now."

Libbie jumped to her feet. "Wait—"

I ignored her, my vision red with rage as I leaped into a run. Sneakers pounding against the concrete, I made my way toward the school.

Aven and Libbie were calling my name, but neither of them was even close to catching up with me.

Sadira was gone.

I was so, so angry. But I knew the fury I felt was, in fact, just a facade. A curtain to cover the fear that lurked behind. Anxious thoughts dashed through my mind. I didn't bother to get rid of them because they only made me move faster.

I leaped over a ditch and landed on a trail. The fence was just up ahead. I could see the walls of my school.

Then, a gunshot rang out. The ground beside my feet sprayed dirt.

I whirled around.

Aven had their gun raised. Libbie stood beside them with her hands over her ears and her mouth agape.

"You could've shot me!" I yelped.

They jogged up beside me. "I've practiced." They grabbed onto my shirt and held up their finger. "Don't go running off like that. The worst things happen when people let anger control them."

My blood chilled at the sorrow in their voice.

It was then Libbie came running up. "What. The. Hell." She gasped for breath. "Where did you get the gun?"

Aven waved their hand dismissively and began to reply, but a blaring alarm interrupted them.

"Students, give me your attention. We are now in emergency lockdown. Please follow all emergency procedures at this time."

I glared at Aven. "This is why you don't go shooting guns within thirty feet of a high school."

They glared right back at me. "We're going back. But you need to calm down first."

"I am calm," I lied.

Libbie cut in, "Can we please talk about why this person has a gun? And you just seem okay with it? They just tried to shoot you!"

"They didn't try to shoot me!" I shouted.

At the same time, Aven said, "I didn't try to shoot him!" They pinched the bridge of their nose. "I was trying to stop him."

"Yeah," I said, turning my attention back to them. Putting my hands on my hips, I asked, "And just why did you do that? You were trying to stop me from coming here not too long ago. Now you want me to stay."

"No. I—" They sighed. "You were mad, Sander. You *are* mad. I've seen people do stupid things when they're mad. And we don't even know who has Sadira. If we told Amias or Eden this without proof…"

"Then we'll get proof," I snapped and faced Libbie. "When did Sadira disappear? Give me the details."

"About a week after you vanished." She rubbed her forehead worriedly. "Your mom said you had gone to help your grandpa, who was recovering from a sudden injury. She and Sadira left together."

It was like a building had fallen on top of me. Mama wasn't here either. Libbie's information flew in one ear and out the other, but I trusted Aven was paying attention.

When she finished, I cleared my throat and shook myself out. "We're going back. Right now."

"I'm coming with you," she said defiantly.

Aven and I shook our heads in unison.

"No way. It's too dangerous."

Her gaze narrowed. "That means Sadira is in danger. She's my best friend."

Aven rolled their eyes. "We're going. If you try to come with us, I'll shoot you in the foot."

Libbie growled and crossed her arms. However, she stayed where she was as we leaped over the fence and hurried inside the school, desperate to beat the oncoming sirens.

It took us a while to get into the building, which we managed to do by breaking a window. By the time we entered the empty hallways, the cops had already made it inside.

Police officers on our heels, I slammed through the doors to the bathroom and climbed up onto the counter with Aven close behind me. Just as I was about to crawl through the Mirror, the doors burst open again.

"Freeze," the cop in the front of the group demanded, gun poised at our heads. "Don't move. You've got yourself cornered."

"Man," Aven chuckled. "Do you really think I'm that stupid?"

The cop's jaw twitched.

"Stop!" cried a voice from outside. The cops whirled as Libbie shoved her way through the crowd of people in blue. "Please, they're not—"

She fell silent as Aven chuckled and shoved me through the

Mirror.

I went tumbling through the silvery liquid, then rolled off the counter in Aven's bathroom and landed on the hard tile. I groaned as Aven crawled through, a crazy grin on their face.

"That was amazing!" they exclaimed and hopped down.

I stumbled to my feet, glancing back at the Mirror. A hand was poking through; a cop on the other side was testing the portal. As any sane person would do.

"Watch out, buddy," Aven brushed their hand against the cop's, and the hand yanked back. Then, Aven wiped away one of the symbols.

"What would've happened if he hadn't moved his hand?" I questioned.

"It would've been chopped off," they said. "We should get cleaned up."

My gut flipped.

Thirty minutes later, I sat on the edge of Aven's bed while they got ready in the bathroom.

The silence was deafening. My hair damp from the shower I'd just taken, I flopped onto the white duvet.

Sadira and Mama were gone. The latter had lied to Libbie. I scoffed. We hadn't ever met our grandparents. On either side of the family. Mama had rarely mentioned her parents, and I had often wondered if they were dead.

I'd gone back home to have questions answered, and once again, I was only left with more worries and fears swimming laps in my mind.

Aven exited their bathroom and leaned against the doorframe, drying their hair with a towel. "Somebody's having a crisis."

I wasn't in the mood to say anything.

They threw the towel at my face. "You went from raging to depressed so quickly."

When it was clear I wasn't going to answer, they sighed and sat down next to me. "Libbie's information doesn't tell us much. But your mom would have a reason for lying. A good one."

I swallowed. What if she knew where I had gone? What if… No. I didn't want to think about that. Instead, I blinked back tears and said, "What do we do now?"

"We're going to find them."

I gaped at them. "We? Why? My family isn't your problem."

They shrugged. "You're my friend. Your problems are my problems."

My throat closed up.

Then, Aven smiled sadly and looked away. "You have a chance at… fixing your family. I wasn't able to do that with mine. I don't want you to feel what I did."

I opened my mouth. To say what? I'm sorry? There wasn't anything I could say to comfort them.

I didn't need to say anything, however, because they shook themself off and rose, plastering a grin on their face as they pulled me up from the bed. "And no need to worry. They're only lost. And lucky for us, our friends are the best damn hunters in the multiverse."

"Huh?"

"Amias and Renna. They were literally *made* to do this kind of stuff. They'll find Sadira in no time."

"No need," said a voice from the doorway.

Aven and I whirled to greet Eden, who noiselessly closed the door and then made her way over to us.

A glance at her expression told me exactly what she was going to say. But still, the words shocked me when she spoke.

"I am already aware of Sadira's whereabouts. The Major is holding her captive."

CHAPTER TWENTY-SEVEN

Captive. The Major. The Rising.

The rage I'd felt earlier began to bubble up like lava rising up before an explosion.

I clenched my fists.

"How do you know?" Aven asked, much calmer than I felt. They squeezed my arm in what I guessed was supposed to be a comforting gesture. However, the physical contact sent a new wave of anxiety through my body.

I stepped out of their grip, crossing my arms as I watched Eden quickly scan the room. Deeming it safe, she leaned against the wall and tucked her hair behind her pointed ear.

"After the events of the party, the Major informed Amias and me of your sister's captivity in an effort to threaten us. He said if we betrayed him in any sort of way, he would kill her on the spot."

I gaped. "And it worked? Amias listened?" They hadn't told me. The feeling of betrayal stabbed my insides.

She inclined her head in acknowledgment, a movement that made the strand of hair she'd just tucked away fall in front of her face again. "Of course he did. You are a dear friend of ours."

I frowned.

"You hesitate to take that information as gospel," she noted. "Why?"

"I didn't think Amias cared for me that much," I grumbled.

Beside me, Aven chuckled.

Eden ignored them. "Amias is a short-tempered man and often puts on a mask of stone to keep his enemies from seeing his weaknesses. But even someone as skilled as him has a hard time determining who his enemies are. So, I assure you, Sander, losing Amias's trust does not mean you have lost his heart."

That hadn't occurred to me. I knew Amias was an untrusting person. But…

Eden continued, "That being said, I have reason to believe he has his own incentive for remaining in Primos. One he has declined to share with us."

I took a seat, eyes trained on the ground. This was almost too much to handle. Everything with Amias and Sadira. Libbie. Mama.

The world around me blurred.

What was even happening? None of this made sense to me. I was a human playing a game of gods. I was nothing compared to these people. Insignificant. A burden, if anything. And now, Aven was planning to fight with me to get my sister back.

Was I really worth their friendship?

A soft hand met my cheek. "Sander. Look at me." Eden smiled softly. "It will be okay. We are going to rescue your sister."

I was surprised when a tear rolled down my face. It didn't stop there. More followed, and soon, I was sobbing in Eden's arms as she pulled me into a hug.

For the rest of the day, we acted as if nothing had changed. It was the most difficult thing I had ever experienced. The urge to scream and rage and tear through the Rising boiled beneath my skin. So, I spent the majority of the day in my room, brainstorming with Aven and Eden. When I asked why we couldn't just tell the others about Sadira now, Aven explained that we had to come up with a plan. Or something like that. I think they just didn't want me raging through the city as we broke her out.

When we were summoned to dinner with Nevena and the

Major, it was all I could do to keep from stabbing them with my salad fork.

Sensing my discomfort, Eden suggested I take a walk. The Major, having overheard, asked me if I would take some of his dogs out with me.

There were three of them, a golden retriever named Sunny, a black lab named Oreo, and a border collie named Teddy.

Renna, who had opted to come with me after hearing the word dogs, carried Sunny and Oreo's leashes, humming quietly to herself. Her long brown hair waved in the breeze, falling back to her shoulders every time the wind stopped.

"Do you like dogs, Sander?" she asked. Her shoelace was untied. It slapped against the sidewalk as we headed toward the woods. She didn't seem to notice. Or care.

"I do."

She smiled. "Amias and I had a dog, you know."

I looked down at her in surprise, desperate to fall into an emotion that wasn't anger. "When did you have time to take care of a dog? Weren't you in prison your whole life?"

"We escaped when we were younger. We stayed at an old shed in the woods. On our third night there, a dog wandered up to the campfire. Amias wanted to have it for dinner, but I stopped him."

"He what? He wanted to eat a dog?"

"We didn't have much food. And we were really hungry," she explained. "We named the dog Bentley. He was brown. Like chocolate."

"What happened to Bentley?" I asked, though curiosity had left a while ago.

"The SSD found us a day later. Bentley attacked them, and they shot him," she said the words almost cheerily like she wasn't telling me how her only pet had died. "Sometimes I wonder if Amias is like Bentley."

I raised an eyebrow.

She noticed it. "He's always worrying about protecting the people he loves. He doesn't even think about the danger in front of him before attacking."

She was right, I realized. All those times Amias had run into danger, he'd been protecting his friends. "Why? Why does he not care about the danger?"

"Would you?" she replied. "If it was your sister or Amias who were in trouble, would you hesitate to save them?"

I hesitated before shaking my head.

She continued, "I think it's because of his sister. The reason he's so protective. It was his fault she died, you know?"

"I—I didn't know," my eyebrows knit together. "Wait—what? What happened to his sister?"

She glanced at me, icy blue eyes scanning my face. She was silent for long enough that I began to wonder if maybe she hadn't heard my question. But eventually, she said, "I think that's for him to tell you."

I frowned and stared at the ground. "Did you and Amias talk to each other after that argument you had?"

"Oh, yes," she nodded. "We talked yesterday."

"So, you forgave each other."

She tilted her head back and laughed. "Amias doesn't forgive, Sander. He forgets."

I was about to ask her what that meant, but she handed me Oreo and Sunny's leashes before racing across the street and into a sweets shop. I threw up my hands in exasperation and leaned back against the nearest building. A few moments later, Renna emerged from the shop, two caramel apples in her hands. She approached and held one out to me.

"I'm good," I declined. "Do you even have money?"

She shook her head and took Sunny's leash. The dog sniffed a lamppost. We walked in silence for a few minutes longer until we exited the city and took a dirt path through the forest. At Renna's word, we took the dogs off their leashes and let them run around us happily.

"They're not going to leave," she assured when I nervously watched Teddy trot away. "I've got treats."

"Are we even allowed to be in the forest?" I looked back toward the city. My view of the buildings was nearly overtaken by trees.

"No one's stopped me before," she replied. "I've been meaning to ask you for a while, actually, but what exactly happened to you during your time alone at the SSD?"

A chill swept over me, and my heart dropped into my stomach.

Renna peered up at me, curiosity alight on her features. "Ah, so she handed you off to Mr. Coldwell."

My throat went dry.

"No surprise there," she continued. "You are an interesting one. Mr. Coldwell wouldn't stop going on about you back when you were in Blackford. He was begging The Director to let him look at you."

"Why?" I croaked out.

She tilted her head, choosing her words carefully. "Your father had a unique mind. Mr. Coldwell wanted to see if those genes had been passed on to you."

I fell silent. Had Warren really done something to me? I'd figured they hadn't finished whatever it was they'd been doing. But maybe… maybe Renna was on to something. I'd never been a normal person, that was for sure. Perhaps Warren had messed up my brain even more than it already was.

It wasn't a comforting thought, and it stuck with me the rest of the day.

CHAPTER TWENTY-EIGHT

The next morning, we met in Eden's room to tell Ivy and Renna about Sadira. Neither of them was as shocked as I thought they'd be. In fact, they just nodded their heads as if it made sense. The ignorance I'd been accustomed to now seemed more and more like a way for them to look down on me.

After a quick discussion about what we should do, it was decided that we should tell Amias about our plan, too. If he had his own reasons to stay, then we would wait until he finished what he needed to do. But we needed to be transparent with each other. No secrets. That was the general consensus.

When it came time to choose who would be the one to find Amias and bring him back to Eden's room, everyone automatically elected me to do the honors. Fed up with everything, I only grumbled a few curses at them before starting my search.

However, I spent over half an hour wandering the building and still couldn't find him. Granted, I hadn't really looked that hard. I didn't want to talk to him.

I turned into an empty hallway on one of the bottom levels of the building.

With or without Amias's help, I was going to break Sadira out. I'd need the other's help, but I had no doubt Aven, Ivy, and Eden would be happy to join me. Renna, on the other hand, I wasn't so sure.

If I was going to break my twin out of prison, I needed to know where she was. And there were only two people I knew of who would know that information. The Major, whom I wasn't going to ask, and Nevena. I debated about it for a long time, half of me telling myself not to talk to her, that she'd alert the Major and we'd all get thrown in prison, but the other half was saying that it was a good idea and Sadira was worth the risks.

I sighed.

I turned to make my way back upstairs but stopped when I spotted something peeking out from under a cracked door. The tip of a finger lay on the tile, the rest of the hand disappearing into the darkness of the closet. Breakfast rising to my throat, I forced a step toward the appendage and pulled open the door.

Limbs tumbled out. Two men I recognized had been shoved carelessly into the closet. I'd seen them the other day, guarding Amias.

They weren't dead. I could see their chests moving.

But if they were here, where was Amias?

The light came before the noise. Lights flashed through the hallway, followed closely by deafening alarms. Screams echoed from the staircase as a crowd rushed past the end of the hallway. Gunshots rang out.

I raced forward, heart pounding, and shouted at the people fleeing. "What's going on?"

No one answered me. A couple glanced at me, sending terrified looks before getting shoved forward.

Someone grabbed my wrist. I spun and met Nevena's panicked gaze with panic of my own.

"What's happening?" I tried to sound demanding, but the crack in my voice didn't help.

"The cell towers," she replied, pulling me further into the hallway. "The ones circling the city. One of them got blown up."

"What? By who?"

"I don't know. But they were the only thing keeping the SSD from finding us."

Nevena gripped my wrist harder and started dragging me down

the stairs.

Someone called my name, and I turned but was swept up in the mob. Nevena's hand slipped from my arm, and she was lost, too.

More gunshots echoed. A woman beside me fell to the ground. A shocking thought ripped through me. If I just stopped, maybe a bullet would rip through my flesh and I'd bleed out. I thought about it as I ran, warm blood leaking through my shirt, a bullet through my heart, falling to the ground with a smile on my face. But then I thought about Sadira, bent over my corpse, shoulders shaking as tears fell from her eyes.

Sadira.

I wheeled around and began shoving back up the stairs. I made it to the nearest landing, but someone grabbed my shirt and yanked me back.

"Where the hell are you going?" Nevena snapped, dark eyes ablaze with fury.

A sudden rage took over my body. I pushed her back onto the landing and took cover behind a bench. "Where is my sister?" I snarled.

I didn't know if the confusion that crossed her face was real. "What?"

An inhuman growl rippled from behind me. "Where is Sadira?" Amias said as he crouched down beside me. My heart jumped, whether with fear or excitement, I couldn't tell.

"I don't know who that is," Nevena replied and began tugging at my wrist. "We need to get out of here before we die."

Amias lunged forward and snatched her by the neck, his movements powered by pure hatred. I followed as he pulled Nevena, gasping and clawing at the hand on her skin, into the nearest room. The gunshots and screams became muffled as the door swung closed.

"You know what we're talking about." Amias threw her onto the glass desk in the center of the office. It came down with a crash.

I took a step forward, then stopped myself. A sick part of me wanted to see what Amias would do next.

Nevena climbed to her feet in the middle of the mess, brushing pieces of glass from her bleeding palms. She coughed and rubbed her neck, not seeming to notice she left behind a red smear. "What is wrong with you? I don't know a Sadira. I didn't even know Sander had a sister."

"You're lying," Amias said and advanced on her.

Nevena straightened. "I know your weaknesses, Blood Bringer. I wouldn't try anything you'd regret."

His blow was so fast I didn't even see it. It was only when she lifted her head to reveal her crooked, bleeding nose that I knew he'd punched her. She hissed, bringing her hand up to her face. Then, she moved. Again, faster than I could process.

Suddenly, Amias was stumbling backward, having taken a blow to his stomach. Nevena didn't waste any time before launching into a roundhouse, but he blocked the kick and sent his own at her knee. The crack of the collision was echoed by her cry. Amias was on her again, knocking her to the floor and pinning her to the ground.

"I thought you were supposed to be good," he chuckled. "Being the Major's Shadow and all."

She spat at him. "I don't know anything."

He smiled thinly and reached for the stapler that had fallen off the desk when it crashed. "Sander, turn around and plug your ears."

I obeyed hesitantly.

Barely five minutes later, Amias opened the door to the office, dragging Nevena by the collar of her shirt. The muzzle of her own gun was pressed against the back of her head.

The screams had stopped. Dead bodies littered the ground. There wasn't a single soul in sight. But despite that, Amias swiveled his head from side to side. Couldn't be too careful.

I wasn't sure what had happened in the room, but Nevena seemed compliant.

"Which way?" he growled.

"Left," she mumbled. "There's an elevator at the end of the hall."

He peered down the hall, and I copied him. There was nothing but a near-empty bookshelf.

"There's nothing there," I noted.

"It's a secret elevator," she snapped and turned to me. "There's a reason Sadira wasn't in the regular prison."

Amias began walking, a muscle twitching in his jaw.

"You did check the prison, did you not?"

He said nothing, so I did the same.

She chuckled. "I thought you were supposed to be good," she mocked. "Being one of the Blood Bringers and all."

"Shut up," he snapped.

She didn't shut up, despite the fact that he had a gun on her. Instead, she turned to me as we walked. "How does it feel? To be friends with such a monster?"

I pulled my gaze away. "Amias isn't a monster."

Out of the corner of my eye, I saw him lift his head.

She laughed weakly.

"Keep your mouth shut," Amias snapped.

I dragged my eyes to his face. His jaw was tense; he was probably clenching his teeth. Looking at him now, I didn't see a monster. I remembered the way he looked as Kayson had crumpled to the ground. The heart in his hands. I hadn't seen a monster then either; I'd just seen Amias. But maybe I'd gotten used to the look of monsters, having seen one in the mirror my whole life.

At Nevena's instructions, Amias pulled at a blue book on the shelf. After a clunk, the bookcase creaked open. Amias pulled it open all the way to reveal the inside of an elevator. He shoved Nevena in first, then deemed it safe for us to walk through.

When the doors slid closed and machines began to whir, the small room was suddenly overtaken by an uncomfortable silence.

Amias still had the gun pressed against Nevena's head, but I could see his mind was somewhere else. Nevena had a slight smile on her bruised and bloodied face. I looked back at the gun. My heart began to speed up.

Nevena was smart. She was the Major's Shadow. Something about her and Ivy told me their parents would have taught them to withstand a lot more than what Amias had done. Which meant—

I opened my mouth to warn Amias, but the elevator stopped, and the doors opened. It was too late. Something whizzed through the air. Amias looked down as a dart pierced his neck. He began to pull it out but was bombarded with a dozen more. He glanced at me, and then his beautiful blue eyes fluttered closed. He crumpled.

Nevena's smile grew wider despite her ruined face. She grinned at me. "It's a shame, Sander. I really like you."

"You—" I started, but then something pricked my neck. I reached to pull it out but wasn't fast enough. My eyes rolled into the back of my head, and I dropped into unconsciousness.

CHAPTER TWENTY-NINE

"This is him?"

A man to the right of me nodded. He was a short man, the hairline on his round head receding. A screen rested in his hands. I couldn't see the text; he had angled it away from me purposely. I didn't mind.

I bent down in front of the young man before me, sprawled on the tiled floor as if he'd been thrown there carelessly.

He was about seventeen, with dark curly hair and sharp cheekbones. Stunning might be a word one would use to describe him. But I could only think about the soul that lurked beneath and how truly hideous it was. Even in his sleep, he looked worried, his eyebrows furrowed slightly. Black crescents rested against his golden-bronze cheeks, and I knew if they moved, if he opened his eyes, I'd see bottle green staring back at me. I knew because they were my eyes. Everything about him was mine. He didn't deserve to look like me.

I reached out to brush a curl from his eyes.

"Don't—" the short man started.

But I didn't listen. My fingers brushed against his skin. A spark of electricity shot up my finger, and I was blown backward. My head collided with the wall, and everything went dark.

When I came to, I was still in the room, except I was lying on the floor in place of the dark-haired boy. The short man was gone.

Instead, it was Nevena in the room with me. She sat on a metal chair in front of a window. Behind the window, a couple dozen more cells stretched down a dark cement hallway.

I rose from my position on the floor slowly, trying to clear my head.

"Morning, sunshine." Nevena smiled.

"Where's Amias?" I growled and hauled myself onto the cot behind me.

"Where's Amias?" she mocked, her smile turning downward. "It's always about him, isn't it?"

"I thought we were friends."

Her scowl deepened. "Well, boohoo. I'm sorry your feelings were hurt, princess. Welcome to the real world."

"You can't keep me in here," I said. "Amias won't fight for you if you do." Even as the words came out of my mouth, I didn't fully believe them.

But she grinned. "Not if he thinks you're with him."

I forced myself not to show my confusion. "What are you talking about?"

She stood. "I told him I knew his weaknesses. He shouldn't have messed with me. Or the Major. I knew hanging Sadira's life over his head wasn't going to work. We should've taken a bigger step."

"And what is that?"

The corner of her mouth curved, and she pressed her hand to a touchpad on the wall that I hadn't noticed before. Something hissed, and then a piece of the window swung open, just big enough for her to walk through.

"Aren't you going to share with the class?" I shouted after her as she stepped through.

She winked.

I burst from my spot and raced after her, but the door closed before I could reach her. I slammed my fists against the glass.

"Tell me where he is!" I screamed. "Tell me where he is!"

But she didn't answer. Why would she?

I cursed at her as she stalked down the hallway, slowly disappearing into the darkness.

"Tell me where he is!"

My head throbbed as I paced the length of the room. Pain lanced through the top of my spine, growing worse with each step. I didn't care. It couldn't be anything more than an annoyance.

My mind raced despite the grogginess that still hugged my limbs. Nevena was wrong. Amias didn't have any weaknesses. He was literally a superhuman. He'd said so himself. He'd been shot in the gut and healed within two weeks; he could survive whatever Nevena was going to do to him.

Ivy was right not to have trusted her. But she knew not to, based on experience.

I tried to peer down the hallway, hoping to catch a glimpse of dark hair or hear Aven's joyful laugh or, hell, even Renna's odd words. But mostly, to see tattooed arms and sapphire eyes.

I placed my hand on the touchpad multiple times, but nothing happened. Of course, I hadn't expected it to, but the hope was always there. I did it again, but it was ineffective. A red light beeped back at me. I growled at it.

I couldn't get out of this damn cell. The walls were made of pure cement and the glass was unbreakable. I knew because I'd thrown everything I had at it, including the cot. But it hadn't even left a scratch.

If Amias was here, he could use his super strength to shatter the glass. Ivy would find a way to hack the touchpad. They'd all know what to do. Yet, I didn't. I was a useless sack of nothing. Worthless. Why they'd saved me all those times, I didn't know. If I were them, I wouldn't have saved myself.

I placed my forehead against the glass.

"Let me go, you sick bastards!" The new voice came from down the hallway. It was a voice I recognized. Libbie Bates blew a strand of shoulder-length brown hair off her glasses and yanked against the guards holding her hostage.

"Libbie?" I asked.

Her head swiveled toward me. Her hazel eyes widened. "Sander? What the hell?"

A tidal wave of guilt slammed into me as the Rising guards shoved her into the cell across the hall. I'd been so worried about Sadira that I hadn't even given her a second thought after escaping through the Mirror.

"What are you doing here?" She flipped off the guards as they walked away.

"I—what are *you* doing here?"

"I don't even know. Not even ten minutes after you guys left, a bunch of people came and grabbed me. Everything after that is blurry, but I remember a forest. I think. Maybe it was a dream." I saw her hand go to the back of her head, then drop. "Is Sadira okay? Have you found her?"

I swallowed back the fear I'd been shoving down. "I don't know. Aven and I—we got close. We were gonna break her out, but—"

"Oh god," she pulled off her glasses and rubbed her eyes. "Oh god, oh god. Are these the people who have Sadira? Is she locked up, too? Where?"

"I don't know where she is," I admitted. "But my friends are probably looking for her. And me." At least, I hoped they were.

Libbie raised an eyebrow. "These friends—are they reliable?"

"What? Of course, they are. Why would you say that?"

"I don't know!" She threw her hands up. "It seems like you've been hanging out with some sketchy people, Sander. We're in a goddamn prison! Forgive me if I'm a little skeptical."

"They've saved my life more than once," I insisted. "Believe it or not, they're really nice murderers."

"*Murderers?*"

I bit my lip. "Umm, to be fair, they only murder bad people. I think."

She pinched the bridge of her nose and closed her eyes. "You're going to explain everything to me. Now."

I obliged.

When I finished, my words were met with silence. For a long time, I wasn't sure if Libbie had even heard anything I'd said. She sat cross-legged on her cot and stared at her hands with a vacant expression. But then she took in a slow breath, held it for a second, then let it out.

"So, this Ivy—" She turned to me. "Is she single?"

I groaned. "Seriously, Libbie? Everything I just said, and that's the first question you come up with?"

"Oh, don't get me wrong, I have a couple dozen other questions, but I don't think you're going to want to answer them."

I winced. After seeing her expressions when I'd told her about our escape from Blackford, I'd opted to leave out what happened with Leland and at the party.

She must've noticed because she unfolded herself from the cot and approached the glass. "Sander—"

I turned and made for my cot. "I'm going to sleep."

I didn't listen for an answer.

I wasn't sure if I actually managed to fall asleep, but I was jolted from whatever quiet I'd found when the sound of a slamming door echoed down the hallway. I rolled over in time to see Nevena appear in front of my cell, carrying two trays.

"The Big Bad Wolf has been sedated," she reported and slid my meager meal of mashed potatoes and bread through a slit in the glass.

"What did you do to him?"

"I didn't do anything." She smiled and handed Libbie her food. "It was all you."

"What the hell does that mean?"

"Why would I tell you? It's more fun when I leave you guessing."

"So, what?" I snapped. "You just came here to taunt me?"

She nodded. "And partly to thank you. Your assistance has been greatly appreciated." Then, she winked and left.

Rage heated my neck as I watched her leave. What was the reason for her visit? To make me even more angry? Because if it was, it had worked.

I slumped against the wall and ran my hands over my face. If there was anything I'd gathered from that conversation, it was that Amias had been taken care of, in one way or another. Whatever that meant. Worry knotted in my chest, and I began to find it hard to breathe.

"Sander…" Libbie began from her cell.

If she finished the sentence, I didn't hear it because my mind had gone fuzzy. I turned to her and squinted when the edges of my vision began to go dark.

"Libbie." Her name was hard to pronounce. I reached up to touch my face, my mouth, to make sure it was still there because everything had gone numb. I blinked, then promptly fainted.

***

Amias was bleeding. Blue blood trickled down the side of his head and over the muzzle on his mouth. His eyes were open, panicked. When he saw me, he lunged forward, pulling at the chains that draped his body, and he screamed my name through the muzzle.

"Amias!" I raced forward and began tugging at the chains. When they didn't budge, I turned to the Major and gave him my best pleading expression.

The Major smiled and handed me the key.

I undid Amias's muzzle first. It fell to the ground with a clatter.

"I'm going to kill you!" were the first words out of his mouth. For a brief moment, I panicked, thinking he'd caught me already. But he was looking at the Major. "I'm going to pin your eyes open and make you watch as I gut everyone you've ever loved!"

The Major raised an eyebrow at me.

"Amias, it's okay," I assured.

He turned to me. "What?"

"He's not the bad guy. Nevena kidnapped Sadira without him knowing."

His enraged expression fell.

I continued, "She thought she could use my sister as a bargaining chip if anything went down. After what happened at the party…"

"But the Major was there," Amias cut in. "He was there when Nevena told Eden and me they had Sadira."

I shook my head. "He thought she was lying. And she was, at first, but then she went and got Sadira afterward. I just saw her, Amias; she's okay."

He eyed the Major warily. I could see the doubt in his expression.

"Trust me," I said and offered a small smile.

His face softened, and he nodded.

Amias didn't see my triumphant grin as I leaned in to unlock the rest of his binds.

CHAPTER THIRTY

I woke drenched in a cold sweat. It clung to my skin like cobwebs as I forced myself to sit up, my head still throbbing. I rubbed my temples, trying to make sense of the unbelievably vivid dream. Except, it didn't feel like a dream; it felt like a memory.

But I was sure I'd never seen Amias like that. The panic in his eyes as I walked into the room, the blood on his face, I would've remembered that. There was no way I would have forgotten it.

Nevena's words flashed through my mind. *It was all you.*

Is this what she meant? Were they planting some weird memories in my brain? Was it a torture method I had yet to discover? Were they trying to get me to switch sides?

Panic flared. I'd spent days in Primos. They could've messed with my brain without me knowing any time they wanted. Maybe they'd snuck me some sleeping pills in my food and knocked me out while they went into my head. Maybe they'd done the same with the others. Was that why they hadn't gotten me yet?

My eyes went to the cell across from mine. Had they done the same with Libbie? Was she planted here to trick me, too?

You're going crazy.

The thought was loud enough that, for a moment, I thought someone was whispering in my ear. I laid back down and faced the back wall, letting my mind wander.

As it always did when I fell into my thoughts, time seemed to have no meaning. So, I wasn't sure how long had passed before I heard something beep and the door to my cell swung open. A set of guards came in and began pulling me toward the door.

I didn't try to fight. They were taking me outside either way. They dragged me out of the cell, doing the same to Libbie. She glanced at me in worry, and I tried to give her a reassuring smile. I had a feeling it didn't look even close to how I wanted it to.

"Where are we going?" I asked.

"The Shadow needs you moved," said one of the guards holding me.

I didn't ask any more questions, not that I could've anyway, because I heard the familiar sound of a blade cutting flesh, and the guard fell to the ground. The second guard holding me went for his gun and, in doing so, loosened his grip on me.

All the training Ivy, Amias, and Nevena had pounded into my brain came rushing back. I ducked under the guard's arm, twisting it in the process, and landed a blow to the back of his knee. He cried out and fell to his knees. I made for his gun but stopped when another blade landed in his throat. He choked, dropped his gun, and then promptly fell forward.

I snatched up the gun and hesitated only for a brief moment before putting a bullet in the last guard holding Libbie.

She looked at me in shock, blood on her glasses.

I turned toward the direction the blades had come from. A figure emerged from the shadows. The familiarity of her jaunty, confident walk was enough to bring the breath back to my lungs. I knew Libbie recognized her, too, given the way her eyes widened.

Sadira smiled as she pulled off her hood, dark curls pouring over her shoulders.

Libbie let out an excited squeal and ran forward into her best friend's arms. "You're alive!"

Sadira laughed, a rich, beautiful sound. I brought a hand to my mouth, vision blurring.

"Sadira?" I asked, voice cracking.

She turned to me, a smile filling her beautiful face. She approached me. The familiar smell of wood and lavender fell over my senses.

I couldn't keep the rest of the tears back. I collapsed into her arms, shoulders shaking as I sobbed. She hugged me tightly. Her embrace felt like happiness, and a wave of homesickness slammed into me like a boulder. My legs wobbled.

"What—" I swallowed and pulled back. Tears filled Sadira's eyes. "I thought the Rising had you."

"I don't know what that is." She sniffed and rubbed her nose on her black sweater. She was wearing a backpack, I finally noticed. Where had she gotten a backpack? Hadn't she been a prisoner? "I'll tell you everything later. We need to move."

I nodded and wiped my eyes, then began following Libbie and Sadira down the hallway. They talked quietly to one another as we went, and I tried to listen, but I had trouble focusing. My mind was still stuck on the fact that it was Sadira who was walking in front of me. Sadira. My sister. Was here. And had killed three men. A pang of guilt stabbed my gut.

Was it my fault she'd become a killer? Or had she learned to throw knives like that in order to defend herself? Did she feel guilty about taking the men's lives?

It didn't seem like it. She grinned happily as she talked to Libbie. But who wouldn't be happy to see their best friend again after so long?

When we reached the end of the hallway, Sadira pushed open a thick metal door. I held up the gun I'd stolen from the guard. As I suspected, we came face to face with a small group of Rising soldiers. I fired. Once, twice. Three guards dropped. I looked at Sadira, whose hand was still outstretched. She winked and hurled another knife so fast I couldn't even see where she'd gotten it from.

I fired again, then shoved Libbie behind the door as opposing gunshots sounded through the hallway. But when Sadira peeked around the doorframe, another knife flying from her hand, the gunshots stopped. She waved for us to follow.

We ascended a cement staircase and emerged into a garage I'd never seen before. It was relatively empty, save for a few army rovers and the bikes we'd ridden on when we'd first arrived in Primos.

It was deadly silent, so the echo of our footsteps stuck out like a broken limb.

"Where are we?" I tried to whisper, but my voice carried throughout the room. I winced.

"I don't really know," Sadira said. "After the attack back at the city, I saw you being loaded into a truck and followed you here. We're in the middle of a forest, about four hundred miles away from a big city I've never seen before."

She was right about being in a forest. We exited the garage and entered a small clearing. The cloudy sky loomed above us, dark and thick with the warning of heavy showers. In the distance, I could hear the faint jumble of voices and began to stride toward it.

Sadira stopped me. "I just broke you out of prison. I think going toward your captors is a stupid idea."

"But my friends—" She tugged me into the safety of the trees before I could finish.

"Listen, Sander." She looked over my shoulder toward the voices. "If your friends are here, then they're either on the bad guy's side or prisoners themselves."

"Or maybe they think I died in the attack on Primos," I argued. "I don't really care. I need to make sure he—they are okay."

Her eyes narrowed. "No. I can't—"

"Sander?"

My head shot up. Ivy emerged from the bushes, carrying a stack of wood in her arms. She tried to brush a strand of hair from her eyes.

"What are you doing here? I thought you were supposed to be helping Amias set up the tents."

"What—" I stuttered. "Wait, Amias is all right? He's here?"

She tilted her head. "Of course, he's all right. You just saw him."

I opened my mouth to speak but was interrupted by another voice calling out Ivy's name, this time from behind me. I spun around just in time to see myself walk out of the trees.

The world was knocked from underneath my feet.

Suddenly, the weird dreams made sense. They'd felt like memories because they were. Just not mine. Not really. They were my Reflection's memories.

My body froze in place. I felt my blood go cold as my Reflection approached us, a slight frown on my, no, *his* face. As he came closer, it grew deeper. I saw genuine confusion flash through his eyes.

"What—who—" he stuttered, slowing to a stop. It was chilling, seeing such a perfect imitation of me.

I was at a loss for words, and it seemed the others were, too.

"Ivy," he said slowly. "Who is this?"

We all turned to her. "Umm," she stammered. "I thought he was you."

Suddenly, I could move again. "What? Ivy, it is me!"

"Don't listen to him!" my Reflection exclaimed.

"Shut up!" I snapped at him, rage rising. "We both know you and Nevena locked me in that prison!" I pointed. "This is what Nevena meant by 'It was all me.'"

"I have no idea what you're talking about," he growled. Again, his voice sent a shiver down my spine. "I've been with my *friends* this entire time. You don't get to come into my life and mess it up."

I turned to Ivy, enraged, "Seriously? You believe this pile of shit?"

She shrugged, her eyes wide. "He's literally you."

"He is not me!" I exclaimed and tapped his chest. "He is the opposite of me. I'm your real friend. I was the one who broke out of Blackford with you! I—"

"Sadira," I heard Libbie say slowly. "Sadira, I think someone's coming."

My sister responded, but I didn't hear it because my Reflection was speaking.

"He's lying! Ask me a question. I can answer it correctly."

Ivy took a step back and set the wood down. "Maybe we should talk to Amias. I feel like he'd be able to tell you two apart."

My Reflection lifted his chin. "All right, fine."

But movement in the forest behind him caught my eye. About a dozen Rising guards emerged, and when they saw us, they pointed and shouted.

Sadira didn't waste any time before snatching my wrist and dragging me behind her with Libbie close behind as we ran into the forest. We scrambled through bushes and over fallen trees and half-swam, half-ran through a murky river. None of the surroundings were familiar.

My breath came in short huffs, the air flying in and out of my burning lungs. At one point, I had been the best runner in the family, but now, Sadira pulled ahead of me easily, even slowing down every now and then to make sure we didn't fall behind. Libbie, however, was not a wonderful runner.

She stumbled multiple times. Her big black boots were not helping her case. She panted heavily, constantly brushing hair off of her glasses, which were now spotted with water from wading through the river.

"Up here," Sadira said, stopping and pointing up a looming pine tree.

I helped Libbie up first, blinking violently as she kicked dirt in my eyes, and then clambered up after her.

Shouts sounded from behind us. My heart raced.

We climbed to the top, maybe fifty feet in the air or so. I grabbed hold of the trunk and helped Sadira through a gap in the branches.

The voices had become more distinct. It sounded as if there was a group right below us.

No one dared to breathe.

"They went this way," someone said.

"I'm going to kill them," growled a voice I recognized. Amias.

How had he gotten here so fast?

"You always say that," replied Aven. "But this time, I give you permission. That jerk doesn't get to get away. He tried to replace our Sander."

"He *tried*." It was Eden. My heart sank. If she wasn't having doubts, then I really was screwed. I wasn't getting my friends back. Not unless I could prove that I really was me. "Thank the gods he did not have a very good plan."

"There's another thing you and your Reflection have in common, Sander," laughed Renna. "You're pretty dumb."

I gritted my teeth.

"Thanks," grumbled my Reflection. Another perfect imitation of me.

Their voices faded as they walked away. Through the branches, I could see my Reflection dressed in a dark green shirt and jeans. He walked closely to Amias, so close their arms brushed. Something tightened in my chest.

Two hours later, the storm clouds finally broke. Rain drenched my clothes as I made my way back down the tree, soaking through the cotton and onto my skin. My hair clung to my head like a saggy, wet mop. The ground squished beneath my feet when I jumped the last few feet off the tree.

I barely got a chance to catch my breath, however, because Sadira demanded that I start explaining everything.

I obeyed, for my sister was not to be ignored.

I talked low as we made our way through the forest and away from the Rising camp. I started with waking up in Blackford and meeting Amias and the others. I left out a few parts. I left out everything Warren had done to me in the tiled room with the metal chair. I left out my conversation with Renna a few days ago. I left out everything that was going on between Amias and me.

Both Libbie and Sadira were silent as I explained. Libbie had heard it all before, but I felt more comfortable with Sadira, so I went more in-depth.

I lied about why I'd been attacked at the party. I couldn't bear to see the looks on their faces when they found out what I'd done.

When I finished, they were quiet for a while. Just as Libbie had been.

"So, you're not sure if Mama's all right?" Sadira asked, her voice wavering.

I shook my head. "I'm sorry."

"I'm sure she's okay," Libbie cut in half-heartedly.

I changed the subject. "What happened to you?" I looked at Sadira. "Where did you learn to throw knives like that?" *Where did you learn to kill men like that?* was what I really meant to say.

Her expression tightened. "The men in blue and gray uniforms—the SSD—took me when I was sleeping. I don't remember much, but I remember waking up in a baseball field—like an overgrown one. There were blackberry bushes everywhere. The men were talking with a woman."

I tilted my head. "Blonde hair? Tall? Walks like she rules everything?"

Sadira nodded. "Exactly. Anyway, I didn't hear their conversation, but they left."

"Did you see where they went?" I asked.

She shook her head. "No, but the symbols you were talking about, I found them in one of the bathrooms in the stadium."

"What happened next?" Libbie questioned, kicking a pinecone.

"I'm getting there," she snapped, then took a deep breath. "I spent a few weeks there until that Nevena—as you called her—came to get me the other day."

I noted but ignored her dance around my question about the knives. "Wait, the other day? How long ago?"

"Yesterday, I think?"

"That means she didn't get you until I was already locked up." I frowned. Which meant she had been telling the truth.

Libbie changed the subject, obviously uncomfortable with everything that was going on. I zoned out, as I often did when they started talking.

Thunder rumbled and lightning snapped, lighting up the dark clouds. My limbs had gone numb. I couldn't move my fingers.

I finally pulled myself back to the present when Sadira stopped underneath a tree large enough to block most of the rain from reaching us. She pulled back its low-hanging branches.

"Welcome to my humble abode. Care to spend the night?"

Libbie crawled in, and I followed.

It was damp, but it would do.

Department 1, Day 7

In my opinion, being left in the dark is one of the most agonizing things there is. Unless, of course, you do not know you are being left in the dark. In Sander's case, he had no idea what was going on outside what he could see. His ignorance was something I sometimes envied.

I envy all the people who live in innocence. Knowing too much can be a burden. I often wonder if it is necessary for someone to know everything. If Sander and our friends needed to see everything. But if we had not, how would everything have ended?

We managed to alter the fate of the multiverse. Hopefully, for the better. But that weight does not lay in our hands anymore. We have done all we can.

Yet, I wonder if it had to be us. If Sander had never seen that mangled corpse outside of Blackford, would any of this have happened? I suppose that is the thing with the multiverse; you can spend forever wondering about what could have been different, and you know you could try to find out. However, finding out would change even more variables.

I am rambling yet again. But if I am to die within the week, it would be nice to leave some of my thoughts behind. And perhaps warn others not to make the same mistakes I did.

–Elyane

CHAPTER THIRTY-ONE

The downpour had stopped by the next morning. The smell of rain still hung heavily in the air, dancing along the folds of a blanket of fog. My boots sank in the sodden, muddy soil as I made my way back to our makeshift camp, a pile of mostly dry branches in my arms.

I dumped the wood on a mound of dry pine needles and crouched down. I stared at my work for a long, silent moment before admitting to myself that I really didn't know how to make a fire, no matter how optimistic I'd been upon setting out this morning.

I turned back to the tree we'd slept under. Libbie was sprawled on her stomach, one arm wrapped around Sadira's legs. Her glasses had been thrown carelessly to the side. I knew because I'd almost stepped on them when I'd gotten up.

Sadira leaned against the trunk, her eyes open, watching me. "You need my help, don't you?"

I nodded, a burning blush creeping up my neck.

She chuckled and heaved Libbie's arm off her lower half. Her best friend grunted in response.

"I don't think I've ever started a fire," I said as I led her to the pile I'd made.

"That's not true," she said and started digging through her backpack. I saw the flash of blades, among other things. "Remember that time Dad took us camping while Mama had that conference thing? You started the campfire the first night."

"Yeah," I answered and rolled my eyes. "I almost burned down the whole campsite in the process."

"It wasn't your fault," she laughed. "Dad was the one who put the paper towels by the firepit."

I fell quiet, as did Sadira. As much as I tried, I couldn't remember that version of Dad. The smiling one. The happy one. Not the pleading, bloodied one. It was like he was a blur in my memories, shrouded by a curtain of fog. Sometimes, hearing Sadira talk about him like that was almost like hearing her tell me a fairytale. It seemed so surreal. So fake. It was almost as if he hadn't existed before he died.

She gestured toward her friend. "Would you mind waking Libbie? She said she saw blackberry bushes a while back."

My stomach grumbled in response.

Libbie actually snarled at me when I woke her, but eventually, she grudgingly pulled herself up. She emerged from beneath the tree, wiping her glasses on her dirt-covered shirt. When she realized her efforts weren't doing much, she grumbled a curse and put them on anyway.

"What's for breakfast?" she asked Sadira.

"Berries," she replied. "Go get them."

"What? Why do I have to?"

"Because I'm making a fire." My sister gestured to me. "Take him with you. He's no use to me here."

Useless.

I clenched my fists but accepted the knife Sadira handed me as Libbie walked off.

"Keep her safe," she said. "Please."

I nodded. "I still have the gun from the guard. I don't need the knife."

She shrugged and turned away as I tried to hand it back. "Knives don't get jammed. Knives don't run out of bullets. Keep it."

After a very sad breakfast of blackberries and a can of beans from

Sadira's backpack, my twin dumped damp leaves and dirt on the fire. It sizzled and cracked, but the flames quickly died, and we were on the move again.

My legs still ached from yesterday and all the days before that, but I kept my mouth shut. Complaining wasn't going to help anyone. Libbie, on the other hand, didn't seem to get that message.

She complained about being cold; she complained about her wet shoes; she complained about her aching muscles. She was a nice person, and I enjoyed being around her. But there were times when I wanted to punch her in the mouth so she would shut up. Eventually, Sadira finally snapped, and Libbie fell silent.

I couldn't blame either of them. We were tired and cold and hungry. No one got a full eight hours of sleep, probably not even half that. There were multiple times when we had to hide from a group of scouts, whether SSD or Rising.

We walked higher into the mountains, and the interactions with the scouts got less and less frequent. The clouds cleared as the sun went down, making way for the blanket of stars that sprawled across the darkness.

I wrestled with my thoughts as we settled down for the night. Common sense told me to stay with Sadira and Libbie. But there was a nagging feeling in my gut. It was screaming at me, saying I needed to get back to my friends. I needed to. I needed to. I needed to.

I need to.

But I couldn't quite figure out why. Not even as I lay underneath the branches of a pine tree, staring into the forest as shadows overtook the world around me.

"I can't believe it," Amias was saying when I opened my eyes. I lay on a cot, the woolen blankets I'd slept with hanging off the edge, the tips draping against the tarp that covered the ground.

Both Amias and Aven stood in the tent, the former pacing the length of it angrily. His fists were balled. "That idiot got away. I should've hunted him down myself."

"Well, he's gone now. As long as we have this Sander, use the buddy system," Aven said. "His Reflection is not going to take his place anytime soon."

"Are you offering to be my buddy, Aven?" I asked.

They both turned to me, startled that I was awake.

"No," they replied. "Amias is."

Amias rolled his eyes, and I smiled. He saw and turned away. I saw his nails dig into his palms and chuckled to myself. Nevena wasn't stupid after all.

CHAPTER THIRTY-TWO

I didn't tell Libbie or Sadira about the memories. I didn't fully understand them and didn't want Sadira to worry about me even more than she already did. They became more frequent, sometimes even happening during the day. Every time, I'd get a terrible headache. A few times, they were so bad I had to stop walking and sit for a minute or two.

They asked, of course, if I was okay. I always shrugged off their questions and changed the subject.

On the fourth day after the run-in with my Reflection, we saw smoke. It was Libbie who spotted it first. She pointed to the plume of gray fog that rose above the treetops and into the cloudy sky.

Despite Sadira's warnings, we followed it toward what I assumed was an outpost town. Immediately, I noticed the smell of rotting meat, so thick it made my eyes water, followed by the buzzing of flies.

As we neared the town, the smell and the sound only became stronger. We took our first steps into the dirt-packed streets and realized why.

Libbie gagged and turned away. Sadira put a hand on her mouth, her face twisting in disgust.

I, however, looked at the first dead body as if I'd seen and smelled millions. I hadn't seen millions. But definitely more than the average person should.

I bent down and checked the man's wrist. "He's part of the Rising," I said and showed Sadira and Libbie the shattered mirror tattoo. "I assume the SSD attacked."

"Sander!" Libbie cried, horrified. "Stop touching the corpse!"

I dropped his wrist.

"My god," she cursed. "What the hell is wrong with you?"

"A lot of things," I replied and began walking deeper into the town. "But it's just a dead body."

"Just a dead body," Libbie muttered angrily to herself. "It's just a dead body, Libbie. Don't be disgusted."

Even though I couldn't see her face, I knew she was rolling her eyes.

More dead bodies littered the streets. In the center of the town, there was a pile of them stacked higher than my head. They were ablaze, sending up a plume of dark smoke. I wrinkled my nose, the smell almost overwhelming. At least the SSD had the decency to burn the bodies, even if it wasn't all of them.

"Help," someone croaked.

I took a startled step back when a bloodied hand reached for my ankle. Then, my heart leaped into my throat. A woman at the bottom of the pile, where the flames hadn't yet reached, extended her arm toward me again.

"How is she still alive?" Sadira asked, her voice quiet.

"Help me," the woman moaned. "Please."

I saw my twin go for a knife. I grabbed her wrist. "What are you doing?"

"Even if we get her out of the pile," she whispered back to me. "She's not going to survive with those wounds." She gestured to a long slash along the woman's neck. "It'd be better to put her out of her misery."

I swallowed a lump in my throat, itching to help her but not knowing what to do. Sadira grabbed me as I made to move toward the woman, giving a small shake of her head.

I pulled my hand from her grip. "I have to try," I croaked out.

"She's gone, Sander."

I turned back to the woman, watching in misery as life slipped from her body and her head slumped.

Sadira led us away from the pile of corpses and wandered into the biggest house, made from strips of steel and wood. As suspected, there was a Mirror in the center, big enough to fit a car through. White, painted symbols lined the edges.

My twin met my gaze. "Do you want to leave?"

I hesitated. I didn't want to, but I thought of the memory I'd dreamed about a few nights ago. The anger radiating from Amias's body as he'd paced the length of the tent. It would be smarter to leave. Nobody wanted Amias as an enemy.

I nodded to Sadira. I'd find a way back. Or they'd find me. Either way, I had a feeling I would see them again.

CHAPTER THIRTY-THREE

I didn't recognize the dimension we arrived in. Neither did Sadira. Libbie, of course, was still shocked that dimensions even existed.

The new dimension we stepped into was peaceful. A small town inside a jungle, with cobblestone roads and glowing plants. The simply-dressed residents seemed wary of us but ultimately paid little attention to our bedraggled trio. The plain fabrics they wore were so stark against the ornate, curved buildings. I wondered if they used all their resources decorating the slabs of cream-colored stone with rainbow mosaics.

We spent the night in a motel of some sort. It had been a struggle to find a place to stay, given that the signs were not in English. Thankfully, the layout of the town was similar enough to those from our home world. The only big difference between our worlds seemed to be the style of buildings and clothes.

When I woke up in an actual bed the next morning, I silently thanked Sadira for knowing how to pick a lock.

Apparently, she knew how to steal as well because there was a small pile of funky-looking food on the table. I took a bite of a triangle-shaped muffin thingy and took note of Sadira counting a pile of silver coins.

"Where did you get that?" I asked, rubbing my eyes and throwing the plain blanket off my legs. The pale floor, made of some sort of orange-toned marble or rock, coldly met my bare feet. My shoes had been discarded by the door, which we'd locked and barricaded with a coffee table.

"Store a few miles down the road," she replied vaguely.

I didn't bother asking for details; I didn't really want to know. "What's the plan?"

She shrugged. "Stay here for a few days; try not to get murdered."

"Sounds good," answered Libbie through a mouthful of bread. She sat cross-legged on the double bed next to the one I'd slept on, not noticing the crumbs she sent spilling onto the covers. "And then we can go home?"

Silence fell over the room. Libbie swallowed and took a sip of water. She eyed me and Sadira. Then, her face fell.

"I—I'm sorry," Sadira said. "We don't know how to get home."

Libbie ran her hands underneath her glasses. When she dropped her arms away, I could see tears forming in her eyes. She blinked rapidly. "It's okay," she choked. "I get it." She rose and brushed off her legs. "I'm going to go take a shower."

Sadira waited until we heard the water start running before speaking again. "Are you sure you don't know how to get back home?"

I shook my head. "I don't. I'm really sorry."

She nodded, running her hands through her hair. Then, she stood. "I'm going to see if I can find us a change of clothes. You stay here."

She departed, the door slamming shut behind her.

I ran my hands through my hair, then reached for the notepad and pen by the TV. My hand started moving, and a picture began to form. Before I knew it, Amias was grinning back at me.

I ripped the drawing from the notepad and shoved it into my pocket. I hadn't even meant to draw him. The perfect, beautiful, strong lines of his figure had just come so easily to me. It was like they'd been burned into my brain. I couldn't forget them, no matter how hard I tried.

Then, a memory hit me harder than any before.

I was on my cot, sitting cross-legged as I sketched to the light of a dwindling candle. I lifted my head to see Amias on his cot. He was on his stomach, his face smushed into the pillow. In the dim light, I could make out the dark lines of his tattoos and the curves of the muscles in his arm.

I smiled.

I pulled myself out of the memory, my heart racing. Anger rushed through me. My Reflection was getting too close. He was getting too close to all of them. I wasn't going to get my friends back. Ever.

I clenched my teeth and pulled the drawing from my pocket. I stared at it for a long time, something sinking in my chest.

I couldn't think of a way to convince them that I really was me. How could I? My Reflection was probably getting all my memories as well. He could easily fool them. After all, he technically was me.

Sadira came back a couple of hours later, throwing a pile of clothes in my face. I changed into them gratefully and emerged from the bathroom the cleanest I'd felt in months. My shirt was two sizes too big, as was the jacket, but I didn't really care. I also didn't care that Sadira had probably found these in a donation bin. Donations were for those in need. I was certainly in need of new clothes.

Sadira had also picked up a pack of clean bandages and a first aid kit.

"There's one thing I don't understand," she said as she began packing them in her backpack. "Who blew up the tower?"

"I have no idea what you're talking about," I said.

"At Primos," she clarified. "You said one of the cell towers fell in a big explosion, and then the SSD attacked. Who blew it up?"

I frowned. I hadn't thought about that much in all the chaos.

"It must've been someone high enough in rank to know what the cell towers did," my sister continued. "And high enough to get supplies for the bombs. Unless the SSD gave them the bombs."

"Why are you so invested in this?" Libbie asked from her spot on the bed. She was flipping through a children's book she'd found in the dresser. "The way I see it, it's not our problem."

"She's right," I agreed. "We got away. Both the SSD and the Rising are distracted by each other. They've probably forgotten about us." I hoped so, at least.

"Nevena," Sadira snapped her fingers. "Maybe it was her. She's the one who stole me from the place the SSD put me in. How would she know where to look unless she was working with them?"

"Her parents," I said. "Ivy told me their parents worked for the SSD."

Sadira frowned and finished packing up.

"Where are we going?" I asked.

"Is the Mirror we came through still open?"

"Possibly. As long as no one erased the symbols on the other side. Or broke the Mirror. Then we wouldn't fit."

"We're going back," she announced. "There's somewhere we need to go."

Libbie rolled her eyes and stuffed the children's book into Sadira's backpack. "Why?"

"I think I know a way we can get home."

When we'd first arrived in this dimension, we'd crawled through a Mirror in a dance studio. Thankfully, it had been late at night and empty, but today, we weren't so lucky. We approached the studio, as well as the crowd that surrounded it. Some sort of party was going on, but we managed to slip through and make our way into the foyer.

Once we got inside, however, we were greeted by a dozen friendly smiles. The dancers, in their vibrant costumes, paused their movements and turned their attention toward us. Their eyes sparkled with curiosity and excitement as they welcomed us into their midst. The pulsating music filled the air, and the infectious energy of the dance floor enveloped us, making me forget the chaos we had come from.

Though they didn't seem to know who we were, they welcomed us to their festivities as if we were already friends.

Confused, I met Sadira's gaze. She shrugged and motioned to the door of the studio we had arrived in. We made our way toward the door but were stopped by an elderly woman. She shook her head at us, spouting a bunch of words I couldn't understand. But the basic message was clear: we couldn't go in there.

We backed off reluctantly, keeping silent in order to avoid more conversation.

"What are we going to do?" I muttered as we approached an empty spot in the foyer.

Sadira crossed her arms and leaned against the wall. "Wait for them to look away, then make a run for it."

I sighed.

It wasn't long before the people by the door departed and we were able to slip in unnoticed. I shut the door behind me quietly, taking in a deep breath as we stepped into the room.

I heard a small squeak.

Before us stood a dozen or so girls, all staring wide-eyed and all half-naked.

Sadira slammed her hands over my eyes seconds before I was able to do it.

Shit. They were using this as a changing room.

The girls shrieked and began yelling at us. I heard apologies spill from Sadira's mouth as she dragged me toward the Mirror. Her hands over my eyes, I waved to the dancers. "Sorry!"

Then, I fell into the silvery liquid. Once again, I was overwhelmed by the feeling of being underwater. It was like a damp, cold substance hung just mere inches from my skin.

Then, I stepped into a dark room. Sadira stepped up behind me.

"Where's Libbie?" she asked, taking in the tight space made

from metal and wood.

"I'm right here," Libbie replied, emerging from the shadows. "That was kind of awkward."

I nodded in agreement. Her face was flushed with embarrassment. I guess she still wasn't used to girls changing rooms, seeing as she hadn't been allowed in them back at school. Even after her mom had yelled at the principal.

I wiped away the symbols on the Mirror.

"This form of travel is kind of inconvenient," Sadira noted as we stepped outside of the building.

The stench of burnt bodies filled my nose almost immediately. Libbie gagged and shoved her face into her shirt.

"I mean, it's unpredictable. You just show up anywhere on any planet. Can't they use the symbols to get more specific?" Sadira looked at me questioningly, like I had all the answers.

I shrugged, grateful that this was a topic I had some knowledge of. "Aven was able to get me into school that one time, but I'm not sure if they can get more specific than a few miles."

She continued, "There should be another way. An easier way."

I blinked, a sudden realization coming to mind. "How far are we from Primos?"

She turned to me, an eyebrow raised. "You got an idea, didn't you?"

"Well, if you already had a plan, I don't want to take over—"

"Spit it out."

The words rushed out of my mouth, and I felt stupid for not thinking of it before. "The Mirror Aven used to take me back home. We didn't erase all the symbols, I think I remember what the missing ones looked like. If it's still intact…"

Sadira shook her head. "The SSD probably has probably taken over that place by now. Getting into the city center would be suicide."

My shoulders drooped.

"But, it's worth a shot. My plan did involve going back to Primos anyway."

"The city that we just escaped from?" Libbie raised her eyebrows. "Seriously? Why didn't we do that when we were already there?"

Sadira let out an exasperated sigh. "Because I didn't think of it when we were there. And plus, we were a little too busy running from the SSD and the Rising."

"And Amias," I added.

"You sound terrified of this Amias dude."

I thought of the way he'd looked with Kayson's heart in his hand. "If you ever meet him, you'll understand why. Especially now that we're on his bad side."

"You never were on my good side," said a voice from beside me. Amias grinned at me, but there was no humor in his eyes. "You shouldn't have come back."

The world fell from underneath me. I felt my knees wobble. Libbie froze.

"This is Amias?" whispered Sadira, her face slack. She, too, was petrified.

"Shut up," he snapped and pulled his gun on her. I had the instinct to step in front of her, but my limbs refused to move. Amias turned back to me, his blue eyes nearly glowing with rage. "You would've been better off staying as far away from us as possible."

A lump formed in my throat.

"Well?" Amias glared at me. "Aren't you going to say something?"

I should say something. Anything. But I'd forgotten how to speak.

He called out to the mess of a village. "I found them."

Only a few seconds passed before more familiar faces appeared. Eden and Ivy. Then Renna. Followed by Aven. And lastly, me.

I gritted my teeth when I saw my Reflection. He saw me and gave a slight smirk. Blinding rage rushed through me, heating my neck and ears.

"How did you find us?" Sadira asked.

Amias chuckled and gestured to Eden. "Never underestimate the quiet ones."

Eden spoke, addressing Sadira. "Who are you?" She then turned to Libbie. "And you."

"Um, I'm Libbie," she stuttered.

"Sadira," my sister growled.

"Sadira," Aven mused. They flicked their gun toward me. "You do know that's not your brother, right?"

She glared at him and gestured toward my Reflection. "You do know that's not your friend, right?"

Aven grinned and turned to Amias. "I like her."

"Well, you can't keep her. If she really is our Sander's sister, then we can't kill her. If she's not, then the Major was telling the truth, and our Sadira died in the chaos at Primos."

"Can't we just kill them both?" Renna asked. "It is quite confusing. Killing them both would clear everything up. And Sander doesn't need a sister, do you?"

I thought for a brief second that she was talking to me, but of course, she wasn't. My Reflection narrowed his eyes.

"I don't think that one's my sister," he said.

Renna clapped. "So, we *can* kill her!"

"No," grumbled Amias. "We're not killing anyone yet."

She frowned. "Then what are we doing?"

"We're taking them back to the Major," he replied and moved toward me. My heart caught in my throat as the smell of smoke and rain washed over me. He reached into his backpack and pulled out a long rope. He tied my wrists behind my back. As he did, he leaned in and whispered in my ear, "Save a spot for me in hell, won't you?"

A chill crawled down my spine.

CHAPTER THIRTY-FOUR

They blindfolded us for the ride back to their temporary camp, which I overheard Aven mention had become occupied after the Primos attack by a few survivors. The rest of their words flitted by me unnoticed as I constantly checked the warmth of Sadira by my side, brushing my fingers against her hand just to make sure she was there. When the vehicle stopped and I was pulled from the trunk, the warmth disappeared, and it felt like someone had ripped away a chunk of my soul.

Darkness overcame the dim edges of my obscured vision as I was thrust onto a chair and tied down. A heartbeat passed before someone removed the blindfold. I lifted my head, blinking in hopes of adjusting my eyes to the dark.

Muted daylight leaked through the cracks in the heavy tent flaps, but beyond a few obscure dark lumps, I was blind.

"Sadira?" I called, biting back a wave of panic.

"She's not in here," Amias said.

I jumped, scanning the shadowed figures for one that looked like him. Beside the entrance, doused in darkness but illuminated in a way that made him seem ethereal, he sat on a chair a few feet in front of me, elbows on his knees.

"Where are they?" I asked, trying to keep my voice from trembling. I'd seen firsthand what being his enemy did to someone. I'd never thought I'd be on the receiving end of those actions.

"They're not dead."

I resisted the urge to roll my eyes. Not that he would've seen. I could barely see my hands. "Are they hurt?"

Amias lunged. One moment, he was sitting; the next, his hand wrapped around my throat, and his breath was on my face. "You don't ask the questions," he snarled.

"Amias—" I choked out.

He released me hesitantly, then turned and paced a few steps away. "Don't call me that."

"What am I supposed to call you, then?" I rolled my neck, heart pounding. "That's your name."

"You don't get to call me anything," he spat. "You don't deserve to call me anything."

"Oh my—" I groaned and leaned back, anxiety forgotten in a rush of frustration. "It's me, Amias! That other Sander isn't your friend. He and Nevena plotted against us and tricked you. Don't be so stupid." If I hadn't been so worried about Sadira and Libbie, I would've thought twice about calling Amias stupid.

He didn't move, though. He was unusually quiet for a long time. Finally, he let out a breath and sat back down. "Maybe."

My eyebrows shot up.

"Prove to me you're really—really the Sander I know, and maybe I'll let you go."

I struggled to figure out what to say. How was I supposed to know my Reflection didn't know everything about me?

He saw my hesitation. "Never mind. This is pointless."

"Wait, Amias." I tried to stop him, but he rose and left the tent through a flap in front of me. As he did, clouded light fell through. The room was lit long enough for me to see a pile of tarps in the far corner, a post to my left, and a few guns and a map lying across a table. But then, the flap closed, and I was immersed in darkness again.

Outside the tent, I could hear Amias talking to someone. His low voice carried through the flaps, but I couldn't understand what he was saying. I heard another voice follow his, but this one was quieter.

I tugged hopelessly against the ropes again, trying to ignore the restless drum beat in my chest. My binds were getting tighter. I could feel them moving. Constricting. Squeezing the life out of my hands and feet.

My breath began to quicken. The walls felt as if they were closing in on me.

"Amias," I choked out. The room began to spin, and I swallowed dryly, wondering if the food I'd eaten was going to make a reappearance. My vision blurred. "Amias… please… "

The ropes continued to tighten. They snaked their way up my arms and legs. Like a boa constrictor choking the life from their prey.

I squeezed my eyes shut, but that didn't stop the tears from coming. Heat waves slammed into me. Over and over again.

"What the hell is wrong with you?"

I opened my eyes.

Amias stared at me, eyebrows narrowed. I couldn't tell if he was worried or angry, but it only made me feel worse.

I bit my lip to keep from speaking. At the moment, I wasn't sure I trusted the words that would come out.

A woman stepped in behind him, silhouetted against the morning light. A woman with hair like snow and skin like tree bark. It only took Eden a second to analyze the situation. She bent before me and started untying the ropes. "Take a breath, Sander."

"What are you doing?" Amias reached to stop her, but she slapped his hand.

"Back off," she snarled. To my surprise, he did. She met my gaze again. Her blue-gray eyes were calm. I found peace in them. "Deep breath," she instructed. "In and out."

I obliged, drawing in a breath and letting it out as if it were the most important thing in the world.

"Focus on something else. Focus on me."

I studied her face. The soft lines of her jawline, the round, almond shape of her eyes, and the curve of her eyelashes.

The ropes dropped away. Relief washed over me like a waterfall.

"Thank you," I whispered.

Eden gave me a small smile, her expression comforting but worried. She rose and made her way to the door. "Do not bind him again. Keep guards surrounding this tent at all times," she ordered Amias.

"Who died and made you queen?" he snapped.

"Do it."

He grumbled a curse and bowed his head mockingly but followed her orders anyway.

I was hit by a memory a few hours later. I was in the place of my Reflection, standing outside a tent with a pile of blankets in my hands. The flap was barely open, just enough for me to see a sliver of what was going on inside.

Aven leaned their head against the tent pole, banging it repeatedly. "This is so confusing. You think the Sander we imprisoned is our Sander?"

"Yes," Eden replied.

"And why do you think that again?" Ivy asked. "That Sander had one panic attack, and you flip sides?"

"I do not understand how I know," Eden argued. "There was something in his eyes when I was helping him. It just…" She sighed. "Never mind. Perhaps, I am wrong."

"I don't think you are." Renna's voice was calm and sweet. A sudden rage I didn't understand rushed through me. "You've always been the most intuitive of us. I agree with Eden on this one."

There was silence. Then, Ivy spoke. "Amias? What do you think?"

"We need proof. We can't just kill one of them."

"Do you have an idea on how to get proof?"

"I think so," he answered.

I gritted my teeth. The blood in my veins turned white hot with rage. I tossed the blankets on a nearby table and stormed off toward the far side of camp.

Just seconds after I pulled myself out of the memory, I heard a commotion outside the tent. I forced myself to sit up from my spot on the floor despite the headache that was rudely pounding against the inside of my skull.

"Sir," said one of the guards. "Sir, you can't go in there."

"Amias said I could," said a voice. "He said to let me in, or there'd be hell to pay."

I could almost hear the guard's fear. He hesitated but inevitably let the person in.

I shouldn't have been so surprised when I saw myself enter the tent. It felt rather odd, seeing a perfect replica of myself walking and talking like another person. It felt like what I imagined it would feel like to be a famous actor, seeing yourself on screens, posters, and all that, or what it would feel like if Sadira and I had been identical. The rage that rushed through me was distasteful, brimming with disgust and uncertainty, almost as if it didn't know why it was there.

"What are you doing here?" I growled.

The corner of his mouth quirked, and he pulled out a gun. "Scream," he whispered. "I dare you."

I kept my mouth shut.

"Good," he applauded and gestured to the chair. I sat without argument. He pulled up the other chair and sat in front of me. "I've been inside your head, Sander Fox." My name spilled from his tongue as if it held a foul taste. "I know the difference between us."

"You're a deranged maniac, and I'm still partially sane."

He chuckled. "In my reality—in my dimension—Sadira died. Do you know what it feels like to lose a sibling?" He pressed the gun to my chest, his face twisting in sorrow and rage. "Do you know what it's like to lose a twin?"

"No," I whispered, lowering my gaze because I couldn't handle the vengeance brimming in his.

He grinned. "Well, you're in luck. Because in your reality, it will be Sadira who learns that feeling."

"Kill me," I snapped quietly. "I don't give a damn."

"Oh, Sander. I know you don't. But Sadira does. And Amias. And Eden. And all the gross little friends you made. Really, killing you would just be doing me a favor."

I rolled my eyes. "Do you have any motive for killing me? Other than the fact you hate me?"

"You've messed up my plans," he snarled. "You were supposed to stay locked up. But then that bitch went and broke you out."

I made to lunge forward, but he held up the gun as a reminder. "That bitch," I hissed, "is my sister. Don't think you're going to get away with calling her that."

He smiled. "Maybe I won't. But who's to say?" He rose and pressed the gun to my forehead. "After all, you'll be too dead to do anything about it."

I straightened, terror creeping into my throat. He saw it, and his grin grew wider. "You really aren't all they've put you up to be, are you?"

I clenched my fists, praying that I wouldn't make this worse than it already was, and swung my hand down on his elbow. Just as I hoped, his arm buckled, and his grip on the gun loosened. I knocked it from his hand and shot to my feet.

My Reflection's eyes widened, and he darted toward where the gun had skidded across the ground.

I sent a blow at his jaw, and he stumbled back a step.

"You're all talk," I said and aimed a kick at his knee, just as Ivy had taught me. It snapped, and he crumpled. "If you'd ever paid attention during the times Ivy and Eden were training you, then maybe you could beat me." I crouched before him. "And guess what? I know that you didn't pay attention." I tapped his forehead, and he flinched. "Because I've been inside your head, too. I know your thoughts and feelings."

"No, you don't." He scrambled backward. "Because if you were inside my head, you wouldn't be able to stand."

"You underestimate me," I said and wrapped my hand around his throat. "I could choke the life out of you and never feel the slightest bit guilty."

"It'd only be because you'd be killing yourself," he gasped, then grabbed a loose plank and slammed it against my head.

My vision went black. I thought I might have fallen unconscious. Perhaps I did because when I opened my eyes, my Reflection had thrown me off and was racing for the gun. I tried to rise and follow, but the room swayed, and I fell onto my knees again.

He approached me triumphantly, gun pointed at my head. I blinked at it, dazed. He said something, but a deafening ringing in my ears drowned out his voice.

"What?" I asked, probably speaking louder than needed.

My Reflection frowned in confusion, but something else grabbed his attention, and his eyes went for the tent flap. I followed his gaze and saw the others enter just as Ivy fired her gun. The gunshot, of course, only made the ringing worse, and I yelped.

Aven ran toward my Reflection, who was staring at the gaping hole in his hand in shock.

Hands grabbed me and helped me up. I turned to thank them but saw the anger in Eden's eyes and decided against it.

Amias stood at the entrance, shouting at the guard, "I told you not to let him in! Do you have any idea which one is which?!"

I shook myself from Eden's grasp and desperately made my way toward him. I needed to tell him that it was me. I spun, trying to face him, but with such a distorted reality, I couldn't see with any accuracy. Instead of falling onto Amias as I'd planned, I fell headfirst into the pole and promptly blacked out.

The ringing had stopped when I woke up. But I certainly didn't feel better. My stomach was uneasy, swimming with nausea. Someone was inside my head and stabbing at the backs of my eyeballs with rude fingers.

I groaned and pressed my hands to my forehead. I forced myself to sit up, only to immediately fall back down, causing an even worse wave of pain to wash over me. The cot I'd fallen back onto was as unforgiving as a bed of rocks, and metal dug into my back as I tried to turn to get a better view of my dark surroundings.

"Do not try to move," said a silky voice. Eden pressed a damp towel to my forehead.

"Thanks for the heads up," I grumbled and weakly swatted her hand away. "I'm fine. I feel fine. Where's Sadira?"

"You feel like shit," she replied in a level tone. "And your sister is safe, asleep with her friend." A lamp lit in the corner seemed to be the only source of light, and its warm glow cast long shadows across her tight expression.

I looked at her in surprise, using the information about Sadira to settle the unease in my stomach. "I think that's the first time I've heard you talk like a regular person."

She rose from her seat and crossed the tent, rinsing the towel in a bowl of water that lay simmering over a portable stove. "I'm afraid I'm not sure what you mean."

"I don't know. You talk so fancy. You talk like you're from the 1800s." I raised my eyebrows. "Unless you are."

She laughed and shook her head. "The world I come from is very different from yours. This was the way I was taught to speak your language. Though I confess, it is confusing."

"Confusing," I scoffed. "That's one word to describe the English language."

She smiled. "You are certainly in a jovial mood."

"I'm just glad you're my friend again." I paused. "Well, are you? What happened?"

Her smile fell. "I am, perhaps, but Amias is not so sure. After you passed out, your Reflection tried to make a run for it, attempting to shoot us in the process. Despite that, our fearless leader has his doubts."

I sighed. "That makes sense. Amias has got some serious trust issues."

She nodded. "Unfortunately. At the moment, Ivy is… encouraging your Reflection to confess. But he is stronger than we believed."

I winced. "What about the Major? Where is he?"

"I am not sure. He was gone when we came back from looking for you. The others say he went on a walk a few days ago and never came back. Scouts are searching for him as we speak."

I closed my eyes. "Can you just, I don't know, tell me everything that happened while I was gone? I feel like I missed so much."

She gave me a comforting smile and sat down beside me once again, dabbing the towel across the sweat beading on my forehead. "After the SSD attacked, the Major and most of the higher-level Chieftains fled here. We spent a few days gathering as many survivors as we could; however, we were unable to find many. Most had been slaughtered at the hands of those monsters." Her face twisted in rage. "After that, you showed up claiming you were the real Sander. And now, we are here."

"What about Nevena?" I asked

Eden shrugged. "Missing. Or dead. No one has seen her since that attack on Primos."

"Huh. So, Sadira could've been right."

She tilted her head.

"My sister has this theory that Nevena is working for the SSD," I explained. "That she was the one who caused the explosion and brought the cell tower down in the first place. And at first, I didn't believe her."

"And now?" she prompted.

"I don't know. She found me barely minutes after the explosion. There's no way she could've set off the explosion and gotten there in time. Unless she had a remote detonator. I don't know," I said again. "She's not here. Running makes her seem guilty. I say we just forget it for now."

"Agreed," Eden said. She reached for my head, gently rubbing my temples in slow, soothing circles.

I blinked away my instinct to shove her away, noticing that the pressure of the headache had already lessened. Instead, I closed my eyes and relished in the short-lived relief. She moved from my temples to my jawline and eventually to the base of my skull. Her touch was delicate but meticulous, and though the pain didn't vanish, enough had subsided for me to decide that Eden knew what she was doing.

A few minutes later, just as I'd begun to drift off, the tent flap burst open and Sadira came racing for me. The pain in my temple came flooding back as Eden pulled away.

My twin skidded to a halt when she saw me. "My god, Sander, you look like shit."

I chuckled weakly. "That's not the first time I've heard that today."

She grabbed a seat on the stool beside me. "What happened? Ivy said your Reflection beat you up."

"Yeah, pretty much." I smiled. "So, you met Ivy, huh?"

She nodded vigorously. "Libbie's talking to her right now just outside. She seems nice."

"Nice." Eden laughed while crossing the tent to take the water off the heat. "Nice. Describe her again once you get to know her."

Sadira turned. "I'm sorry. Who are you?"

"Oh, Sadira," I tried to sit up again but failed. "This is Eden. She's a really good friend."

She looked at Eden skeptically but eventually brought her attention back to me. "I talked to Amias. I tried to convince him that you're the real Sander, but he's really set on finding more proof before trusting either of you."

"That's Amias, all right," I grumbled.

"And I also talked to your Reflection," she added, which surprised me. "Well, I talked to him after beating him up a little."

"Just a little," I laughed.

"Just a little." She smiled. "And once we get you all healed up, we can start searching for a way home."

"I apologize," Eden interrupted, stepping up. "But Sander's not going anywhere. He was hit pretty hard in the head, and until I know how bad it is, I need him to stay here."

"Excuse me," Sadira snapped, rising from her chair. "But we have family to get home to."

Eden met Sadira with a calm expression. "If you really care about your brother, you will let me treat him."

Sadira, clearly ruffled, sat back down. "Never mind. We'll go when you can."

"Thank you," Eden said.

CHAPTER THIRTY-FIVE

I barely slept, as would be suspected after getting whacked in the head with a wood plank and then walking into a post, but when I did, it was fitful. I woke up every ten minutes or so, and my nightmares kept getting worse. Finally, the light of the sunrise began to seep through the cracks in the tent. Eden, who had slept in a makeshift bed beside mine, stirred.

"Eden," I whispered. "Eden, are you awake?"

She rolled over, smushing her face against the blanket she'd bunched up and made into a pillow. "I am now."

"Good morning."

She glared at me.

A few minutes later, the tent flap opened, and Sadira approached Eden. "Did you figure out what was wrong with him?"

"No," Eden replied, rising from her bed. She rubbed her eyes. "I did not. But I know someone who can."

"Great." Sadira clapped her hands. "Let's go get them."

Eden gave my twin a smile of daggers. "They are not on this world. Nor are they on a world protected from the SSD."

"Then where are they?" I asked.

She didn't respond; instead, she brushed past Sadira and out the door.

Sadira rolled her eyes. "Wonderful."

I sighed. "That's just Eden."

She smiled, but it didn't reach her eyes. "I'm glad you're happy with your friends," she said. "And I'm glad you have friends. I can't remember the last time you were this comfortable around people outside of Libbie, Mama, and me."

"Speaking of Libbie." The tent flap opened, and Libbie strode in, arms wide. She laughed to herself. "Sorry, that was like perfect timing." She pulled up the stool from Eden's desk. "You look like hell."

"I feel like hell," I replied.

"No, I mean, have you even seen yourself?" She began searching the room for a mirror, probably. "You have a huge bruise on the side of your face."

I reached for my face instinctively. My fingers met swollen, tender skin. "Ow," I muttered. "I didn't know it was that bad."

"It's really bad," Libbie continued. When she didn't find a mirror, she sat back down. "Are you—no, you're not okay. That's a stupid question. *Will* you be okay?"

I shrugged. "Eden's taking me to some magic doctor who's supposed to find out. I honestly don't know why we can't just hop dimensions and find a hospital."

"Two reasons," Aven said as they walked through the entrance. They had my old backpack in their hands and dropped it on the ground beside my cot. "One, the SSD has tabs on every hospital. Please, don't ask why."

"Why?" Libbie asked immediately.

Aven glared at her for a long moment before continuing. "And reason number two, the people Eden is talking about can also help us take down the SSD. If they're willing."

"Who are they?" I questioned, reaching for my backpack.

"Witch doctors," Aven replied and handed my backpack to me.

"Really?" Sadira raised an eyebrow.

"No," they chuckled. "Actually, I don't know. My mom took me to convince them to join the SSD a while ago, but I was really young and barely remember anything. I remember it being cold and windy. And birds."

"Birds?" I tilted my head, bringing my gaze from my backpack to Aven. "Like parrots?"

They shook their head. "Big birds. Birds of prey. Like eagles. And falcons."

"I still want to know about the hospitals," interrupted Libbie.

Aven sighed. "Are you sure?"

"Yes."

They launched into a dramatic story, but I blocked it out. Mainly because I didn't really care, but also because as I dug through my backpack, my hands met my sketchbook. I grinned and pulled it out.

Eden came back an hour later, carrying the food from Sadira's backpack. Aven, Libbie, and Sadira all cried out in happiness and reached for the treats joyfully. I didn't feel like eating, but the gnawing in my gut made me force the food down my throat.

"Good news," Eden announced as she finished the last of her tart. "Amias has agreed to let us go. However, he and Sander's Reflection have to go as well."

My heart dropped. "What? Why?"

"He does not trust the guards here to keep an eye on him. And he also does not want to let you out of his sight."

I frowned.

Aven coughed. "So, Eden, I assume that means you need help trying to get to this place?"

She nodded. They both rose and made their way out the door, but as they stepped out, they quickly backtracked and made room for Amias to enter.

I forgot about my headache when I saw him. His stunning eyes flicked over me. Worry filled his face but was gone so fast I wondered if I'd imagined it. Silence hung in the air. Everyone was frozen until he cleared his throat.

"Can I talk to him alone?" he asked.

Everyone filed out. Sadira, despite her hesitancy, departed after I gave her a small nod. I could feel my heartbeat behind my ears, loud and persistent. It only got worse as Amias made his way over to me. He didn't sit, I noticed, and he continuously tapped his fingers against his thumb.

"I don't trust you," he blurted.

"Um," I searched for the right words. "Excellent way to start a conversation."

"Sorry," he muttered, rolling his eyes. "Except it's true. My gut says that you're the real Sander, but I don't know. I can't trust you. Not until I have proof."

"I know." I looked down.

"But for now, I'm willing to believe. At least, as much as I can." He dropped his hands. "So, I'm sorry for hunting you and trying to kill you."

We were silent for a brief moment. When I realized that was all he had to say, I offered a slight smile.

"It's okay," I assured. "I would've done the same."

He raised an eyebrow. "Really?"

"Probably not, actually."

He laughed, then put a hand over his mouth as if refusing himself a second laugh. I pulled my gaze away from him, longing tugging at my heart. I wanted him to trust me again. I wanted to make him laugh again. I wanted to be his happiness because God knows he didn't have enough of it.

"Do you want to see the camp?" he asked.

I nodded and threw off the blankets. As I rose, my head began pounding harder than before. I gritted my teeth and pushed through it, forcing my legs to swing over the edge of the cot.

Amias held out his arm tentatively, and I took it. My arms shook, as did my legs. I hated how weak I felt.

A weird tingle ran up my shins when I set my feet on the ground. I pushed myself off the cot and, then immediately collapsed.

Amias bent to help. "Are you okay?" he asked quietly.

I nodded, biting my lip and hauling myself up. This time, as I rose, my legs didn't give out. I managed to take a step. After I felt strong enough to walk on my own, I shook Amias off, and he stepped back almost gratefully.

Outside the tent, a light fog hung lazily over the camp. The damp air clung to my skin and sent a shiver through my body. A few early risers eyed Amias and me as we passed. The hair on the back of my neck rose.

"Did you build this entire camp after the attack?" I asked.

He shook his head. "Not really. A few of the tents were already set up. It was being used as an outpost and a prison. But the Rising kept provisions in the garage just in case."

"I'm glad they did," I said.

He nodded slightly.

Amias led me to the center of the camp. On the way, we passed about a dozen firepits, all crackling and glowing. We stopped at a circular building frame with a cone-shaped ceiling carved from wood and spiraling toward the cloudy sky. Inside, Aslen, the Chieftain of the Second Station, was bent before a circular firepit and feeding the flames with a pile of twigs.

"Aslen." Amias bowed his head in acknowledgment.

Aslen turned. His eyes furrowed when he saw me. "I thought Mr. Fox was on bed rest."

"He was," Amias replied and then added authoritatively. "He will be joining us for the meeting."

I could see the Chieftain wanted to argue, but he kept his mouth shut and nodded bitterly.

"Since when do they answer to you?" I questioned Amias as we walked away. "Also, what meeting?"

"Since their leader disappeared and I took charge," he answered bluntly, his expression unmoving. I didn't fail to notice his lack of an answer to my second question.

I frowned, deciding not to push it, and looked away just in time to see Ivy barrel into me. My legs buckled, and I would've fallen backward if it hadn't been for the firm hand against my back. She pulled away, a grin on her face. I turned to thank Amias for catching me, but he had already walked away.

"Sander! Hi!" She grabbed my hands, forcing my attention back on her. "I'm so sorry I haven't visited you. You wouldn't believe how busy I've been. You heard about the Major, right? About how he disappeared?"

I nodded.

"Well, Renna and I have been leading the scout groups, and yesterday, my group found a deserted SSD camp. And then we got attacked. But that doesn't matter. It means we're getting close." She took a breath, then continued, "By the time we got back, everyone was already asleep. And then, this morning, I had to brief Amias. I was actually on my way to visit you when I saw you."

I offered her a weak smile, but she didn't seem to notice. She grabbed my arm and started leading me away from the round building. "How are you?"

"Um, good," I said. "I think."

She nodded. "I heard Eden's taking us to some fancy doctor."

"Yeah, they're supposed to be really powerful. According to Aven, they turned down an alliance with the SSD a few years back."

Ivy whistled. "Wow. They must be super strong, then. I wonder how Eden knows them."

"Me too," I said quietly. I already had my suspicions, but I didn't bother sharing them with her. I cleared my throat. "Do you really believe that I'm me?"

She shrugged. "I have my doubts. But mostly, yes. I do believe."

"Why? Amias doesn't."

She tilted her head as if confused by the question. "Why do I believe you're you?"

I nodded.

"The other one acted differently. He's too angry. You're not an angry or careless person. I can tell that's what he is, though."

I didn't respond, thinking of the way the guards had crumpled when Sadira, Libbie, and I had escaped. The way I didn't care if they were breathing or not. I rubbed in between my eyes. "Yeah."

"And," she continued. "Amias doesn't trust anyone. Not fully. Don't sweat it. He'll come around eventually."

I highly doubted that but smiled as if I didn't.

She changed the subject and began rambling on about her grudges against Nevena, whose disappearance had been met with unease throughout the Rising.

I peered at her attentively, my mind running in constant circles with worries and fears. Amias didn't trust me. And he never was going to; that was obvious. The more I thought about it, the more I realized it was hurting me.

God knows I couldn't be trusted. Who knew what would happen? It wasn't the fact that he wasn't going to trust *me*; it was the fact that he wasn't going to trust anyone. And with the life he'd had, I understood why.

Eventually, we made our way back to the tent I'd woken up in. Ivy said goodbye, and I tried my best to fall back asleep. I didn't think I'd have much luck, but before I knew it, Aven was shaking me awake.

"Wake up, dude," they said. "You're supposed to come to the meeting with us."

"What meeting?" I grumbled and tiredly pulled myself from the cot.

They held the tent flap open for me. "We meet with the Chieftains every few days. Just to update each other and everything."

We gathered in the round wooden room Amias and I had stopped at earlier that day. I took a seat on one of the benches in between Renna and Aven. Sadira and Libbie hadn't been invited, I noticed, but it was easy to understand why.

From what I could tell, five of the seven Chieftains had shown up along with their Shadows, most of whom I recognized. Aslen and a woman with features similar to his sat across the fire from me. Kenneth and Asher, I remembered from my first day in Primos. And Rosa and Carlos from the party. The last two, the duos I'd never seen before, had their eyes pinned on me.

The hair on the back of my neck stood, and I shifted my gaze from their dark eyes.

Amias stood by the firepit, picking at a scratch on his arm. For someone who was supposed to be in charge, he didn't strike me as professional.

The Chieftains and their Shadows muttered amongst themselves impatiently. Aven, Renna, Ivy, Eden, and I, however, sat in silence.

Based on the position of the sun, I had slept through most of the day. I figured we had maybe two hours left until sunset. The fading light cast a golden glow across the pit, illuminating the skin on my hands and bare arms.

"Should we just start?" Kenneth asked. "Even without the twins?"

"Wait!"

Two sets of footsteps came pounding down the stairs and into the pit-like room. A girl and a boy, both surprisingly young. Both had light brown hair and pale skin, along with a splash of freckles across their small noses. Maybe fourteen or fifteen.

"Wait!" cried the girl as she stopped and bent over herself, breathing heavily. "We're here. Sorry. We're here."

"Whatever," grumbled Amias. "Just take a seat."

They sat on the bench beside Aven and stared at Amias attentively.

"Everyone, in case you don't know," Amias gestured to me. "This is Sander Fox. Hopefully the real one. I'm pretty sure you all were told about the mix-up we had between him and his Reflection."

"Is that what happened to his face?" The young girl asked. "Did his Reflection beat him up?"

"Um, yes. Anyway, Eden's pretty sure he has a bad concussion, maybe even worse. She's taking us to some special people who can fix him. It's not a hospital, don't worry. However, the SSD has tried to win them over in the past. No one's sure if they have tried again."

"Why don't you just ask the Director's kid?" The Shadow with dark silky hair turned her death stare to Aven.

I blinked through the fog in my head, surprise lighting my features. How had they figured out about them? Last I'd checked, we had all agreed to keep it a secret.

Amias let out an exasperated sigh. "Listen, I know you don't trust us—"

The man beside the Shadow scoffed. "And we have every right, too. Tanith was my friend. And you and your little friends butchered her like an animal."

"Oh, please." Amias rolled his eyes. "Don't act like you've never done worse. I know all about you, Jonas Lee Kinsley. You're not as secret as you hoped. Tell me, how's Dara?"

His face went slack.

"She's six now, right?"

"Keep our daughter out of this," the woman beside Jonas snapped, fists clenching. "And we know about you, too. Amias Wolf, brought to the SSD at age seven, genetically experimented on. You're Warren Coldwell's lab rat and the Director's dog. You and Renna have killed hundreds for them. You've helped take down entire governments. Why in the hell are you helping us now?"

Pain throbbed in my temple, her words dancing between nonsense and understanding. I focused my attention on Amias, studying the way his jaw clenched, if only to keep conscious.

"Listen to what you just said," he said. "We were errand kids for the SSD. I'm done being on their leash." He drew in a deep breath, trying to regain composure.

Silence fell over us, maintained by the fear of speaking up.

"So, about these doctors," Aslen cleared his throat. I was grateful for the change in subject, no matter how slight it was. "For all we know, you could be walking into a death trap. If you're talking about who I think you are, your entrance into their world won't be welcomed."

"I'm well aware of the risks. We all are. But this is a necessary trip."

"To save one life?" Asher raised an eyebrow. "Is he really that important?"

"Hell yes," Ivy snapped, leaning forward so she could glare at Asher. "Maybe if you had a heart you'd understand."

"Maybe if you were anything like your sister," Asher argued. "Then we would've found the Major already."

Ivy's whole body tensed, and she shot to her feet. "At least I'm doing something. All of you are just sitting on your asses. It seems to me like you don't even want to find the Major."

Asher's eyes flared. "You have no idea what is going on at our Stations. Thousands of refugees from Primos are seeking a safe place. It's chaos. I can't help them and look for him at the same time."

"Shut up!" Amias snarled. Everyone fell silent. My heartbeat thudded uncomfortably against the walls of my ribcage, each beat sending new aches up my neck.

Renna dragged Ivy back into her seat.

"Take a breath," Amias snapped. "Both of you. We're all stressed. Ivy, the Stations are sending out scouts; it's just not their main priority. And Asher, talk like that to my friend again, and I'll break every bone in your body. I don't care if you're a Shadow."

Fury flashed in Asher's eyes, but he remained silent. A few of the other Shadows shifted nervously.

"Anyway," Amias turned to Aslen. "Any updates?"

Aslen straightened. "The Primos refugees are only growing. They come by the dozens every day. I'm not sure how much longer we can keep housing them."

Amias bit his lip worriedly.

"You can send them to my Station," offered the young, freckled girl. "We have plenty of room. It's like people forget we're there."

Amias nodded in agreement. "Sage is right. Brentor is highly secure; it would be a good place for temporary residents."

Aslen eyed Sage. "No offense, but are we really sure we can entrust the care of thousands of lives to one little girl?"

Sage narrowed her eyes. "My parents left me in charge for a reason. I may be young, but I'm not stupid. And other than Primos, my Station is the strongest and best protected."

"And look what happened to Primos," Aslen said. "Who's to say it won't happen to Brentor?"

"Primos fell from the inside out. It was probably Nevena who brought the tower down. I assure you, there is no way we could have a mole inside Brentor."

I knit my eyebrows together. Someone must have informed them of Sadira's theory. Or maybe they figured it out on their own.

The boy beside her nodded. "Our security is elite. No mole could get in."

"Nevena can get in anywhere," Ivy said. "I know because I can get in anywhere, and she was trained for longer than me."

"You overestimate your sister," the boy said.

"You overestimate your security," Ivy argued.

"Actually," I cut in. Everyone's eyes darted toward me, and I glanced down at my hands, hoping the trembling in my bones didn't reveal itself through my voice. "Nevena didn't blow up the tower. She showed up beside me barely a minute after the tower fell. The timing doesn't add up."

"Unless she had a remote detonator," Aslen said.

"I thought about that, too," I said. "But it was too far. It wouldn't have reached. Your technology is impressive, but I doubt even it can do that."

"If Nevena didn't set off the bombs," Aven said. "Then why did she run?"

"I don't know. Maybe she was involved somehow. Maybe she knew we would point fingers at her. I'm not saying she isn't guilty; I'm just saying that I don't think she's working alone."

Silence echoed my words. The Chieftains and Shadows were quiet, taking their time to digest what I'd just said. Amias took a seat on one of the lower benches across from me. His fists were clenched, his jaw set.

Why was he so angry? It's not like he really cared about traitors in the Rising. I knew him; he wouldn't lead the Rising unless he was hoping to gain something from it. But I couldn't ask him. He didn't trust me enough to tell me. He didn't even think I was me.

"There are two moles," Sage whispered. I didn't think she meant for everyone to hear it, but we did anyway.

"One of them could still be here," added the boy next to her.

We all looked at Amias. He didn't notice. He was staring at the flames, the golden light illuminating his wolf-like features.

"Amias?" Renna tilted her head.

He looked up. "What?"

"What are we going to do about the traitor?"

He glanced back at the flames. "Sage and Atlas, if your security is really as good as you say, then send small troops to each Station. They'll interview each person from Primos. Look at their backgrounds. Eden, Sander, Aven, Ivy, and I will go to the magic doctors and try to get them to join us in fighting the SSD. While I'm gone, Renna is in charge."

The room burst into a commotion of angry shouts.

"Another thirteen-year-old?" Asher exclaimed. "Before we know it, we're going to be ruled by babies!"

"Shut your faces!" Renna shouted. "I'm qualified. If any of you have a problem with that—" She paused, frowning. "If you have a problem with it, then keep it to yourself."

Amias nodded once. "You're all dismissed."

Angry grumbles floated around as the Chieftains and Shadows

made their way up and out of the room. I trailed behind Aven, my legs feeling ready to give out. My head pounded, and the ringing in my ears was back, but I ignored it.

When I left the room, I spotted Amias hurriedly making his way toward the forest.

I forced myself to speed up. "Amias!" I called. He didn't seem to hear me. I leaned into a jog. Pain splintered through my legs. "Amias!"

He turned.

I caught up to him, head throbbing hard enough to make my vision spot black.

"Should you be running?" he asked with only a slight bit of worry in his words.

"Probably not," I admitted. "Um, I need to ask you something. And I know you don't trust me, so you don't have to answer. It's fine if you don't want to—"

"What's the question?"

"Right. Um, why are you leading the Rising? Surely there's more to it than you being in the right place at the right time."

"Truth be told." His eyes darted around, and he lowered his voice. "Truth be told, I'm hoping we can defeat the SSD once and for all."

"You're going to use their army?" I asked.

He nodded. "Think about it. Their army, two Blood Bringers, a super spy, and the child of the Director. This is the most power we've had against them in… ever."

I nodded, unsure if he was telling the truth.

"I need to go," he said. "But I'll talk to you later." He smiled slightly and continued making his way toward the forest.

My heart dropped. He was lying. I had no doubt now. Because he'd smiled at me.

I would've followed him into the forest were it not for Aven tapping me on the shoulder.

"Where'd you go, man? I looked behind me and you were gone."

"I—I was talking to Amias."

They grabbed my elbow and began leading me back to the tent. I looked over my shoulder once, just in time to see Amias glance around before slipping into the darkness of the trees.

Department 1, Day 8

Some people have a way of sneaking into your heart and staying there. I, myself, believe in fate. My belief is that of a higher power guiding us with love toward where we need to be. If someone is meant to be in your life, then so they shall be.

Even through the struggles, the heartbreaks, and the pain, they will come back if they are meant to. There are many names for these types of people. Soulmate. Twin flame. And so on. But a single word alone cannot epitomize the true and entire definition.

The connection with this person is one that transcends the normalcy of commonplace relationships. Through whatever challenges, this person becomes your leading light. At times, it may be hard to see, but this person guides you to the best version of yourself. They are your reason. Your life. Even if you break apart, your person will find their way back to you, and you to them. Because that is how it was written.

Among this group of killers and thieves, Sander found his person. Deep down, he knew it but refused to accept it. However, love takes time.

To who ever may be reading this, if you find your person or people, for it may be many, never let go. Always fight for them. Even if they leave, trust that when the time is right, they will come back.

–Elyane

CHAPTER THIRTY-SIX

The next morning, Amias was acting strangely. He seemed absent from conversations, giving short answers and keeping quieter than usual. I could tell something was on his mind. Given the timing, I could only assume it had something to do with last night.

I didn't say anything despite him acting so apprehensive. I didn't want to falsely accuse him and have their suspicions of me raised. But worries plagued my thoughts. Though I couldn't bring myself to imagine anything too far-fetched, I couldn't help but wonder the extent of what he wasn't sharing.

After breakfast, we met at a rather large tent near the center of the camp. Full-length Mirrors lined the wall, and when I stepped inside, Eden was working on one near the flap, copying the symbols from a piece of paper in her hands.

My other friends had gathered in the middle, along with Sage, Kenneth, Sadira, and Libbie.

"We'll be back in a few days," Amias told the Chieftains and Renna. "Keep the Mirrors guarded. Don't let any strangers through unless they're with a Chieftain or a Shadow you know."

I shifted my backpack as I approached Sadira and Libbie. It was heavier than usual but still relatively light. Along with my sketchbook and sweatshirt, I'd shoved in a gun Eden had snuck into my possession last night, the knife Sadira had given me, and a bag of chips I'd found in the tent. I didn't really care whose they were.

"Are you packed?" Sadira asked, worry in her bottle-green eyes. She wasn't coming with me. Neither was Libbie. Amias worried they wouldn't be much help and hadn't wanted to be responsible for them.

I nodded, pulling her into a hug and trying to savor the warmth her company brought. "I don't really have much, but yeah. I'm as prepared as I can be without knowing what it's going to be like."

"Cold," Eden said from her spot by the Mirror. "And windy."

"Helpful," I muttered. "I meant people-wise. Are they nice?"

"Do not anger their goddess," she advised. "They will bleed you dry and throw you off a cliff." Her expression was calm. I couldn't tell if she was joking or not.

"That's nice," Libbie said, turning to Sadira with wide eyes.

My twin mouthed to me, "Is she joking?"

I shrugged.

The fear in their eyes only grew.

"I'll be fine," I assured. "I'll just do what she says. I won't anger their goddess."

Amias approached us. "Are you ready?" he asked me, ignoring my sister and her best friend entirely.

I glanced around the room. "I thought my Reflection was coming with us."

He shrugged. "Renna will take care of him."

I frowned at the sudden change but turned my attention to Sadira as she pulled me into another hug.

"I love you, Sander," she said into my ear, her voice sorrowful. "Don't die."

I smiled as she pulled back. "I can't promise anything. And I love you too."

Eden finished the last symbol and rose, brushing off her legs. She stuck her arm through the Mirror, and the familiar silvery liquid rippled around her wrist. Aven gave Eden a thumbs-up.

"I call first," Ivy said and slung her bag over her shoulders. She didn't wait for a response before stepping through the Mirror. Aven followed. Eden then gestured for me.

I stepped up.

"Are you feeling okay?" she asked.

I nodded despite the persistent headache pounding in my skull.

"Perfect. Hopefully, you do not die." She began pushing me toward the Mirror.

I dug my heels into the ground. "Whoa, whoa, whoa. What do you mean, *hopefully* I don't die?"

She pulled her hands away, causing me to stumble, and sighed. "Jumping between dimensions is physically demanding. In your weakened state, I am not sure how easy it will be for you to make it through."

"And you couldn't have told me this before?" I exclaimed.

"No time like the present to try something new," Amias grumbled, and he shoved me forward.

I stumbled into the Mirror. A boulder of white-hot pain slammed into me. I let out a pained cry. My vision darkened. My head felt as if it were going to explode. My brain pushed against the edges of my skull, begging for release.

I would've screamed if I could, but the breath had been snatched from my lungs. For a minute, I thought I saw a flash of an unfamiliar face, but it faded faster than I could register. Panic seized my heart, wondering if it had been my father trying to welcome me to the afterlife.

I brought my hands to my head and took a step forward. My feet hit solid ground. I opened my eyes, not realizing I'd had them closed. The pain only intensified. I caught a glimpse of rocky walls and Ivy's terrified expression before I crumpled, unconscious.

It felt like a century had passed when my eyes finally opened, but according to Eden, who sat beside me in a chair writing in a leather-bound journal, it had only been a few hours.

I lay on a small, wooden-framed bed covered in thick wool blankets. Underneath the bed, the tan and black pelt of an unrecognizable animal sprawled across the stone flooring. The stone continued up the walls and ceiling as if the room had been carved right into the side of a mountain. Given the way the exit of the room led to a dim tunnel, it seemed very possible. Golden light illuminated the room, coming from the few dozen lanterns that hung from the curved ceiling.

There was very little furniture as well. A small couch to my left and a desk to my right. My backpack had been thrown onto the desk, which Eden currently had her feet on. She leaned back and set the leather journal down.

"How are you feeling?"

I raised my eyebrows, realizing the headache had faded. It wasn't gone, but it had lessened. "Um, actually not too bad."

She smiled. "Good. Can you stand?"

I did so, then nodded.

She grabbed my arm and led me into the stone hallway.

"Where's Amias?" I asked.

She arched an eyebrow.

"Um," I coughed. "And everyone else."

Eden chuckled, a deep, pleasant sound I'd heard before and had grown to love. "They're waiting for you."

The walk was short. We strode through long, winding tunnels, all illuminated by strings of lanterns. We passed about a dozen more rooms before the tunnels began off-shooting and stretching further away. The air began to change. The chilled, smoky breeze I'd felt before began to get even colder. A breeze whistled through the tunnels, stirring the lanterns.

As we walked, I began to notice shapes taking form on the walls. Pictures of dragons, birds, and stars had been carved into the stone. I wondered how long it must've taken to finish. Years, probably. I wouldn't be surprised if it had taken a century. They were deeply intricate so much so that they seemed to be real. As if the dragons would step off the wall and begin walking beside me.

Every now and then, tunnels would merge and grow, and soon, we stepped into a room large enough to fit half a football field.

The wall to my right fell away, revealing a stunning view. As I'd guessed earlier, we were in the mountains. A rounded ledge shot out approximately fifty feet over a valley. The ledge contained what looked like a rounded, sunken auditorium, much like the wooden room we'd met in with the Chieftains.

Unlike in the tunnels, there were people out here. People that looked like Eden. They were dressed heavily in furs and leather, some with hats that covered pointed ears.

I was in awe. I barely noticed the frigid wind until Eden wrapped a long coat around me. I thanked her, and she led me to the group of people before us.

There weren't a lot of them. Five or six, at first glance. I was entranced by the white swirls and lines that adorned their dark complexions. I found myself staring as the eldest of the group, a stout man, greeted Eden with a bowed head. He then raised his gaze to me, wrinkles creasing as he smiled warmly.

The words that came from his mouth seemed like gibberish, but from his tone, it sounded like a hello.

"He does not speak our language," Eden clarified when she saw the ignorance on my face.

The old man blinked in confusion, then spoke again. This time, in English. "Ah, my apologies, young one. I merely wished you a warm welcome."

I nodded, too stunned to speak.

It didn't faze this man, and he simply gestured toward the auditorium. "Your companions are waiting."

Eden and I made for the auditorium. A group of people I recognized sat by the fire in the bottom of the pit.

When Amias turned and saw me, I nearly tripped and fell down the seemingly endless staircase. He'd taken a shower. Even from the distance, I could tell. I tried and failed to remember the last time he'd done that. His black hair whipped around in the harsh wind. He wore sweatpants and a thick wool coat that hung to his shins.

"You look like you're feeling better," Ivy noted as we approached.

I nodded through the off-beat thrumming in my head. The pain was still there, but not nearly as intense as before. "Yeah. I am. Where are we?"

If anyone answered, their replies were cut off by a devastating roar that seemed to shake the entire mountain. I stumbled.

Then, when I began to search for the source of the noise, a scaly, winged figure shot up from behind the ledge. A gust of wind slammed into us, putting the fire out and sending anyone standing to the ground.

Impossibly huge talons landed on the edge of the auditorium. Wings flapped and folded against the side of the body.

I blinked. Apparently, there was a reason for all the dragon carvings.

The gray dragon shook out its head, causing dirt to rain down on us. I pinched myself to make sure I wasn't dreaming.

Beside me, Eden was beaming. "Welcome to Avrix," she said. "Land of the Moonstone Healers, homeland of the Moon Goddess Lua, and my birthplace."

"God," Amias muttered to himself, an almost wistful expression carved onto his features as he stared at the drop below. "Renna would love this."

I sat on the edge of the cliff, peering at the dozens of dragons that flapped through the valley below. We'd exited the auditorium when the dragons arrived, racing to higher peaks for better views of the creatures that soared through the valley and beyond. Amias and Aven stood on either side of me, pointing out each new beast that appeared. Ivy was talking with Eden a few feet away. The wind blew away their voices, yet I strained to hear them.

"Maybe we can show her when this is all over," Aven offered, somewhat hopefully.

I doubted that this would ever be over, but I bit back my thoughts as Amias started to complain.

"Eden," he whined. "What's taking so long? I thought these people were supposed to be important. Doesn't that mean they shouldn't keep guests waiting?"

Her boots scuffed against stone as she sat down behind me. "We barge into their home unannounced, and you have the audacity to demand their lord's presence? It is a miracle we were not thrown in prison."

I wasn't sure what we were waiting for. For once, I wasn't anxious about it. The land around me was one from a dream. It zapped my worries away as quickly as they came.

I lay down, embracing the way the wind seemed to blow away the pain lacing my muscles and skull. There wasn't a single thought in my head as I stared up at the gloomy sky, watching a distant dragon dance through the dark clouds.

It wasn't until the elderly man I'd previously met came to announce that the people we were waiting for had arrived that I allowed myself to be pulled from the peace.

I rose, brushing off my pants and helping Aven with the dirt on their back.

"Stand straight," Eden hissed at Amias. "Pretend like you have some manners."

On the far side of the platform, a man finished his ascent of a flight of stairs hugging the mountainside and stepped onto the flat stone landing. A metal crown vanished into long, braided white hair, from which poked a set of pointed ears. A step behind him, a plump woman with white spirals beneath her eyes struggled to keep up with his long, purposeful strides.

Beside me, Eden trembled.

I wasn't sure why she was so nervous, but I squeezed her hand anyway. She leaned into my touch gratefully.

The couple stopped a few feet away from us, greeting the group of people that I'd first seen. The man with the metal crown swept his gray eyes across our group, not seeming to notice Eden. Probably because she had half-hidden herself behind me. Also, because his gaze lingered on Amias, who stood in front of us in a position of authority.

"Many apologies," the man spoke. The richness of his voice carried over to us on the wind. His white markings were like a strap across his nose, as well as a line connecting his lower lip to his chin. "Had I known we were having visitors today, I would have freed my schedule."

It was Amias who spoke first. "You are not the one who has to apologize. We should've sent word before coming here."

"And may I ask, how did you come here?" His eyes narrowed. "Your language and appearance suggest you are not from Eprijuan or any other nearby kingdoms."

"Indeed, we are not. We've come from another universe in seek of your assistance, both medically and in battle."

His mouth tightened. "I find it ill-mannered that you have not introduced yourself."

I swallowed. Now, I was nervous.

Amias lowered his head. "My name is Amias Wolf, and these are my—"

A collective gasp went through their group. "Amias." The name rippled through the air, followed by a tense silence.

The silence was broken when the man with the crown reached for a blade. "Amias Wolf. I'm afraid I'm going to have to ask you to leave."

Amias bared his teeth. "You've heard of me."

"Blood Bringer," the man spat. "An omen of death to thousands."

Amias sighed. "Sir, please. I don't work for the SSD. Not

anymore."

"Leave, or we will kill you." His companions drew blades and swords, which had lurked beneath their heavy coats. The crowned man stepped in front of the woman with whom he'd entered.

Both Ivy and Aven reached for their guns, but Amias shook his head at them.

"We're not here for a fight."

"I will not ask again. Depart from this world immediately."

"Please—"

The man hurled his blade. Had it not been for a dark hand that wrapped around the handle, it would've gone straight through Amias's throat.

Eden lifted her head and tossed the dagger to the ground. "Fighting is impractical. We come on behalf of peace."

The man's face went slack. A ghost of a name formed on his lips. He cleared his throat and tried again. "Adar?"

The woman shoved the man aside. Tears filled her eyes almost instantly as she locked eyes with Eden.

Eden smiled. "Eth ek ka kothrar."

Shocked murmurs swept through the crowd that had gathered behind the man.

"Aham," the man brought a hand to his mouth. "Aham, ur horrems eth rok baam ku rums kemca e'qa kaam iui." Both the man and the woman held out their arms, and Eden raced forward. She tripped and fell into their embrace, laughing with delight.

"Please tell me I'm not the only one who didn't understand a thing they just said," Aven grumbled.

No one replied to them.

Eden pulled away from the man and gestured to us. "Vo vo, thraka ora ki kreamhk."

She then addressed us. "Friends, please allow me to introduce my parents, Lord Osiris and Lady Nerezza of Avrix."

Ivy gaped at Eden. "What?"

Amias's jaw dropped. "Are you kidding me?" Fury bristled beneath his words. He was going to start yelling.

I grabbed his arm. "Shut up," I said. "Don't say anything you'll regret."

He glared at me but snapped his mouth closed as the lord approached us.

"I offer my apologies. Had I known you came with my daughter—"

"Excuse me," Aven cut in. Hands on their hips, they faced Eden with a look of betrayal. "You're telling me this whole time you were a goddamn princess and declined to inform us?"

Eden laughed, then clapped a hand over her mouth. "I am no princess."

"Your dad is a lord. If not princess, then you're some kind of royalty."

She dismissed them with a wave of her hand. "We have more important matters at hand. Please, Aven, let us not get sidetracked."

Aven grunted but didn't argue.

"As Amias said," Eden turned to her father. "A dear friend of ours has been injured, and we are unable to seek help from other places. Avrix's medicinal expertise is—"

"Say no more." Lord Osiris smiled. He then turned to me. "I am assuming this is the one who has been injured?"

"Is the bruise that noticeable?" I muttered under my breath as he approached.

He took me in and nodded to himself. Then, he brushed his calloused fingers over my bruised face. I did my best to resist pulling away, both from the pain that sparked at his touch and the unease I felt at being so close to a stranger. Sensing my discomfort, he drew back.

"Your name?" he asked.

"Sander. Sander Fox."

He tilted his head. A look I couldn't comprehend crossed his face. Fear? Recognition? Maybe both. He turned to face his wife, who had an equally perplexing expression.

"Sander Fox," he mused. "Interesting."

My eyebrows knit together. "Excuse me?"

He turned back to Amias. "We can fix him, but it won't come freely."

"Papa—" Eden started.

He sent her a glance. One that I couldn't read. She fell silent. "You are a Blood Bringer," he stated. "I would like it if you would let a few of my people take a look at you."

"Why?" Amias bristled. "So, you can poke at my brain and see how it works?"

"No," Eden's dad said bluntly, unruffled by Amias's outburst. "I believe your story could be of use to our intelligence group."

"He'll do it," Ivy cut in, then sent Amias a silent threat with her dark eyes. He straightened but didn't argue. "But unfortunately, the other Blood Bringer is back at our camp. She's trying to keep everything under control while the Major's gone."

"*Ivy*," Aven hissed.

Her eyes widened when she realized what she'd said.

"The Major's gone?" Lord Osiris asked.

"Um, no," Ivy stammered. "He's just…"

"He's missing," Amias grumbled. "The SSD attacked Primos, and now he's gone. As is his Shadow, Nevena."

Eden's dad was quiet, his hand resting on his daughter's shoulder. Then, he nodded to himself and addressed Amias and Eden. "We shall bring Sander to our healers now. They can get started right away. As for the rest of you, please allow us to help you get settled in."

Lord Osiris and Lady Nerezza gestured for me to follow them. I glanced back at Eden warily, but she waved me on. I trailed them through the maze of lantern-lit tunnels. How they managed not to get lost, I couldn't understand.

The ground sloped, and we descended deeper into the mountain.

It got warmer, I noticed. Every now and then, a faint roar from outside would shake the ground. Despite the… unnatural elements of Avrix, it felt surprisingly comfortable. It felt like a home. And to Eden, it was.

She was home. Her family was here. This was where she had been born. This was where she'd grown up. Her friends were here. I wondered if she was even planning on leaving. I wouldn't be surprised if she wasn't. In fact, as much as I wanted her to come back with us, she'd be happier here.

Eventually, we stepped into a larger cave. I was immediately washed with a sense of calmness. Serenity. I wasn't sure what it was that made me feel that way. Low-set beds lined the edge of the circular room and were covered in white sheets and gray knitted blankets. A red and brown crochet carpet covered most of the rocky ground, stopping at the end of the beds. On the far wall, a curtain had been hung over the entrance to another cave, and behind it, I heard voices.

Eden's mother grabbed my hands; her own were warm and calloused. "I am Nerezza. The lead healer. I shall do my best to help."

I nodded my thanks.

She chuckled and gestured for me to sit on a nearby bed. She inspected the bruise, using gentle hands to tilt my head. "My dear, you have suffered a severe head injury. Would you mind telling me how this happened?"

"I hit myself in the head with a board," I said. Her eyebrows knit in confusion. It took me a moment to realize how that sounded. "I—I didn't hit *myself*. It… My Reflection attacked me."

Nerezza raised her eyebrows. "You have experienced an encounter with your Reflection?"

I nodded again.

"That is pretty rare," Osiris cut in. I jumped, having forgotten he was there. "The few who have talked to their Reflection…" he trailed off, his expression solemn.

A sudden chill ran through me. "What happened?"

He shook himself out, then smiled. "Nothing. It is not important."

I eyed him but didn't push him.

Nerezza spent some time peppering me with questions about my injury, asking mainly about my symptoms. Though she spent some time inquiring about my Reflection. I suspected she was just curious.

She rubbed an oil across my face that smelled of mint, a scent so strong I sneezed. But the pain lessened. After she mentioned that was all she could do for the day, we continued talking.

She felt like a fireplace after coming home from playing in the snow. Such a comforting feeling. One that reminded me much of my own mother. By the time dinner rolled around, I'd nearly told her my entire life story.

We met in the sunken auditorium for dinner. It was just the five of us, along with Eden's parents, both of whom sat beside their daughter, utter joy written across their faces as their laughs echoed through the valley.

The fire blazed before me, the tips of the flames reaching my shoulders.

"This is delicious," Aven said through a mouthful of steak and potatoes. "Thank you."

Nerezza inclined her head. "We are most grateful for you bringing our daughter back."

Besides me, Ivy shifted uncomfortably. "But that's not the only reason we came here."

Lord Osiris cleared his throat. "Correct. Let us address the matters at hand now, shall we?"

Amias informed them of our situation. At times, Aven or Ivy would interrupt and add something. I stayed silent, focusing on my food as Amias spoke about Primos falling and Sadira's theory about Nevena.

Silence hung heavily in the air after Amias finished.

It was Osiris who spoke first. "You come here asking for our alliance, knowing we have turned down the SSD in the past?"

Amias nodded.

The lord continued, "The Director's child." He turned to Aven. "You were there. Do you not remember why we refused?"

They shook their head. "No, sir. I was pretty young."

"Hm. I suppose you were." He sighed and leaned back, resting a hand over his eyes. "It was not the first time those from another realm came to us when the Director came to offer friendship. She claimed she wished to catalog and study our world. However, she was after something else."

He gestured to his wife, who held out her hand, palm open. The white swirls and curves along her skin began to glow.

I gaped in astonishment as the silver light illuminated the darkness around us.

Then, Osiris pointed to the night sky, where we could just see the moon peeking through the clouds.

"Our world was created by the gods. Avrix, our home, was the place where the Moon Goddess chose to lay her roots. She blessed our kind with a drop of her powers.

"It was power that the Director wanted, for she had not come across a world with such a close connection to the divine. Our gods had made this so. The chance of her coming here... " He looked down, a shadow falling across his face. "It was only because of a mistake someone made. She was playing with the power of the multiverse and opened a connection to the SSD."

A chill ran down my spine. Something about the images Osiris was painting was hauntingly familiar, and yet, I couldn't place memory behind the feeling.

"Due to this, the SSD discovered they had limited access to the multiverse. But we, however, were free to go wherever we wished."

Eden rested her hand atop her father's, sympathy falling across her features.

"And so, under the illusion of friendship, the SSD gained our trust. The truth was revealed by a young man who had once worked closely with the Director. Overcome by guilt and fear, he helped us hide this power." His gaze flitted to me. My blood went cold. "The SSD has not come back since."

"What happened to the man who helped you?" Aven asked.

Osiris sighed. "He left. Claimed he wanted to live a life before the SSD found him."

Amias's face was white. "The SSD doesn't have free access to the multiverse?" His voice was low. I could see the terror in his eyes, brought to life by the reflection of the fire.

"No," Osiris replied. "And I can see you understand the tragedy that would befall this world and many others should they gain that freedom."

"Which is why we need to stop them." Amias shook himself out. "With your help, we could. You said it yourself; you have powers—"

"Boy." Osiris's voice was hard. "The secrets of these powers lie among my kind. By fighting with you, we would be getting ourselves involved with the SSD again. It is a risk I cannot take."

"But—"

He held up his hand. "I said no."

I was about to speak. I was going to plead for their help. I would get on my knees if that's what it took. But I was interrupted when a woman came running down the stairs.

She bowed before the lord and lady. "Sodfe ke fet. Wertchum zal Lua utame opine."

Eden's eyes widened.

Osiris shot to his feet. He faced us. "There's been a disturbance on the Northern Borders. I must go." He began to depart, then turned to address Amias one last time. "You may stay until Sander is healed. That is as far as my hospitality will go."

CHAPTER THIRTY-SEVEN

The headache returned as a dull throbbing in the back of my eyes. The oil that smelled of mint was chilled by a small breeze, and I resisted the urge to rub it.

Our group had dispersed after dinner. Eden had run after her parents, Ivy only a few steps behind her. As for Aven and Amias, I hadn't seen where they'd gone. I'd stayed by the fire for as long as I could manage, the wind nipping at my skin despite the flames before me.

Unlimited access to the multiverse.

I understood why Osiris couldn't risk fighting with us. But we could take precautions. We wouldn't send fighters who knew about the whereabouts of this power.

Still, there were many uncertainties. Hazards we wouldn't be able to predict.

I wasn't sure where my alliances lay. I knew it wasn't with the SSD. I wasn't entirely sure it was with the Rising, either. But when Osiris had said no, I would've done just about anything to get him to change his mind. If only because of the looks on my friend's faces.

I traced the carvings on the walls, distracting myself with the delicate patterns as I made my way back to the hall with my room.

I wanted to go home. That's what I had wanted before. But now, with Mom missing and Sadira back at camp, I wasn't sure where home was anymore.

Then, I had to ask myself, where did I want home to be? *Who* did I want home to be?

Mama. Sadira. My friends.

I had no chance of going back to my life before. I knew that now. This feeling, the drop in my stomach, the way my heartbeat seemed too slow and too fast at the same time, I'd felt it all before when I was lying in the hospital bed the morning after Dad had died.

I hated it.

It was the same thing all over again. I couldn't do anything. I had no plans. I was too scared to fight.

I wanted to run away and hide like I'd done in the bathroom. Like I'd done every time something in my life got a little bit stressful.

Amias was right. I truly was a coward. And I was surrounded by fighters.

Footsteps echoed in the tunnel behind me.

My heart leaped to my throat, and I spun. An empty lantern-lit tunnel greeted me.

"Hello?" I called out, but no one answered.

I frowned and turned back around, only to run straight into a muscled figure. Pain burst through my bruise, and I pulled away, frantically apologizing. My voice fell away when I looked up at Amias.

"Hey." He was unruffled. "Where were you?"

"Outside," I replied, neck flushing. "By the fire."

"Oh. You smell like smoke."

"That's probably why." I tilted my head. "Are you okay?"

He shrugged. "Disappointed. It's okay, though. We can take down the SSD without help from Avrix."

I swallowed the question in my throat.

Amias noticed. "Say it."

"Why fight at all?" I blurted. "The SSD can't get us here, right? Why can't we just stay?"

He clenched his fists. For a long moment, he was silent, contemplating his answer. Finally, he said, "No one else is going to. Someone has to give those shitholes what they deserve."

There it was. That little drop in my stomach. I dug my nails into my palm.

"Oh." It was all I could say.

He looked me up and down. "You don't have to fight with us, Foxy. You have nothing to do with it. Believe me, I'd understand if you bailed right now."

The next words to come out of my mouth were possibly the stupidest words I could've ever said. I knew that, even before I spoke, but I couldn't help it. The look in his eyes… that deep blue filled with heartache.

"I'll fight with you. Until the end."

The smile that lit his face was something I had never seen and wished I could see forever. He held out his pinkie. "Pinkie promise?"

"Pinkie promise." I couldn't help the small curve of my lips as I grasped his pinkie with my own. "Why do I feel like you're warming up to me?"

He glanced down; his silence answered enough.

I bit my lip to keep from smiling and yet still failed. "So, you believe it's me."

The corner of his mouth bent, and he turned away slightly. "Don't get too comfortable. I still don't trust you."

"You don't trust anyone," I said.

He chuckled but tilted his head in agreement.

"Night, Wolf," I said and gave a small salute. I pushed past him and began making my way to my room.

"Night, Fox." His voice was soft enough that I thought I had imagined it.

I was awoken by a tray of breakfast being set down on the table beside my bed. Eyes opening groggily, I managed to get a glimpse of Nerezza's smile before she slipped out through the bearskin curtain.

I felt like absolute shit. My skull throbbed, my neck ached, and my feet felt like they were going to fall off. Nerezza had warned me that her treatment would have these side effects, but I hadn't cared at the time. It would be worth it, though, she'd also said, because I'd be completely healed within the week. Which, scientifically, was impossible, but I'd begun to think impossible didn't exist. Especially now that my life consisted of traveling between universes.

Before I could finish my breakfast, which consisted of eggs, something that looked like oatmeal but tasted more like pumpkin bread, and peppermint tea, Aven came to announce that Eden was looking for us.

Eden said she wanted to show us something, so we followed her to a set of stairs tucked on the far side of the mountain. The trek did nothing to help the ache in my bones, but my heart lifted when I saw the others already waiting for us.

"When is your dad going to be back?" Ivy asked Eden as we approached.

Eden shrugged. "He declined to give me the details. It could be days or weeks."

"Where'd he go?" Amias asked.

"Northern border. To check out the disturbance." She put air quotes around the last word. One of the most human things I'd seen her do.

"You don't think anything's really going on?" I rubbed my forehead.

"I am unsure." Eden sighed. "However, I do know he is not telling us everything."

Aven shifted. "Anyways," they said. "You wanted to show us something?"

Eden nodded. "Sander especially. Since we have the opportunity, I would like to give you all a tour of my home."

Eden led us into a dark corridor lit by lanterns strung along the walls. The sound of the wind dulled as we ascended an endless flight of stone stairs.

"There are a bunch of places I wish to show you, but we shall start with the hatchery." She smiled at me. It didn't reach her eyes. "I used to spend all day up here."

"Hmph," Aven grunted. "What could possibly be worth all these stairs?" They brushed a blonde strand of hair out of their eyes. "By the way, Sander, why did Amias want your sister to stay behind? And her friend, Lily?"

"Libbie," I corrected. "He didn't want them ruining our chances at a possible ally." I was glad Libbie wasn't here. She would've complained endlessly.

Aven frowned.

"Not getting too attached to Sander's sister, are we, Aven?" Amias chuckled.

Aven lifted a brow at me. "Would you be upset if I did?"

"No," I replied truthfully. "But I would strongly advise against it."

"Why? Because you'd beat me up if I hurt her?"

I laughed. "Because she'd beat you up. And let me tell you this, she's sent more than one guy to the hospital because they hurt her."

Aven swallowed. "Oh."

"But by all means," I said. "Break her heart. It'd be fun to see her shatter your hip bone."

Their face had gone pale. "Did she actually do that?"

I nodded, grinning at the memory of her ex-boyfriend stumbling frantically out of our apartment after she'd found out he'd cheated.

"Date her," Ivy said. "I'd like to see how it turns out."

"I wouldn't." Aven rubbed their eyes. "I really wouldn't."

Ivy laughed.

We arrived at the hatchery a few minutes later.

There was already someone in there—a girl a bit younger than me with long, wavy brown hair. The strands in front of her face had been braided and tied behind her head and dotted with small white flowers. She blinked at us from behind dark eyelashes and bowed her head at Eden.

The two of them exchanged a few words in Avrix's language, then the girl turned to us.

"I am Daesyn. Pleasure to meet you all."

We said our greetings, and she gestured for us to follow her through a blue-tinted glass door lined with branches. A wave of stuffy heat washed over me when I stepped inside.

"We need to keep it warm for the hatchlings," she informed us. "Their scales aren't fully formed, so they have trouble producing and maintaining body heat." Her accent was thick, the English words tumbling off her tongue sloppily.

I took in the room. A few feet to my right, the floor dropped away. When I peered over the ledge, I saw the room continued down for a few levels, connected by a spiraling wooden staircase. A long window stretched along the far wall of those stories, showing off the rest of the mountain range, which continued into the horizon.

But the view wasn't the thing that took my breath away. It was the dragons.

They came in all shapes and sizes, scampering around the room and staircase as if they were puppies. A few of the larger ones flapped their wings unsteadily. The highest level, the one we were on, was empty of dragons.

Daesyn pointed to my left. The back of the room had been layered with smooth, black stones, sitting atop a crackling pile of embers. On top of the stones, however, were shimmering oval-shaped eggs.

"Oh wow," I whispered and took a hesitant step toward them.

"It is okay," Daesyn assured. "You may take a closer look. Just don't touch."

I bent down in front of the eggs, holding in a breath. The eggs were large, approximately twice the size of a basketball. They varied from shades of lavender and deep blue to the darkest black. One of them, a greenish-blue that changed colors depending on the angle of the light, had begun to crack.

I turned to face Daesyn, then nearly fell backward when I realized she'd crouched down beside me. She giggled lightly.

"How long do they take to hatch?"

She shrugged. "It depends quite a lot on the type of dragon. Most take seven to eight months."

"There are different types?" I asked. "Like fire dragons? And earth dragons?"

She frowned and gave a small shake of her head, then led me over to the drop-off. Eden had led the others down the stairs and was messing with a dragon just beneath us.

Daesyn pointed to a smaller dragon perched on a ledge and gnawing on what looked like a bone. The dragon was blue, with horns that curved like a ram.

"Her name is Laylyn. I am unsure of how to say it in your language…"

"Ablaninan Ridgeback," Eden finished for her.

Daesyn sent her a grateful look. "Yes. They were raised and bred in the chilly lands of Ablana. Rare creatures. Solitary, too. She is only here because one of our hunting troops discovered her mother wounded in a cave. If it were not for them taking care of her, Laylyn wouldn't have survived."

"She's beautiful," I said, admiring the shining indigo scales.

"She is." Daesyn nodded approvingly, then began leading me down the stairs.

I ran my hand along the wooden railing, following the staircase as it curved around a tree growing through the middle of the hatchery. This room was easily one of the most breathtaking rooms I'd ever stepped into, despite it being mostly made of simple stone and wood.

The dragons crowded around us curiously, and I felt my heart rate rise in excitement. It was like being surrounded by fire-breathing, winged, scaly puppies. One of them brushed up against my leg, and I nearly jumped.

At the bottom of the stairs, the floor was carpeted with pelts of different animals. A few of the dragons perched on a small bench by the window, their snouts pressed against the glass. I smiled.

Daesyn bent down in front of them, and they attacked her joyfully. She laughed. I bent down beside her, but they were more cautious with me.

I held out my hand to a deep green one, who took a hesitant step forward. He sniffed my fingers, then decided I was decent. He leaned the top of his head into my hands. I had the urge to scratch him, just like I would a dog, but the rough scales underneath my fingertips stopped me from doing so.

"We should go." Aven looked around nervously. They stood in the far corner, almost pressing themself against the wall. Ivy knelt in front of them, playing gently with a cluster of baby dragons. She answered them without turning.

"Don't tell me you're scared of the dragons." She chuckled, then addressed the one in front of her, "You're not scary, are you? No, you're as scary as a puppy."

"I'm not scared," they insisted, gritting their teeth.

"Really?" Eden laughed, who held a smaller one in her arms. She approached Aven and held the dragon out to them. "Take her."

They shook their head and took a small step away. Then, they looked down, let out a shriek, and jumped. A dragon, one who had been chewing on Aven's pant leg, sniffed and fluffed its wings, then walked away defiantly.

Aven closed their eyes and pressed their head against the stone. "Can we *please* get out of here?"

Daesyn smiled and rose. "Follow me."

"Oh, thank god," they muttered and pushed past Eden, nearly knocking the dragon from her arms.

"What is your problem with them?" Ivy asked as we followed Daesyn through a gated door on the bottom level.

"They remind me of goats," Aven muttered.

"Do you have something against goats?"

They glared at her. "They're creepy. They have stupid, creepy little eyes and weird mouths. And horns." They shuddered. "And they eat your hair while you're sleeping. And then you wake up, and their face and demon-spawned eyes are just—" They held their hands close to their face, "—right there."

Ivy broke into a fit of laughter. "When did something like that happen to you?" she asked breathlessly.

They pinched the bridge of their nose. "I've gone with Amias and Renna on a few of their slightly less dangerous 'missions' before."

Eden grinned. After giving Daesyn our thanks, we followed the princess of Avrix up another set of stairs.

It wasn't long before we got to the top.

"Holy…" Aven didn't finish their sentence. There was no need. No words could describe the view that was spread out before us.

It felt like we were on top of the world.

Gray clouds blanketed the sky. A fog had settled over the mountain ranges. The mountain we stood on was by far the largest in the range and didn't yet have snow on it. I had assumed it was fall when we'd arrived, but it was hard to tell so far up in the mountains.

The wind swept through my hair, rippling my clothes. I'd thought it had been cold down there, but this was a whole new level.

Eden grinned and reached into a nook in the stone. She pulled out a large, pink conch shell and pressed it to her lips. The sound it produced reminded me of a whale's call, only deeper. After she finished, silence filled the air. But a few moments later, a distant roar called out in response.

Then, behind one of the closer mountains, a large figure emerged and began making its way toward us.

"Don't get so nervous," Eden warned Aven. "Shana is friendly."

Shana, it turned out, was even more beautiful than the view.

She was a Rubied Frostback, Eden told us. A dragon breed that typically lived in the Southern or Northern poles. Shana was smaller than the first dragon I'd seen, maybe two or three times the size of a horse. Gray-blue scales lined most of her body, along with a strip of bright red down her spine. Spirals danced on the underside of her pale, almost translucent wings. White horns curved upward, and a snow-colored mane trailed along her neck, flapping as she neared.

Eden pushed us backward as Shana landed, for there wasn't much room for a dragon on the balcony.

"The big ones aren't so bad," Aven said.

Shana whisked her pointed tail back and forth, bending so her snout was nearly pressed against us. Eden grinned.

"Hello, baby," she crooned happily and set her hand on Shana's scales. The big beast leaned into her touch. "I missed you."

"Wait." Ivy narrowed her eyes. "You're telling me Shana is—"

"Mine," Eden finished for her. "Yes. We bonded when I was four."

"Bonded?" I prompted.

"Dragons are more complex than most animals out there," Eden explained. "They have feelings and emotions rather than just instincts. You see, when they first emerge from their egg, they automatically begin searching for their mother. In the wild, their mother is right beside them. But here in Avrix, we have riders in need of mounts. They wait beside their chosen egg until the dragon has hatched. When the dragon begins to search for his mother, they find the human instead. Most of the time, they bond with them. Just as Shana and I did."

"Most of the time?" I prompted, tentatively reaching to pet Shana. She eyed me warily but let me stroke her snout.

"Yes. There are times when the dragon knows that the person in front of them is not a good person. If the person is mean or loud, they tend to try to escape."

"You call them complex creatures," Amias said. "But they can't even tell a human apart from a dragon?"

Eden shook her head. "That is not what happens. If their mother is not there, they bond with the thing closest to a mother. It does not matter what species. I have even seen a dragon bond with a dog."

"Oh wow," I said and pulled away from Shana. She snorted, blowing smoke onto all of us. I coughed and blew the smoke away. When it cleared, Shana had her front legs curled underneath her and had turned her neck away. "What's she doing?"

"She wants you to ride," Eden said.

"I—What?"

She grinned and grabbed my hand. "Come. Let me show you the world from the view of a dragon."

"I can't," I said and pulled away. "What if I fall off?"

"She will catch you," Eden replied and tied her hair back. "I promise, you will not die."

I eyed the beast, who was flicking her tail impatiently. As much as I trusted Eden, I wasn't sure if she was telling the truth. And how could she know? Maybe Shana would have a heart attack midair, and we'd fall and die. Could dragons even have heart attacks?

"I don't know," I said.

"Just go, you chicken," Amias said and shoved me forward. "How many chances are you going to get to ride a dragon?"

He was right. I'd missed out on once-in-a-lifetime opportunities before; I wasn't about to make the same mistake again.

I nodded toward Eden and she grinned, then raced back inside. I went with her, and she pulled a saddle and goggles from a cupboard tucked in a corner I hadn't seen earlier. As she began strapping it to Shana, I stared at the drop in horror, my stomach in knots and my heart in my throat. Then, Amias patted my back, peering over the ledge beside me.

"On the bright side," he said. "If you die, you won't have to fight a war."

"You're so helpful," I muttered.

He laughed. "Relax, Fox. It'll be fun. You should live once in a while. Don't be a scared mouse inside your little bubble your whole life."

"Is that what you tell yourself when you're about to do something stupid?" I asked him.

He shrugged. "I used to. Now, it's just a voice in the back of my mind saying, 'Well, hey, if you do die during this, at least it'll be a cool death.'"

I rolled my eyes and began walking back toward Eden.

"And it works," Amias called after me.

"I'm sure it does," I grumbled.

Eden handed me a pair of leather-strapped goggles. I put them on and followed her onto Shana's back. Her scales were hard underneath my hands as I climbed up her forearm. I felt bad, stepping all over her, but she didn't seem to care.

Once settled in the saddle with Eden in front of me, I suddenly felt a wave of panic rush over me. I wanted to get off, but it was too late. Shana rose and unfolded her glassy, spiral-patterned wings.

I'd never ridden a horse before, but I imagined it felt something like this. The tilting as Shana turned, the way I leaned forward when she bent down. It felt like I wasn't in control of my body.

"Put your hands around my waist," Eden instructed. I did so, touching gently. She sighed and pulled them tighter. "You will fall off if you do not hold on."

"Got it," I said.

"Come on, Shana," Eden patted the dragon's side. "Let us give him a ride he won't forget."

Shana tilted her head back, a low growl rumbling through her throat. She shifted her footing, folded in her wings, and promptly stepped off the edge of the cliff.

Even if I wanted to scream, I wasn't sure I could. The wind rippling at my face knocked my breath away. Even with the goggles, my eyes watered. I gripped Eden so hard I could've sworn I suffocated her.

Had Shana forgotten how to fly? Why were we just falling?

The rocks below got closer. Eighty feet away. Sixty. Thirty.

Twenty. Just as we were about to crash into them, Shana snapped out her wings, and we shot up into the sky.

Eden whooped, her braid flapping behind her.

We shot back up past the balcony, from which I could hear Ivy, Aven, and Amias's shouts. I clenched my jaw, heart pounding hard enough I didn't think my rib cage could hold it in. Maybe that's how I'd die. Maybe my heart would beat right out of my chest and explode into a mess of blood and tissue.

Oh well. At least it would be a cool death.

Shana leveled out, slowing down. I let myself relax and glanced around. For the third time today, beauty took my breath away.

The jagged peaks of the mountains and valleys stretched out beneath us, rolling in every direction. The gray blanket of the sky had begun to part, allowing the mid-morning sun to stream through.

Shana let out a happy roar. A few other dragons answered it.

I grinned.

The terror and fear that had clutched my throat before had cleared. Eden let out a shout of glee. Without hesitation, I answered it with my own.

All my worries had been left on the balcony. All my fears and sadness. Everything. I was, without a doubt, the happiest I'd ever been.

Shana flew until a lake came into view. She glided toward it and landed in an empty clearing.

"Lua's fist," Eden announced and pulled off her goggles. She slid down Shana's back, and I trailed behind her, much less gracefully. She pointed to the lake. "That is what it is called."

"Who's Lua?"

Shana trailed behind us as we made our way toward the water; her hulking body almost didn't fit between the trees. Branches rained down from where her wings ripped them from the trunks. She didn't seem to care.

"The Goddess of the Moon," Eden replied. "One of twenty

gods that created and rule this world."

She knelt down before the water, reaching for a flat stone. She then sent it skidding across the water.

Shana lay down beside the lake, sprawling across the rocky shore. I took a seat on a log, picking at the peeling bark.

"Goddess?" I echoed.

It wasn't hard to believe it, the concept of gods and goddesses existing in this world. What shocked me, however, was the intimacy Eden seemed to share with this goddess.

I found myself staring at the water's surface, almost hoping for a glimpse of the elusive Lua herself.

"Do you have faith in these gods?" The question leaped from my mouth before I had time to think about it. It was always a question that lingered in my mind when it came to religion. Never before had I the courage to ask it. But with Eden, I felt safe.

Eden's expression turned thoughtful as she skipped another stone across the water. Each skip created a ripple that expanded outward, echoing the uncertainty of my thoughts. "I suppose I do. Though it indeed has wavered at times."

"Like when you got thrown into Blackford?"

She turned sharply, eyebrows raised.

I looked down. "Sorry," I mumbled. "Just a thought."

To my surprise, she chuckled. "That day… was certainly a surprise."

Shana let out a contented rumble, her eyes half-lidded as she observed the sky above through the canopy of leaves. Her massive form, both fearsome and majestic, contrasted sharply with the serene atmosphere around the lake. I couldn't help but feel a mixture of awe and trepidation in her presence.

Eden glanced over at me, a sympathetic smile on her lips. "Do not think too hard, Sander. We have nowhere to be."

It took a moment for her words to sink in. But when they did, I smiled. I wished I could stay here forever.

We spent the rest of the day by the lake. When the sun began to melt into the horizon, we mounted Shana and made our way back to Avrix. We stopped at the auditorium, where Eden said goodbye to her dragon and then waved as she flapped away.

The tables were being cleared. Daesyn, who sat on the edge of the cliff with her friend, told us we'd just missed dinner, and plates had been put in our rooms. We thanked her and stepped into the tunnels.

They were more crowded than usual. Avrix citizens, men, women, and children alike were decorating the halls with white fabric streamers and star paintings. For the full moon tomorrow, Eden told me.

Amias was sitting on my bed when I arrived. Eden squeezed my elbow, then disappeared down the hallway.

"What are you doing?" I asked him.

He had my sketchbook on his lap.

My heart seized. Had he looked through it? Then, I took a breath and told myself it wouldn't be so bad if he had. He'd certainly seen worse.

"The man," he said and tapped the journal. "The one that looked like a character from *The Walking Dead*, is he your dad?"

I nodded slowly.

He drew in a breath, then rubbed his temples. "I need you to do something for me."

"Anything," I said—and I meant it.

"Name every drawing in this book."

"Why?"

"Because fake you wouldn't be able to."

"Um, the first one is a drawing of my dad. On the chair. The Rising soldiers standing over him. The second one is a drawing of Sadira. In that one, she's standing over the coffin at my dad's funeral." I half expected him to make some sort of joke, but he stayed silent. He didn't open the book either. Like he knew each one as well. "The third one is a mountain range, as well as just a bunch of random sketches. The fourth one is a lake. Pine Lake. We went there on vacation all the time… " I stopped because Amias was smiling. "What?"

"I knew it," he grinned and made his way over to me.

"I—knew what?"

But then he hugged me. I went stiff. My limbs had turned to stone.

He pulled back, worry crossing his features. "What? I'm sorry if I pushed your boundaries. I just—I got—" He stumbled over his words, panic rising in his voice. "I got really happy for a second."

Something inside me broke. It was like I was seeing him for the first time. The real him. The lonely, sad boy who'd grown up as an experiment. Who'd become a killer against his will.

I wrapped my arms around him, feeling awkward yet wanting to show him that I cared. He went quiet and hugged me back. My heart sped. The smell of metal and rain washed over my senses. I felt overwhelmed, nervous, but also comfortable. Like I was home.

He then sniffed and pulled away, making for the door.

"Amias," I said.

He stopped, not turning to face me. "Yeah?" he asked, but his voice sounded choked.

"You can—you can come to me," I stammered. "If you need anything. Or just someone to talk to."

He gave a quick nod. The curtain rippled as it closed behind him.

CHAPTER THIRTY-EIGHT

The next day was the full moon, a time when the Avrixians renewed their connection to Lua by dedicating the day to her. To me, it just sounded like a party. But Daesyn and Eden insisted that it wasn't. Calling it "just a party" would be insulting. Either way, I was told the festivities didn't begin until after the sun went down.

I found that hard to believe, considering I woke to the sound of drums, laughter, and roars.

The sun was already high in the sky by the time I stumbled outside, rubbing my heavy eyes and shaking off the sleepy exhaustion that resulted from a good night's sleep. A feeling I hadn't felt since before pain had become a natural part of my body. I marveled at the speed at which my wounds had recovered, though a soreness still laced my movements.

Dragons lined the edge of the cliff, swaying their tails to the rhythm of the music. People danced and chatted happily.

The front pavilion with the auditorium had been decorated with white sheets, lines of hanging lanterns, and paper stars that looked like they'd been cut by children.

I spotted Eden with her parents, talking by the carving of Lua decorating the back wall, the goddess's gaze slanted toward the valley spreading before her and the people below her. Eden had dressed up for the occasion. They all had. The men wore robes of silk, varying from blues to grays to purples. The women wore dresses of the same. Eden wore a white one, the hem sewn with gold stars. Crescent silver earrings offset the dark tone of her skin. As I approached, I suddenly felt very underdressed in the jeans and fur coat I'd been given.

"Good morning, Sander." Eden smiled.

I offered one back. "Hey. Why didn't you wake me up earlier?"

"My mother said not to disturb you."

Nerezza nodded.

Eden looped her arm through mine. "Come, I have your outfit in my room."

My outfit had been laid on her bed, consisting of forest green silks and silver hemming.

"Do I have to wear it?" I asked, feeling my face twist. I wasn't disgusted by it. In fact, I found it very beautiful, but the thought of wearing it in front of the others made my cheeks flush.

"Yes," she said. "It would be disrespectful to Lua if you did not."

"Really?"

"No, but it would be disrespectful to the people who made it."

"Oh." I hadn't thought of that. Grudgingly, I dressed. When I emerged from the room, Eden clapped her hands, a smile of pure joy filling her face.

Seeing her like that, it was easy to forget she'd slaughtered her way through a dozen men and hadn't flinched. It was also easy to forget we were in the middle of a war, the Major was missing, Nevena was on the run, and someone in the Rising was a spy.

Back in the auditorium, Eden led me to Ivy and Aven, who were sitting by Shana and feeding her chunks of raw meat. Aven, dressed in silver, shook out their hand in disgust when the meat brushed against their skin. Ivy laughed at them, brushing a strand of wavy dark hair from her eyes.

She seemed to be enjoying dressing up. Her hair had been braided into a crown and decorated with violet flowers. The lavender silk dress she wore was simple but elegant. When she noticed me, her eyes lit up and she waved.

"Hi!" she said cheerfully. "About time you got up."

"Hi," I replied and sat down beside them. Shana brushed her

snout against me, nearly knocking me over. I chuckled and patted her scales. "Where's Amias?"

"He went back to the Rising camp," Aven answered, scooting to the side to make room for Eden. "Apparently, Renna beat someone up because they looked at her funny."

I ignored the stabbing dismay in my gut.

"That is in character," Eden smiled.

"Yeah." Aven nodded. "But he'll be back tonight. I wouldn't let him miss this party."

"Maybe Renna could come too?" Ivy suggested. "It'd only be for a few hours. She could leave Kenneth or Aslen or someone in charge. Besides, I really think she'd want to see the dragons."

Shana grumbled in response.

Eden nodded. "I like that. I shall go see if my parents will allow it."

As she left, I saw Ivy's smile fall a little. But then she rose and brushed off her legs. "Want to see what Aven and I found yesterday?"

"Oh yeah!" Aven jumped up, sending the plate of meat tumbling over the edge of the cliff. Shana glared at them. "Oops. Anyway, you've got to see this place, Sander. It's so cool. As long as you don't fall in."

"That doesn't sound safe," I said as they grabbed hold of my arm and hauled me up.

"It's perfectly safe." Aven grinned.

"Kind of," Ivy added. "It's safe if you're careful."

I rolled my eyes but followed them into the tunnels anyway.

They led me deeper into the mountain than I'd been before. Like the healer's room, it slowly became hotter. The cool breeze was gone. The tunnels were stuffy, and as I ran my hand along the wall, it felt warm, as if it had been held over a flame.

When we turned a corner that opened up into a large cave, I saw why.

The mountain, it seemed, was not a normal mountain. It was

a volcano.

A lake of orange-red lava bubbled before us. We stood on a small ledge that circled around the entire lake. Thankfully, it had a fence of stone stopping anyone from falling in.

I turned to Aven, wide-eyed. "Is it going to explode?"

They laughed and pointed to the wall of the cliff below us. As I leaned over the fence and peered closer, I saw the rock had been carved with those same white swirls Nerezza had on her hand. The powers from Lua.

"Apparently, they're keeping the lava level low. They help it not explode. And don't worry, they have evacuation plans in case it does become dangerous."

I looked back at the lava. That wasn't as comforting as it should've been. It wasn't as hot as I expected, either. I assumed that was because of the magic as well.

"Isn't it cool?" Ivy said, resting her arms on the ledge. "Daesyn showed it to us while you and Eden were out with Shana."

I nodded, then noticed a bulge in the lava slowly growing bigger. I frowned as scales began to emerge, then wings and a tail. A dragon lifted its head, craning its neck and peering at us curiously.

"What the hell?"

"Oh yeah. There's another thing." Aven grinned. "Dragons are fireproof."

The dragon turned over, laying on its back as it floated in the lava.

"Is it—is it just swimming?"

Ivy shrugged, fixing the strap of her dress. "I don't really know. But if you were fireproof, wouldn't you want to float in lava?"

"No," I said immediately. "Not at all."

"I would," she replied almost wistfully.

"Who knows," chuckled Aven. "Maybe they have dragon scale suits you can go swimming with."

"I should ask."

I opened my mouth to object, but my words were cut off by a thunderous boom from outside, followed by a pained roar. No one hesitated before racing toward the tunnels. As we neared the exit to the auditorium, I saw the problem.

The tunnel had collapsed. Something from outside was clawing at the pile of boulders.

A few people, those who had been inside, were crowding around the pile.

"Get back," Ivy ordered. "The rest could collapse."

"This should not be possible," said a man, his arm slung protectively over his son's shoulder. "Those rocks are stable."

"Obviously not." Aven rolled their eyes.

The boy whimpered.

"Not helping." I jabbed Aven with my elbow.

"Is there another exit?" Ivy asked the man. He nodded. "Take them there. And stick together. Right now, outside is safer than inside."

The group followed the man as they disappeared into the tunnels. Ivy turned back to the pile just as the top few boulders came tumbling down. A red-tipped, icy-gray snout poked through the hole.

"Shana," I said and lunged forward, clambering up the pile of rocks.

The dragon whined when she heard my voice.

"Sander?" said a voice from outside. "Shana, move." The dragon pulled her snout from the hole and revealed Eden.

"What happened?" I asked.

"Are you all right? Is Ivy all right?"

"Yeah, we're okay. No one's hurt."

I heard Aven snort. "Physically, maybe. She didn't ask if I'm okay."

I ignored him. "What happened? Did someone attack?"

"I do not think so. I can't see anyone." Eden turned away from the hole. "Is anyone else in there?"

"There was, but we sent them to another exit. Ivy figures outside is safer."

Eden shook her head. "It won't work. The scouts just came back. They said all the exits are closed."

"Then this was an attack," Ivy mused. "A planned one."

"Amazingly planned," said a voice behind us. We turned in unison. Renna brushed blood from a wound on her forehead nonchalantly. "All the Mirrors are broken."

"Renna?" Ivy exclaimed. "What are you doing here?"

"Amias told me about the party. I wanted to come. But I stepped through the Mirror and someone nearly bashed my skull in. I just woke up."

"Is Amias here?" I asked.

She shrugged. "The Mirror was broken when I came to. I assume the person who knocked me out smashed the Mirror before he could come through. That is, if you haven't found him already."

"Who do you think could've done this?" Eden called through the hole.

"Nevena," Ivy replied, hatred twisting her features. "A hundred percent. She's perfectly capable of pulling this off."

"It makes sense, but—" Eden's voice was cut off by a piercing shriek. She turned so fast I could've sworn her neck broke. I saw her face go slack. Then, a roar carried through the air. "Shana!" Eden cried and raced away.

"Eden, what is it?" I shouted after her. I peered through the hole, but my limited vision only let me see part of what was going on. Shana was out of view, but I saw Eden running toward her, pulling a knife that had been strapped to her leg.

People were screaming. Panic had taken over. Osiris was shouting, trying to get everyone to calm down, but wasn't having much luck. Nerezza knelt by her husband, tending to a woman with a giant gash through her leg.

I'd only begun to wonder what it was from when a white flash darted into the corner of my vision. Then, I felt hands on my back and was yanked down just as a pale and bloodied creature came tearing at me.

My heart dropped away as I recognized the cracking skin. It was the monster from the SSD. The one that had attacked us in the garage.

Long, sharp teeth snapped at us, dripping with red blood.

"Oh my god," I breathed.

"Come on!" Renna urged, helping me up. "We need to find a way to get out there."

"Can't you get it to stop?" I asked, trying to ignore the panicky feeling in my chest. "Like you did last time?"

"Stop," she called out half-heartedly. She knew it wasn't going to work. And so did I.

As I'd predicted, the monster didn't pause.

We ran.

Aven veered off into their room, coming back out with a backpack full of guns. They handed them out to each of us.

"Is that the only thing you brought?" Ivy asked, checking the magazine.

"You better be damn thankful it is," they snapped back.

She rolled her eyes. "We're going to split up. Renna and I will head down this way. Try to find as many people as you can and get them out."

"When did I sign up to play hero?" Renna grumbled but followed Ivy as they veered off down a hallway.

Aven and I took off the other way.

Another tremble echoed through the mountain, followed by a piercing scream. When we turned the corner, a girl slammed into us. Her face was bleeding, three deep slashes stretching from her cheek to her neck.

"Help me," she cried, tears streaming down her face. "It is

coming."

The monster skidded around a corner and came tearing down the long hallway.

The girl screamed and started running down the hallway we'd come from. Aven pulled out their gun and fired once. As to be expected from big, creepy monsters, the bullet bounced off. They cursed and took off after the girl. I followed, my heart beating faster than my footsteps.

The monster roared. I heard a crash and turned to see that it had slipped and slammed into the wall. A crack stretched to the ceiling.

I raced faster after Aven and the girl. But then, a boom shook the tunnel, and the ceiling in front of us exploded. Rocks rained down. Someone grabbed my hand and pulled me back just as a boulder smashed into the ground in front of us.

I turned to see who had grabbed me, but there was no one there.

Aven helped the girl stand, then faced the monster in defiance. They held up their gun.

"Lua save us," the girl prayed softly.

Aven fired. Once. Twice.

The monster growled but didn't slow.

I glanced up at the cracks in the ceiling. An idea came to me. I sent a silent prayer and then aimed at the ceiling. The gunshot echoed. And then, the ceiling split and sent boulders falling. Out of the corner of my eye, I saw Aven as they were yanked back by an invisible force. Maybe it was adrenaline, or my concussion had gotten worse, but I could've sworn I saw a girl take form in the air. Her eyes met mine; her mouth opened in warning. But a rock slammed into my head, and I fell from consciousness.

CHAPTER THIRTY-NINE

The girl met me in my dreams.

She was small, with skin like the midnight sea and tattoos of constellations dotting her shoulders. Her eyes were a pale silver, pupils blue and white with stars dancing along her cheekbones. Wavy pale hair waterfalled over her shoulders and brushed against her hips in shining locks. A silver dress hugged the edges of her body, revealing the skeletal shape.

"Who are you?" I asked.

She looked up from her hands, which I noticed were tattooed with white swirls. Her face twisted in surprise as if she hadn't expected me to see her. But what else was there to see? There was nothing else around but empty, black nothingness.

When she spoke, her voice was like liquid moonlight. "Why?"

I didn't understand. "Um, because you're standing in front of me."

She frowned, taking a few graceful steps forward, then pressed the palm of her hand to my forehead.

"Sander!"

Someone was screaming my name.

"Sander, wake up!" they kept screaming.

Something hard jabbed into my back. My eyes opened in a flash. A gasp ripped through me as I was flung into the air. Something wrapped around my ankle.

I barely got a glimpse of the cracked skin of the SSD's creature and its gaping, bloodstained jaws before I was slammed against the ground.

Something cracked. I let out a yell, my breath zapped from my lungs. Pain burst along every inch of my back and neck, brutally stealing any sense of physical peace I'd found in the last few days.

A bloody stench washed over me, and I looked up to meet the twisted, cracked, bleeding face of the morphed man. Impossibly round, bloodshot eyes locked onto my gaze.

Adrenaline took over. I reached for a fallen, jagged piece of stone and slammed it against the creature's skull. For a moment, it paused, stunned, and I scrambled to my feet.

The creature roared, lunging for me, but a gunshot splintered the air, slicing through the creature's eye and into its brain.

Blood splattered onto my face.

"Come on!" yelled a panicked voice. Aven grabbed my wrist and began pulling me away from the creature.

I began to follow them but slowed when I noticed the creature hadn't fallen. It had frozen, but its ribs were heaving. It was still breathing. How was it still alive?

I didn't have any more time to think about it because the creature shook out its head, the hole in its eye slowly closing over.

Aven let out a string of filthy curses, and we both burst into a sprint.

Barely able to keep upright, we tumbled over fallen boulders and debris, screams echoing from the surrounding tunnels.

Heavy footsteps thundered from behind us. Aven yanked my arm and pulled me through a small gap in between a set of cracked boulders. I tripped and rolled onto the ground. Gasping for breath, I shifted onto my back and grabbed my chest. It felt like it was on fire, but there was nothing out of the ordinary on the surface, aside from a couple dozen scratches.

There was a roar and a crash as the creature rammed into the gap, failing to fit through. It howled angrily at us, disappointed in losing its meal.

I stumbled to my feet and away from the entrance of the small cave, reaching for the wall to support my trembling body.

"Don't worry," Aven panted, hands on their knees. "It can't get through."

"What—" I drew in a sharp breath, lifting my hands above my head. "—is going on?"

"Long story short, monsters showed up, you got knocked out, Ezlyn and I tried to move you somewhere safer, but then you got attacked and woke up."

I blinked. "Ezlyn?"

Aven's expression fell. "Um, the girl we ran into earlier. She, uh… she didn't make it."

My heart broke, remembering the terrified expression she'd been wearing when I'd last seen her. The last words I'd heard her speak were of a prayer to a goddess she didn't even know existed.

Faith was a dangerous thing. She'd believed, just like they'd told her to, and she'd still died. What good was believing if it didn't do anything?

I closed my eyes and sank down, leaning against the wall.

"What happened?" I swallowed.

Aven didn't reply for long enough that I thought they weren't going to answer. I opened my eyes to see them seated next to me, furiously blinking back tears.

"I couldn't—I couldn't save her," they choked out, bringing a hand to their mouth. "I tried, Sander. I really tried, but—" A sob rippled from them. Regret filled their eyes as their gaze landed on me. "I tried."

I squeezed my eyes shut, dropping my head between my knees. "I'm sorry," I whispered.

"It's not your fault."

"I don't know," I clenched my fists. "I'm sorry you've had such a terrible life, and now it's going to end before you have had a chance to change it.”

They sniffed and wiped their nose. “Please, don’t say that. My life hasn’t been terrible. Not recently, at least.”

I raised my head.

“Escaping the SSD was the best thing I’ve ever done. Even though we almost died countless times, I’ve been free. And I’ve been with people who actually care about me and want me around.” Their voice began to crack. They buried their head into their shirt, shoulders starting to shake.

“Aven—”

“I really tried, Sander,” their voice was muffled. “I thought that maybe I could at least save one person, and it might make up for all the damage I’ve done, but—”

“Hey,” I snapped, my voice reverberating off the stone walls.

Aven lifted their head, a strand of their messy hair falling in front of their face.

“You have saved people,” I continued. “You saved me, remember? When we escaped from Blackford.”

They gave a weak shrug. “That was mostly Amias. It was his plan.”

“I don’t care. You helped, didn’t you?”

They grunted and ran their hands over their face. “Barely. I’m not a very helpful person. I can’t even get us out of this stupid cave.”

I didn’t argue because I was becoming increasingly aware of the rise in temperature. Sweat beaded on my brow, and I spotted something bubbling in a crack beside Aven.

Aven followed my gaze to where an orange molten liquid was peeking through the stone.

“Is that—” I began.

“Lava,” Aven finished for me, scrambling away.

I rose to my feet. “I thought the white lines were—” I started but was cut off when the ground rumbled. Cracks began to appear in the back wall and floor, lava seeping through.

A wave of heat washed over us.

They cursed and faced the exit, where Warren's experiment was viciously clawing at the stone.

"Shit, shit, shit." They backed against the wall near the cave entrance, farthest from the lava.

The lava continued to spill through the cracks, which were growing. They crawled along the floor, like long, spindly hands creeping toward us at a quickening pace.

We should be dead.

That was the only thing going through my mind as I backed into the corner of the cave.

The heat was growing. I wasn't sure what the minimum safest distance from lava was, but without the magic rocks, this definitely wasn't it.

Aven was furiously scanning the walls, desperate to find another way out.

The cracks grew wider. The monster snarled at us from the exit. My skin burned. The heat rippled the air, blurring Aven's face as they approached me, a hopeless expression across their features.

"I can't save you." They crumpled to the ground, exhaustion and reality hitting them like a boulder.

The cracks split further. The wall opened up, and the lava burst through.

A future flashed through my mind. One that was peaceful and happy enough that I knew I would never have it. I saw myself, curled in a hammock on a porch I didn't recognize. The porch wrapped around an old, rustic cottage. The door to the cottage opened, and a German Shepard padded through, followed by a tall figure carrying two cups of coffee.

I lifted my gaze to see the figure, but I was snapped back into the present as something slammed into me. The taste of blood filled my mouth. My head launched backward so hard I heard a crack. I must've blacked out for a second or two because I was awoken by a deafening roar. Loud enough the ground shook. Or maybe that was just me.

I blinked a few times in an attempt to clear my blurred vision. A bloodied face approached me. Daesyn helped me to my feet, asking a question. I couldn't hear what she was saying. Behind her, a mud-brown dragon with thick limbs and heavy scales was finishing off the monster.

Aven and I had been set on a small ledge on the side of the tunnel. The lava was now spilling out of the room we'd just been in, the entrance made wider by its force. About as big as the dragon fighting below us.

Daesyn patted me on the shoulder. "Where's Ezlyn?" she asked.

"Ezlyn…" I trailed off, realization dawning.

"She was with you, wasn't she?" Daesyn's expression fell. "My dragon could smell her, that's why…"

"I'm so sorry," I said.

She brought a hand to her mouth, tears forming in her eyes. She glared from me to Aven, who had just stumbled to their feet. "Why didn't you save her?" she cried at us in anguish.

Aven seemed desperate for words, but none came.

"There was nothing we could've done," I tried.

"You should have saved her," she sobbed, shoulders trembling. "Why didn't—"

She drew in a shuddering breath, visibly trying to pull herself together. It failed. She let it all out with a piercing shriek, then punched Aven in the nose.

They stumbled a few steps but didn't bother fighting back as she punched them again. I knew they let her because they felt like they deserved it, but I couldn't let them get beaten up.

I grabbed Daesyn's wrist as she swung again. She turned to me, infuriated.

"There was nothing we could have done," I said again firmly.

Daesyn dropped her arm, sadness once again crashing over her features. She brought her head to her hands, biting her lip to stop the sobs from escaping. In her grief, she stumbled away from us, then fell to her knees.

"I'm sorry," Aven whispered.

She didn't reply.

Daesyn's dragon guarded us as we made our way outside to where a group of Avrixians had gathered. One of which I recognized. I didn't even see Eden before she had her arms around me. Her shoulders shook as if she were sobbing.

I'd never seen Eden cry. Seeing her in this state, weakened and broken, arms shaking, made my heart ache with a deep sense of helplessness.

I let her lean into me, pulling her closer.

When she heard Aven's approaching footsteps, however, she pulled back so quickly that she nearly fell. She hastily brushed her eyes and addressed them with a nearly composed demeanor. "Have you seen my father?"

We both shook our heads.

Her composure faltered for a moment, but she managed to maintain it.

"What exactly happened?" Aven asked.

She glanced at the ground. "Let us gather the survivors first."

Department 1, Day 10

I have many regrets in my life. Everyone does. But now that I am on the verge of death, everything I have or have not done has been racing through my thoughts. Everybody dies with regrets. It is a truth I have known since my first years; however, I have always thought myself to be the one to break the cycle.

But alas, I was mistaken. It should have been expected, given the life that I have led. Regret is a formidable opponent, one that even I, a fighter since birth, have lost the battle against.

Regret is inevitable, I realize now. We all make mistakes that cost us. We all do things that we wish we had not, or do not do things we wish we had. What is important about regret is what you do with it. I ask myself, as I sit here, my life running on repeat in my mind, how did I learn from my choices? How can I use my regret to make myself a better person?

There is not much I am able to do. Not much that I want to do. However, if this week was not going to end in death, I would tell her everything. All the words I have yearned to say since the day I realized I loved her.

It should have been clear that my love for her would be the end of me.
-Elyane

CHAPTER FORTY

We worked late into the night, hauling debris and clearing piles of boulders. Dragons pulled long carts of rocks over the edge of the cliff. People recovered bodies, lining them up outside and covering them with white cloth.

We'd offered the bodies of the monsters to the dragons—which they'd killed off together—as food, but even they seemed to know there was something wrong with them. Instead, we dumped them into the auditorium and burned them until the flames rose higher than my head.

Eden was quiet as we worked. Everyone was. The only words spoken were the occasional order or apology if someone bumped into another.

Out of the nineteen thousand citizens who had lived in the mountain, only nine thousand had survived. And the number was decreasing. Nerezza and her team did their best to heal the wounded, but even they couldn't get to them fast enough.

Everyone had lost someone. And we weren't excluded.

Ivy was missing.

I hoped for the best, as one should, but deep in my gut, there was the sinking feeling that she wasn't okay. I kept telling myself that it would be fine. Ivy was strong. She'd been raised to get herself out of situations like this. She could do it again.

The sun had just begun to peek out from beneath the horizon when a young boy and an older woman helped a familiar man from the tunnels.

"Papa!" Eden cried, dumping her end of the boulder we'd been carrying and racing over to him.

I raced after her, leaving the forgotten rock. We took the places of the boy and the woman and helped Osiris to the makeshift beds we'd made for the wounded along the cavern wall.

"Eden," Osiris coughed, blood spilling from his mouth. There was so much blood staining his silk shirt that I couldn't even see where he was injured.

"Where's Nerezza?" I cried to the ever-growing crowd.

"She went back into the tunnels to look for more bandages," said a woman who rose from her spot by another wounded man. She began to make her way over to Osiris, but he held up his hand.

"Don't," he ordered. "Finish with him."

"But—"

"Do it," he demanded, then coughed again. "I am no more important than he is."

She seemed hesitant but didn't want to disobey him.

Aven pushed their way through the crowd, Renna tailing them. They bent beside Osiris and began ripping away the bloodied satin. As they did, I saw the wound and stifled a gag.

There was a long, deep slash extending from his sternum to his stomach. How he'd gotten away alive, I had no idea.

"Someone, go find a bucket of water or something," Aven demanded and began scanning the surrounding area. They grabbed a pile of semi-clean rags and pressed them onto the wound. Osiris let out a pained groan, teeth clenching.

Every Avrixian around us winced and reached forward to help.

"What are you standing there for?" Aven snapped.

No one argued. The crowd dispersed.

"Eden and Sander," Aven said. "Go find Nerezza."

Eden started to protest but stopped when they glared at her.

"Do it. You're no use here."

She looked at her father. "I will see you again," she affirmed, more to herself than him. He gave a slight nod, face twisting in pain.

We raced into the tunnels, past the room that had been turned into the hatchery since the original one had been destroyed. The surviving dragons yapped at us as we went.

Eden stopped a boy passing us. After a quick conversation in their language, she thanked him, then took off again in the direction he'd directed us.

We found Nerezza bent over a nightstand next to a canopy bed decorated in blue and purple weaving. I barely had time to register the beauty of the room before Eden grabbed her wrist and began tugging her out.

"It's Papa," she told her. "He's hurt."

Nerezza didn't waste any time. We sprinted through the tunnels, Eden muttering prayers under her breath. I didn't know how much good it would do, considering the last person I'd heard praying ended up dead.

Way to be optimistic, Sander, I thought to myself.

Back outside by the auditorium, Aven was bent over a bleeding Osiris, doing their best to stitch up the wound. They'd done a pretty good job, all things considered. Osiris, however, had passed out.

Nerezza bent down and pressed her fingers to his neck, then let out a sigh of relief. She turned to Aven. "Thank you," she said and gripped their hand. "You saved him."

Aven shrugged, but I could see the pride lifting their shoulders.

Nerezza set her palm on her husband's forehead. Life rushed back to his face. The long wound running down his chest began to close. Not all the way, but it seemed better than it had been before.

Aven disappeared through the crowd. I made to follow, squeezing Eden's shoulder before I went.

"Where are you going?" I asked as I caught up with Aven.

"To find some clean towels," they replied.

"Can I come with?"

They nodded and headed into the tunnels.

"You did good," I said as they peered into one of the nearest rooms.

"You don't have to try to make me feel better," they grumbled and stepped back. "Saving one person doesn't ease my guilt."

"I'm not—" I took a breath. "You're never not going to feel guilty. That's the way life works. Unless you're a complete sociopath, you're going to feel something. But you can do your best to forgive yourself."

They clenched their jaw.

"Aven." I reached for them.

They yanked their arm away. "I don't need you to preach about life. I'm fine. I'll be fine. Just leave it alone."

"Why do you feel like it's your job to save everyone?" I snapped, following them down the hall anyway. "What happened in your life that made you feel the need to redeem yourself?"

Their eyes flared as they spun and faced me. I backed up. At the moment, angry Aven seemed a lot scarier than a hundred-foot cliff dive. I took another step back.

"You don't get to ask that," they snarled. "You don't know anything about me."

"Maybe," I shot back, bristling. "Maybe not. But I do know that you're not heartless. In fact, you probably have the biggest heart out of anyone I've ever met."

"Will you shut up?" They continued making their way down the hall, fists clenched at their side.

"No. Because you're angry-sad, and you need my help."

"Angry-sad?" For a moment, they seemed to forget their anger and let it be taken over by confusion.

"Sorry, that's what Sadira calls it. But seriously, Aven, please talk to someone about it. Even if it's not me. It's not healthy to keep everything bottled up. One day, you're going to explode."

"Says you," they muttered and ducked into a closet, then came back out with a pile of white rags. "And I have talked to someone about it. But they're dead now."

"Oh. Well, um, maybe you should talk to someone alive?"

They stopped walking. "I don't need a therapist. Stop trying to be one."

"I'm not trying to be a therapist," I protested. "I'm trying to help my friend because I don't… I don't want to watch you go through something like this without trying to help you. As you know, I've never had friends before, but I at least want to try to do something right."

Their features softened. "I'll talk to someone," they promised. "Just not right now."

I didn't believe them.

It was mid-afternoon when Osiris forced Aven, Eden, Renna, and me to take a break. We'd worked nonstop throughout the night. Finding Ivy was the first thing on everyone's mind, but sleep came in at a close second.

I fell asleep nearly the second I lay down on a cot in one of the front rooms. As soon as I slipped into unconsciousness, I was hit by a memory.

The walls were illuminated bright white, casting a cold glow over the man's face. A man I recognized. Troy.

His face was set in a scowl. The sharp features of his cheekbones and jaw, so similar to Aven's, were tight with anger. He sat on a desk, hands gripping the edge tight enough to turn his knuckles white. "Sander," he growled.

I felt a twinge of fear, followed by a hot burst of anger. I was mad at myself for fearing him. After all, he was nothing but a pretty face in a suit. What could he really do to me? I suddenly became aware of someone behind me. I could see their reflection in the shiny surface of the metal cabinet but couldn't quite make out who they were.

"I messed up," I admitted. "But it wasn't my fault. If you'd kept

Sadira on lockdown—"

Troy sent a punch to my face. I stumbled back a small step, pain rushing through my jaw.

"You messed up. Period. You failed. We can't send you back in. They'd be too suspicious." Troy leaned back onto the desk, turning his attention to the person behind me. "What do you think? You know the real Sander pretty well."

I felt myself turning and heard the person begin to answer, but then I was snapped out of the memory and into reality.

"Sander!" Aven was shaking me. "Sander, Amias is back."

"What?" I grumbled, rubbing my eyes. They'd thrown a tarp over the entrance to the room, and it now flapped noisily in the wind.

"Amias," Aven repeated, then dragged me off of my cot.

Outside the room, the lanterns along the stone walls stretched into the darkness to my left, and to my right, the tunnel opened onto the landing. Rain poured from the sky in heavy, thick sheets. The wind whipped so fiercely that, as I made my way out with Aven, I thought it was going to knock me over.

The dragons huddled along the mountain on the other side of the valley in caves I hadn't noticed before. I stared at them as we walked, counting. I spotted at least a dozen before a figure stepped into my vision. Amias.

I blinked. "How'd you get here?"

He gestured to a Mirror that had been set up underneath the carving of Lua. "Eden found it in one of the rooms higher up. She came to tell me about everything that happened right away." His face fell. "So, still no word about Ivy?"

Eden, who had sidled up between us sometime during the conversation, shook her head. "We have groups clearing as much debris as possible, but there is a good chance we will not be able to get to her in time. That is—" She didn't finish because we were all thinking about it.

That is if she wasn't dead already.

We worked the rest of the day, hauling boulders over the side of the mountain, and fetching fresh food and water for the wounded. Amias's strength was a welcome addition to our efforts. I spotted more than one person eyeing him haul boulders twice the size of himself through the tunnels. The rain didn't stop. In the evening, thunder rumbled through the sky, followed closely by a crack of lightning that sent a few children running into the arms of their mothers.

When I asked Eden why we hadn't buried the bodies that were stretched out across the platform, she told me it was because all of those who had died, had died together, so they ought to be buried together.

Daesyn didn't speak to Aven or me, although she passed us multiple times. Her eyes were bloodshot, cheeks stained with dirt. But she didn't stop working. Only the children and elderly took breaks. We were allowed to, of course, but no one could stop with the hope of lives hanging over our heads.

In total, we found about a dozen survivors that day, with four times that number of corpses. The sun had just set when Amias, Eden, Renna, Aven, and I sat around the dwindling fire at the center of the auditorium.

I picked at the scraps of cheese on my lopsided, wooden plate. I'd spent the day carrying mangled, bloody bodies; I wasn't in the mood to eat. It was obvious the others felt the same because they hadn't touched their food either.

Amias drummed his fingers against his plate, a worrying frown on his beautiful face.

I cleared my throat. "Do you guys remember my Reflection?"

"How could we not?" Amias said, lifting his head to meet my gaze.

I couldn't meet his eyes. "Well, I didn't tell you guys this earlier, but I think somehow we're… connected."

"Like physically?" Aven said, their face twisting in disgust.

"What? No!" I shook my head, horrified at what they might have been thinking. "Like his memories are mine. Some of them, at least."

"I guess it makes sense," Renna added. "You might not be from the same reality, but you're still the same person. And you've had physical interaction, so that might help."

I knit my eyebrows together. "Yeah. But what I need to tell you is that I had one of the memories earlier today. They're kind of like dreams from my Reflection's point of view. Anyway, I was in an office and Troy was there."

Aven's face fell. "Why are you telling us this?"

"Because," I said, turning to Amias forcing myself to look at his face. "Most of the memories are pretty recent and, well, was my Reflection at the camp when you were there?"

He seemed confused. But then he shook himself out. "Oh, yeah. I meant to tell you, but I just—with everything that happened—um, he escaped."

Renna chuckled. "Yeah. That happened a couple of days ago. I was planning on telling you guys, but I got distracted."

"Seriously?" I blurted out, anger building up. "What is wrong with you? He tried to ruin your guys' lives! What is more important to you than that?"

Her eyes flared. "In my defense, I was a little busy running the Rising. Do you realize how unorganized they are? There's no social structure at all. It's just chaos."

"Would you two relax?" Amias rubbed his eyes. "I can't deal with this right now. Sander's Reflection escaped. There's nothing we can do about it. No need to whine about it."

Renna opened her mouth to protest, but he sent her the type of death glare only he could manage. She shut her mouth, frowning.

Eden sighed, running her hands through her hair. "We need to take a break. How about I show you all Lua's temple?"

"What about Ivy?" Aven asked.

"We are not going to find her any faster in this state," she pointed out, then set her plate down. "Come."

No one argued. Honestly, I guessed we all secretly wanted a distraction.

Eden called Shana, and we filed onto her back somewhat gracefully. Amias, sitting behind me, let out a small huff as he adjusted his goggles. "Do I have to wear these?"

"If you want to see," I replied.

He grunted and wrapped his arms around my waist. I shifted uncomfortably, a flush rushing up my neck.

Lua's temple was placed on a small bridge connecting two sides of a bare, rocky valley. Shana landed on the bridge, which was just big enough for her. The rain let up as we walked into the temple, a circular, open-air structure supported by ornately carved pillars. A mosaic of a moon embedded with sapphires and diamonds decorated the stone ground.

"Why are we here?" Renna asked.

Eden sat cross-legged and gestured for us to do the same. When we did, Eden closed her eyes and clasped her hands in her lap, tilting her head toward the clouds. I followed her lead. There was something about not being able to see that brought a sense of peace washing over me. As soon as one of my senses was blocked, all the others came into hyper-focus. I could hear the rain pattering lightly against the stone roof. I heard Shana shuffling along the cliff, knocking rocks into the canyon.

I shifted. The cold, hard floor pressed against my legs. A soft wind swept through my hair and brushed my face. I drew in a deep breath.

It was quiet for a while. Aven, of course, was the first to speak.

"Are we meditating?"

"Shh," Eden replied.

I heard them move. Even with my eyes closed, I could see their frown of frustration. They didn't like being told to shut up.

"Sander."

"Eden told you to shut up," I said.

"Sander. Your name is Sander."

I realized then it wasn't Aven talking. Or anyone I knew. I opened my eyes. The same girl I'd seen before stood in front of me, peering down with unusual silver eyes.

My heart nearly jumped out of my chest, but I drew in a breath and rubbed my hands over my eyes. When I dropped my hands, she was still there.

She tilted her head, long white hair falling over her shoulder. "Why can you see me?"

"Wha—Should I not be able to?"

"No," the girl replied.

I poked Eden, who was sitting beside me. She didn't move. "Eden? There's a weird girl here."

"She cannot hear you," said the girl. "Or feel you. We are in your mind."

I tilted my head, a lock of hair falling in front of my eyes. "You're not real, are you?"

Now, it was her turn to show confusion. "Of course I am real."

I unfolded myself and stood to meet the girl at eye level. She was shorter than me but somehow seemed as if she was taller.

She said something in a language I didn't understand. When I didn't reply, she frowned. "You cannot comprehend my words?"

"No."

"Then how can you see me?"

"Listen, lady," I sighed. "I'm sorry to disappoint you, but I know you're not real. You're just in my head, trying to make me believe I'm going even crazier. I've had a really bad couple of days, so if you could just leave me alone, that would be great."

She nodded slightly.

I sat down and closed my eyes. What was going on? Was it the stress of the past few days? Was my head injury making me hallucinate? I shrugged it off, focusing back on my breathing.

Feet shuffled against the stone. I felt the wind move as the girl took a few steps forward. I opened my eyes again.

She was sitting in front of Eden, hands on my friend's cheeks and eyes closed. She was smiling. "I hear you, child," she whispered. "Your friend is safe, but not for long. Find her while you can."

"What are you doing?" I snapped.

The girl turned to me. "I am answering her prayers."

"Why?"

"It is my job."

"No, it's not. You're not real. Get away from my friends."

She lifted her hands. "I apologize. I did not mean to cause you harm. I would never wish that upon any human." She paused, then looked me up and down. "Or whatever you are."

"Would you please leave?"

"I am done here," she said.

"Thank you," I grumbled. She vanished.

A few more minutes passed before I heard Eden rise. I opened my eyes, blinking off the sleepiness that had settled over me. Aven had sprawled across the ground and was snoring slightly. She kicked them in the side. They grunted, curling in on themself.

"We need to hurry," Eden said. "Ivy needs help."

"Now you decide that?" They grunted as Renna helped them to their feet.

Amias walked in front of me as we made our way back to Shana. "Why did we come here at all if we were just going to go back?"

"We needed to clear our heads," she replied. "Stress does not do well for anybody."

I knew she was lying. That wasn't the whole truth. She'd come here to pray to Lua. And she didn't want to tell us because she was afraid we'd laugh at her for believing in something like that. I hated that she felt like that, so I sidled up beside her as we walked down the bridge, out of earshot of everyone else.

"What do you think Lua looks like?" I asked.

Eden smiled. I could tell she was happy I had asked. "I do not see a human when I imagine her. I see the innocence of a child. The kindness of a mother and the protectiveness of a father. I see her loving us as if we are her children."

"That sounds nice," I said honestly. "To have faith in something like that. How do you do it? Is it ever hard to believe?"

She nodded. "There were times at my lowest when I had doubts about her. When I was first taken from my family, I hated her. I resented her for letting the men capture me. But I see now she was setting me on the right path. If that hadn't happened, I would never have met you or Ivy. Or the others."

"So, you honestly believe you were meant to live a life like this?"

She nodded.

I stared at her in amazement. "How? I mean, you see death nearly every day. After everything that has happened to you, how can you believe you deserve something like this?"

Eden looked toward the horizon, a slight smile on her features. "It is not about what we deserve. We were chosen to suffer more to ease the suffering of some others."

"Why us? Why you?"

She turned to me. The serene look in her icy gray eyes made me feel stupid for even asking. "Would you really wish this life upon another?"

She didn't need to wait for an answer because she knew what it was going to be. I wouldn't wish this on anyone else. Never in a million years.

Approaching Avrix, we scanned the mountain once before landing on the top balcony where we'd first met Shana. Start from the top and work our way down. That's what seemed like the best way to find Ivy.

The mountain was small yet tall, and the city only took up a third of it. We explored parts of it that even Eden had never seen. There was a grander dining hall in the center, or I assumed it had been grand. Half of one wall had come down. Blood stained the ground. Tapestries had been ripped. Eden told us we had never eaten in here because the Avrixians liked to be closer to Lua when they said their prayers before eating. The dining hall had once played host to visiting nobles from other kingdoms, but time had split apart cultures, and now, they no longer received visitors so far in the mountains.

There were large tunnels stretching deep into the mountain. Most of them had been cleared out, but the ones that hadn't were filled with people constantly hauling boulders.

Eden walked fast. Extremely fast. Despite her being the second shortest, Aven and I had to jog to keep up with her. She was quiet, too, her face tight with worry. She was showing what all of us were feeling.

I thought of what the girl had said to Eden: *Your friend is safe, but not for long.*

Why was Eden suddenly in such a hurry? Had Eden heard her? Or was she rushing only because of her worry for her friend?

We wound through back tunnels, around an underground lake, and back to the outside dining hall. A woman ran up to us as we exited the tunnels.

"Eden," she said. "We found your friend."

I saw Amias's face go slack. "Where?" he demanded.

"Come," she guided us to a small hallway deep in the mountain that had been blocked off.

Osiris leaned against his wife at the front of the ever-growing crowd. Eden shoved the way forward, then stopped, her body going rigid.

I saw why. The tunnel had been blocked off because it dropped away into a chasm, leading deep into the mountain. At the bottom, I spotted the molten liquid I recognized as lava. My breath caught. On the far side of the chasm, Ivy clung to the wall, her feet resting on a small ledge.

"Ivy!" I called.

"Sander?" she shouted back. "Is that you?"

"And me," Aven added. "And Renna and Eden and—"

"How are we going to get her?" Amias interrupted. "Why can't a dragon get her?"

Nerezza shook her head. "The tunnel gets too small to fit a dragon in here."

I scanned the tunnel anxiously. She was right. It was cramped. A car couldn't even fit. A dragon certainly wouldn't be able to. "What about climbing over to get her?"

"That's suicidal," Amias snapped at me. "Even Renna and I can't survive lava."

"We could make a bridge?"

He shook his head. "How would we get it over to her?"

"I don't know!" I threw my hands up. "I'm giving suggestions! I'm trying to help. I don't see you giving any ideas."

"I don't have any ideas," he snapped. "And your ideas are stupid. Do you not see the two-thousand-degree lava below us? Because I do."

"Would you two shut the hell up?" Renna growled. "I can't think."

"Why should we listen to you?" I snarled. "Your ideas are probably even more dangerous than mine. Why do you even care about saving her? It's not like you give a shit about any of us."

She punched me in the gut. "I might not feel things, but I know it's wrong to let her die."

Everyone was staring at us now.

"Wrong? It's wrong? Was that even in question?"

But then Nerezza shrieked.

We spun to see Eden clinging to the cracks in the wall, slowly making her way toward Ivy.

"Eden!" Aven shouted. "What are you doing?"

"Do not talk to me," she grunted. Her foot slipped. Someone

passed out. She adjusted her grip and continued moving. "You will make me lose concentration."

"Are you stupid?" Amias pushed past Nerezza and Osiris so he was standing at the front. "You'll never make it that far. Even if you do, what are you supposed to do when you get to her? You can't carry her back."

"I know what I am doing."

"No, you don't. Your feelings have blinded your judgment. Get back over here!"

She didn't listen to him. He cursed, running his hands through his hair. "Someone needs to get her."

"I can," I offered.

"No way in hell," he snapped, sudden anger flashing in his eyes.

I stepped back unconsciously. Aven and Renna exchanged a glance.

I straightened. "I can do it. I used to go rock climbing all the time."

"It's no use," Aven cut off Amias before he could yell at me. "Eden's not going to listen. Not when our friend is in danger."

"Aven's right," Renna said. "The only thing we can do now is pray they don't fall and burn to their deaths."

"That's not true," I protested. I did not want to believe there was nothing I could do, but it was true. I felt helpless. And I hated it.

We watched in silence as Eden inched her way down the wall, grunting every now and then. It was nerve-racking. Every time she slipped, it was as if my heart plummeted a thousand feet. Halfway through, I could see her limbs begin to shake. Sweat glinted on her forehead, and she pressed herself against the wall, pausing.

"Eden?" I heard Ivy say, her voice distant.

"I'm fine," Eden breathed. "Just—" The ledge beneath her feet cracked. She let out a small yelp. Nerezza pressed her face into Osiris's chest.

Ivy closed her eyes, biting her lip. "You're so stupid, Eden. There's no point in this."

Eden found her footing again. "I do not care."

"Go back," Ivy pleaded.

Eden didn't go back. She wouldn't until Ivy was safe. I supposed that kind of loyalty was admirable, but it could also be dangerous if it was for the wrong person.

When Eden finally clung to the wall beside the small ledge where Ivy stood, she said something to her that we couldn't hear, then pulled a dagger from her belt. I watched in shock as she held the handle in her mouth and dragged the blade over the skin on her palm.

"What the hell are you doing?" Ivy snapped, her voice carrying across the chasm.

Eden's arm shook as she lifted her bloodied hand and began drawing with her blood on the wall. I watched in shock as words in a language I didn't understand took form on the rock. Osiris drew in a sharp breath.

"Eden—" he started, his face twisting in fear and worry.

"I have to," she said, the words distorted by the knife's handle.

"What is it?" Aven stole the words from my mouth.

"An ancient spell," Nerezza replied. "Used by our ancestors to draw among the power of the gods."

"And it'll work?" Amias seemed skeptical.

"It will, but at a price."

"That's never good," Renna pointed out.

Nerezza's answer was cut off by Ivy's piercing shriek. I snapped my attention back to them only to see that Eden had fallen and was now dangling above the chasm and the lava below, her bloodied hand clutching Ivy's. She caught my eyes and sent a pleading look.

Amias saw it, too, but he didn't have time to stop me. I had already kicked off my shoes and stepped onto the wall.

"Sander," he warned. "I told you not to."

"I don't give a shit," I snapped, reaching for a handhold.

Hurt flashed across his features, but it was gone within a second, blocked by a wall of anger. He didn't stop me. He didn't reach for me. He couldn't risk accidentally knocking me over.

I tuned him out as he started grumbling curses. What I'd said was true; Sadira and I had started rock climbing together when we were eight but stopped a few weeks after Dad died. My bare feet scraped against rock. As I made my way across the wall, I felt them begin to bleed. Despite it, I was glad I'd taken my shoes off. My boots had been big and clunky. I wouldn't have been able to stand on the minuscule ledges I stood on now.

By the time I was halfway across the chasm, my limbs were trembling. Sweat beaded on my forehead. Despite the magic rocks bordering the lava, the heat still wafted up in nearly unbearable waves. It reminded me of the desert outside the SSD. I remembered how happy Amias had been then, how glad he was we'd finally escaped.

More than once, I slipped and saw my life flash before my eyes. Every single regret slammed down on me with the force of a thousand elephants. The guilt, every time I'd lied, the things I hadn't said, all of it. I closed my eyes, pressing my head against the rock.

"Sander?" I heard Amias call to me.

I ignored him and continued inching across the wall. I was close to Eden and Ivy now. A few feet away. My heart beat against my ribcage. My blood flowed in hard, pulsing waves.

I reached for Eden. Ivy winced as Eden shifted to grab my hand. Our fingers met, and I realized then that I couldn't lift her back up to the blood painting. There was no way I was strong enough, especially not now, with my arms trembling as much as they were.

"You have to finish it, Sander," she said. "You will not be able to get me up there."

I shook my head. "I don't know how."

"I can guide you through it, but you have to be prepared."

"For what?"

She didn't answer, only stared up at me with wide eyes.

I guided her toward a ledge wide enough for her to rest her knee on and regain her footing. She dropped her hand from mine. I climbed up a few feet toward the painting and jabbed my palm into a particularly sharp spot on the wall. Blood bloomed. I held up my bloodied finger and began drawing the letters per Eden's instruction.

"This is the last one," Eden said. There was something fearful in her voice, not the steady calm that had been guiding me thus far.

My heart sped up even more, if that was possible. Blood rushed in my ears. The only thing I could hear was Eden's voice as she helped me draw the last one. I pulled my finger off the wall.

The words began to glow.

"Is that supposed to happen?" I asked Eden. She didn't answer. When I looked down, she was gone.

My heart stopped. I looked toward Ivy, but she was gone, too. I noticed then that everything had gone silent. Everyone who had been standing on the ledge by the chasm was gone like they had never been there in the first place.

I shifted, then realized that the pain in my arms and legs had disappeared. The blood on my hand had vanished.

"Sander?"

I jumped. My hands slipped. My stomach flipped. I expected to fall, but instead, my feet met hard ground. I looked up to see the girl with white hair and blue-black skin standing before me. Her eyebrows knit together. She flicked her hand, and suddenly, we were standing in the outside dining hall with my back to the carving of Lua.

The girl's face fell as she brought her hand to my cheek. "You should not have done that."

"What—"

CHAPTER FORTY-ONE

My friends' voices drifted in and out of my consciousness, throwing around heated accusations.

"I saw him!" Ivy was nearly screaming. "He's the one who broke all the Mirrors! He's the one who led the monsters here!"

"Why would I do that?" Amias shouted back.

I blearily opened my eyes.

"Ivy, calm down, please." Aven reached for her, but she swatted them away.

Amias was red with fury. "No, no, no. Don't stop her, Aven. Please, Ivy, continue with your explanation as to why I am working with my enemies."

"I don't know who you're working with!" she shrieked. "But it sure as hell isn't us because I saw you lead those monsters into Avrix."

Eden's face was distraught. "I think it would benefit us all if we were to quiet down."

Ivy didn't seem to hear her. "Give us a goddamn reason, Amias!"

Rubbing my head, I rose from my spot on the ground. The blisters and scrapes on my feet cried out, but the pain was the least of my worries at the moment.

"What's going on?" I asked.

"Oh, thank god." Ivy turned to me and grabbed my hands, a pleading expression on her face. "You agree with me, right? You seem like someone who would."

"Agree with you on what?"

Her voice was panicked. Words fell from her lips almost faster than I could process. "Amias—right before everything went to shit—I saw him leading a pack of those monsters through a Mirror. He saw me and tried to catch me, but then I got trapped in the lava. And—"

"Shut your face," Amias growled. "Are you seriously suggesting that I would betray you all? After all I have done for you guys? I was the one who got you all out of Blackford. I've been the one leading you and protecting you."

"Liar." Ivy was shaking; her voice choked. Tears brimmed in her eyes. "I—I know what I saw. I think."

His expression went slack. "You're accusing me of being a traitor because of something you *think* you saw?"

"You need to leave." Ivy swallowed.

Amias gaped. He turned to the rest of us for support.

Aven averted their gaze.

"Eden?"

"I—" She slumped forward. "I am unsure. Ivy is not a person to lie about something of this significance. We do not have solid proof, but if she were to be right…" she trailed off, letting the silence speak for itself.

Renna clapped Amias on the back. "Well, I'll go pack our stuff."

I blinked furiously, trying to hold back the confusion that rattled my mind. Ivy was mistaken. Amias couldn't have done that.

His jaw was set, fury raging in the blue of his eyes. But he didn't fight. He accepted their decision bitterly, but he accepted it all the same. Concerned, I narrowed my eyes. No one else seemed inclined to find an alternative route.

"You're going with him?" Aven shot up from their seat on the floor.

Renna glared at them. "I certainly don't want to stay with you all if he's not going to be here."

Then, everyone turned to me. My worries about Amias zapped away.

My heart began to pound. "W-what?"

"Well?" Amias prompted. "Are you staying or going?"

My face went cold. I turned to Eden. She had her arm around Ivy and wore a pleading expression as she glanced my way.

To leave would mean to be on the run again. Wandering through the multiverse, sleeping in different places every night. It also meant being with Amias.

Was Ivy telling the truth? I couldn't tell. I sure as hell hoped she wasn't. Amias was one of the first people I had ever considered to truly be a friend, and if she was right…

A knot formed in my chest.

But Ivy could be lying. What if she was the one who had released the creatures? Maybe she'd pinned it on Amias because he had found out about her. No, that wouldn't fit. Amias wasn't saying that.

I bit my nail.

Staying, however, meant being with Eden and her family. Staying at Avrix would mean guaranteed meals and predictable days. Somewhat, at least.

A deep, silky voice chuckled. "My, my, Sander. Your person or your place? Whatever shall you choose?"

I blinked in surprise. Although I was sure none of my friends had spoken, I'd heard the voice as if it was coming from beside me. Whoever it had been was right, though.

I lifted my head to meet Amias's eyes. "I'll come with you."

We weren't in the mountains anymore.

That was the first thing I noticed when we hustled our way through the Mirror. The constant whistle of the wind was gone, as was the dampness of the rock walls hanging over me. Instead, I felt the warmth of the sun beating down on my face. My feet, which Nerezza had so blessedly offered to heal, were stuffed into wool boots that strode through long lines of golden blades of wheat.

Renna let out a pointed, deep breath beside me as we walked. I turned to see her raise an eyebrow at me.

"What?"

"Are you going to tell us why you decided to come with us?"

"Lots of reasons." I glanced at Amias, who walked a couple paces ahead. His pale linen shirt did nothing to hide the inked patterns and drawings that sprawled across his shoulder blades. "But I don't believe Ivy." I swallowed. *I don't want to believe Ivy,* is what I didn't say.

Amias tensed. "Why not?"

"I just—I just don't understand."

"What's there to not understand?" Amias grumbled. "They think I'm a traitor. You and Renna are the only ones who believe the truth. Now, we're stuck here on this world because no one knows how to get back."

"Seriously?" I lifted my head. "All that time at the SSD and you never bothered to learn the one thing we need to get anywhere?"

"I didn't have much time to learn stuff like that," he argued. "I was a little busy being bred into a death machine."

Our conversation slipped into silence, and we stopped to eat the rest of our packed lunch, sitting quietly.

While eating, I caught myself admiring the golden hills of grass rolling in every direction. Mountains rose up in the distance. Birds chirped. The wind brushed through my hair. It was peaceful. I hated it.

I'd grown used to the fierce whistle of the wind slamming against rocks, the faint roar reverberating through the stone tunnels. Although I hadn't been there long, it had felt more like home than home ever had. Mama would've liked it at Avrix.

When I was little, we'd spend our mid-winter breaks at a vacation house in the mountains. Mama would take me up a trail through the woods, and we'd sit on a large boulder together. Just sit. Listening to the sound of the wind.

"Do you hear that, Sander?" Mama would say, tilting her head back to let the fading sunlight fall over her warm features. "That's the spirits of the forest. They're singing for you."

"Why?" I'd ask her.

She wouldn't answer. Maybe because she didn't know. I'd thought it was because she wanted me to find out on my own. The wind today was different. It was strange. Cold. Screaming at me to turn back.

I tucked my hands in my pockets, remembering the fearful expression on Eden's face when I had finished writing the letters. What had happened after that? How had we gotten out of there?

I had a feeling Amias and Renna weren't going to say anything about it. They seemed on edge, Amias especially. I found myself doubting that he was telling the truth about everything with Ivy, then immediately regretted the thought. Of course, he was telling the truth. Why would he lie about it?

Amias whispered into Renna's ear. She gave him a disgusted look but snorted and walked away. When she was out of earshot, he rose and took a seat next to me. His leg brushed against mine. Heat washed over me. He didn't move.

"Sorry for everything." He picked at a rip in his cargo pants. "Sorry for almost getting you killed multiple times. Sorry for, well, like I said, everything. I never wanted to see you hurt, you know that, right?"

My eyebrows knit together. I opened my mouth to ask him why he was saying this, but he cut me off before I could get the words out.

"Listen, Foxy." He didn't meet my gaze. "I know I suck at apologies. I've never really had much practice, but I want you to know that I truly am sorry for everything I've done to you. Past, present, or future."

"What's that supposed to mean?"

"Well, I don't—" He cleared his throat and lifted his gaze to me. Sapphire eyes darted across my face. "Knowing me, knowing our life, there's probably going to be a point in time where I mess something up again. So, I apologize in advance—"

I grabbed his hand. He stiffened but didn't pull away. "Don't say that. You're not going to mess up."

"But—"

"You're my friend," I said, then chuckled to myself. "Hell, you're one of the first real friends I've ever had. There is nothing you could do that I wouldn't forgive you for."

"You never know," he insisted. "What if I murdered your sister?"

"You wouldn't do that."

"You don't know that."

"Yes, I do." I felt my heart rate begin to quicken. "Because I know you. You're not the type of person who would do something like that."

He shook his head. "You can't see the future. What if I do something really, really bad, like end a world, and you're too dead to be mad at me? Or what if you die, and you can't forgive me because you're dead?"

"If I die, then I'll forgive you from wherever we go when we die."

"I don't believe we go anywhere when we die," he said. "I think that's just it. Boom, you're dead, the end."

"You don't believe in heaven or anything like that?"

"Nope. Why should people be punished for just living their life? Or rewarded for living a life like hell? I'm just saying, everyone's life is different, so why should we be judged by the same rules?"

I didn't reply because I knew he was right. "I hope there's something good after death," I said. "Because I don't think I could live a life like this and not wish for a reward."

He squeezed my hand and smiled slightly. "We'll make our own heaven. After this is all over."

I smiled back. "I'm going to hold you to that."

His face flushed.

We had a measly dinner of canned beans and—hopefully safe—berries Amias had stashed in his backpack. For emergencies, he'd said. I guess this counted as an emergency.

Both of them decided it would be better to travel at night and sleep during the day, so that's what we did.

No one knew where we were going. Our only option was to wander around and hope to stumble across civilization. Sure enough, at about midnight, we stepped out from within a forest and onto a road. We followed it as it wound around the mountains and through tunnels.

The events from the previous days flashed through my mind on replay.

I looked up at Amias, walking beside Renna and speaking to her in a low voice. I couldn't hear what they were saying, but it looked private, so I didn't try.

We'll build our own heaven after this is over.

I found myself thinking about what that would be like. I imagined living at Avrix, spending the days out riding and exploring the mountains. Taking care of the baby dragons. Watching them grow up. It was just a dream—I knew that—but I liked to pretend I was there.

Mama was there as well. She'd wake me up every morning with a big, happy smile on her face. The type of smile I hadn't seen her wear since Dad died. Sadira, Libbie, all of them were happy.

The more I thought about it, the sadder I got. It would never happen. I knew this would never be over. And if it ever did end, there was no way we'd all make it out alive. Then, as to be expected from my morbid mind, I began imagining ways we could all die. For some reason, I saw Eden go by falling off a cliff. Ivy was crushed beneath a falling wall. Amias—gunshot to the head. Renna—stabbed, then bled out. Aven—probably in some sacrificial way. Blocking a shot meant for someone else and giving us time to escape.

I saw myself die, too, but I wasn't sad about it. At least I wasn't as sad as I should've been. I found myself hoping that Amias was right. That there wasn't anything after life. I saw my death as peaceful. An end to the madness that I lived in now. I enjoyed that peace. I wanted to feel that peace. But I didn't want to leave my friends.

CHAPTER FORTY-TWO

The sun had just set when we encountered our first car. We were in the middle of playing Never Have I Ever, a game neither of them had played before, when we heard the rumble of a distant engine. I dropped my hand, turning to see headlights speeding toward us. Out of the corner of my eye, I saw Amias's hand go to his gun.

I stuck out my hand as the car neared. It slowed to a stop beside us, engine purring. The window of the old Camaro rolled down, and a balding man with dusky skin peered at us from inside. He was silent for a moment, taking in our stained clothes and messy faces.

"You kids need a lift?"

"Kids?" Amias muttered angrily under his breath.

I rolled my eyes at Amias. "Yeah, that'd be great. If you could."

The man gestured for us to climb in.

The car smelled like cigarettes and dog hair, but I said nothing as Amias and I slid into the backseat and Renna into the front.

"Where are you going?" the man asked as the car started moving.

"Anywhere with food," Renna replied.

"I'm Todd," he said. "Pleasure to meet you."

"Renna," she said, then pointed to us. "Sander and Amias."

"Nice to meet you, too," I said, then nudged Amias.

He looked at me, and I jerked my chin toward Todd. He rolled his eyes and forced a smile. "Yeah. Nice to meet you."

Todd glanced at us in the mirror through round glasses. "I gotta ask, what were you three doing on the road at this time of night? There's no town for miles."

I stammered for an answer, but Renna spoke up. "We were

camping. Our car broke down, and we needed a lift back to town to get replacement parts."

"Well, I could help," Todd offered. "I'm an expert with cars. Just point me in the right direction."

"No thanks. Amias here is a little egotistical when it comes to fixing things. He likes to think he doesn't need any help."

Todd chuckled. "My son is exactly like that. You two would get along."

Amias didn't seem to know what to say. He looked around the car. "Your car is old. Are you, like, an antique collector or something?"

"Old?" Todd raised an eyebrow. "What century were you born in, boy? This car came out five years ago. Top of the line '69 Chevy Camaro."

"Oh." Amias gave me a look. I tried to resist the urge to smile but didn't have much luck. "Right. Because it's 1974 now. Because that's what time it is here. The 70s. Yay."

Amias didn't sound very enthusiastic.

"Do you not like the 70s?" I asked under my breath.

"I hate the 70s," he replied, then fell silent because Todd was staring at us through the mirror. He raised an eyebrow.

"You lot are by far the weirdest group of kids I've met."

Renna laughed. "Man, this is only the tip of the iceberg."

Yeah, I thought to myself. *You're sitting in a car full of murderers. What's weirder than that?*

"Where'd you say you were from again?" he asked.

Renna launched into our impromptu fake backstories, and I fell silent. She was really good at lying. A master at it. I shouldn't have been admiring her skill at deception and manipulation, but I was. I'd never been one to be able to do that. Sadira had always been able to tell when I had stolen her Halloween candy. Mama had told me it was a good thing, not being able to lie. So, I'd never practiced. Now, sitting in the backseat of a stranger's car as he peppered us about our fake lives, I really wished I had.

Eventually, Todd fell silent and let us drift to sleep. I rested my head against the window and closed my eyes.

I wasn't sure when I'd fallen asleep, but a while had passed by the time I felt the car slow to a stop. We were at a gas station. Todd noticed me and pulled a ten from his pocket. "Go get something for you and your friends. You look like you need it."

I thanked him and made my way into the convenience store. The bell rang as I pulled open the door, and a harsh breeze followed me inside. A young man at the counter gave me a quick nod before turning back to his book.

I didn't recognize a lot of the food. So, I grabbed a box of what looked like Cheez-Its, a couple of sodas, and a bag of Ruffles. When I stepped out of the aisle, the cashier had gone. I rang the bell and waited, but nothing happened.

I peered over the desk, then spotted a trail of blood leading to the back room. Chips still in my hand, I raced out the door and back toward the car. Todd was just pulling the nozzle out of the car. He spotted my panicked expression.

"What—"

"Get in the car," I demanded. "Drive! Drive! Drive!"

Renna shifted sleepily as I slammed the car door shut and threw the box of Cheez-Its at Amias's head. The engine roared to life, and Todd pulled the car forward.

"Amias," I snapped, shaking him.

He murmured something.

"Amias, they found us."

He was upright instantly. "What? Where?"

I pointed behind us where a dozen men in SSD suits were bursting out of the store. They saw the car and fired. Todd nearly lost control of the wheel.

"What the hell?" he shouted.

"Just go!" Renna, Amias, and I all shouted in unison.

Amias pulled his gun and fired through his open window. One

of the men crumpled, and I found myself impressed by his aim, then realized that was a dark thought. I shouldn't think like that.

Todd slammed his foot on the gas pedal, and we sped down the highway. He didn't lift his foot until we were about a dozen miles away. Then, he pulled the car over. The vehicle shook as he stood up and slammed the door shut with almost enough force to break the windows.

We watched him awkwardly as he paced the length of the car, hands on his head. He yanked open Amias's door and stared at us with fury in his eyes. We filed out of the car. Soon, we were sitting on the side of the road, watching Todd as he leaned against the Camaro, trying to process what had just happened.

"Do you want a chip?" I asked, holding the box out to him.

He glared at me.

I pulled the box back. "Sorry."

After a few silent moments, he spoke. "Are you going to tell me anything about what just happened? Because I think I deserve to know."

"We can't tell you everything," I said. "But basically, we got into some deep shit and now people are trying to kill me and capture them."

"What deep shit?"

"We can't tell you," I repeated.

"Why not? Is it money-related? I can loan you—"

"It's not money-related." Amias let out an exasperated sigh. "Thank you for trying to help us, but I think it would be best if we went our separate ways."

Todd didn't seem to like that idea. I watched as he contemplated it, chewing on his bottom lip. "How about I drop you off in town? We can talk to the cops, get this all sorted out."

I shook my head. "No cops. Trust me, they're not going to be any help."

Renna stood. "We'll let you take us to town. But that's it. After that, you never talked to us. You don't even know who we are."

He gave a hesitant nod.

CHAPTER FORTY-THREE

Mid-afternoon the following day, Todd pulled to a stop in the parking lot of a dog park. We sat in silence for a moment, watching the dogs race through the green grass and bark playfully at one another. Their owners were oblivious to the group of inter-dimensional criminals that had just pulled up. I envied their ignorance but found it amusing at the same time.

"Thanks for the ride." Amias broke the silence and started to open the car door.

"What? That's it?" Todd turned in his seat to look at us. "You're just going to leave?"

"Um, yeah? Unless you want to hug and kiss goodbye?"

His face tightened. "Amias, I don't think this is a good idea."

"We're saving you trouble," Amias argued. "You said you have a son. Do you really want him to live the rest of his life without a father?"

Todd turned back to face the windshield, on which rain had started to patter. The doors locked. "I'm sorry. I can't let you—"

Amias pulled out his gun and set it on the space between the driver and passenger seat. His finger hovered over the trigger. "Let us out."

Todd's eyes grew wide, but to his credit, he shook his head. The rain pounded harder. "You're not going to shoot me. You're not heartless."

Amias leaned forward, his mouth near Todd's ear as he said, "Try me."

"Amias," I started, heart pounding. "You could just break the door."

He turned to me, eyes narrowed. "And how do we know he won't run to the cops? The last thing we need is the law trailing our asses. Especially since we have no way to leave this world."

"Can't you try asking him?"

"I did ask him. Just now." Then, he turned back to Todd. "Unlock the doors."

I mumbled an anxious curse and reached for the gun. "Give me the gun, Amias."

He pulled away, nearly yanking my wrist from its socket with the movement. "No. I don't see why it's such a big deal. It's one threat."

"You really don't know the effect you have on people, do you?" Blood rushed in my ears.

Todd's face was permanently etched into an expression of terror. Debate echoed through his movements as he subtly reached for the car door.

"What's that supposed to mean?"

I reached for the gun again, trying to give Todd more time. When Amias tried to tug it out of my hands, I could tell his grip had softened. "Give it."

"Stop talking like that."

"Give it."

"Stop talking to me like I'm a dog."

I pulled at his wrists, trying to pry his fingers from the gun. He elbowed me, refusing to let go.

"Stop," Renna said, pressing herself against her door. "You're going to accidentally—" Her words were cut short as a gunshot ripped through the air. We dropped the gun.

"Oops." Amias raised his eyebrows.

"Yeah," Renna cut in and reached across the seats to poke at a lifeless Todd. "Oops."

My heart dropped into my gut. Amias's face went slack.

"Todd?" he said, his voice laced with false hope. Renna nudged

Todd again, and he slumped over, revealing the hole that had ripped through his back.

"Oh god." I pressed a hand to my mouth, bile rising in my throat.

"That's not good." Renna shook her head.

"It's really not."

"Should we just… leave?" Amias offered awkwardly but fell silent when we noticed a woman standing wide-eyed outside of the car, just behind Renna's door. She caught our gazes and burst into a sprint.

"No, no, no. She's going to call the cops!" I tried and failed to open the door.

Panicked, Amias reached over Todd and unlocked the doors.

I raced after the woman and into the park. "Hey! Don't call the cops! It—"

She plowed through a small group of bystanders, shouting and pointing at me. I couldn't make out what she was saying, but the others started running with her. Dogs barked as I leaped over the fence, but I soon slowed to a stop. They were too far ahead.

Then, Amias raced past me. As should be expected from a genetically enhanced super-being, he caught up to them within seconds. He grabbed the woman by the shoulder. She screamed.

"It's too late!" she was saying as I jogged up beside them. Her face was flushed, tears streaming from her eyes. Her arms trembled as she presented her weaponless hands to Amias. The rest of the group had scattered. "Once one of the others reaches a phone, they're going to call the cops. You're going to jail!"

"Dammit," Amias cursed and shoved her away. He ran his hands through his hair, turning to me. "Dammit. Dammit."

"What do we do now?" I asked.

"We get out of here." Renna stepped up beside us, staring at the woman who had frozen with shock. Renna handed her the rest of the Cheez-Its. "Sorry for making you see that." Her words lacked empathy. I could feel their bitterness reverberating through my skull.

The woman glanced at the box, then Renna, then Amias, and

finally, at me. Renna waved as the woman ran away, still clutching the snack box.

"Shit," Amias said as he watched her go. "I should've asked for her car keys."

In the distance, sirens wailed. That was fast.

I followed them at a sprint through the dog park and down the street. When the sirens veered closer, we ducked into a nearby alley, hiding behind a dumpster that reeked of fish and rotten eggs. Cars whizzed past. My fingers trembled. Although fear still pulsed through my body, I'd gotten used to the feeling of imminent doom.

"Take your sweatshirt off," Amias said to me as he pulled his own off and tossed it aside. "Someone from the park has probably given the cops a description, including our clothes."

As I took off my hoodie, Amias peeked inside the dumpster and pulled out a hat. He set it on my head.

"This is disgusting," I grumbled, shaking bread crumbs from the hat.

Amias pulled out a pair of sunglasses and handed them to Renna. She took them grudgingly.

We walked down the street hurriedly, taking care not to run. It would be too obvious. I kept my head down, hands in my pockets, and shied away as cop cars slowly drove past. They were searching for us.

"We need a car," said Amias as we neared the edge of town. He pointed to the endless ocean of pale yellow grass. "We're not going to be able to sneak through that."

"What do you suggest?" I glanced around. "Steal one from a parking lot?"

He shook his head. "I don't trust 70s cars. As easy as they are to break into, last time I stole one, it broke down before I could even get twenty feet."

"Maybe that was because it was broken to begin with." Renna rolled her eyes. "You smashed the engine when you fell on it."

"That wasn't my fault," he snapped. "If you hadn't pushed me off the roof—"

"We're stealing a car," I interrupted. "Because we don't have any other option. Unless you want to go to jail, I suggest you pick one."

He chose a pale blue truck parked outside of a malt shop and punched the window in. I kept watch as he hotwired the car. A cop car slowed down as it passed us.

I elbowed Amias. "Hurry up. I think they spotted us."

The cop car turned around, making its way back toward us. I saw the cop's hand go to his gun, and he said something into his walkie-talkie.

"Aw, hell," I cursed. "He saw us."

The engine roared to life. The cop car stopped, and the officer jumped out onto the pavement. Before we could pile into the truck, he fired twice. One bullet went into the side of the car. The second hit the wheel. It hissed and deflated.

"Wonderful," Amias grumbled and pulled out his own gun.

"Don't shoot him." I slapped his arm. "He's just doing his job."

"I'm just trying to live," he snapped back and fired. But the bullet hit the ground beside the cop. I knew Amias had done that on purpose.

We ran into the shop, slamming the door closed behind us. A few dozen heads swiveled to stare at us.

Without hesitating, Renna fired her gun into the air. "Everyone out!" she shouted.

They didn't hesitate before screaming and pushing past us toward the door. The crowd created a diversion. The cop couldn't risk shooting at us without hitting one of them. We raced through the kitchens, pushing past workers and chefs.

Renna snatched a handful of fries and shoved them into her mouth as we ran. She caught my glance.

"What?" Her voice was muffled by the food.

I shook my head. Amias pulled the back door open so hard it almost fell off its hinges. Two cops, who must've been searching the space behind the shop, turned our way. Amias slammed the door as they shouted and ran toward us. With inhuman strength, he pulled a fridge across the path of the door. I watched the muscles in his arms ripple as he did so, even underneath his sleeves.

There was pounding at the door. Amias turned to face me, but his wild grin fell when his eyes caught on something behind me.

I had a sinking feeling that I knew what it was.

"Don't move," said a voice, false confidence masking the fear behind it.

A gun cocked.

We were loaded into separate cars, which was probably for the best. For the cops, of course. Not for us. I sat in the back of the 70s cruiser, hands cuffed behind my back, and peered out the window at a dozen cops. Amias grinned at me from his car and held up a set of broken cuffs.

If I could, I would've given him a thumbs up. But since I wasn't some superhuman, I was defenseless against my handcuffs. I was about as useful as a piece of wet cardboard.

I watched as he snuck out the far door. No one noticed. At least, not until Amias had grabbed Renna and disappeared behind the malt shop.

One of the cops pointed. I didn't see the rest of what happened because another cop opened the car door and sat down in the driver's seat.

"Sir," I said, frustrated and hungry. "If you have any snacks, I haven't eaten in a while. It would be great if you could get me something."

"Sorry, Sander," said a voice I recognized. Troy Coldwell grinned at me in the rearview mirror. "There are no snacks on the ride to hell."

Breathing had become difficult, I found, as Aven's brother tugged me through the terrifyingly familiar pristine white hallways of the SSD. Men and women in blue and gray uniforms formed a circle around us.

How had they found us? And so quickly. Almost as soon as we'd left Avrix, they'd been on top of us.

I dug my nails into my palms. Where was Amias? Shouldn't he have noticed I was gone by now? Unless they weren't going to come after me. Maybe they had decided I wasn't worth risking their own freedom. If I was being honest, I wouldn't be surprised if that's what they thought.

I lifted my head and took a few deep breaths, trying to ignore the possibility that I would never see Sadira again. Or Mama. Or any of the other friends I'd made. I never even got to say goodbye.

But that should've been expected. Deep down, I'd always known it would end like this. Maybe I should just throw myself on a knife and get it over with.

I was thrown straight into Blackford, which I found surprising. I'd been expecting to see the Director. Or Warren. Or someone.

Instead, they threw me through the doors of the cafeteria and slammed them shut behind me. The rest of the prisoners, who were eating lunch, fell silent as their eyes landed on me, sprawled in a pitiful heap.

I shook out my arms as I climbed to my feet, rubbing my wrists. The hair on the back of my neck rose. I felt their gazes as I made my way up the ramp circling the rotunda and into my old hallway.

My cell was empty. I hadn't been replaced, as if they had expected

I would be back. I ignored the prison uniform that had been laid out for me and collapsed onto the cot. It was a fitting end, to die in the same place my life had truly started.

CHAPTER FORTY-FOUR

Fortunately, I didn't die overnight. Although I wouldn't have been terribly upset if I had.

Apparently, I had become famous during my time outside of the prison. Famous enough that I was appointed two guards to watch my every move. Even though their faces were covered by the dark visors on their helmets, I could sense their piercing stares as I made my way to breakfast. Five feet away from me at all times. Even in the bathroom.

It made me wonder why they hadn't done this from the beginning. From what I'd gathered, the SSD took pride in Blackford being one of the strongest and most secure prisons, yet the six of us had escaped. If Amias and Renna were so powerful and important, why hadn't they upped the security on those two? The SSD didn't necessarily seem like a corporation that had been built on trust.

As I walked through the prison, I could feel the inmates' curious and skeptical stares. Whispers echoed as I passed.

"Seriously? This is the boy who broke out?"

"He's awfully scrawny. Must be all brains."

Oh boy. I guess they hadn't gotten the full story. I had barely done anything in our escape.

"I heard he manipulated the Blood Bringers into helping him."

I perked up a bit at that one. I wasn't sure what type of story the SSD had woven about us breaking out, but it seemed they hadn't included the betrayal of their biggest weapons.

I had to scoff. Me? Manipulating Amias and Renna?

But after a morning of pondering the rumors, I had to think

that maybe they were on to something.

A plan began to form in the back of my mind. I guess spending all that time with trained assassins and spies hadn't accounted for nothing.

A spark of hope lit inside me. Determination to see Mama and Sadira coaxed that spark into a bright flame, and I couldn't help but smile as the pieces started to fall together.

At lunch, I asked around for some art supplies. After dancing from person to person, I was finally directed back to my guards, whom I had to nearly beg for something to draw with. In the end, one of them sighed and came back with a piece of paper and a crayon.

After thanking them, I took a seat at our old table and began to sketch.

Time went by slowly. Too slowly. While doodling, I observed my fellow inmates.

For a while, I studied a blue-skinned woman with fins behind her ears and gills on her neck. She walked with a purpose, but by the way she slumped when she thought no one was looking, I could tell her confidence was forced. Probably due to a subjugating need to act like she knew what she was doing, stemming from being forced to be the parental figure for a group of people—a group I noticed quickly.

They followed the blue-skinned woman around, asking for her when they got confused or when they needed help with something. But this woman and her followers weren't the type of people I was interested in at the moment.

About mid-afternoon, a commotion shook the cafeteria. A deeply androgynous person with long purple braids and dark skin began shouting at a younger boy. Their English was choppy, but their anger got across. The boy skidded away as quickly as possible.

A couple of guards attempted to settle the situation, but that only made the person with the braids angrier.

Temperamental. Hot-headed.

For the next few hours, I continued to observe them. They got into arguments often. They had trouble backing down. Obvious stress laced their every movement, even when it was time for the inmates to head back to their cells for the night.

One of my guards stopped me as I started toward mine. They motioned to the drawing. "Can't take it to your cell."

I resisted the urge to roll my eyes. What was I going to do with a crayon and paper? Still, I ducked my head in compliance and hustled my way through the crowd to get to the trash can.

The guards fell behind. The wave of exiting inmates swept them aside.

Heart racing, I eyed the purple-haired person.

They were also in the crowd. I ripped the paper and, as I squeezed past them, shoved part of it into their hand. I met their confused gaze with a hard stare.

Their face morphed from uncertainty to recognition. They knew who I was.

I tilted my head toward the guards—still struggling to catch up with me—then met the person's eyes.

They caught on, gave a small nod, and then pushed past.

I bit back a sigh of relief and smiled, then slipped the crayon into my pocket.

Department 1, Day 11

I am not a good person. That much is obvious.

But for years now, I've been pondering a question I haven't yet found an answer to. What makes a good person? Is it moral decency? Unbiased kindness to others? If that were true, would being nice to a bad person be considered a good act?

I asked my friend what she thought about my question. She said she didn't think good people existed. We all have our own opinions.

I can't know for sure what a good person is. But I do know that those who harbor more hatred toward themselves tend to be kinder to others. As sad as it is, society sees these people as gullible. Someone whose kindness can be taken advantage of. Sander is one of these people.

At the beginning of his story, he didn't know how to fight for himself. He didn't know when people were using him, or even if he did, his selflessness won him over. It was because of his nobility that he was seen as weak. But he was far from weak, even before he could fight. Because physical strength and intelligence cannot make someone spiritually strong.

Unlike my friends and me, Sander doesn't fight for himself. He fights for the well-being and happiness of others. And that, I think, may be the key to becoming a good person. Being someone who can put aside their own selfish needs to support their loved ones without expecting anything in return is a feat that only those who are truly good can pull off.

–Elyane

CHAPTER FORTY-FIVE

I wasn't sure what euphoria felt like. But I imagined it was similar to what I was feeling now because, at the moment, I felt invincible.

An unstable giddiness danced through my body. It overwhelmed my limbs, forcing my leg to bounce impatiently in the white fur chair I sat on as I scanned the minimalist furnishing of the office around me.

My plan was genius. Even though I could easily point out a few flaws and errors, every inch of me was absolutely certain I would succeed because if I didn't, well, no one was coming to save me.

I stifled a pained laugh.

That was the best part about this new feeling. I wasn't worrying. In fact, I didn't care about anything at all.

The giddiness overtook me, and I jumped up, pacing the cement floor. I padded to the windows on one side of the room, overlooking a large, concrete room similar to the garage I'd seen on my previous adventures around the SSD, but not quite the same. I pressed my face against the glass, trying to see further, but there wasn't anything to see. The room was empty, save for a few gray posts.

"What are you so happy about?" Troy walked through the office door, and I caught a glimpse of a dozen or so uniformed guards waiting in the hall.

This meeting with Troy hadn't been part of my plan, but I knew it would be okay. As long as he got rid of me soon, it would all turn out just fine.

I shrugged and turned to face him.

Troy perched on the armrest of the sofa and brushed a strand of his slicked-back hair from his face. I hated how much he looked like Aven. "You've changed. You're not the scared little boy I remember."

"Yeah, well, that's what happens."

"That's what happens when you become a murderer." He grinned.

My eyebrows knitted together. "How—"

"I know lots of things. Of course, your friend has been quite helpful." He pressed a button on the remote sitting on the coffee table. Somewhere nearby, a door swung open on noisy hinges. I turned to the window in time to see a figure stumble out from underneath us.

The Major turned to face us, craning his neck. His face was bloodied. The pink of his hair had been washed and bleached. An open burn scarred his neck, starting on his chin and disappearing underneath his tattered, bloodied shirt.

My mouth went dry.

The Major's eyes landed on me. His mouth fell open. Then, he narrowed his eyes at me accusingly. "I knew it!" he shouted, his voice muffled by the glass separating us. "You traitor! You sold us all out!"

"No, I didn't!" I called. "Nevena did! She's been manipulating you since the beginning."

The Major shook his head. "She wouldn't dare. My own Shadow."

"Give up," Troy said. "Whatever Nevena did to make him trust her worked well. We gave him all the proof he needed, but he refused to believe it."

We'd been right, then. About Nevena. "Why are you showing me this?" I snapped. "The Major may be an asshole, but he doesn't deserve to be treated like this."

Troy smiled, a thin, cruel smile laced with malice and sadism. "You really are quite a legend around here, Sander Fox." He leaned onto his desk. "The boy we thought of as nothing turned out to be one of the SSD's biggest threats."

"Biggest threats," I snorted. "What type of threats are you facing?

A rat infestation?"

"You escaped," he said simply. "You are one of the first to do that. You know our secrets. You walked through our halls. Letting you live would be a danger to all of us."

I groaned. "Wow. You took forever to say that. I know you're going to kill me. You don't need to tell me a whole story as to why."

A muscle in his jaw twitched.

Rage trembled through me, building into a roaring wildfire. "You need to stop pretending to be the big bad villain. Honestly, you're not that scary. You're just a boy, trying to fit into the shoes of someone better than you."

He shot to his feet, eyes flaring. "I could kill you right now."

I leaned back. "Go ahead."

"You don't believe me?" He pulled out a gun.

"Oh, so scary." My expression remained bored, but the trembling in my bones didn't lessen. "You can't threaten someone with something they're not afraid of."

Troy lifted his chin and put his gun down on the table. However, he didn't let it go. His finger danced over the trigger, and I watched it with a composed demeanor that I didn't truly feel. "I'm not going to kill you."

I raised an eyebrow. "Do you change your mind like that often?"

Troy rose and made his way to the window, where he gestured to the Major, who was sitting in the middle of the room with his head in his hands. My eyes trailed over the burns on his face. It'd been weeks since I'd seen him last. Had he really spent all this time here?

"Would you like to know why your little group is still free?"

I didn't say anything. He was going to tell me anyway.

"Believe it or not, they weren't our first priority."

I straightened, curious. "Then what was?"

He seemed pleased to get a reaction out of me. "My father and I have been working on something. Something that could change the entire multiverse." He grinned at me. "Allow me to demonstrate."

He pressed a button, and I heard the sound of a garage door opening. The floor beneath us trembled. Then, a low growl shook the window panes. The Major's face went slack.

I approached the window.

The growl rippled through the air again, and a figure stepped out from underneath us. Its pale, cracked skin, unnaturally long limbs, and deadly sharp teeth were horrifying enough, but even worse, it hadn't torn the Major to shreds yet.

The last time I encountered one of those monsters, it went straight for the nearest snack, SSD or not. The Director had been terrified of them. Terrified because she hadn't been able to control them. But if I had to guess based on the scene laid out before me, I'd say that was exactly what Warren and Troy had been working on all this time.

My whole body went numb as I watched the monster slowly approach the Major.

"We call them Phantoms. The creatures, once human, are now nothing but mindless drones ready to follow orders."

"How—" The question stuck in my throat.

"I'm sure you wouldn't understand," Troy said. "But in words you could, we stopped treating the Phantom's brain like it was a human's and started treating it like the creature it was. Although, some seem to show signs of still being conscious."

"And it worked?" I asked, breathless.

"Obviously." Troy gestured to the Phantom now pacing in a circle around the Major. "Of course, we've only managed to complete a few transformations. We will begin mass-producing soon."

"Mass-producing?"

"The serum, of course." He chuckled and glanced at me. "It's quite similar to the one we used on you. Did you ever wonder what that did?"

I went silent. I had wondered. For the first few weeks after my second escape, it had gnawed at the back of my mind. But when nothing happened, I'd tried to forget about it. I'd hoped Troy wouldn't bring it up. But of course, he had. He loved talking about his experiments.

I didn't want to talk about it, so instead, I shifted my gaze back to Troy's slate eyes and changed the subject. "Do you have him?"

"What?"

"Did you capture Amias?"

The corner of his mouth curved, and my body went numb. "Oh, Sander," he crooned. "If only I could be the one to break it to you."

"What's that supposed to mean?" I called after him as he made his way back to the door.

Troy answered over his shoulder. "It means you overestimate Amias's attachment to you." His grin grew wider when he saw my crumbling expression. "Come with me. I suppose I can show you now."

I didn't have much of a choice. But before I could make my way toward the door, it swung open.

The Director stepped in, wearing a tight black suit. Her hair was pulled back into a flawless low bun. Her eyes narrowed at Troy, and he appeared to shrink into himself.

"Son," she growled, her voice as sharp and deadly as ice.

Troy bowed his head. "Mother."

She took a step forward, heels clicking against the white tiled floor. "How long has Mr. Fox been here?"

"He arrived midday yesterday, ma'am."

She turned her gaze to me. "It's been a while since I've seen you." She addressed one of the guards standing outside of the room. "Escort my son out of here. I will deal with him later."

The Director gestured for me to take a seat on the couch. As I did, a guard grabbed Troy by the arm and pulled him out the door.

There was a long moment of silence.

"What did he tell you?" The Director said, her voice strangely even. Sometimes, I wondered if she was a robot.

I struggled for words.

"What did he tell you?" she said again.

"Nothing," I blurted. "Nothing. Not really. Just that you can control the Phantoms now."

The conversation slipped into silence again as she studied my expression. She frowned. "You are spoken so highly of. But I don't see your significance. You look like nothing more than trash picked from the street."

"Um…" I didn't understand. What did that mean? Who had talked to her about me? "Thanks?"

She lifted a perfectly trimmed brow, then turned to the window and faced the Major. She tapped on the glass twice. The Phantom backed away from him.

The Major glanced up at us. When his gaze fell on the Director, I got the impression his whole world had shattered. I recognized surprise, betrayal, and utter shock cross his face all at once, followed instantly by a wave of guilt.

He mouthed a word. A name. An emotion I couldn't understand passed over the Director's face. She turned back to the guards.

"Put Mr. Fox back in Blackford."

They reached for me. I didn't bother fighting as I was dragged back to prison.

The plan had changed.

I gritted my teeth as I stormed up the ramp of the rotunda, my guards trailing closely. Troy and his big mouth had to go and brag about the Major. Now, I had to add another step to my plan.

I grumbled a curse, scanning the prison for the purple-haired person.

The giddiness from earlier had morphed into annoyance. Not only would I have to get myself out of Blackford, but now, I had to get the Major out from wherever they were keeping him.

I rubbed my face and told myself to calm down. Not that it helped.

It would be okay, though. I just had to get back into Troy's office. Which, if I managed to escape Blackford unscathed, wouldn't be too difficult. If everything went to plan, that is.

My eyes landed on lavender braids. Their gaze was on me already, and when they realized I had seen them, they began shoving their way up the ramp. I headed down to meet them.

As we neared, their milky white eyes flicked to my guards.

"When?" they whispered as we brushed past each other.

"Now," I muttered back.

Even as they disappeared from my line of sight, I could feel them tense up. I crossed the cafeteria and headed into the bathroom. My limbs threatened to give out from the nervous buzzing that ran through my entire body.

I slipped into the nearest stall and waited, pulling the crayon from my pocket.

It wasn't long before sounds of a commotion slipped through the doorway and into the bathroom. My guards, who stood at attention just outside the stall door, quickly conversed about who was going to check it out.

As soon as I heard a set of footsteps depart from the room, I stepped out of the cell and, in a flash, jabbed the crayon into the remaining guard's Adam's apple.

The guard choked, hands going to his throat. I pulled the Taser from his belt and zapped him. He let out a strangled cry and collapsed. Just for reassurance, I tased him again. Once he stopped moving, I pulled off his helmet.

I blinked at the face before me. I recognized it. Brown hair, a simple face with messy stubble. Where had I seen him before?

I shook my head. He had a plain face, one that was surely similar to enough people I'd seen to account for the familiarity.

Although I felt weird about it, I made quick work of stripping him of his uniform and putting it on. I shoved the man into a stall and locked it, then slipped out into the chaos.

Whatever the purple-haired person had done worked because the prison was in absolute chaos. Relieved that my message had worked, I shouldered my way through the panicking crowds.

Inmates were screaming, shoving past each other in their efforts to get out the door. The guards had their guns out but weren't firing. Perhaps they were under orders not to harm us. I didn't have time to consider the reason because another guard began yelling at me.

"Why are you just standing there? Go get help!"

I gave a brief nod, my giddy smile hidden by the helmet. Someone grabbed my arm.

A pleading face stared up at me. "Please," cried the boy in a prison uniform. "I can't turn into one of those things. I want to live."

I jerked my arm away from him and advanced toward the exit. I swallowed, ignoring the blooming guilt in my gut.

The note had been a lie, obviously. But seeing as it had come from someone who had stepped outside the walls of Blackford, someone who was known to have a relationship with two of the SSD's biggest assets, they'd be stupid not to believe it.

Through murmured whispers yesterday, I'd learned that news of terrifying creatures under the SSD's control had spread throughout the prison, as had the fear. Demonic humanoid creatures with a thirst for blood that had once been people. I hadn't said much in my note, merely that the next batch of the monsters were to be made from the remaining Blackford prisoners. Based on the temper and anxiety of the person with purple hair, I knew I could count on them to act on their emotions without adhering to logic. My faith in their emotional instability hadn't been misplaced, for the chaos they'd wreaked now enveloped the prison in a wave of shouts and screams and the sound of bodies being thrown to the floor.

In my new uniform, I announced I was going for backup and

was let right through the doors toward Troy's office. I resisted the urge to skip down the sleek hallway and instead walked briskly until I was out of sight.

Making my way back to Troy's office was easy enough. But once I got there, carefully shutting the door behind me, I soon realized a flaw in my plan: if I were to break the Major out, I would first need to figure out how to get into the cement room he had been in before.

I scoured the office, searching desperately for the remote Troy had used earlier. As I did so, my hand brushed against a keyboard, and a holographic screen lit up.

I paused, for one of the files on display was titled with my name.

Come on, Sander, my mind snapped. *We don't have much time. Get the Major and go.*

Curiosity took control of me. I clicked on the file. The first thing that came up was a report. A summary of my time with Warren.

My breath caught in my throat.

Sweat beading on my hands, I scanned the words.

Week 1

Compared to the previous subjects, Sander's reactions to my replica of Substance A seem to be taking longer to show. By slower, I mean they are almost nonexistent.

It went on with a lot of sciency stuff I didn't fully understand. Blood rushed in my ears.

Week 2

It's remarkable. At first, it seemed like his body and cells were rejecting the serum, but I realize now that it is the serum that is rejecting his body. Samrah designed this serum to adapt depending on the living organism's DNA structure. Sander is not like a being I have ever encountered.

My mouth went dry. What did that mean? I wasn't human?

Voices echoed from the hallway, getting closer by the second. One voice I recognized. Troy.

Heartbeat louder than my thoughts, I raced for the door and struggled to find the lock.

"Goddammit," I cursed, hating the stupid, fancy technology. I pressed a button, and something clicked. It seemed to work, so I raced back to the computer, frantically searching for a way to print the files.

The door shook.

"He's in here!"

Then, I heard a familiar voice. "Don't make us do this, Sander." It was Troy. "I truly don't want to see such a mess."

I didn't have time to ask what he meant because a low growl rippled through the air. The floor underneath me began to vibrate. A Phantom emerged from the space beneath the office. My throat went dry as it turned to pin its bloodshot eyes on me through the window.

The Phantom's muscles rippled as it took a step back, then launched itself at the window. The glass cracked underneath the impact of its hulking body but didn't shatter.

My eyes snagged on a vent in the ceiling. I used the desk chair as support and heaved myself into the cramped metal vent. Below, the monster leaped for the window again. Pieces of glass sprayed across the room as the Phantom burst through the window, landing in the office with a thud.

I let out a desperate cry, tossing the vent cover downward at the creature fruitlessly. It roared in retaliation, claws clicking against the tile as it made for me.

My elbows and knees banged against the metal as I pulled myself through the opening and then army crawled forward, away from the opening.

I screamed as something grabbed my foot. I slid against the metal despite my useless attempts to stop.

Dammit. Dammit. Dammit.

I didn't want to die like this.

For some reason, as I was pulled out of the vent, I was struck with the image of my broken body hanging limply as a set of SSD guards tossed it into a fire. I wasn't even sure where the image had come from.

I landed on the ground with a thud and quickly scrambled to my feet.

Bloodshot, crazed eyes pinned on me. My body froze in place. My limbs turned to stone. It took another step forward, slowly, not with the brainless ferocity I'd seen before. It was stalking me. Teeth bared, it knocked me aside with its free forearm and pulled the door open in one swift movement, nearly ripping it off the hinges.

A dozen guards burst in, guns raised and trained on me. I rose from my spot on the ground, pain splintering through my hip. I faced Troy as he walked in. He had something like a phone pressed against his ear and was yelling angrily at the person on the other side of the line.

"We got him, all right? I know you warned me." He rolled his eyes. "You win. You know him better. But I promise you, from now on, he's not going to be a problem." His eyes narrowed at me. "Keep in mind, you're not the one in charge. No, I don't care that you could kill me without breaking a sweat. My mother left me in charge, and if you want to talk to her about it, be my guest." The person he was talking to said something, and Troy's face twisted in rage. He hung up without another word.

My limbs went numb as his eyes flicked over my body. There was silence for a long moment, the only sounds being the raspy breathing of the Phantom and the ticking of the clock hanging on the wall. It had gotten to the point where I'd begun to find the ticking annoying before I spoke.

"How did you find me?"

"The guard's uniform you took. Once we found out what you

had done, we tracked you with that to here." He let out a tired sigh. "I underestimated you, despite being warned. My mother is going to be disappointed."

I had to fight hard to resist the urge to roll my eyes. "Is that seriously all you care about? Proving to Mommy you're not as useless as you seem?"

His eyes flared, and I knew I'd hit a sensitive spot. Based on what Aven had told me about his brother, Troy had always been angry at Aven for being favored. Today, I was angry at him. I didn't care that a dozen guns were pointed at us. This could be my last chance to piss him off. I wasn't going to let it go by.

"Do you even realize how childish you are?" I asked. "What are you? Twenty years old, and you haven't mentally grown past five? Maybe that's why the Director favors Aven."

"My brother," he spat. I bristled. "Is a broken idiot with the mental capacity of a toddler. Not to mention a traitor and a disgrace to our family name. He could never become like me. I worked while he played. I always have."

"And yet, somehow you're still the disappointment." I gave him a pitiful frown. "Even after your *sibling* ran away."

He took a step back, eyes narrowing. "How do you know that?"

I let out a small chuckle. I hadn't known. I'd taken a chance. Looks like I'd guessed right. "You're never going to be loved by your mom," I taunted. "I mean, what did you expect? You can't even keep me in a prison. Me, of all people. Do you realize how low you've sunk?"

Troy turned on his heel. "Shut him up."

A soldier grabbed my wrists, placing the tip of his gun at the back of my neck. "Don't speak," he growled, shoving me forward. I stumbled but held my chin high as I was escorted out of the office.

The Phantom's long claws clicked against the tiles, bringing everyone's eyes toward our group. Guards posted at doors went still. People in black suits and long white coats stopped to stare. I felt like I was at school again, which was odd considering the situation. But the way they stared at me as I walked past reminded me so much of the way the other students would. I half expected to turn and see Sadira and Libbie walking behind me.

Up ahead, the crowd began to part as a figure stormed around the corner, coming straight for us. Beside me, Troy's face went slack.

It was the Director. The click of her heels joined the scrap of the Phantom's claws. I couldn't tell if the complete lack of expression on her face was terrifying or not. The only thing that gave away her anger was the way she gripped a pen tight enough to make her knuckles turn white. Her cold, gray eyes flickered over me and the Phantom before finally landing on Troy.

"Explain."

It wasn't a request.

"Mother—" Troy swallowed. "I—"

"He called me. Told me everything that happened." Her eyebrows narrowed, the first emotion she'd shown since walking up. "Should I trust his word, or would you like to explain your side of the story?"

Everyone's eyes darted to Troy. He bit his lip. I could see the debate flickering across his expression. Should he tell the truth? Or lie to his mom in hopes of her taking his side? If he chose the second option, what were the chances that she'd believe him? Eventually, he lowered his gaze and spoke. "He was right. About everything. I underestimated Sander and thought it wouldn't do any harm to put him back in Blackford."

A muscle in the Director's jaw twitched. She took a step forward and backhanded Troy across the face. The slap echoed through the silent hallway. "Useless boy," she hissed. "Have you learned nothing from the last two times he was here?"

He lifted his head, gesturing to us. "But I got him back! See!"

"At what cost? You revealing our control over the Phantoms to the enemy?"

I raised my eyebrows.

"If he had gotten out, then what would you have done?" she continued. Everyone was staring at us. Troy's face was turning red, shame creeping over his features.

"He wouldn't have gotten out," he protested. "This building is too secure! And you know the only reason he got out the last two times is because we wanted him to!" His eyes widened the moment the words spilled from his lips. He clasped a hand over his mouth and turned to me.

"You…" My voice fell away. I tilted my head in confusion. "What?"

The Director's face was red with fury. She slapped Troy again, then pointed down the hall. "Go tell your father to find me, then wait in my office. I need to clean up your mess, once again."

Troy hung his head shamefully but walked quickly down the hall. When he turned the corner and disappeared from sight, the Director faced me again. A cold expression had fallen over her sharp features.

She faced the Phantom. "Go back to your siblings."

It grunted and lumbered off without hesitation.

The guards shoved me forward, following the Director as she led us toward an elevator. I watched the Phantom as it made its way down a different hallway. People nearly pushed each other over to get out of its way.

The elevator doors chimed open, and I was thrust inside with not-so-gentle hands. The doors closed, and it was just the Director, two guards, and me.

"You probably have questions," she said. It took a moment for me to realize she was addressing me.

"I… um, some?"

She sighed through her nose. "My idiot son has already spilled two of our biggest secrets, so I don't see the point of not answering a few of them."

"What did he mean when he said I only escaped because you wanted me to?" I blurted.

"A little experiment of ours to see where your journeys would take you." It wasn't really an answer, but she didn't seem inclined to share more, so I shifted my question.

"So, when Nevena came to break me out, she was working for you?"

She gave a short nod.

"Who helped her with the bombs back in Primos?"

The corner of her mouth curved, and I felt a chill run down my spine. "I'm surprised you haven't figured it out already. But I suppose emotions are more blinding than we'd like to think."

I frowned, even more confused than before. "What?" Was she suggesting I was close to this person? My heart began to sink as realization settled upon me. Everything had been moving so fast lately; I hadn't really stopped to wonder if maybe—no. *Stop thinking like that. He wouldn't betray us. He hates the SSD and the Director more than anything.*

"What about the Major?" I said, shoving the horrid thoughts away. I could deal with them later. If the Director was willing to answer some questions, then I wanted to get as many out as I could. "What did you do to him?"

"I didn't do anything," she said. "That was all my husband. He has somewhat of a… grudge, against the Major."

"What do you plan on doing with him?"

The elevator slowed to a stop, and the doors pinged open. The guards nudged me forward and I jumped, having forgotten they were there.

"That's none of your concern." The Director led me into a narrow, empty hallway clad in white tiles and LED lights. Her impossibly tall high heels clicked as I trailed behind her. Every twenty feet or so, we'd pass a door marked with a large black number, starting from one and continuing up.

"Now that I've answered a few of your questions, why don't you answer some of mine?"

I silently cursed myself. Of course, she wasn't going to give up the answers to her questions without asking for something in return. I'd been stupid to expect otherwise. "I'd rather not."

"Oh, I understand." She let out a light chuckle, little more than a huff of breath. "But I'd suggest you do as I say. It'd make this whole thing a lot easier on you and me."

I gritted my teeth.

"Is Aven still alive?" she asked. "Our tracker on them cut out about a week ago."

"Last I saw they were," I grumbled, trying to hide the worry that had started seeping in. "What do you mean, the tracker on them?"

She stopped and tapped the back of my neck. "We put small trackers in your neck. How do you think we managed to find you after all this time?"

I didn't answer.

She continued, "The trackers monitor your vitals, heart rate, and all the necessities. But Aven's stopped transmitting. As did Ms. Harrison's and Ms. Kavan's. Either they're all dead, or they found a way to block the signal."

"Like the towers back at Primos," I said in realization. "That's why you had Nevena take them out."

She nodded. "Indeed."

"But why? If you already had two spies there, then why would you need them to take out the towers when you already knew where we were?"

"Because the towers didn't just stop the signal; they stopped us from using Mirrors to gain access to Primos. Well-built city, I might say. The Major certainly knows some smart people."

"What makes you think he didn't build it himself?" I asked bitterly.

The Director laughed. Really laughed. I raised my eyebrows in surprise. "Have you met the man? He spends his days at the bottom of a wine bottle. Even if he didn't, I've known him for longer than you'd think. There's no way he'd be able to create something as complex as that."

"If he didn't build it, then who did?" My question wasn't necessarily for her, but she answered it anyway.

"I think I have an idea," she mused, eyeing me.

I curled in on myself, hating myself for allowing her to scare me this much.

The echoes of our footsteps stopped as the Director came to a halt beside door number thirty-three. She stepped in front of the keypad and punched in a set of numbers, using her body to shield it from my sight. The door clicked and swung open automatically.

The room we walked into was small, and I was struck with an overwhelming sense of claustrophobia.

There was a man curled into a ball in the center of the floor. I couldn't tell if he was sleeping or dead. But when the Director nudged the man with the tip of her foot, he jerked back, eyelids flying open.

My heart dropped to my stomach.

The man's eyes were bloodshot, his pupils covering his irises and looking in different directions. From a blackened spot on the side of his neck, his skin had begun to crack, allowing blue blood to trickle over his skin and stain what was left of his tattered shirt.

"What is this?" I said, bringing my hand to my nose to cover the stink.

"The beginning stage of a Phantom," the Director said, kicking the man again.

He rose, his breathing labored and raspy. His arms dangled in front of him, seemingly longer than typical. He turned to me, mouth hanging open as if he wasn't able to close it.

"God," I mumbled. "Why are you showing me this?"

The Director grabbed the man's warped face, holding one of his eyes wide open with no particular kindness. I watched for a moment as she inspected the man, turning him this way and that. "I truly despise you, Sander Fox. I hope you know that."

"Is there any special reason? Or can you just not handle my personality?"

She turned to face me again, blue blood on her fingertips. She pressed those bloody fingertips to my face, grabbing hold of my jaw with surprising strength. Her face twisted in disgust as she sneered, "You have your father's eyes."

I fell quiet.

I'd been told that. Many times. By his friends, by Mama, by Sadira, too. But even more so after he'd died. So many people said it with pity or jealousy behind their words but never anger. No one had ever been mad about that.

"You have his jawline, too," she said, tracing her finger over it as she spoke. "And his cheekbones. Hell, you even sound like him."

I swallowed. "You must've known him pretty well if you can remember what his cheekbones looked like."

She released me, taking a step back. "I did know him pretty well. In fact, he was almost the father of my children."

The world went silent. My knees weakened. Shock blanketed me with the strength of a thousand boulders. "What?" I was barely able to get the word out.

"But then he met your mom," she continued, then faced the man again. "Which is why it's going to be so fun to turn you into that."

CHAPTER FORTY-SIX

They left me in the cell with the twisted, bloodied man. He spent the night pacing the length of the room, groaning and mumbling incoherently. I sat in the corner, head in my hands, and tried to process everything that had happened. Everything she had said.

She was lying, right? There was no way my dad would ever… Oh, god. I was disgusted just thinking about it. But if she was telling the truth, it would explain why my dad never talked about his past. Maybe—

"Shut up," I snapped at myself.

"Shut up," the man mocked me.

I glared at him.

"Shut up. Shut up. Shut up," he muttered to himself on a loop, as if he had forgotten all other words but those. I hadn't even known him for a day, and I already despised his presence, though he made me feel better about my sanity.

He continued mumbling the words, circling the room.

I squeezed myself further into the corner when he passed me, blocking my nose to keep the stink from bombarding me. As I did, the door beeped and swung open. A guard entered, his helmet obscuring his face. Carrying two trays, he passed one to the man carelessly but approached me slowly.

I lifted my head when he extended the tray with gloved hands. I looked at myself in the black visor that protected his expression from my view. "I'm not hungry," I said blandly, shoving the tray back at him.

"Please," he said quietly. His voice sounded familiar.

"I said I'm not hungry," I repeated.

He turned his head toward the corner of the ceiling above me. I followed his gaze to find he was looking at a camera I hadn't noticed earlier. I frowned.

"Are they watching me?"

The guard set the tray down in front of me and moved to scratch his wrist. His sleeve shifted, revealing the tattoo of a snake spiraling his wrist. My head snapped up, desperately searching the masked face for any sign of familiarity. He didn't seem to notice my reaction because he rose and left the room without another word.

I shot to my feet, but the door slammed in my face before I could chase after him.

Tattoos were normal, common. It was possible the guard had tattoos on his arms. It was possible it was just a coincidence. But I'd seen the snake tattoo before.

I ran a hand over my face. That hadn't been Amias. Had it?

I ended up eating the stale bread and peas the guard had left, and after, I managed to fall asleep. My dreams were filled with blood. Blood that stained my own hands.

Fires blazed around me, the heat waves blurring everything in the distance. A few feet ahead of me, I could see Amias on his knees, coughing blue blood. I took a step forward but froze when my foot landed on something soft.

Fear clutching my chest, I looked down and bit back a shriek. Ivy's cold brown eyes stared back at me, empty and vacant. There was a bullet hole in her forehead. I scrambled backward, only to trip and fall onto another familiar corpse. White hair stained red sprawled across the ground. Eden.

I leaped to my feet.

Beside Eden, Renna's body hung limp, a pole emerging from her back.

Behind me, I heard the snap of bones and spun. A Phantom crouched on its hindlegs, munching on something in its claws. Oh god. I nearly threw up as Aven's head dropped from the monster's clutch and rolled along the bloodied ground.

"Fox!"

I looked back at Amias. "Wha-what's happening?" I asked.

"Why didn't you help?" he cried, coughing up more blood. "I thought we were friends."

"Amias—"

His hands fell from a gaping hole in his chest. His face was full of anguish. "You were my friend." Then, he crumpled to the ground.

I jolted awake, heart still pounding. The smell of blood and vomit washed over me, and I gagged, opening my eyes to see the man leaning over me. His sunken, morphed face was inches away from mine, close enough I could feel his hot breath against my cheek.

I couldn't keep back a yelp and instinctively kicked him away.

He took a few shocked steps back. "Shouting," he enunciated slowly, thinking about the word before it came out of his mouth.

I sat up. "You smell disgusting."

He didn't seem to understand. Instead, he'd become absolutely fascinated by a crack in the wall. I tried to ignore the sinking feeling in my gut.

I was going to become like that. If not worse. Warren would somehow figure out how to mess me up. The Director had made a promise, and I didn't see her backing out of it.

Desperation moving my limbs, I made my way to the door and tugged on the handle. I hadn't expected it to work. I'd tried earlier and it hadn't budged, but this time, it gave, and the door swung open. My eyes widened as I stared into the empty hall before me.

This had to be a hallucination.

I thought about what Troy had said. *The only reason he got out last time was because we wanted him to.* Was this one of those times? If so, should I do the opposite of what they wanted and stay behind? But how would that make the situation any better?

I felt someone brush against my shoulder. The man with the

cracked skin grinned wildly as he stepped up beside me.

"What's going on?" I asked, not really expecting an answer.

"Feeding time," he answered, wiping his mouth.

"What?"

Then, the other doors swung open. All fifty-something of them. What emerged sent a chill down my spine.

More than a hundred Phantoms, whether complete or in progress, stepped out of the rooms and began pushing past each other toward a door at the far end of the hall. I backtracked into the room. My cellmate looked at me worriedly but didn't do anything to stop me.

The crowd was moving slowly, the pale, deformed creatures pushing past each other desperately as they tried to reach wherever they were going.

I grabbed one of the empty trays from the ground and waited for them to pass. When they finally dispersed and the only few left were the weaker stragglers, I took a tentative step out of the cell. I shifted my grip on the tray and peered toward the door through which they'd disappeared.

Roars and screeches echoed down the hallway, followed by human screams. Horror gripped me. Were they really feeding humans to those monsters?

I didn't have time to worry. I made my way toward the elevator door and greeted the keypad beside it with a curse. I pushed on the door beside it, the one labeled "Stairs," but that, too, was locked. Gritting my teeth, I crept into the room with the Phantoms. Would they attack me, too?

The walls were made of concrete. The doors on the far side were thick and heavy and, again, blocked with a keypad. Even if I did try to guess the passcode, it probably had a failsafe.

The Phantoms ignored me as I paced the circumference of the room, running my hand along the wall in hopes of finding another way out. The people who had been released to the beasts paid no attention to me, nor did the Phantoms. I tuned out the screams and snarls, my heart thundering in my chest as I looked the other way. It was so loud I almost didn't hear when someone hissed my name.

"Sander."

I turned.

"Sander Fox," a bloodied man stumbled from the crowd toward me. The Major lifted his scarred face to meet my gaze. His deep brown eyes were full of pain. "You traitor."

"What?"

"Don't play innocent," he snarled. "I saw you talking with that whiny, desperate son of a bitch."

"Who, Troy?" I began to see why he was confused. "It's not what you think—"

"Save it," the Major started to turn away from me. "If you're down here, then we're both going to die anyway."

"But—"

"You should shut up, traitor."

"I'm not a traitor," I said, exasperated. "I'm a prisoner here, just like you. Troy just wanted to brag to me about his control over the Phantoms. I don't know what you thought was going on, but I can assure you, I would never in a million years work for them."

He peered at me. "And how do I know you're really you? Not a Reflection."

"Because I know you have a secret room in your office, and I don't think my Reflection has been in there."

He frowned. "How did you know that?"

"Ivy, Eden, Renna, and I snuck in a while ago because Ivy was being paranoid and didn't trust you." A crash sounded on the other side of the room. I ignored it, as did the Major. "We opened the door by accident."

He seemed hesitant to trust me. I studied the bruises on his face and the burn on his neck. Eventually, the Major let out a sigh and herded me to the back corner of the room. He took a seat on a stack of crates and gestured for me to do the same.

"The Phantoms haven't seemed to notice us," I noted, watching the massacre but turning away when I felt my meal from earlier begin to rise.

"I'm on the no-kill list," he said, touching his burn tentatively. "And since you haven't already been eaten, I suppose you are, too."

"No-kill list? Then why are you here in the first place?"

He shrugged. "The Director likes to use every chance possible to make me feel worse about myself."

"Why? I mean, I know you led a revolution against her, but this feels personal."

A shadow crossed over his face. "I'll tell you later, perhaps. Have you talked to Amias yet?"

My heart lurched to a stop. I struggled to speak for a short second, then managed to say, "Amias is here?"

His expression fell, eyes filling with sympathy. "You don't know, do you?"

"Know what?" I had a feeling I knew what he was going to say. "Is he okay?"

"Sander," his tone had gone soft. "Amias is working for the SSD. He always has been."

Before I could even process his words, the entire room fell silent as all the Phantoms suddenly went still. They turned their heads toward the door and began making their way back to their cells in sync. Then, another door clicked and opened.

The Director's cold eyes landed on me, and she stormed over to us. The click of her heels had grown annoying to me, I noticed. That said, I wasn't sure whether to be thankful or fearful when the clicking stopped and she was silent, staring at us.

"Good morning," the Major said cheerfully, a mask falling over his terrified expression. "I was wondering when I'd see you again. I was just telling Mr. Fox here that his friend still works for you. Care to explain the rest?"

Her mouth tightened into a thin line. "Come with me. Both of you."

I made to follow her, but the Major held me back. "Why should we?" he called.

She held up a small remote I hadn't seen before and pressed a button. A zapping sensation radiated through the back of my neck. It wasn't painful, not that much, at least. But it was enough to let us know that she could do worse if she wanted.

The Major grumbled something under his breath and shoved me forward.

"You're lying, aren't you?" I whispered to him as we trailed the Director. "About Amias working for them?"

He shook his head, pity in his eyes. "I wish I was. I trusted him, too. But I saw him myself. Amias is on their side, which means Renna probably is, too."

I didn't want to believe him, so I fed myself the same lie I told him. "You're wrong. He's probably working as a spy for the others. Eden will know what he's doing. Amias can get us out of here. He did it before."

The Major didn't answer. I hadn't expected him to.

We walked through the door and were led into a slightly smaller room lined with TVs displaying the room we'd just come from. There were a few other people, but their conversations died off as soon as we entered.

A man approached us, giving the Director a small bow before saying in a thick accent, "Apologies, ma'am, we should have kept them apart."

"Yes, you should have," she said.

I eyed the man with the accent as we passed. He had braided black hair tied back with strips of leather and dark skin that offset the unique grey-blue of his eyes. White swirls crawled up his neck and around his pointed ears. My mouth fell open. He seemed to know that I recognized him because he turned away, dropping his chin shamefully. My steps faltered to a stop.

An Avrixian. Working for the SSD. God. Was everyone working for them these days?

The zapping sensation tingled my neck again, this time sharper. "Keep moving," the Director snapped.

I forced my feet to move again. We were led down a hall and up an elevator, then through another series of hallways before finally arriving at our destination, which turned out to be a part of their stronghold I had never been to before.

The Director pushed through a set of glass doors, revealing what looked like the bottom level of a strange hotel. The concrete walls, trimmed with vibrant light, stretched upward for dozens of stories, each level lined with dozens of doors connected by a steel walkway. At the top of the structure, I could just make out a domed ceiling.

We circled around the back of the room and entered a glass elevator. Inside, the Director pressed the button for floor number seventeen and leaned against the back corner as the doors slid closed.

"Where are we going?" the Major asked, taking a seat on the ground. He grunted and stretched out his legs.

She ignored him. "I made a promise to you, Mr. Fox. I intend to keep it. Keep that in mind as we move forward with our day."

We spent the rest of the elevator ride in silence, as well as the walk around the circular hotel. I ran my hand along the railing, staring at the massive drop below us in awe. How had they built this?

The Director pulled a keycard from the jacket of her suit and slid it through the handle of Room 717. What we stepped into was not what I'd been expecting.

I assumed it was her room, but I found it odd. She was the leader of this place, and yet the room was small and bland, consisting of little more than a kitchenette, bathroom, bedroom, and couch. A few pictures hung on the walls, a blue rug had been laid across the hardwood, and a mahogany desk peeked out from beneath piles of papers.

The Director opened the door to the bathroom and shoved the Major in.

"Ooh, I've always wanted to be murdered in the bathroom. Make sure you do it over the drain though. Easier to clean up the blood."

"Get in the shower," she growled. "You smell like shit."

His response was cut short as she slammed the door behind him. She made her way over to her desk and began sorting through the papers. Barely a second later, the water began running in the bathroom.

"The Reflector and his council are on their way," she reported to me, sensing my confusion. "They are not a fan of the work we've been doing."

"So, you're trying to cover your tracks," I realized.

She nodded and turned to me. "You will behave. Don't even think about letting a word about the Phantoms slip through that mouth of yours, or we'll blow your brains onto the wall."

"Um, okay."

I stood awkwardly in the corner of the room while the Major finished his shower. When he stepped out of the room, gingerly drying his burned head with a towel, the Director shoved me in, pushing a suit into my arms along the way.

I stood quietly as the water ran over me, trying to find peace in the rhythmic pulse of the water. I couldn't remember the last time I'd taken a shower, and it should've felt good, but the sense that the Major was right about Amias weighed heavily on my happiness. If he was right, then that would mean it was Amias who had helped Nevena with the bombs. It also meant that he'd been the one to let the Phantoms in and the one who'd smashed the Mirrors back at Avrix. Which meant… Ivy hadn't been lying.

Meaning I'd made the wrong choice.

Someone banged on the door. "Hurry up!" the Director called.

I switched off the water and reached for a towel. After pulling on the suit the Director had given me, I stared at myself in the mirror for a while, unable to recognize the tired boy who stared back. I found myself worrying that if I ever saw Mama again, she wouldn't recognize me either.

I pulled open a drawer and reached for the nearest weapon I could find, which turned out to be a pair of nail clippers. I tucked them into my back pocket and shook myself out. I didn't care if she wouldn't recognize me; I couldn't die without seeing her again. Without seeing any of them again.

As much as I wanted to, I couldn't give up. Not yet.

The Reflector. Aven had mentioned him during my first week at Blackford. I clawed at my memories, trying to recall what they had said. From what I remembered and what I'd gathered from the Director's words, he was the man in charge. Something about an inter-dimensional government, right? Something even bigger than the SSD.

We walked briskly back to the main part of the SSD's stronghold. The Major did his best to keep up, but a limp I hadn't noticed before became apparent.

"Does the Reflector even know about the Rising?" the Major asked when we piled into an empty elevator. "Because honestly, I'm really surprised the big man hasn't shown himself until now."

"He does not know that you are involved. He still thinks you're working for me," she snapped.

I bit back my surprise. The Major had once worked for the Director?

"Your only job during this meeting is to sit beside me and keep quiet. Say nothing about the Rising or the Phantoms."

"Why is he coming then? If he doesn't know about the Phantoms or the Rising?" I asked, then immediately regretted it when she sent me a cutting glare. Why was I even coming to the meeting? I doubted the Reflector knew who I was. I kept my mouth shut as the elevator opened and we stepped into a room large enough to fit my family's old apartment.

Simple black-bordered white walls stretched nearly thirty feet, curving into a dome decorated with sparkling chandeliers. A window took up the far wall, slanting outward and overlooking some sort of cafeteria. The cafeteria was nearly empty, save for a janitor and an older lady bent over her meal. The Director gestured to the vacant table beneath the chandeliers, and I took a seat beside the head.

"When's he going to get here?" The Major's words were echoed by the sound of doors opening and the clamor of voices. A group of well-dressed men and women entered, crowding around a gray-haired man and peppering him with questions.

The man seemed bored. He ignored his followers and stepped up to the Director, offering her a cold smile. "It's nice to see you again, though I wish it were under different circumstances."

"As do I," the Director said with a bowed head. In her heels, she was taller than the man. It was awkward to see her bow to someone who seemed so inferior. Was this the Reflector? The short, rounded man who grunted with effort as he made to sit in his chair?

His beady eyes met mine. "Ah, you must be Sander Fox. Am I right?"

I nodded, mouth dry.

The Major took a seat next to me. "How does he know who you are?" he whispered into my ear as more people began to fill the seats, including Troy, who sat across from me.

I didn't answer him, mainly because I didn't know, but also because the lights in the room flicked off and the Reflector rolled a small metal ball onto the table. It slowed to a stop and opened into a triangle. From the triangle, an image projected into the air.

I held back a shocked gasp. Holograms were things I'd only ever seen in movies, but surely the rest of the people in this room had seen them dozens of times.

The image flickered for a moment and changed from the blue ball it had been to a mountain. A mountain I recognized.

"Eleven days ago, a small town on Department 978 was attacked by an unknown species of creatures. Their leader reported to me that these creatures had come through the Mirrors." The Reflector turned to the Director. "Did you know of this?"

Oh. So that's why he had come. But why so late?

The Director stayed quiet.

"Of the nineteen thousand living there, ten thousand were killed, and many more permanently injured."

I looked down, shame creeping over me. It hadn't necessarily been my fault, but I could've done more to help save them. The Major looked at me curiously, though he couldn't have known I'd been there.

"But sir," Troy spoke up. "Why are we worrying about these creatures? I mean, we've seen worse, haven't we?"

"They went through the Mirrors, Mr. Coldwell." The hologram image morphed into a picture of the Avrixian outdoor dining area. Through the image, I could see Osiris and Eden bent over a table, arguing about something on the paper sprawled out in front of them. "This is a live feed. The Avrixians gave me permission to set up small cameras around their town. As the Reflector, it's my duty to keep the crossings of the dimensions strictly for those who need it—and to stop creatures, such as these ones, from wreaking havoc among the multiverse."

The rest of his words were drowned out by the thoughts in my head. I had become focused on the image before me. A live feed, he'd said, which meant the Eden in front of me was the real one. They were safe. A knot in my chest loosened, but at the same time, something else tightened. Before now, I hadn't realized how much I missed them. They'd been the first friends I'd ever truly cared about. If what the Major had said about Amias was true…

"Mr. Fox."

I snapped my head around, searching for the person who had called my name.

The Reflector raised an eyebrow at me. "Is it true you were at

Avrix at the time it was attacked?"

I stayed silent, casting a glance at the Director. This seemed like a topic I should avoid. She spoke for me.

"Yes. Sander, as well as Amias and Renna, were sent to Avrix to try and convince their leader one last time to join us."

I scanned the occupants at the table as they talked. Most of the faces I didn't recognize, but the ones I did were Warren, Troy, the Director, and the Avrixian I had seen earlier. His gaze was solemn, eyes on his hands. Shame shaped his features.

The Reflector sighed. "They gave us their answer a while ago. I ordered you to respect their word."

"With all due respect," the Director said, "having the Avrixians on our side could do wonders. They can do the things we can't. They can bring people back from the dead."

My heart stuttered to a stop.

The Director's stony facade slipped as the words continued spilling from her mouth. The rage boiling beneath her surface seemed just about ready to burst. "Ambrose and I have both seen it firsthand. Imagine what our future could be like if they sided with us. There'd be no more loss. No one would have to suffer. We could rule the multiverse and—"

"Verena," the Reflector snapped, shooting to his feet. His chair screeched across the marble. "We are not gods. We do not get to play at being gods. We are here to keep the dimensions from becoming a pool of chaos, and that is it. The only reason I have brought this case to you is because, last time we talked, I remember Warren saying something about a failed experiment. These creatures look awfully close to the image he described."

Verena. That was the Director's real name. Why did it sound so familiar?

"I'm only going to ask once," he growled. "Do you or do you not have something to do with the creation of these creatures?"

She met his gaze with unwavering intensity. Her cold, calm

composure had taken back over her body. "I do not."

I bit back a retort.

The Reflector didn't seem to believe her. I sent a pleading glance his way, but it was useless because his eyes were on the Director. If I could somehow let him know that she was lying, then maybe he could get the Major and me out of here. And maybe we could take down the SSD while we were at it.

More importantly, maybe I could see my friends again.

There was silence for a long moment. No one dared to even breathe. Eventually, the Reflector sat back down.

No. No, no, no. Don't believe her. Stand back up. Keep pushing.

But he didn't. He leaned back in his chair. "Let's take a break. I'm starving."

The Director glanced at me and the Major, but then bowed her head again. "I'll go see if I can find something." She and a few others, including Troy, left the room without another word.

The door closed, leaving just the Reflector, the Major Warren, the Avrixian, me, and a few others I didn't recognize.

The Reflector locked his gaze onto me. "I'm so pleased you've joined our cause. Your father really made a name for himself around here. It's going to be hard for you to live up to."

I had no idea what he was talking about. My father had never once mentioned a place like this. I hadn't joined his cause. All I wanted was to get out of here. I didn't know what lies the Director had fed him. The only choice I had was to play along.

"Yeah," I muttered.

"It's horrible what happened to him. Car accidents are such a shame. Some worlds have such poor technology."

I nodded. If he thought it was a car accident, then he had taken the Director's word and didn't further investigate my father's death. So far, the Reflector seemed like a very lazy person. Maybe I was better off trying to figure out a way to escape on my own.

He met my gaze, then rose to his feet and gestured for me to follow him. I did as he said.

The hallway was empty, but he still lowered his voice when he said, "You know what's funny? The report I was given about your father's death said he was killed in a home invasion."

A chill swept down my spine.

"So, Sander. Do you want to tell me what's really going on?"

I swept my gaze from side to side, double-checking the hallway. "I—" I cleared my throat. I wasn't even sure where to start. "She's been lying to you. For years, from what I've gathered."

"Lying to me about what?"

"A lot of things," I said. "But first, I need you to get me and the Major out of here. She's implanted some sort of device in our necks that emits a shock whenever she presses a button on a remote."

He frowned, bushy eyebrows furrowing.

"Please, sir," I begged. "You have to get us out of here. I left my friends and—"

"I can't."

The hope that had begun to fill me shattered. "What?"

The Reflector glanced toward the door we'd just walked through. "I'm sorry. If you're lying about this, I can't risk losing her loyalty."

I gaped at him. "You can't be serious. You lost her loyalty years ago. She's been playing you all this time. The Major—you know him? He's been leading a revolution against her for years. They only managed to capture him recently. That's because Nevena was spying on them and—"

"Nevena? Nevena Harrison?"

"Yeah, do you know her?"

"Of course, I do. She set my house on fire. Her parents are mercenaries. I hired them to do a job for me a while back. They didn't do everything I asked, so I refused to pay. In return, they sent her to get their money."

"Well, she's working for the SSD now," I said. "The Major also believes Amias is still working for them, but that can't be true because we escaped a few months ago and—"

"I saw Mr. Wolf ten minutes ago," he said.

"What?"

"He was the first one to greet me when I arrived. He's in the cafeteria."

My body moved before I could think. Within seconds, I had pulled open the door to the stairwell and thundered down the steps faster than I'd ever gone before. I burst through the doors labeled *Staff Cafeteria* in no time.

More people had come in since I'd last looked through the slanted window in the meeting room, and now a light chatter filled the air. I scanned the room frantically and went entirely still with rage when my eyes landed on a familiar face.

He was sitting with a boy I'd never seen before, leaning over the round table as he talked and picked at his food. The boy was listening intently, nodding every now and then.

It felt like a dream. A nightmare, to be exact. It was terrifying to see him sitting there so casually. In this place. In this hellhole. I was seeing it; it was playing out in front of me, but I couldn't believe it.

But then the boy, looking around my age, said something and tilted his head back, laughing. And Amias smiled. He smiled. His features lit up in a way I'd never seen before. Like he was truly happy.

I didn't understand the hatred running through me. But I didn't have time to ponder over it because the doors behind me burst open again, and the Reflector came rushing through, panting and yelling my name.

We'd caused a scene.

Amias and the boy looked over at us.

Our eyes met, and Amias's expression fell, taken over by utter shock. It was then I knew that Ivy hadn't been lying. Nor had the Major.

Amias was a traitor. He had been from the start.

CHAPTER FORTY-SEVEN

I couldn't remember if I'd passed out or been knocked unconscious. All I knew was that when I woke up, the back of my neck was screaming in pain. My head was fuzzy. I couldn't seem to think straight. I heard voices, but it took me a moment to understand what they were saying.

"What exactly are we planning on doing with him?" I didn't recognize the voice. Its timbre was smooth, reminding me of rounded sea rocks.

"We can't kill him." I recognized that one. A deep, gruff voice laced with constant anger at the world. Amias.

Hatred shot through me, sharper than I'd ever felt before. Still, I kept my eyes closed. I wasn't sure I could open them, even if I wanted to.

"Why not?" asked the calm, smooth voice.

Amias took a moment to answer. "Because he's useful to our plan."

Traitor.

"I should've trusted Ivy," I muttered, lifting my head despite the soreness spiderwebbing through it. I took in the faces of those around me. The Director, whose expression was calm as ever. Warren, standing behind his wife and picking at his nails nervously. Troy, sitting in a chair beside them, hands clasped in front of him and jaw clenched. Then, the boy I'd seen earlier, now standing in front of me. His face was almost as calm as the Director's. And finally, Amias. His eyes were pinned on me, fists bound into tight balls at his side.

"Glad to see you're awake," he said through gritted teeth.

"Don't fool yourself," I snapped.

"There's no need for anger," the boy interrupted. I hadn't gotten a good look at him earlier, but now that he stood in front of me, I slowly studied his features. A strand of his hair had been dyed orange and braided back, nesting among his dark curls. A strip of leather held the braid together. It dangled in front of his amber eyes. The roundness of his eyes and the soft curves of his jaw gave him a naturally kind complexion, but there was something about him that seemed slightly off—aside from him standing among all of my enemies.

The boy in front of me looked exactly like a young version of the Major. I began to get a sinking feeling in my stomach.

I shifted in my chair, pulling against my bindings. My eyes flickered over the conference room we'd had the meeting in, its seats now empty.

"Who are you?" I asked.

He chuckled. If he'd been my friend, it was a sound I might've liked. "How rude. I forgot to introduce myself. I'm Caspian."

He said his name with pride as if it was supposed to mean something to me. What was his importance? Who was he to the SSD? And why was Amias so close to him?

My hands shook violently from both fear and rage. I dug my nails into my palms. "Why aren't you planning on killing me? It would be a hell of a lot easier than keeping me alive."

"Perhaps," the Director agreed. "But, at the moment, you're of importance to us."

I didn't even look at her. My gaze had shifted to Amias. He stared right back at me, unmoving.

I cracked my neck, eyes still pinned on Amias. "How long?"

"Since the beginning."

I did my best not to show the way my heart split. "I trusted you," my voice cracked, ruining my attempt at composure.

A flicker of guilt passed over his face, but it was gone as soon as it had appeared.

"I trusted you!" I screamed, lunging forward despite the ropes on my wrists and feet. The chair didn't budge.

He took a small step back anyway but righted himself quickly. Caspian's eyes turned to Amias. There wasn't worry in his expression. Instead, he seemed curious. Curious to see how Amias was going to answer.

"That mistake is on you."

Kill him now, said a voice. I scanned the room, surprised. *Now, Sander*, said the voice again. I couldn't tell where it was coming from, but its deep, urging tone reminded me of a voice I'd long forgotten.

"Maybe I should," I said aloud. Confusion flickered across everybody's faces. "Maybe I should gut you like the animal you are."

Amias's face fell.

I hadn't meant to say that. It was so… vivid. I couldn't control the words that spilled from my mouth.

"You're not just a traitor or a murderer," I spat. "You're a monster. I thought you at least had a conscious, but now, I know you're barely even human. You'd be better off dead."

Amias bent down in front of me, sapphire eyes dancing across my face. "I might be a monster. I might not have a conscience. But at least I'm not like you. Hopeless. *Weak*. At least I can fight for myself. At least I'm actually of use to my friends rather than just a weight on their shoulders." He sighed and patted my shoulder. "Because that's who you are, Fox. You're a burden. You cause nothing but grief for those who have to carry you. You say I'd be better off dead, but we'd all be better off if you had never existed."

I was speechless as he rose and exited the room. Was that really what he thought of me? The words spun in my head as I stared at the floor, my vision beginning to blur. Those words confirmed the thoughts I had day after day. *You're a burden. You cause nothing but grief for those who have to carry you.* If that's what he thought of me, then what did others think?

Caspian shifted, his boots scraping against the floor. "You seem like a nice person, Sander," he said. "I'm truly sorry you had to find out about Amias this way."

I lifted my gaze to his amber eyes. They were beautiful eyes, the color of sunlit honey framed by long black crescents. I hated them. I hated every part of his stupidly stunning face. I hated the way he gave me a sorrowful smile, his expression full of pity.

"If I might suggest, you could always leave your foolishness behind and become part of our cause."

I couldn't believe what I was hearing. My limbs were trembling, from fear or anger, I couldn't tell. "Your cause. Tell me, what exactly is that?"

"The Director's plan to make the multiverse better for all."

I scoffed. "I'd rather go to hell."

He frowned, seeming genuinely disappointed. "Do you have a problem with me?"

"Do I—" I was unable to finish the sentence.

"You were close with Amias, weren't you?" Caspian tilted his head. "I understand your anger toward me. You saw me bring out a side of him that you were never able to. Are you… jealous, maybe? Did you like him?"

Again, I was at a loss for words.

We'll make our own heaven.

"I didn't like him—I don't—"

"Right. Of course, you didn't." The mildly curious, content expression on Caspian's face was gone. In its place was an image of undiluted rage that I'd never in a million years have imagined he could wear. And it was directed at me. "After all, who could love a monster?"

Everyone exited the room shortly after Caspian's comment. I was left alone, trying desperately to come to terms with everything that had just happened.

The ropes around my wrists were mocking me. Rope. Because they knew I couldn't escape it. Ivy would be able to get out of this mess. And Eden. Renna. Hell, even Aven could. Amias was right. I really was a burden.

If I ever did manage to get out of this place, maybe it would be best if I never saw them again.

We'll make our own heaven.

Son of a… I threw my head back almost violently as if I could throw the thought out of my mind. What had he meant by that? Was that part of his act? Was that a lie, too?

Probably. At this point, I should just assume everything Amias did was a part of his act.

I groaned and shifted my wrists, flexing them against the rope. As I did, I felt something fall from my bindings and clatter to the floor. I craned my neck and spotted what had fallen. It was a scalpel, about the size of my pointer finger. Someone had wedged it in the rope.

Whoever had tried to help me obviously hadn't thought that far ahead because now I had no way of reaching it. I mumbled a curse, trying to pivot the chair with violent jerks of my body. The chair moved but only slightly. I leaned forward and tried again. Unlike my recent failed attempts, this one caused the chair to tip sideways. Before I knew it, I had slammed into the ground with a crash.

I let out a moan of pain. Now what was I supposed to do?

My feet were still bound, but the rope had been bound around the leg of the chair. Now that there was nothing blocking the end of the chair leg, I could slide my foot down and unhook the rope from the chair. I strained my body, stretching through my toes. After a few moments of silent struggling, I managed to free my right foot, followed closely by my left.

With my feet free, I was able to turn myself around so the

scalpel was by my face. I grabbed the handle with my mouth and heaved myself onto my knees, then rose to my feet. I bent forward, the chair still attached to my back.

In most TV shows, people got out of this position by jumping onto their backs and breaking the chair. However, since my chair was made of metal, I doubted that would do much good. Instead, I spit the scalpel onto the table and turned around. I ran my hands along the rim of the table, feeling for the scalpel. When my fingers closed around the cool metal handle, I silently applauded myself. As quickly as I could, I managed to begin sawing through the rope.

Voices sounded from outside the door.

My heart leaped to my throat.

Hurry, Sander, hurry.

The handle started to move.

I sawed faster.

Just as the door began to swing open, the rope snapped and the chair tied to my back fell to the ground with a crash. Without a second of hesitation, I hurled the scalpel in my hand at the figure who had opened the door, just as Ivy had taught me. The sound of the blade sinking into flesh made me want to gag, but I held it back and raced forward.

The second figure, a small woman with a round frame, stared at me wide-eyed as I pulled the scalpel from the first man.

"But—" her eyes darted to the space behind me where the chair and ropes were lying on the ground. "They said—"

I held up the bloodied blade, guilt smashing into my chest. Who were these people? Why were they in here?

I looked to where the first man had fallen to the ground. He was clutching his chest, blood seeping through his hands. His stomach heaved. He stared at me with a fearful expression. There was a moment of silence between us before his eyes glazed over, and he went limp.

I faced the woman, who'd frozen in shock. To the best of my

ability, I forced a threatening expression onto my face. "Help me out of here, and I'll spare you."

Her face went pale. I hated the way terror filled her eyes, but I had to do this. I had to see my friends again. I couldn't die without them knowing the truth about Amias.

"Ma'am? Is everything all right with the prisoner?" a voice sounded from further down the hallway.

I took a few frantic steps backward, praying they couldn't see me or the man.

The woman looked from me to the voice in the hallway to the corpse between us, then back to the voice. Her voice shook as she said, "Yes, we're all right. You can be on your way."

Footsteps faded away. The woman waited until they were gone before turning back to me. I grabbed the man's feet and pulled him inside the room, then shut the door.

"Where's the Director keeping the Major and the Reflector?" I asked her.

"The—Who?" Her hands were shaking.

"The Reflector. The one in charge. Short dude, looks like he needs to stop eating at fast food places."

Her confusion didn't let up.

I rubbed my head, barely noticing the blood on my fingers. "What about Amias? Amias Wolf."

"The Blood Bringer?"

I nodded.

"They're in a conference room a few doors down."

"All right listen. I'm going to need you to do a few things for me, okay? First, tell me where I can get a guard's uniform."

"Twenty-fourth floor," she said. "There's a room labeled *Equipment*. But you'll need a key card to get in."

"Do you have one on you?"

She pulled one from her pocket and handed it to me.

"Thank you," I said before remembering I was supposed to be

mean. I cursed at myself, tucking the key card and the scalpel into the pocket of my suit.

I tied the woman to the chair, hating each second of it. I apologized to her and double-checked the rope before slipping out of the room and pressing the button for the elevator.

The metal doors slid open, and a group of strangers stared back at me. I felt the hope drain from my limbs. Luckily, they saw me but did not react.

I forced myself to move. They didn't recognize me. They couldn't tell I was a prisoner.

"What floor?" a man asked me.

"Twenty-fourth," I replied, hoping they couldn't hear the panic in my voice. "Thanks."

He gave a tight nod and went back to reading a hologram projected in the air before him. I wasn't sure if holograms were a common thing in this place. Maybe I just hadn't noticed during my previous stays. I'd been a bit preoccupied.

As the machine whirred into motion, I found my gaze slipping toward the hologram. At the top, in bold print, it read, "Operation Rising: Complete." The rest of the page went on to report what happened back at Primos. As I read the paragraph he was on, my heart began to sink.

"Early this morning, a group of our scouts reported stumbling upon their main base. It seemed as if it were being run by a trio of girls. Two were unrecognized, but the third was said to be the second Blood Bringer. They were able to get out unnoticed. We plan on moving in on them midday, two days' time, at the Director's permission."

Oh god.

I swallowed a lump forming in my throat. The trio it had talked about… could that have been Renna, Sadira, and Libbie? If so, that meant Renna had managed to get off the dimension we'd been on and back to Primos. Which also meant Renna wasn't working for the SSD; otherwise, she would've come back here with Amias.

"Excuse me," I tapped the man on the shoulder. "When was that report written?"

He scrolled back to the top. "Looks like it was updated yesterday."

"Okay, thank you."

He eyed me warily but said nothing.

I had to get off of this Department. I had to warn them. If I didn't, the whole camp would be slaughtered.

The elevator slowed to a stop. The number above the door read twenty-four. I stepped out along with a few others.

The elevator deposited me in another identical hallway. I should've expected it. It seemed hallways were the only thing in this place. It was a rather large hallway, however, and I was surprised when I was able to make my way down the hall without recognition. It seemed as if I was always at the center of the Director's plans. Either she didn't share what she planned with her followers, or they were just not paying much attention.

Either way, I kept my head down and did my best to avoid anyone's attention.

The room the woman had mentioned was at the end of the hall. Silence greeted me as I pushed open the door. I took a few steps forward. Lights clicked on, illuminating endless rows of crates stacked high on towering shelves. I made my way through the rows, scanning the labels on each shelf. Most of them were for weapons. There was a whole section for chains. I didn't want to think about what those were used for. Twelfth row down, I stopped at the label that read *Uniforms*.

A name marked each bucket. I recognized one of the very first names. Aven V. Coldwell. Their bucket was empty.

I grabbed the first uniform that looked like it would fit me and slipped it on over my suit. It took me longer than I'd hoped to clip on the belt and harness, strap the gun to my hip, and tighten the helmet. Just in case, I hid a few extra guns and grenades inside the unusually big pockets.

As I was making my way back toward the door, I heard a voice in my ear.

"Welcome back, Mr. Strickland."

The inside of the helmet's visor flicked to life.

"Whoa," I muttered in awe, pausing for a moment.

Then, the door opened, and a man entered. He gave me a nod of acknowledgment. As his face came into view, however, the screen changed, and a box appeared next to the man's head. The box contained a picture of him, along with his name, age, birthday, and a bunch of other data that made no sense to me.

I returned the nod and stepped back out into the hallway.

The crowd in the hallway had thickened in the time I'd been gone, which didn't help with the anxiety that had started to tighten my chest. I clenched my fists, drawing in deep breaths. I had to save Sadira, Renna, and Libbie.

But how was I supposed to find the correct symbols for their Department? I silently cursed myself for not asking the woman from earlier if she knew. But maybe…

I made my way to a less crowded part of the hallway and leaned against the wall, trying to act like I was doing something while I pondered over the dilemma.

There had to be someone in Blackford who had been part of the Rising. Maybe they knew the symbols of one of the Stations. Unfortunately, it would take too long to figure out which prisoner I needed. I'd be found out by then.

If I were to free them all, however, they'd lead me straight to where I needed to go. They would run straight back to the Rising, and from there, I could make my way back to my sister.

It was a risky gamble, but one I was willing to take. Deep in my gut, I knew the odds of escape were slim. But truth be told, I didn't care that much. If I was going to go die, I wanted to die fighting.

Easier said than done.

"Now how am I supposed to get to Blackford?" I muttered to

myself in frustration.

As if in response, the same voice I'd heard in my ear in the storage room flicked back to life. "Are you looking for a map, Mr. Strickland?"

"Um, yes?"

The visor's screen changed. There was a map of the stronghold in the bottom left corner. I spotted Blackford and traced a path back to the red dot that signaled my location.

The walk was longer than I'd expected it, but it felt like it couldn't be long enough. Panic had started to seep into my bones. I had no plan. I was walking into a prison and hoping that the guards wouldn't recognize me. Even with the helmet on, I felt exposed.

I opted for the stairs instead of the elevator. I didn't want to risk getting trapped in it. As I climbed the steps, I studied the map on my screen. From what I could see, there were three ways out of this place. Through the garage or the door through which I'd escaped with Nevena, both of which led to the desert. I crossed those off the list immediately. It wouldn't do much good for me if I escaped the SSD only to die of dehydration or starvation.

That left the Mirror. I vaguely remembered the room it was in from the last time I'd been in there. Oddly enough, at the time, it hadn't been heavily guarded, but I had to expect the worst.

About a dozen guards stood outside of Blackford.

I lifted my chin and rolled back my shoulders, trying to act like I was supposed to be there. One of the guards tilted his head when he saw me.

The box next to his face showed a kind-looking man with a crooked smile. Joseph Mason was his name.

"Back from break already, Strickland?"

I nodded, thankful that the person's uniform I'd taken fit in at Blackford. However, if I spoke, he'd realize I wasn't who he thought I was, so I kept my mouth shut.

Joseph didn't stop me as two other guards opened the door to the prison to let me through. The inside set of guards turned to face me in unison, and I felt my heart speed up to a thousand beats per minute.

"I thought—" One of the guards began to speak but was cut off when I pulled a grenade from my belt, pulled the pin, and threw it at the guards behind me.

The explosion threw me forward. I skidded across the ground and slammed into one of the cafeteria tables, any guilt I would've felt being knocked out of my body and replaced with an overwhelming rush of adrenaline.

"What the hell?!"

I climbed to my feet, facing the prisoners at the table. I let out a crazed laugh when my eyes met the purple-haired person. I pulled the extra guns from my pockets and slammed them on the metal tabletop in front of their group. "I told you I wasn't going to leave without you."

"Sander Fox?" They said, tilting their head.

One of their friends grinned. He lunged for a gun and fired at someone behind me. I spun, clutching my own larger gun and aiming it at the group of guards, some of which had started to climb to their feet.

The explosion hadn't killed them all. It had knocked a few out, but the majority of them were groaning and staggering toward us.

The gun in my hands was different than any I'd ever used before, but it seemed simple enough. I loaded it and pulled the trigger. The kickback nearly knocked me off my feet. A string of laughter burst from me. Oh god, I was going crazy. But it was okay because sometimes, you need a little bit of crazy to get out of tough situations. I couldn't help but smile as the faces of my friends flashed through my mind along with that thought.

I pulled the trigger again. This time, the bullets spilled from the gun in an endless stream of metal. I aimed blindly, sweeping it back and forth until all the guards had fallen to the ground.

The purple-haired person frowned at my gun. "I want that one."

I handed it to them without another word, staring at the bodies. I'd just killed them all, but I wasn't sure if I cared. I didn't feel a thing. My remorse must've been drowning under the waves of adrenaline flooding my veins, sending breaths from my lungs in short bursts. I shrugged it off, sure the guilt would come later. That is, unless I'd truly become a monster, too.

I turned to face the increasing number of prisoners who had begun to file out of their hallways and into the rotunda. I pulled off my helmet, and a collective murmur rose around Blackford. "Listen up, people!" I shouted. "More guards will be here soon. We're leaving this shit hole. All of us. Grab whatever weapon you can. Don't expect this escape to be easy."

A cheer rose around the prison cafeteria.

At the moment, I didn't really care that these people were probably murderers. Not after what I had just done. I needed a way out of this place; this was how I would get it.

Besides, I was blowing a hole in the SSD's reputation.

"You are not going anywhere, Fox," said a low, angry voice I recognized.

I turned to the doorway. Amias tilted his head toward me.

"Who would've thought a coward like you could do something as big as this?" He motioned toward the bodies littered around him, not the prison break.

"One man?" Someone in the crowd chuckled. "They sent one man to stop us?"

He must've been new.

"That's not a man," another prisoner said. "That's a monster."

Then, Amias moved. He raced forward, lunging for the man nearest to him. One blow to the head and the man crumpled to the ground, unconscious. Someone lifted their gun and fired, but Amias was faster. He moved with such strength and speed that I barely had time to register what was happening before I was shoved onto the table, gun at my temple.

Amias's face was inches from mine, breath hot on my cheek. He straddled me, one hand pressing my wrists into the table. "You made a mistake, coming back here, to Blackford, and not leaving when you had the chance."

Another gun clicked. The purple-haired person had the tip of their weapon pressed against Amias's head. "Let him go."

Amias let out a deep chuckle, one that sent a chill down my spine.

The panic was gone. Instead, it had been replaced with adrenaline. My body was trembling with raging energy, red-hot and burning.

"I'm giving you one chance," Amias said to them, then said louder, "To all of you. Leave this prison now. Leave Fox to me, and I'll spare your lives."

They hesitated. Leaving would be the smart choice. "How do I know you're not lying?"

"All of you are useless to me," Amias said. "You were brought here to be pawns and guinea pigs. Fortunately, there's a surplus of prisoners back on Primos. However, Fox here is one of a kind. He carries something the Director needs."

What? What was he talking about?

They dropped their gun.

My heart sank.

"Sorry, Sander," they said, gesturing for the prisoners to move out. "If I see an opportunity, I take it. That's just how I work."

I kept my mouth shut, angry but already accepting my fate.

They leaned into a run, and the other prisoners exited Blackford in a stampede of murderers, thieves, and spies.

"Son of a…" I closed my eyes and waited for the sound of footsteps to fade.

"Open your eyes, Fox." Amias pulled himself off me. His voice had softened, but anger still trembled along the edges of his words.

I obeyed. "Why did you let them go?" I asked.

"Were you not listening? I just said so."

"No." I shook my head. "You wouldn't let a whole prison free just to get me."

The corner of his mouth curved. "You have no idea the lengths I'd go for you."

His words confused me. I didn't respond, however, because there was a small click, and Amias's eyes went wide. I grinned, looking down at the grenade from which I'd pulled the pin.

"Think fast," I said and tossed it to him, then threw myself over the table and onto the ground, hands over my head.

The explosion shook the cafeteria. I was sent rolling and slammed into the far wall. My ears rang as I staggered to my feet, back aching. My vision blurred, but I could make out a figure emerging from the prison entrance. It wasn't Amias.

Amias was in the far corner of the cafeteria, blue blood trickling from a gash on his forehead.

The figure that approached me had a slender, lean build, as if there wasn't much muscle on his bones. By the way he walked, I could tell he hadn't done much fighting. I blinked hard, and Caspian's face came into view.

White-hot anger rushed through me, blinding me with rage as I raced forward, screaming in fury. Caspian barely had time to react before I leaped on top of him. He crumpled under my weight, and I threw punch after punch, fueled by anger.

My knuckles were bleeding by the time I pulled myself off him.

"Sander," Caspian started.

I pulled out the last gun I had and cocked it.

"No!"

My head shot up. That hadn't been Caspian's voice.

In the corner of the room, Amias had risen to his feet. He stumbled toward me, his hands raised in surrender. "Fox, please, put the gun down."

"What do you care?" I snapped. "It's not your head about to be blown off."

Caspian's stupidly beautiful eyes were wide as they darted from me to Amias.

"Or are you more capable of caring than I thought?"

Amias's expression was pleading. He looked like he was ready to beg. I couldn't deny the fact that it brought me joy to see him like that.

"I never wanted to hurt you," he said. "Please, you have to believe me."

I wanted to. I really did. "Then why?" My voice cracked. "Why did you do it?"

"Lower the gun."

I shifted my grip on the trigger.

Caspian whimpered.

"Is this seriously who you care about?" I asked in disbelief. "He's a coward. Weak. He's a mouse desperate to crawl back to his hole in the wall."

"I'm not that different from you," Caspian shot back but fell silent when I took a step forward. The muscles in my pointer finger clenched as I tightened my grip.

"I'll give you anything you want!" Amias shouted. "Please, just let Caspian go."

Something in me snapped. I pulled the trigger.

Caspian yelped as the bullet slammed into the ground beside his head.

My eyes were on Amias. "You betrayed me. You betrayed all of us. The least you could do is tell me why."

He didn't answer.

"You betrayed us!" I screamed, tears brimming in my eyes.

Kill them both, a voice whispered in my ear. *Slaughter them like the heartless monsters they are.*

"I trusted you! I cared about you! And I was stupid enough to believe you cared about me, too! But it was all a lie, wasn't it? You never gave a shit about any of us! So how do you feel now, Amias? Are you happy that you managed to tear my life apart? Are you happy that you—you got me to care about you? To like you? Do you delight in the fact that I thought we could have a future together? Do—"

"*I did care about you!*"

It took me a moment to process what he'd said. When I did, it was hard for me to speak. "I—What?"

"I did care about you," he said, pain lacing his voice. "I do care about you."

It was like the world had been knocked from underneath my feet. "What?" I couldn't seem to comprehend what he had just said.

"I wasn't supposed to." It was odd to see this side of him. The broken, emotional boy who had spent years within walls of stone. "I didn't want to. But I couldn't help it."

"But… I thought…" I was crying now. "You said you hated me!"

"I hated you because I couldn't get you out of my head!" he snapped.

He's lying, the voice said. *He's telling you what you want to hear. Shoot both of them before it's too late.*

"You're lying," I said to Amias, shaking my head and backing up. My vision blurred. Tears streamed down my cheeks. "I'm not—I don't—"

"You're addicting, Sander Fox."

Why was he saying this? Surely, it couldn't be true.

"You can't do that. Being friends with you was like hanging off the edge of a cliff. You'd pull me up, make me think I was someone important to you; only then would you shove me back down."

"I'm sorry," he pleaded. I hated seeing him so sad and hated myself for caring. "I didn't understand."

"You didn't understand?" I screamed. "You didn't understand? Amias, you can't play with people like that! I'm not a toy for you to experiment on! I have emotions, too! Did that even cross your mind?"

He wasn't able to respond because there was a flash of movement in the corner of my eye, and before I knew what was happening, the gun had been snatched from my hand, and I was thrown onto the floor.

Caspian. God, I'd completely forgotten he was there.

He stood above me, the gun trained between my eyes. He kept his gaze on me as he asked, "Should I kill him?"

"Kill him?" Amias echoed, confusion taking over the pain. "What? Caspian, what the hell is wrong with you?"

Caspian said something back, but I didn't hear his words because my attention had gone to the man who had materialized behind him.

Dad grinned at me and waved a bloodied hand. "Long time no see, son."

My heart dropped. "What?"

Caspian swiveled his head. Dad vanished. I blinked, then took advantage of his momentary distraction and swung my foot upward toward his hand. The gun flew from his grip, and I lunged forward, snatching it out of the air.

Just like that, the gun was in my hands again. Sometimes, I surprised even myself.

I swung the gun from Amias to Caspian.

"Would you kill them already?" Dad appeared again, ruffling Caspian's hair. "The slightest movement of your finger and boom—" He clapped, and I flinched. "They're dead."

"You're dead," I choked out.

"Dead, maybe. But not completely gone."

"Sander," Caspian said, raising his hands. "We're not the bad guys here."

"You're—" Once again, I was dumbfounded by his stupidity.

"Please, Fox," Amias pleaded. "Don't kill him."

I swiveled my gun to face him. "And why shouldn't I kill you? You're no better than he is, with your cheap little lies and annoyingly perfect poker faces. You're a liar, Amias."

"Kill them," Dad encouraged.

"They hurt you," said a voice I hadn't heard in a while. Leland set a hand on my shoulder. "Don't you want to hurt them back?"

I jumped. *What the hell?* "No, I don't. Get away from me."

Confusion flickered across Caspian's face.

"I'm not a monster," I said, eyes deliberately going to Amias. "I don't hurt people for fun."

"Really?" A guard stepped out from behind Dad. His helmet was shattered, revealing the kind face that had talked to me before I'd entered the prison. Joseph, if I remembered correctly. "Is that not what happened with us? I remember you laughing as you filled my friends with bullets."

"I—"

"I believe you," Amias cut me off. "You're not a monster. You're better than me. You're better than all of us. And you're right. I don't feel guilty about the people I kill. I was trained not to. I'm begging you; prove you're better than me, and let Caspian go. I'll get you out of here. I promise."

"Stop it!" I screamed, bringing my hands to my ears. "Stop pleading for his life! Can't you see? He's not worth it!"

Amias seemed shocked.

"Why do you care about him?" I shouted, voice cracking. "Why does he get to be your first priority?"

"Kill them now!" Dad yelled, anger engulfing his features. "Embrace who you really are!"

"*Shut up!*" I swung the gun toward him. "You're not real! You can't tell me what to do!"

"He may not be real," Leland said. "But you know he's right. You're a murderer, Sander Fox. Just look around."

The other guards began to rise from the floor, surrounding us. My heart lurched. They stumbled toward me, bleeding from the bullet holes peppering their bodies. Then, a new face emerged from the crowd. Todd.

"Do you remember me?" he asked. "You should. It's your fault I never went back to my family, even though you knew how they would feel."

"Stop," I pleaded.

"You killed them all!" Dad screamed at me, forcing my attention back to him. "And it's because of you I'm dead, too! You weren't able to get out of those ropes. If you had, maybe you could've stopped them."

"No! It's not my fault!" I swung the gun from person to person, unsure of who to aim at. With my attention split, I hadn't noticed Amias inching forward. He now stood a few feet away from me, hands raised and expression pained.

"Please," he said again. "Put the gun down."

"Stop saying that!" I shouted.

Dad was still screaming at me. "Pull the trigger, Sander! Pull it now before it's too late!"

I couldn't breathe. It felt like my ribcage was slowly closing in on my lungs. I drew in short, desperate breaths as I took panicked steps backward, hands on my ears. It didn't stop the voices. They were all yelling at me. Every single person in the prison was telling me to kill. Begging me.

I bumped against a table and stumbled.

"Please stop," I begged.

But they didn't. Why should they?

Someone was approaching me. Tears blurred my vision, and I wasn't able to see who it was.

"Give me the gun, Fox," Amias held out his hand. "I don't want Caspian to get hurt."

The anger that took over me was blinding. The second his name escaped Amias's lips, I was in motion. I moved before I could think, and before I knew it, I'd pulled the trigger.

A deadly silence fell over the prison.

I blinked once. Amias looked from the hole in his gut to me. Blue blood trickled from his lips.

I froze in shock. My body had turned to solid stone, and I was forced to watch as my friend fell to the ground, gasping. No, no, no, no. I didn't mean to do that. I didn't—the anger—

Someone slammed into me. I fell backward, my leg hitting the edge of a bench. Another gunshot echoed through the prison.

I looked at the person who had pushed me over. Sapphire eyes raked over me with worry.

"Are you hurt?" Amias demanded, helping me to my feet.

"I—"

Had it been a hallucination?

I didn't have time to answer him, because someone fired again. This time, I felt the bullet whizz past my ear.

Then, a shout sounded from the hallway. "Don't kill him!" It was Troy, along with a few dozen guards. "The Director wants him alive."

Amias reached for the nearest table. With inhuman strength, he lifted it off the ground and hurled it at the group racing toward us. I didn't see what happened next because he grabbed my arm and pulled me toward the rotunda's ramp. As we ran, my eyes flicked over the spot where I'd seen Amias fall to the ground, bloodied, but there was nothing there.

"Amias!" Caspian called after us. "What are you doing? Orders were to bring him back!"

Amias didn't slow. I pulled my arm out of his grip and raced along beside him.

Gunshots peppered the air. Amias snatched the gun from my hand and fired the last few rounds at the men behind us. When the gun clicked, the magazine empty, he threw the gun toward Caspian with scary accuracy. It rammed him on the forehead, and he crumpled to the ground, unconscious.

"Where are we going?" I asked, confusion and rage wrapping themselves around my heart. "There's no other way out of here."

"That's what they want you to think," he replied, slowing down as we neared the upper level. He pulled the door to the hall open so hard the hinges nearly snapped.

In the dusty room with the piano, Amias began pulling piles of junk off the wall to reach a painting I hadn't noticed before.

Nearby, there was a crash followed by pounding footsteps. I peeked into the hallway. Troy was leading the group of guards, his face red with fury. I turned back to Amias, who had pulled aside the painting to reveal a dark hallway.

"What the—"

"Go, go, go," he ordered, shoving me forward.

I stumbled down the hallway, lights clicking on as I went. Amias pulled the painting closed.

"Don't slow down!" he snapped.

"What is this place?" I asked as we raced down the series of twists and turns.

"That's a story for another time."

"How—" my response was cut short by a jolt zapping through my body. I cried out, falling to the floor. Amias hoisted me up and pulled open the door at the end of the passage. He shoved me through and locked the door behind us.

The electricity didn't stop. I spasmed on the floor, gasping for a breath that only seemed to scorch my lungs.

"This is going to hurt," Amias warned as he pulled the scalpel from my pocket. I felt the blade on the back of my neck, digging into my skin and splitting apart my flesh. He kept apologizing, but I could barely hear him. The edges of my vision were drawing in, tunneling to blackness.

Then, the zapping stopped. Amias cursed, tossing a buzzing microchip aside.

The cold floor pressed against my cheek. Warm blood ran down the back of my neck. I stayed there for a moment, doing my best to resist the urge to fall asleep right then and there.

"Get up," he said. "We don't have time to nap."

Unsteadily, I rose to my feet and took in the small room. There was a metal cart to my right, filled with syringes and bandages. In front of me, Amias was changing the symbols on a Mirror with a white marker.

I opened my mouth to speak, but no words came out.

"You don't need to say anything." His voice had dropped so dangerously low I strained to hear it. "None of this is your fault."

"But—"

He finished the symbols and pulled away from the Mirror. "You were right. Everything you said about me." He was talking fast, not letting me get a word in. "I'm not mad at you. I have no right to be mad at you. So, please, just don't say anything."

Voices sounded from the hallway. Someone started pounding on the door.

Amias reached for a syringe on the cart and jabbed the needle into my neck.

I swatted him away. "What the hell?"

He gave me a sad half-smile.

My head swam. Nausea crept up my throat. "What did you do to me?" I tried to say, but the words came out slurred and nearly unintelligible.

I wasn't sure if he had heard what I said or not, but he answered my question anyway. "It's a tranquilizer." He went quiet, expression falling. Sapphire eyes studied my face. "I meant what I said, Fox. I do care about you. And I hope that, eventually, you can forgive me for everything I've done."

I couldn't speak. My whole body had turned to slush, and I stumbled forward, crumpling like paper as I fell into his arms. He hoisted me back against the wall and brought a hand to my cheek. His fingers brushed against my skin. I'd never noticed their warmth before. We were both silent for a moment.

I wanted to tell him how beautiful he looked, even with blood on his face, but I couldn't get the words to leave my mouth.

The pounding on the door grew louder. I heard the familiar growling of a Phantom.

"I'm sorry," he whispered.

My heart lurched as I realized what he intended to do next. I tried to stop him, but my limbs were like lead. I couldn't move despite how much I wanted to.

He wrapped his arms around my torso, lifting me toward the Mirror.

"No," I tried to say.

He gave me a pitying look and shoved me toward the Mirror.

The silvery liquid embraced my back like a cold fog. For a split second, I caught a glimpse of the door behind Amias as it burst open, the gaping jaws of a Phantom looming over him. And then, I was falling.

Department 1, Day 12

It feels like having your heart ripped out. Betrayal. Like an important piece of you is suddenly gone. People advise you not to blame yourself when that happens, but I find such a task to be impossible. Whether or not the betrayal was your fault, you get swept up in a cycle of self-loathing and hatred. You think back to every conversation, every expression, every detail, hoping they will lead you to an answer as to why they did what they did.

When you've been denied clarity on a situation regarding another's actions, you do the only thing you can: hate yourself for making them betray you.

Of course, it was my fault. Why else would they leave me like this? I was a terrible friend. I never truly gave them the time they needed. Or perhaps, I am just uncomfortable to be around.

We were friends. I thought you cared about me. Was it really that easy for you to leave?

I had hoped not.

-Elyane

ACKNOWLEDGMENTS

This book was originally made for a version of myself who needed this world and these friends in order to live in a way she couldn't do on her own. But more so, it belongs to the readers. It belongs to everyone who holds the story close to their hearts. So, first and foremost, I want to thank you, the reader, for giving Sander's journey a shot.

Writing a book alone would've driven me to insanity, but with the help of my friends and family, I was able to build something that brought me to a life I had always thought of as a fantasy. So, to my editors, Kailee, for helping me through the mess of a first draft. And to Emily, for putting the icing on the cake. Both of you have been invaluable people in my growth both as a writer and storyteller.

Bryan and Alice, your support and dedication were instrumental to my success. I don't have enough words to describe how grateful I am for the opportunity to make my dreams come true.

An artist would be nothing without inspiration, so for that, I turn to my sister Julia. Though you may feel embarrassed about your published works, it was those things that drove me toward this path. Your passion was my motivation. And to Nicole, because you've sat through so many of my rant sessions. Your genuine excitement for me to achieve my goals has made me feel more than appreciated. Thank you, both of you, for bringing the rainbows into my thunderstorms.

On the topic of family, there's one person I would never have been able to do this without. Thank you, Mom, for stressing about the things that I didn't think needed stressing and for giving me the foundation to rise to greater heights. I love you most.

Teachers are often some of the most influential people in our lives, and that rings true with my high school advisor, Victoria. I had the inspiration, I had the dream, and I had the passion, but you gave me the tools to make this all happen. I know teachers don't get paid enough, but I hope knowing your support led me to reach my life-long goals helps with knowing your work is appreciated.

To the girl who believed in me most, even when I didn't. Rowan, I owe you more than I can give you. You know better than anyone what these worlds mean to me, so thank you for giving me the confidence to share them with others.

And Cammie, who may have noticed, this book is dedicated to you. Though every person who has helped me along this journey has been essential in my success, you were the first person whose voice I could hear cheering me on. And even though we have grown separate ways, you will always be such a special person in my life. Thank you for sitting by my side every day as I dumped out the first draft and for encouraging me the rest of the way. I hope you know I am cheering you on, too, and I can't wait to see the changes you are going to make in this world that so desperately needs your kindness.

ABOUT THE AUTHOR

Ravyn Brown is a passionate storyteller and artist whose journey into writing began in earnest during her early years of high school. Over those formative three years, she crafted her debut novel, *Broken Reflection*, weaving intricate worlds and deep emotions, inspired by a rich inner life. She aims for her writing to be a bridge, inviting others into the solace and wonder she's discovered in stories.

She grew up in the forests of Washington State and takes pride in calling the rainy city her home. Through her work, she aspires to connect her readers with the adventure and exquisite tranquility of the Pacific Northwest, offering them the same peace she's always found in the world of books.